THE FIRST CORRUPTION

Book One of

THE FRACTURED SIGILS

C. B. NAVA

Ashfall Press

THE FIRST CORRUPTION

Book One of *The Fractured Sigils*

ISBN (Paperback): 979-8-9943930-0-0

ISBN (Hardcover): 979-8-9943930-1-7

Published by **Ashfall Press**

www.cbnava.com Printed in the United States of America

First Edition

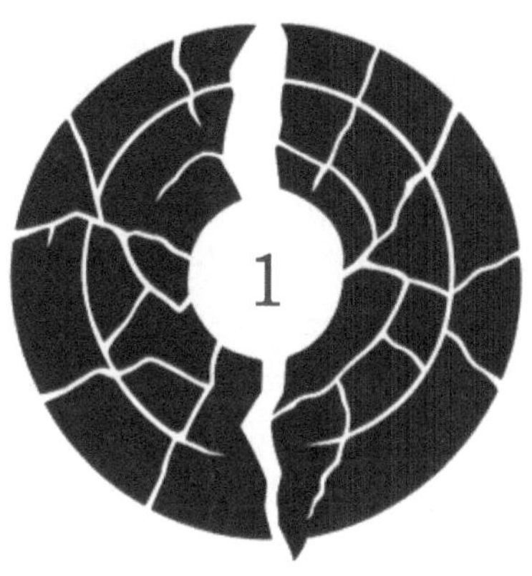

The Warning

The world was burning again. Loran ran through smoke-thick air, half-blind, his lungs aching as a roar rolled across the sky—so deep it vibrated through his ribs. The ground shuddered beneath him, splitting open like cracking ice. He didn't recognize the village around him, yet somehow he did. Every crooked door. Every narrow street. Every voice screaming in terror. He'd never been here, but he knew this place.

"Loran!" The voice was distant, warped, as if it traveled through water. He spun toward the sound just as shapes emerged from the smoke. Animals—at first glance. But their bodies bent at grotesque angles, skin bulging with black, pulsing veins. A horse stumbled into view, its eyes filmed white, dark tears steaming where they hit the dirt. Behind it came goats, a pig, something that might have once been a hound—each twisted, each jerking as though pulled by invisible strings. A chill stabbed down Loran's spine. These weren't creatures anymore. They were being changed by something ancient. Something malignant. Something hungry. The earth erupted beside him with a thunderous crack. A hand the size of a wagon wheel burst upward—stone-colored, faint runes glowing along its skin. Dirt rained like hail as something enormous dragged itself from the ground.

A giant. Taller than the stories. Taller than reason. Its eyes opened—twin pools of molten gold that burned through the smoke... and found him. "You must wake," a voice boomed. But the giant's mouth didn't move. The voice came from everywhere—the sky, the shaking earth, the air in his lungs. Smoke twisted nearby. A shadow stepped out, its form shifting like ink in water. It tore itself apart—ribbons of blinding color ripping free: red, white, green. They spiraled upward, streaking across the sky.

What remained collapsed inward, reshaping into a darker, denser shadow. Black tendrils whipped outward. One wrapped around a silhouette of a person. Someone small. Almost familiar. Loran's heart dropped. No. No, it couldn't be—The figure screamed. The tendrils burrowed deeper. The shadow poured into them like smoke filling a vessel—"Wake," the giant thundered again. The world shattered like glass. A burning pain seared across Loran's forearm, as if a hot poker had been pressed to his skin. He looked down just as a faint red glow pulsed beneath the surface—once... twice... then faded to nothing.

Loran lurched upright in his bed, choking on a gasp. His room was still. The darkness ordinary. But his heart raced as if he'd been running for miles. Sweat chilled his skin. The nightmare clung to him like it had hooked needles into his spine, sending aftershocks through every limb. He looked down at his forearm, half expecting a wound. There was nothing. But the memory of the glow made his breath tremble. It was only a dream. It had to be. Yet deep in his chest, something cold coiled tight. It wasn't a dream. It was a warning.

Loran sat at the edge of his bed, breathing hard, waiting for the last shreds of the vision to fade. But it clung to him like smoke. His palms were damp. His heartbeat wouldn't slow. He pressed a thumb to the place where the glow had been. Just skin now. Ordinary. So why did he feel like something beneath his life had cracked, and he was only now realizing he was standing on thin ice? A rooster crowed outside—shrill and impatient. The familiar sound loosened something in his chest. Morning was ordinary. Life would be ordinary. Whatever he'd seen was nothing more than a dream brought on by too little sleep.

He forced himself up and got dressed. The village was already stirring when he stepped outside. Cool dawn air brushed his face. Smoke curled from chimneys. Someone laughed across the square—Lila, probably, chatting with the baker as she always did. A cartwheel creaked as old Herrin hauled wood toward the smithy. Normal. Completely normal.

He let out a slow breath. "Morning, Loran!" Lila called, waving a warm loaf of bread. "You heading to the wells? My mother said they're running slow again." "Yeah," he said, managing a smile. "I'll take a look." "You should take a look at yourself," she teased. "You look like you fought a bear in your sleep." If only she knew. He shook his head. "Bad dream, that's all." "Then dream better ones," she said with a wink and ducked back into the bakery.

Loran continued down the path, passing small homes and familiar faces. Yet everything felt... distant. As if he were watching someone else walk his morning route. At the well, he knelt and checked the rope, the pulley, the stones around the rim. All fine. Ordinary. But an uneasy crawl ran beneath his skin with every beat of his heart. He kept thinking of the giant—the golden eyes locking onto him. Wake. He splashed cold water on his face and inhaled sharply. It was just a dream. Nightmares didn't mean anything. They didn't show the future. They didn't— A loud voice interrupted his thoughts.

"You've got a foul odor about you, Loran! Need to bathe right here and now, do you?" Braum boomed, laughing deeply. Loran snorted. "Oh, shut it, Braum. I only needed to wake myself a bit." "Lila said you needed help waking up—or was it help fixing the well?" Braum grinned, broad-shouldered and solid as the smithy's anvil. He'd been Loran's closest friend since Loran and his mother had arrived in Two Stone Grove when he was nine. Years of work at his father's forge had left Braum towering, muscular, and callused to the elbow.

"She sure is low, isn't she," Braum said, leaning over the well. "It doesn't make sense," Loran muttered. "It's almost like something clogged it... or drained it." Suddenly, water began rising again—filling the bottom of the well as if nothing had been wrong. Or worse: as if something beneath the well had shifted just enough to cause the drop. A low, distant boom rolled across the hills. Loran froze, heart seizing. Probably thunder. Probably. He exhaled and wiped his hands on his shirt. Work helped. Routine helped.

He checked the well again even though there was no reason to. He lingered in the square, helped an elder lift a crate, repaired a loose shutter on a neighbor's window. Anything to distract himself from the knot tightening in his chest. But every time he paused, the dream crept back—twisting animals, the giant's molten eyes, the black tendrils wrapping around someone familiar— By late morning, he'd convinced himself he was being ridiculous. The dream would fade. Life would settle. It always did. Still, as he sat for his midday meal, he kept glancing at his forearm, half expecting it to glow again. It didn't.

The world was calm. Peaceful. Ordinary. But as the sun dipped low and villagers closed their shutters for the night, Loran couldn't shake the feeling of something watching from the edges of the world. And somewhere deep inside him, beneath all the rational thoughts, a whisper curled through his chest like a warning: This was only the beginning..

CHAPTER TWO
The First Signs

Loran woke to screaming. He shot upright, heart hammering, as another cry tore through the morning air—raw, frantic, too real to be a dream. He stumbled into his boots, shoved open his door, and stepped into chaos. The sky was still dark, dawn only a pale smudge on the horizon, yet half the village was already awake.

Lanterns bobbed between houses, throwing frantic circles of light across the ground. People shouted to one another. Someone ran barefoot down the path, dragging a terrified child behind them. "What's happening?" Loran called to a neighbor rushing past. "The animals!" the man shouted without slowing. "They're... wrong!" A cold weight settled in Loran's stomach. He followed the noise toward Mara's barn. Even before he reached it, he smelled it—the heavy, metallic scent hanging thick in the air. Sharp. Wrong. Like hot iron cooling after a forge strike. The barn door was shattered outward, its wooden planks splintered and hanging at odd angles, as though something massive had forced its way out.

Inside, shadows moved in slow, jerking motions. Loran crept closer, pulse quickening. A low, guttural bleat drifted out—warped, bubbling, almost liquid. Then a goat staggered into the lantern light. Loran froze. Black veins writhed beneath its skin like living worms. Its mouth hung slack, dark saliva dripping to the dirt where it sizzled faintly. Its eyes were pure white—sightless, unblinking. The creature lurched toward him with stiff, unnatural bursts of movement, its limbs bending too sharply, as if its bones no longer knew where they were supposed to go.

"Back!" Mara shouted, charging from the side with a wooden staff. "Loran, move!" Mara was not a fighter by any stretch—short, wiry, with brown hair always falling loose from its braid—but she was stubborn as a mule and twice as fearless. She ran the small orchard beyond the ridge and usually smelled faintly of apples and hay. Loran had known her since they were children; she was the sort who would sprint into a burning barn if someone needed help, even if her hands shook the entire time.

He grabbed her and yanked her aside just as the goat slammed into the doorframe with a sickening thud. The impact cracked the wood. More animals pressed behind it—cows, pigs, even Mara's old dog—each marked by pulsing black veins, each twitching in grotesque spasms. Villagers scattered, screaming. Loran dragged Mara away as another warped animal burst through a side wall of the barn, planks flying like broken arrows. The ground trembled beneath Loran's feet—a subtle vibration, not like normal quakes. It was rhythmic, pulsing upward from the earth itself, as if something deep below shifted in its sleep.

He spun around and saw the earth behind the barn darkening. A perfect circle of dying grass spread outward in all directions, like spilled ink seeping through fabric. Plants curled in on themselves. Soil blackened. The air shimmered above it, warping the morning chill into something hot and suffocating. "What in the gods' names...?" Loran whispered. A deep boom echoed across the distant hills. Not thunder. Not anything natural. It was the same low sound he had heard in his dream, vibrating through bone instead of air. Something enormous was moving beneath the world. Fear stabbed through him, but something else followed—a warmth blooming beneath his skin. His forearm burned.

Loran swallowed hard and rolled up his sleeve. A faint red glow pulsed beneath the skin. Once. Twice. Brighter each time. His breath caught. He wasn't sick. He wasn't imagining it. The dream hadn't lied. Whatever was happening to the animals... was happening to him. Mara followed his gaze and gasped. "Loran...

what is that?" "I—I don't know," he said, though he did know. Somewhere deep inside, he knew exactly what it meant. The mark. The glow. The giant's warning. "Is it contagious?" Mara asked, voice trembling. "Loran, did—did one of the animals scratch you?" "No." He backed away instinctively, not wanting her too close. "This started last night." "You should see the healer." "I don't think the healer can fix this." Another boom rolled across the hills—louder this time, closer, rattling the windows of nearby houses.

People poured into the open square, shouting over one another. A woman cried that her chickens had torn each other apart. Another claimed her horse had spoken her name in a voice that wasn't its own. Someone yelled that the river near the grove had turned black. Braum barreled into view, breathless, hair half-tied and boots unlaced. "Loran! Mara! Are you both—" He saw the animals, the corruption, the shaking earth, and faltered. "Gods..." Loran had never seen Braum look afraid. Not even when a bear wandered too close to the forge last winter. But fear was etched plainly across his face now. "What's happening?" Braum asked. "I don't know," Loran said. "But it started last night. I... think I saw this." "In a dream?" Braum asked. Loran nodded.

"I didn't think it was real," he said quietly. "But now—" The ground lurched beneath them. A crack split the soil near the barn, spreading fast, jagged like a lightning bolt across the earth. A sound followed—deep, groaning, as if the land itself was being pried open. Mara grabbed Loran's arm. "We need to leave. Now." But Loran stood frozen. Because from deep within the widening crack, a faint glow pulsed. Not red like his... but black. Thick and oily, rising like smoke. The same black he had seen wrap around the silhouette in his dream. Braum stepped in front of him, pulling Loran back. "Don't go near that," Braum growled.

"Whatever this is—it's spreading." The air trembled.

A second crack split open. Then a third. Loran's forearm flared with heat, brighter this time, almost painful. The red glow throbbed beneath his skin like a heartbeat—his heartbeat—or something else's. Mara stared at the glow, voice quivering. “Loran... you’re connected to this.” “Yeah,” Loran whispered, unable to deny it anymore. “I think I am.” A shriek tore through the village—the sound of something that had once been alive but no longer remembered how to be. Loran clenched his fists, heart racing. The dream was no longer just a warning. It was happening. And something beneath the earth was waking.

CHAPTER THREE
The Healer's Warning

Morning never came properly. A gray, sickly light bled into the sky as if the sun were afraid to show its face. The villagers gathered in the square, voices overlapping in panicked waves. Children clung to their parents. Someone sobbed. Someone else prayed. Loran stood with Braum and Mara near the shattered barn, trying not to look directly at the twisted bodies of the corrupted livestock. Men had dragged them into a pile, but even dead, they didn't look right. Their skin was waxy. The veins beneath had turned a deep, unnatural black that made his stomach twist. "We need the healer," Mara whispered. "She'll know what to do." Loran nodded, though his chest tightened. He didn't want anyone to see the mark again. He was still hoping it would fade, as if pretending it wasn't there might erase what was happening.

The healer's hut sat at the far edge of Two Stone Grove, past a row of apple trees and a narrow stream running along the ridge. Braum strode ahead, jaw set, but Mara stayed close to Loran, studying him with a worried frown that made him feel even more exposed. "Your arm..." she said quietly. "It glowed, Loran. That wasn't normal." "It's fine," Loran lied. "It's not." He didn't answer. They reached the healer's hut, and before they could knock, the door swung open. Not the old healer. Arlyn. She couldn't have been much older than Loran, maybe seventeen, with dark curls pulled into a messy knot and hands stained green and brown from crushed herbs. There was a smudge of ink along her cheekbone, like she'd wiped her face with the back of an inky hand and forgotten about it. Her eyes were wide and tired. "You saw it too?"

Braum frowned. “Saw what?” Arlyn glanced past them toward the square, where shouting still carried on the wind, then jerked her head for them to come inside. The hut smelled of mint and sage and something sharper Loran didn’t recognize. Scrolls lay scattered across the table, weighed down by jars of dried flowers and cloudy glass bottles. The healer’s staff was gone from its usual corner. Arlyn shut the door and lowered her voice. “Something is happening to the animals. But it isn’t sickness.” “We know that much,” Braum muttered. Arlyn shook her head. “No, I mean—this isn’t like anything I’ve studied. Their bodies don’t break down like they should. The veins are... wrong. They’re not just dark. They move. When I cut into a goat this morning, they twitched on their own, like roots searching for... something.”

Loran swallowed hard. Mara’s fingers tightened around the edge of the table. “Can you fix it?” “If it were a disease, maybe.” Arlyn’s voice cracked. “But this feels more like someone poured something into them. Something that doesn’t belong in anything living.” Loran felt that warmth in his arm again—a faint flutter under the skin, like the echo of a heartbeat that wasn’t entirely his. Arlyn’s gaze slid to him. “You’re hiding something.” Braum bristled. “He’s not—” “Yes, he is.” Arlyn stepped closer, eyes narrowed, not unkind but sharp in the way of people who notice things they wish they didn’t. “Your pulse is too fast. You keep favoring your left arm. Arlyn nodded once. “Show me.” He hesitated. Mara touched his elbow. “Loran. Please.”

He set his jaw, then slowly rolled up his sleeve. The skin of his forearm looked normal at first—no scars, no burns. But as all three of them stared, the faintest trace of red shimmered beneath the surface, like buried embers catching a breath of air. Arlyn sucked in a breath. “Gods... That isn’t a wound. That’s a mark.” “A mark of what?” Braum demanded. “I don’t know.” Arlyn chewed her lower lip. “But the healer did.” Loran’s heart stumbled. “What do you mean?” “She left before dawn,” Arlyn said. “Took her pack, her salves, three of the oldest scrolls. When I asked where she was going, she said, 'The signs are here. Keep the boy safe.'"

Braum's brows knit. "What boy?" Arlyn looked straight at Loran. "She meant you." Silence pressed in on them. Loran's throat felt too tight to speak. "Safe from what?" "I don't know," Arlyn admitted. "She said the old protections wouldn't hold much longer. That something buried was waking. I thought she was just tired, but then the animals started—" A scream cut through the hut walls. Not an animal this time. A person. Arlyn's face drained of color. "That came from the square." Braum was already moving. "Come on!" They bolted out of the hut and sprinted back toward the heart of the village. People had formed a wide, shaky circle around something thrashing in the dirt. Loran pushed through the crowd, Braum and Mara at his heels.

Teren lay on the ground, back arched, hands clawing at the air. Loran recognized him from hunts and harvest festivals—the quiet hunter's son with the easy smile and a knack for tracking birds. There was nothing easy about him now. Black veins crawled under his skin, pulsing and shifting like they were alive. His mouth foamed dark. He gagged, coughed, and spat something thick and tar-like into the dust. Arlyn dropped to her knees beside him. "Hold him!" she snapped. Braum lunged forward, pinning Teren's shoulders, grunting as the boy's body bucked with unnatural strength. Teren's eyes rolled back until only white showed. His legs kicked, heels digging furrows into the earth.

"Get something in his mouth so he doesn't bite through his tongue!" Arlyn barked. Someone handed her a leather strap. She tried to wedge it between his teeth, but Teren's jaw snapped shut with a frightening crack. "Loran," Mara whispered, clutching his sleeve. "This is like the animals. This is the same." Loran's gaze locked on the black veins rippling beneath Teren's skin, spreading from his chest outward like ink in water. He couldn't move. Teren convulsed—and then, suddenly, he went still. Too still. His chest rose slowly, shuddering. His eyes, still rolled back, rolled down again until his gaze fixed on the sky. For a heartbeat, his irises were the familiar brown Loran knew. Then they darkened. Black seeped across them, swallowing the color until his eyes were bottomless pits. He turned his head. And stared directly at Loran.

A voice tore from his throat. It was Teren's voice and not, layered with something deeper and older that scraped along Loran's bones. "Found you..." The word slithered through the square, silencing every murmur. Loran's feet felt rooted to the ground. Braum shifted to block him, but Teren only craned his neck further, eyes never leaving Loran. "The vessel..." Teren hissed. His lips split in a grin that wasn't his. "The vessel... the vessel..." Whispers rippled through the crowd. Loran shook his head. "No." Teren's hands scrabbled at the ground, dragging his body forward even with Braum's weight on him. His fingers dug grooves in the dirt. Mara's nails dug into Loran's arm.

"He means you." "Teren," Arlyn pleaded. "Fight it. Please." Teren's body jerked. His limbs bent at wrong angles, joints popping. The veins beneath his skin throbbed faster, black threads weaving into something like a symbol across his chest. His voice deepened, three tones at once. "The vessel calls the dark. The vessel opens the way." Loran stumbled back, his forearm burning—no longer a faint warmth but a sharp, searing heat. The mark under his skin flared bright red, light bleeding through like molten metal. "Loran—your arm!" Mara cried. Teren lunged. And the mark on Loran's forearm erupted. Crimson light blasted from his skin in a sudden flare, bright as lightning. It struck Teren square in the chest. The force threw Teren backward. Braum toppled with him, swearing as he hit the ground. Several villagers cried out, shielding their eyes from the glare. The light spread across the square, washing over cobblestones, boots, and faces.

For a heartbeat, everything hung silent and still, like the world was holding its breath. Then the light snapped out. Teren lay sprawled in the dirt, chest heaving, eyes wide and staring at nothing. The black veins that had twisted beneath his skin were fading, receding like spilled ink being sucked back into a bottle—leaving only faint, darkened traces behind. Arlyn scrambled to his side, fingers pressing against his throat. "Is he—?" Mara whispered. "Alive," Arlyn said, relief and fear tangling in her voice. "Barely. Whatever that was, it broke the hold on him. For now." Slowly, sound leaked back into the square. Murmurs. Prayers. Someone began sobbing in earnest. Then a voice cut through it all. "The boy did that," a woman said sharply. "I saw it with my own eyes." Loran turned. Lila's mother stood near the edge of the crowd, face pale, eyes hard. Her hands trembled as she pointed straight at him.

"He lit up like a demon," she said. "First the animals, now Teren. It started when that mark appeared, didn't it?" "That's not how it—" Braum began, pushing himself up. "How else do you explain it?" another villager demanded. "The livestock were fine until yesterday. Teren was fine until this morning. Now there's a mark, and red witch-fire shooting from his arm." "It saved Teren," Mara snapped. "You all saw that too."

"Or finished whatever started," the woman shot back. "We don't know what he's bringing down on us." Eyes turned to Loran. Too many eyes. He felt flayed open beneath them. The mark on his arm had dimmed, but he could still feel it throbbing in time with his heart. "I didn't mean to—" he started. "And if you can't control it?" someone else called. "What happens when that light doesn't stop with the corruption?" Arlyn stood, squaring her shoulders despite the fear in her eyes. "He's not the cause. He's reacting to it. The healer knew something like this would happen—that's why she left to look for answers."

The crowd muttered, uncertain. "We'll bring this to the council," an older man said, stepping forward. Loran recognized him—Master Deren, one of the village elders. Deep lines creased his face, but his gaze was sharp. "Everyone calm yourselves. Panicking won't help anyone." Lila's mother glared but fell silent.

Deren's eyes settled on Loran. For a moment, there was something almost pitying in them.

"Boy," he said quietly, "you and your friends will come to the hall at dusk. Until then, stay close. Don't leave the village."

It didn't sound like concern. It sounded like an order. "Yes, sir," Loran said, though his voice barely came out. The villagers slowly dispersed—some helping Arlyn move Teren, some dragging tarps over the corrupted carcasses, some casting nervous looks back at Loran as they went. When most had gone, only Braum, Mara, Arlyn, and Loran remained in the square. Braum clapped a hand on his shoulder. "Don't listen to them. They're scared." "They're not wrong to be," Loran said. Mara stepped in front of him, eyes fierce.

"You saved Teren. Whatever this thing is, it's not all bad." "It lashed out," Loran said. "I didn't call it. I didn't even know what I was doing." "That's why we find out," Arlyn said quietly. "We find the healer. We find whoever taught her. We find out what that mark is before fear decides for everyone else."

Loran looked down at his forearm. The skin was smooth. Normal. But he could still feel the echo of the light, humming there like a caged storm. "What if they're right?" he asked. "What if I really am a vessel? The one calling this down on all of us?"

Mara's jaw tightened. "Then we figure out how to make sure it doesn't destroy you. Or anyone else." Braum squeezed his shoulder harder. "You're not alone in this, Loran. Remember that." Loran lifted his gaze toward the hills. Far in the distance, a low rumble rolled across the land. Not thunder. Not wind. Something deeper. Something shifting beneath the earth. The villagers might wait for the council to speak. But the world wasn't waiting for anyone. And as the sound faded, Loran couldn't shake the feeling that whatever had marked him had just taken a step closer

CHAPTER FOUR
The Village Fractures

By dusk, the entire village felt like a held breath. The sun dipped low behind the ridge, casting Two Stone Grove in long, uneasy shadows. The square, usually filled with the warm clamor of people finishing their day, was strangely silent—save for hushed whispers and the creak of shutters being pulled closed early.

Loran walked between Braum and Mara toward the council hall, trying not to notice how villagers stepped aside as he passed. Not with courtesy. With fear. "Don't look at them," Braum muttered. "They stare because they're cowards."

Mara shot him a look. "They're scared, Braum. Cowards and scared aren't the same." "They're treating him like a monster." "They saw a boy nearly die," she said softly. "And they saw something strange save him." Loran kept his eyes on the ground. "Strange is enough." They reached the hall—an old stone building with thick oak beams and a carved emblem of two stones crossing one another above the door. At least fifty villagers had already gathered, filling the entryway and spilling into the square.

Lila stood with her mother near the front. Lila's eyes were wide, worried—but her mother's expression was tight and hard. As soon as Loran stepped forward, she pointed at him. "There," she said, voice sharp. "The boy with the mark." Whispers thickened instantly. Loran felt Mara press closer to him. Braum's arm shifted protectively across his chest. Elder Deren appeared at the hall entrance and raised both hands. "Quiet." The murmurs died.

"Let them in." Loran, Braum, Mara, and Arlyn walked inside, taking seats on a long bench before the raised platform where the five elders sat. Torches flickered along the walls, casting tall shadows that jittered with every breath of wind sneaking through the eaves. Elder Deren, the oldest and most measured of the group, studied Loran for a long moment before speaking. "Tell us again what happened today," he said.

Loran swallowed hard and described the morning—the screams, the animals, the way Teren had changed, and the light that had erupted from his arm. Mara and Arlyn added what they saw. Braum's version emphasized the panic and how Loran had saved Teren's life. When they finished, the hall fell into heavy silence. Then Elder Varra, a thin woman with a sharp beak of a nose, leaned forward. "The boy's mark reacted to the corruption. This cannot be coincidence."

"Nothing about this is coincidence," Arlyn said. "This is ancient magic—older than the village, older than any of us. The healer left because she expected something like this." "That doesn't mean we should trust him," Varra snapped. "He saved Teren," Mara said. "You saw the boy yourself—he's still alive because of Loran." Varra's mouth tightened. "And how long until he stops saving and starts harming?" A murmur rippled through the hall.

Lila's mother stepped forward from the crowd. "My cousin in Glassmere wrote about a wandering sickness years ago. Started with animals—ended with whole families gone black-veined. Maybe that's what's happening here. Maybe he's the cause." "I'm not," Loran said quietly. "How do you know?" she shot back. "How can any of us?"

Braum stood. "Because we grew up with him. Because he's never hurt anyone. Because he's more likely to save your life than curse it." "Enough," Elder Deren said, raising a hand. "Accusations won't help us understand what this mark is." He turned to Loran. "May I see it?" Loran hesitated, then rolled up his sleeve. The mark didn't glow now, but the faint outline beneath his skin was unmistakable—a red pulse buried deep, like a coal waiting for breath.

The elders leaned in. Elder Harven, the scholar among them, frowned. "This is no wound. It looks... crafted." "Crafted?" Varra echoed. "By who?" "By something powerful." Harven looked troubled. "There are old stories—fragmented and half-lost—about the Sigils. Color-forged marks that guided the first wielders." "You think the boy is a wielder?" Varra scoffed. "He's barely grown." Harven ignored her. "Red, White, Green, and—" He stopped. "Black," Arlyn finished quietly. The room chilled.

"We don't know what he is," Varra said. "But we know what he brings. Chaos. Danger. Death." She pointed at Loran. "I say we quarantine him. For the safety of the village." Braum bristled. "Over my dead—" "Braum," Deren warned. "Let her speak." "She's spoken enough," Mara snapped. "And she's wrong. Loran didn't cause this—this happened TO him."

Elder Deren closed his eyes briefly, exhaling through his nose. "We are not exiling the boy," he said. A stunned silence swept the hall. "But," Deren continued, "we must protect the village. And we must understand what role he plays in this corruption." Loran's stomach twisted. "What do you want me to do?" "You and your friends will remain within sight of the guards tonight," Deren said. "At sunrise, you will speak to Elder Harven and Arlyn about your dream and the mark. Perhaps the healer left clues behind." "And if things worsen before then?" Varra asked coldly. "If they worsen," Deren said, "we will make another decision."

Loran felt the weight in the room shift—a fragile, uneasy balance. He wasn't exiled. But he wasn't trusted. Not fully. Deren dismissed the gathering. Villagers filed out, muttering to one another. Some cast Loran confused, fearful glances. Others wouldn't look at him at all. Lila passed him on her way out. She hesitated, biting her lip, then offered a small, shaky smile. "I don't think you're dangerous," she whispered. "Just scared. Like the rest of us." Her mother grabbed her wrist and pulled her away.

When the hall emptied, only the four of them remained. Loran sank onto the bench, shoulders heavy. "They think I'm cursed."

"No," Braum said. "They think you're important." Arlyn nodded. "The healer wouldn't have left without saying more if she didn't believe something big was coming. And she said to keep you safe." Mara knelt in front of him, her eyes warm despite the shadows under them. "We're staying with you. No matter what they decide." Loran looked at each of them—Braum's stubborn strength, Arlyn's quiet determination, Mara's fierce loyalty. A strange mix of hope and dread stirred in his chest.

"Tomorrow," Arlyn said, "we start searching for answers." "Tonight," Braum corrected, gripping his hammer, "we make sure nothing comes for us." Outside, another low rumble drifted over the hills—distant, but unmistakable. Something moved in the dark beyond the ridge. Something watching.
Waiting. And Loran knew, deep in the burning echo of his mark:
This village would not stay whole much longer

CHAPTER FIVE
The Council Summons

The night felt heavier than any Loran could remember. He managed a few restless hours of sleep at best, jolting awake every time a shadow shifted outside his window or the wind scraped across the boards of his room. Each time he drifted off, Teren's blackened stare followed him into his dreams. By dawn, he was sitting upright in bed, too tired to sleep, too tense to move.

A soft knock broke the silence. "Loran?" Mara's voice. He opened the door. She stood with her cloak wrapped tight around her shoulders, hair braided hastily, her expression still bruised by the night's events. "Braum and Arlyn are getting food," she said quietly. "We thought... you might not want to walk to the hall alone." Loran nodded gratefully.

They stepped outside together. Frost crackled beneath their boots. The morning sun was pale, hesitant, as if the sky itself feared what daylight would reveal. They met Braum and Arlyn on the path, each carrying a small pack. Braum handed Loran a piece of bread. "Eat," he said. "Council mornings drain the life out of anyone." Mara shot him a look. "Not helping." They entered the council hall. Elder Harven was already there, pacing before a large table scattered with brittle scrolls. His normally neat hair was smudged with ink, and fatigue dragged at his eyes.

"You're early," Harven said. "Good." He motioned for them to sit, then unfurled a large, yellowing scroll across the table. Faded symbols covered it—circles, jagged lines, and four colored sigils. Red. White. Green. Black. Loran felt heat coil under his skin, right where the red light had flared. “What is all this?” Braum asked. “Pieces,” Harven said, “of stories older than Two Stone Grove itself. Before the Sealed War. Before the guardians slept.”

He tapped the red circle. “This is the Red Sigil. Fire of the Firstblood. These are said to awaken when balance begins to break.” Mara glanced at Loran’s arm, anxiety rising behind her eyes. Arlyn leaned closer. “Awaken for what?” Harven hesitated, then touched the black sigil. “To oppose the Vessel.” Loran stiffened. “The... Vessel?” Mara whispered. Harven nodded. “The one who carries the Black Core. The source of all corruption. A Vessel is not born—it is chosen when the seals weaken.”

Loran swallowed hard. “But Teren said *I* was the vessel.” “Teren was not in his right mind,” Harven said. “The corruption twists thoughts. It lies.” “But how do we know?” Arlyn asked softly. Harven reached for a smaller scrap of parchment, barely held together by years. He unrolled it carefully, revealing a short, rough line of ancient writing. “This,” he said quietly, “is the only clear phrase that survived the damage.” He read aloud: “The Vessel wears a mark.”

Silence pooled through the hall. Loran felt his stomach drop. Every pair of eyes turned to him—his friends, the elder, even the distant stares from the villagers gathered near the door. “But we don’t know what kind of mark,” Harven continued quickly. “Or even when it appears. Ancient texts are symbolic. Poetic. Sometimes wrong.” Varra entered the hall like a winter draft. “Or sometimes very clear.” Braum bristled. “Here we go.”

Varra ignored him and pointed to Loran’s arm. “A mark appears. Strange light bursts from the boy. And corruption follows him wherever he goes. How much clearer could it be?” Loran’s throat tightened. “I didn’t choose this.” “And we didn’t choose to suffer for it,” Varra shot back. “That’s enough,” Elder Deren said as he stepped inside. His voice carried a weight that silenced the room. “Fear does not excuse cruelty.” Varra’s lip curled, but she said nothing more.

Deren turned to Loran. "Your mark is not proof of anything except that you are involved. But involved does not mean responsible." "But the villagers—" Loran began.

"The villagers are frightened," Deren said. "And frightened people look for simple answers. You are not a simple answer." Arlyn nodded firmly. "He saved Teren. That matters more than anything."

"Perhaps," Varra muttered. "Enough," Deren repeated. He gestured to the scrolls. "Harven, explain your plan." Harven drew in a slow breath. "The healer left before dawn carrying old texts and medicine. She has knowledge we do not. Her hut may hold clues about why she named Loran directly in her warning." Mara's brows knit. "You think she foresaw this?"

"I think," Harven said carefully, "she expected someone to bear a mark. And she believed Loran's life was important enough to protect." Varra snorted. "Or dangerous enough to flee from." Deren slammed his staff against the floor. "Varra!" The sound echoed, shutting her up instantly. Harven cleared his throat.

"I want to search the healer's house for any records she left behind—notes, scrolls, anything she may have hidden. But the corruption is unpredictable. If her magic failed... her home may not be safe."

"We'll go with him," Mara said immediately. "No," Deren said. "Only Loran and Arlyn." Braum stood so quickly his chair scraped the floor. "Why?" "Because the healer asked Arlyn to keep him safe," Deren said. "And the more people we involve, the more panic will spread. We need quiet. Caution." Mara clenched her fists. "He shouldn't go alone."

"He won't," Arlyn said, stepping closer to Loran. "I'll be there." Loran managed a faint smile. "It's fine. We'll be back before sunset." Mara looked like she wanted to argue—but then she exhaled shakily and nodded. "Be careful. Both of you." Braum gripped Loran's shoulder. "Shout if anything tries to eat you. I'll hear."

Varra snorted. “We should be so lucky.” “Varra,” Deren warned again. She held up her hands mockingly, but stepped aside. Loran and Arlyn walked toward the hall doors. The moment they stepped outside, the cold hit them like a wave. The village watched them again. Only this time, the fear in their eyes felt sharper. More directed. Whispered words followed them like shadows.

“Marked...”

“Cursed...”

“Vessel...”

Loran pulled his cloak tighter around himself, jaw clenched. His arm tingled faintly beneath the fabric, as if reacting to every stare. Arlyn walked beside him in silence for a moment, then said quietly, “Don’t listen to them. Prophecies are rarely what they seem.” Loran nodded. “But the mark—” “Isn’t the only one that exists,” Arlyn said. “We just haven’t seen the others yet.” He looked at her sharply. “What do you mean?” Arlyn hesitated. “Just... that magic this old rarely chooses only one person.” Loran’s heart thudded unevenly. “And if someone else also wears a mark...” Arlyn whispered, “the scroll doesn’t say what it looks like. Or how late it appears.” The path to the healer’s cottage stretched ahead of them, quiet and empty.

CHAPTER SIX
The Night Raid

The healer's cottage sat nearly a mile beyond the village boundaries, tucked into a bend of orchard trees and brush. Loran had walked that path a hundred times before—for herbs, for advice, for the occasional scolding when he scraped his knees as a boy. Today, the path felt different. Wrong. Even the wind felt thinner. Arlyn walked beside him, clutching her satchel to her chest, her breath visible in the cold air. The sky had already begun to dim—sunset bleeding orange and red across the hills.

"They'll be watching for us," Arlyn murmured. "Villagers?" "No." She pulled her cloak tighter. "The corrupted things. If they're drawn to your mark... they may not let us reach the cottage quietly." Loran exhaled slowly. "Then we stay alert."

They followed the winding path beyond the last row of houses. Behind them, the village shrank to distant shapes and scattered lanterns—each flicker like a heartbeat pulsing in the dark. The deeper they walked into the trees, the quieter everything became. No birds. No crickets. Not even the usual rustle of squirrels in the brush. Just silence. Loran felt the hair rise on the back of his neck. "Do you feel that?" Arlyn whispered. "Yes," he said. It wasn't wind. It wasn't sound. It was... pressure.

A subtle weight pressing down on everything, flattening the air until it felt hard to breathe. And then— A soft crunch behind them. Not loud. But unmistakable. Loran stopped. Arlyn froze. Something moved in the brush. Slow. Dragging. Too slow to be natural, too deliberate to be wind. Loran lifted a hand, palm out. "Stay close." The brush rustled again. A low, soft sound followed—

wet, almost like something breathing through flooded lungs. Then a figure stepped out. A deer. Or what had once been a deer.

Its body was gaunt, ribs jutting sharply beneath peeled patches of fur. Black veins pulsed beneath the flesh, writhing like worms. One of its eyes was gone entirely—replaced by a swirling pit of darkness. It lifted its head, nostrils flaring. It smelled him. Arlyn clamped a hand over her mouth to keep from screaming. The deer took one stiff step... then another... moving in jerks like its bones didn't fit correctly anymore.

"Don't run," Loran whispered. "If we run, it chases." Arlyn nodded, trembling. The deer jerked forward, drawn to the faint heat pulsing beneath Loran's skin. The mark. The Vessel wears a mark. The words echoed, unbidden, in his mind.

The deer lurched—and its legs buckled beneath it. It slammed into the ground, twitching violently, hooves digging trenches in the dirt as black corruption writhed under its skin. "No—no—no—" Arlyn whimpered. Loran grabbed her arm. "Back. Now." The deer spasmed, twisted, and then let out a howl so human it sent ice down Loran's spine. He didn't think. He moved. "Go!" he shouted, dragging Arlyn down the path at a sprint. Behind them, the creature thrashed, snapping branches as it flung its broken body into the trees. But it didn't follow. It just screamed. A long, terrible sound that echoed down the hills.

Arlyn stumbled beside him, breath ragged. "Why didn't it chase us?" Loran swallowed. "I don't know." Because it recognized him. Because it feared him. Because it was calling to something else. None of those answers comforted him.

They hurried the rest of the way to the healer's cottage, arriving breathless and shaken as the sun finally dipped behind the ridge. The cottage looked abandoned—shutters closed, tools missing, the front door cracked open as if someone had left in a hurry. Loran and Arlyn exchanged a look. "Stay behind me," Loran whispered. He pushed the door open. Inside, the cottage was a mess. Drawers yanked open. Papers scattered. Jars knocked over and spilled into multicolored stains across the wooden floor. "Someone searched this place," Arlyn breathed.

They stepped inside, careful not to step on the loose glass. The air smelled faintly of herbs—mint, sage, and something else. Something sour. Arlyn knelt near the healer's writing table. "These aren't her notes. These are references. She was studying something." Loran scanned the shelves. Many of the oldest scrolls were missing, their usual places empty. He stepped toward the back room—and froze.

Something had scratched deep gouges into the wall. Long, jagged marks. Arlyn's eyes widened. "Those weren't here before." "Something came through," Loran whispered. He reached up and pressed a hand to one of the grooves. It was cold. Fresh. Another sound drifted through the window. A distant scream. From the direction of the village. Arlyn stood so quickly her chair toppled backward. "No—Loran—" "I know." The screams multiplied—several now—panicked, echoing through the trees. The Night Raid had begun.

"We have to go," Arlyn said, voice breaking. "Now." She grabbed a handful of scattered papers—anything that looked important—and stuffed them into her satchel. Loran rushed out the door behind her, heart pounding so hard the mark pulsed with each beat. The path back to the village was already alive with flickering light—lanterns being raised, torches lit, shadows racing. And over it all, the unmistakable sound of terror.

Corrupted creatures were in the village. They sprinted toward the chaos, branches whipping against their faces, cold air burning in their lungs. Lights burst into view as they reached the edge of the square. People were running. Screaming. Smoke poured from a burning roof. A cow—twisted, black-veined, frothing—charged through a group of villagers until Braum tackled it with a roar. Mara stood in the center of the square, staff in hand, swinging desperately at a corrupted fox snapping at a child's heels. "Mara!"

Loran shouted. She whipped around, eyes wide. “Loran! Thank the gods–help me!”

The fox lunged. Loran didn’t think–he grabbed the nearest tool, a shovel leaning against a fence, and swung it hard. The fox hit the ground, twitching once before going still. Mara grabbed his arm, shaking. “I thought– I thought something happened to you–” Before he could respond, a scream tore through the air.

Elder Deren staggered into view, clutching his side. Behind him, something huge slammed into the ground–a corrupted bull, its horns dripping black sludge. It turned toward Loran. Toward the mark. “Get behind me!” Braum roared, sprinting toward the creature with his hammer raised. Loran pulled Mara back. Arlyn raced into the square, scrolls spilling from her satchel. “The healer wrote something!” she shouted. “Something about the corruption seeking–” The bull charged. The ground thundered. The air cracked. Loran’s arm exploded in heat. “No–no, not now–” he gasped, clutching his forearm. The red mark flared beneath his skin, bright enough to cast shadows across the square. The bull stumbled mid-charge, bellowing in pain as the light washed over it. Braum took the opening, slamming his hammer into its skull with a sickening crunch. The creature collapsed. Silence fell. Broken, trembling silence.

Villagers gathered, panting, staring at the carnage. “What did the healer write?” Loran managed, turning to Arlyn. She looked up at him, face pale. “She wrote... that the corruption seeks a mark,” Arlyn whispered, shaking. “Always the mark.” A murmur rippled through the crowd. Some eyes filled with fear. Others with accusation. Loran swallowed. This was only the beginning.

CHAPTER SEVEN
The Healer's Secret

Smoke still curled above the village when dawn crept over the ridge. Loran barely slept. Neither did anyone else. Fires smoldered, villagers dragged the last of the corrupted carcasses into piles, and exhausted guards patrolled the edges of the square with shaking lanterns. Two Stone Grove felt smaller this morning. Tighter. Held together by fear and fraying rope. Braum met Loran at the well, hammer slung across his back, dark circles carved beneath his eyes. "Arlyn's going back to the healer's hut," he said. "She wants us there. Says we missed something." "What about the village?" Loran asked. "Deren told me and Mara to stay with you." Braum's jaw flexed. "Varra wanted to lock you in the council hall. Deren shut that down. Barely." Mara hurried toward them, staff clutched tight enough to whiten her knuckles.

"We should go before Varra changes her mind." They left the village behind, following the same path Loran and Arlyn had taken the night before. The morning air was crisp, but wrong somehow. The forest was too quiet, as if the entire world held its breath. Then they saw it. The deer. Its body lay twisted where it had fallen, but it was different now—horrifyingly so. Black veins had thickened, splitting the hide like roots breaking through dry soil. The horns had spiraled, jagged. One hind leg had warped into something longer, bonier—*becoming something else.* Mara gagged. "It looks worse than last night..." "No," Arlyn whispered as she knelt beside the carcass. "It looks... changed." Loran stepped closer. "Changed how?"

Arlyn didn't answer immediately. She touched her dagger tip to a patch of warped skin—it stretched like rubber, not flesh. "It didn't look like this before," she murmured. "The healer wrote something about this. I saw part of it in her notes last night but didn't understand." Braum frowned. "Wrote what?" Arlyn swallowed, gaze fixed on the twisted leg. "...that corruption does not stay one thing. It progresses." "Progresses?" Loran echoed. "Into *phases*," Arlyn said quietly. "She didn't explain how many." A cold ripple traveled through Loran's spine. "So this isn't the same creature we saw before." "No," Arlyn said. "It's something worse."

They left the deer behind, dread coiled in their stomachs. The healer's cottage looked even smaller in morning light, its door still cracked open, claw marks gouged deep across the back wall. Inside, Arlyn had already cleared the writing table, spreading parchment scraps and torn scrolls across it. Mara gasped. "Someone tore this place apart." She bent and pulled something from a loose floorboard. A brittle scrap of parchment. Ink smeared along the edges. "This was hidden." Loran leaned in. The handwriting was thin, hurried:
"The corruption adapts.
Phase One: Instability.
Phase Two: Mutation.
Phase Three:—"

The rest was torn clean off. Braum exhaled sharply. "So these phases... she'd been studying them?" Arlyn nodded. "And she hid her notes. She didn't want this found." Mara sifted through more scraps and pulled another fragment free. "*The mark is never wrong. Light awakens to oppose the shadowed. The Vessel wears a mark.*"

Loran froze. Braum muttered, "Meaning what?" Arlyn shook her head. "Meaning Loran's mark isn't proof he's the Vessel. Only that he's part of this. The healer must have realized the truth just before she fled." Mara swallowed. "So if Loran isn't the Vessel..." "...someone else is," Arlyn said. Loran's stomach knotted. The idea that another person—somewhere—was tied to all this felt like a stone sinking into his chest. Arlyn handed him a final scrap. *"The corruption seeks the light."*

The words punched the breath from his lungs. "The bull came straight for me." "Because your mark glows," Arlyn said softly. "Not because it belongs to the Vessel." A heavy thump shook the outside wall. They froze. Another thump. Slow. Heavy. Testing the boards.

Braum crept to the window, peering through the shutters. His breath hitched. "Stay quiet." "What is it?" Mara whispered. "A fox," Braum said. "But not like last night." Arlyn tensed. "Phase One?" "...No," Braum whispered. "Worse."

Loran risked a glance. The fox moved with unnatural grace, elongated and sleek like a living shadow. Its eyes glowed—no longer white, but a dim, predatory yellow. Phase Two. Maybe Phase Three. It sniffed the air. Its head snapped toward the cottage. Toward *them.* Loran felt the mark throb beneath his skin—burning, warning.

The fox stepped back. Then another. Its muscles coiled. Deciding. It made a low, guttural sound—then bolted toward the village. Braum cursed. "We have to warn them." "Take everything," Loran said, grabbing the parchment fragments. "Deren needs to see this." Arlyn stuffed the scrolls into her satchel, fingers trembling.

They burst from the cottage and ran. Branches whipped past. Boots pounded earth. The fox was unnaturally fast, weaving through the trees ahead of them. Shouts rose from the edge of the village. A scream split the air. Mara seized Loran's arm. "We're too late." The corruption was evolving. And Two Stone Grove had no idea what was coming.

CHAPTER EIGHT
The Last Words of Deren

The smoke hit them first. Thick. Burning. Bitter. Loran broke into a sprint the moment the village came into view — or what was left of it. Two Stone Grove was drowning in firelight and shadows. Roofs burned orange against the morning sky. Shattered fences lay like broken rib cages. The smell of charred wood mixed horribly with something metallic. Blood.

Mara choked on a sob as they entered the square. "No... no, no—" Bodies lay everywhere. A man slumped against the well, throat torn open. A woman lay face down in the dirt, a trail of blackened footprints beside her. A child's small wooden toy was crushed in the mud next to a hand too small to belong to anyone grown. Braum trembled with fury. "Those monsters..." Loran couldn't speak.

He recognized faces. Neighbors. Friends. People who had fed him, scolded him, laughed with him since he was a boy. People who he had considered family after his mother's untimely death to sickness just a few years prior. Now their eyes stared blankly at the sky or were missing entirely, ripped away. Arlyn knelt beside a young girl half-hidden behind a wagon. She reached for a pulse, but her breath hitched — the girl's chest had been torn open, ribs splintered like cracked pottery.

"Gods..." Arlyn whispered. "They didn't stand a chance." Mara pressed her forehead to Loran's arm, shaking with silent sobs. "My mother... my mother was in the square this morning—" Loran pulled her close. He couldn't bear to say he hadn't seen her yet. Not alive. Not dead.

Braum staggered toward what was left of his home— a collapsed frame, burning slowly. "Ma! Pa!" His voice cracked, raw and terrified. "Ma! Answer me!" He dropped to his knees in the ash. Loran's chest tightened. He had never seen Braum break. Then a weak voice rasped through the smoke: "...over here..." Loran spun toward the council hall. A cracked beam had toppled across the entry, and beneath it – Elder Deren.

Half his body was pinned, robes soaked in blood, breathing shallow and ragged. "Help me move it!" Loran shouted. They rushed over. Braum shoved the beam aside with a roar, muscles straining until it rolled free. Mara knelt immediately, pressing cloth to Deren's wounds, but the blood kept spilling through her fingers. Deren coughed, dark red trickling from his lips. "Don't... waste your cloth, child. I'm past saving."

Arlyn trembled. "What happened here?" "They came... from the north edge..." Deren wheezed. "Not animals anymore. Something... worse." His eyes drifted toward a mangled shape near the blacksmith's door – a creature that might once have been a boar, now twisted, spine arched upward, extra bone pushing through its back like budding horns. Phase Three. Full mutation. "We tried to fight," Deren whispered. "But they were faster. Smarter. They hunted us." Mara's tears fell faster. "Why... why would this happen to us? To our home?"

Deren's gaze softened. "Two Stone Grove has stood for a hundred years... but even old stones crack. I feared this day would come." Loran frowned. "Feared what?" Deren's hand twitched weakly, reaching toward Loran's tear-stained cheek. "When I was a boy... there were stories. Ancient ones. Of a place the old ones fled to when darkness took the land. A place of stone and silence. The... Hollow." Arlyn leaned closer. "Stonewake Hollow?" Deren nodded. "A forbidden place... carved into the mountains beyond the eastern ridges. They said the stones still remember the truth of the past. Said anyone who sought answers went there."

"Why tell us?" Mara whispered. "Because..." Deren coughed violently, blood spraying. "You're the last of this village. The only ones left who can carry its memory. And the world... is changing faster than any of us understand." He gripped Loran's sleeve, desperate, eyes bright with pain. "You must go. Not because of prophecy. Not because of marks or magic. But because if you stay..." His voice cracked. "You will join the dead."

Loran swallowed. "We'll go together." Deren smiled faintly. "Good... good. Stick together. Trust each other..." His gaze flicked briefly to the destroyed square. "You'll need something solid to hold onto... while the world falls apart."

Mara squeezed his hand. "Please don't leave us." Deren's breath faltered. His eyes began to dim. "Child... I left you years ago. I just didn't know it yet." One last exhale. Then nothing. Mara collapsed onto Loran's shoulder, sobbing. Arlyn covered her mouth as tears streamed down her cheeks. Braum bowed his head, fists clenched so tightly his knuckles bled. Loran wiped his face, but more tears came.

Their families were gone.

Their friends.

Their childhood. Two Stone Grove — the world they knew — was dead.

Braum rose slowly, eyes burning. "We leave. Right now. Before those things come back." Arlyn clutched the scroll Deren had mentioned in his youth. "Stonewake Hollow... whatever it is, it's our only lead." Mara wiped her face, voice trembling but steady. "Then let's go. We can mourn later. We survive first."

Loran looked at the burning ruins of his home. He felt something break quietly inside him. "Together," he said. And for the first time, without hesitation, the other three answered: "Together." They stepped into the smoke and flame, leaving the only home they'd ever known. Behind them, the corrupted moved in shadows — evolving, hunting, waiting. Ahead of them, toward Stonewake Hollow, lay the truth. And the Vessel.

CHAPTER NINE
Weeks in the Wild

Three weeks. That's how long they'd been walking. Through forests that once felt familiar and alive. Through valleys where only silence remained. Through the lingering scent of smoke that clung to everything like a memory that refused to fade. Loran wasn't sure when the days began to blur together, but somewhere between the jagged cliffs and the Blackwater marsh, time lost its shape. Each sunrise felt heavier than the last. Each night darker. Grief didn't fade in the wilderness. It simply settled deeper.

Braum walked ahead, broad shoulders more hunched than they used to be. He'd barely spoken the first week. He swung his hammer at anything that moved, even harmless creatures, until Mara finally grabbed him one night and forced him to sit down and breathe. Arlyn became quieter too. She spent her evenings writing notes, cataloguing what they'd seen – corrupted tracks, abandoned settlements, strange movements in the sky– but her hands always shook a little when she thought no one was looking.

And Mara... Loran watched her as she walked beside him now, her eyes fixed on the path. The grief in her face had softened, but not disappeared. It was quieter, deeper. She had lost her mother the same day Loran lost his own home. They all lost something. The only thing they hadn't lost was each other. The forest around them had changed as well. Trees leaned at odd angles. Bark split in spiraling patterns, as if something beneath it was trying to escape.

The leaves had darkened, some turning black along their edges. Corruption seeds. Arlyn warned them not to touch any. "Do you think Stonewake Hollow is close?" Loran asked quietly. "Closer than we were yesterday," Arlyn said, though her voice lacked confidence. "The healer's scroll said east past the ridges. And the last village we passed— what's left of it— had carvings showing the same sigils." "You mean the ones scratched into the well stone?" Braum asked. "Yes," Arlyn said. "Someone there knew about the sigils. Or feared them."

Loran's arm tingled again, a faint warmth pulsing beneath his skin. Not the painful flare from before — this was something else. Calling. Reacting. Reaching. Mara noticed. She always did. "Does it hurt?" "No," Loran said. "Feels... like it's listening." "That's worse," Braum muttered. They stopped around midday at the edge of a cliff overlooking a vast stretch of forest. From here, the eastern ridge looked like a jagged spine rising from the earth. Beyond that, mountains towered under a veil of cloud.

"We're close," Arlyn murmured, studying the map. "Stonewake Hollow should be within a day or two. If nothing slows us down." "Something always slows us down," Braum said. As if on cue, a low rumble trembled through the ground. All four froze. It echoed across the valley — slow, heavy, impossibly deep. Trees shivered in its wake. Birds shot into the air, scattering like startled ash. Another rumble. Closer. Mara grabbed Loran's hand. "What is that?" Arlyn's face was pale. "Not corruption. Something older." Braum scanned the horizon. "Something giant."

Loran felt his stomach twist. He had seen one before— in his dream. But dreams shouldn't bleed into reality. Arlyn folded her map, forcing her voice steady. "The stories say the giants sleep beneath the ridges. If they're waking..." "Then Stonewake Hollow might be connected," Loran finished. The rumbling stopped. Silence returned to the valley. But the eerie stillness felt worse than the sound. Mara sat on a stone, pulling her cloak tighter against the wind. "Do we... do we even know what we're going to do when we get there?" Loran sat beside her. "We survive. We learn. We find answers about the marks." Mara's gaze softened. "And if the truth is worse than the monsters already chasing us?" Loran swallowed. "Then we face it together." She leaned her head against his shoulder– something she hadn't done in weeks. Something she needed more than she'd admit.

Braum cleared his throat loudly. "Right. Together. Which means not dying here on a cliff." Arlyn nodded. "Let's keep moving. The more distance we put between us and that... thing... the better." They gathered their packs and continued east, the forest thickening around them as afternoon light dimmed under rising clouds. Hours passed in steady, uneasy silence. Until the silence broke. A snap echoed through the underbrush. Sharp. Close.

Loran held up a hand. "Stop." The group froze. Another snap. Branches rustled in unnatural rhythm – too many legs, too smooth, too deliberate. Arlyn's face went pale. Mara gripped her staff. Braum raised his hammer. The sound circled them. Not one creature. Several. A chill crawled up Loran's spine. Phase Two. Or worse. The rustling came again – faster, closing in. Arlyn whispered, "Something's stalking us." Braum bared his teeth. "Let it try." Another sound. Claws. Scraping bark. But none of the corrupted emerged. Not yet. They were waiting. Testing the group's reactions. Learning. Corruption was evolving... and growing smarter.

CHAPTER TEN
Creatures of the Canopy

A low hiss drifted from the branches overhead. Mara's breath hitched. "There—above us—" But before she could finish, a dark shape leapt from the canopy— fast, sinuous, impossible to track— It dropped between them like a shadow given flesh. The creature landed on all fours with a sickening, bone-cracking thud. Leaves and dirt scattered. Loran staggered back, heart hammering as he finally saw it fully.

What stood before them had once been a wolf. Now it was a nightmare. Its legs bent at wrong angles, long and spiderlike. Muscles twitched under mottled, hairless patches of skin. Thick black veins crawled across its torso, pulsing as though something inside was pushing to break out. Its jaw unhinged far too wide, ringed with rows of serrated teeth—some broken, some still dripping thick, dark saliva. But the worst part... Was its eyes. Yellow. Focused. Intelligent. It didn't snarl like a wild animal. It watched them. Studied them. Testing. Another hiss came from above. Then another.

Three more shapes shifted in the canopy, their movements precise—coordinated. Corruption had learned to hunt in packs. "Back-to-back!" Loran shouted. They moved instinctively: Braum with his hammer held low and ready, Mara gripping her staff tightly, Arlyn clutching her dagger and breathing unevenly, Loran trying to quiet the rising heat under his skin. The lead creature stretched its limbs, bones popping, then let out a vibrating hum that rippled the air. A signal.

Two more monsters dropped from the branches—one birdlike and twisted, talons elongated into needle-sharp hooks; the other serpentine, its body rippling with too many legs. Arlyn's voice shook. "Phase... Phase Three." The wolf lunged. Braum swung, catching the monster's shoulder with a brutal crack. Bone broke—Loran heard it—but the creature didn't fall. It stumbled, then righted itself unnaturally, head snapping toward Braum with a grotesque, humanlike grin. It was mocking him. Mara thrust her staff forward, striking the creature's flank so hard that bark and corrupted hide scraped together, sending tiny black drops of blood and corruption bursting outward from the impact, buying precious seconds.

The bird-creature swooped down on Arlyn, wings twitching independently like dozens of tiny hands. "Down!" Loran yelled. Arlyn ducked just in time—but the creature wheeled mid-air, talons reaching. Loran felt the mark ignite. Not the flare from before. Not the accidental burst. Something different. A pressure surged inside him—sharp, electric, coiling upward from his chest into his arm. His fingers tingled with heat. His vision sharpened, the world narrowing to the exact angle of the creature's wings. He threw out his hand. A spiraling bolt of red and white erupted from his palm. It wasn't clean. It wasn't controlled. It was raw power. It hit the bird-creature mid-flight, spinning it violently. It screeched, spiraling through branches before crashing into the underbrush with a bone-splitting thud. Loran fell to one knee, gasping as the aftershock shook his bones.

His arm throbbed violently, as if the mark itself were alive. "Loran!" Mara shouted. "Are you—" A serpentine creature lunged for him, fangs dripping sizzling black venom. Mara intercepted it, swinging her staff with a force she didn't know she had. She struck its head, flaring as it recoiled. The wolf charged Braum again, faster this time. Braum grunted, barely dodging a swipe that tore a chunk from a nearby tree. "Would've liked a warning before you did that flashy thing!" "I didn't know it was coming!" Loran shouted back, struggling to his feet.

The wolf snapped at Braum's leg. Braum slammed his hammer upward, driving the monster back with raw strength. But the serpent-creature recovered faster than expected, slithering low, aiming for Arlyn's legs. Arlyn slashed—the blade skittered uselessly off its toughened hide. "Not good," she whispered. The serpent creature coiled, ready to spring. Loran felt the heat spike again—painful, blinding. His heartbeat merged with the pulse of the mark. Something inside him twisted, reached outward. He didn't have time to think. He thrust both hands forward. A wave of red force blasted outward – a concussive shockwave that rippled the air like a heat haze. The serpent-creature flew backward, smashing into a tree.

The trunk split, wood exploding outward in a rain of splinters. The wolf staggered, dazed. Braum seized the moment, roaring as he brought his hammer down on its skull with a thundering crack. The creature convulsed and fell limp. Mara struck the wounded creature again, wood cracking against bone with a loud pop as she forced it still, ensuring it didn't rise again. The forest fell silent except for their gasping breaths. Arlyn wiped blood from a shallow cut across her cheek. "Is... is everyone okay?" Braum spat dirt. "That depends. Was that supposed to happen?" Mara turned to Loran, eyes full of fear and awe. "Your mark—what was that?" Loran clutched his arm, wincing at the burning beneath his skin.

"It feels like... it's waking up. Or reacting. Or—" "Or it has a mind of its own," Arlyn said, voice trembling. "We need to be careful. Very careful." Braum rested a hand on Loran's shoulder. "Kid... you saved us. Again. Whatever that power is—learn to use it before it kills you." Loran swallowed hard, heart still pounding. "I'm trying." Mara stepped closer, touching his arm lightly. "We'll help you. All of us." The words steadied him more than the forest ever could. But as they regrouped, Loran noticed something horrifying. The wolf-creature – the first one he struck – wasn't decomposing. It was changing. Black veins twitched, crawling inward toward its chest. Bones cracked and rearranged. New growths pushed against its skin from inside. Evolving. Arlyn paled. “It’s not stopping. The corruption… it’s still active even after death.” Braum stepped back. “Meaning what?” “Meaning…” Arlyn whispered, voice breaking, “that something is accelerating it.”

The forest creaked around them. Branches swayed though there was no wind. And in the distance — far beyond the tree line — a low, earth-shaking rumble rolled through the valley. Not corruption. Not beasts. Something older. Awakening. Loran gripped his burning arm. “We need to reach Stonewake Hollow,” he said. “Now. Before something finds us that we can’t fight.” They pressed onward, deeper into the forest that felt less like nature and more like a living nightmare. The canopy watched them. And something watched from beyond it.

CHAPTER ELEVEN
The Stonewake Path

The forest thinned as the sun sank toward the jagged eastern ridge. Hours after the attack, their bodies still ached, their nerves still frayed. No one spoke for a long time. Every broken branch and shifting leaf sounded like another creature stalking them. But the deeper they walked, the more the world changed. The trees here were older— towering pillars of silvered bark, their roots weaving through the earth like veins. The air took on a cold, mineral scent. Moss grew in coiling patterns that looked almost like writing. The corruption had not reached this place yet. Or it feared it.

Mara finally broke the silence. "...Does it always feel like something's watching us?" Arlyn wrapped her cloak tighter. "It's the Hollow. Old places tend to listen." "That doesn't make me feel better," Braum muttered, rubbing his shoulder where the wolf-thing had struck him. Loran walked a few paces ahead, staring at the faint trail winding between ancient stones. The pressure in his arm had settled into a deep throb— not painful, not urgent. Just... present. Alive.

He didn't know if it was reacting to the Hollow, or if he was just nervous. Maybe both. He stopped at a break in the tree line. "Look," he whispered. The forest gave way to a wide clearing of stone and earth. Massive slabs jutted from the ground at crooked angles — like the ribs of some ancient beast long dead. Vines wrapped around each stone, but none grew across the carved sigils etched into their surfaces. Red. White. Green. Black.

Familiar and wrong all at once. Braum let out a low whistle. "Stonewake Hollow is real." Mara stepped beside Loran. "It feels... colder here." "It is colder," Arlyn murmured. "Old magic chills the air. Even if there's none left." Braum raised an eyebrow. "Magic. Real magic? Like... in the old stories?" "A long time ago," Arlyn said softly, touching one of the carved stones. "Before the Hollow fell silent. Before the sigils vanished from the world." Loran swallowed. "And before the corruption." Arlyn hesitated. "...We don't know that. But something happened here. Something big enough that people built their lives around not remembering."

They moved deeper into the clearing. The stones grew taller, forming crooked paths. Some bore weathered glyphs, others deep claw marks as though something had fought to escape. Or... fought to get in. Mara knelt by a shattered pillar half-buried in soil. "Look at this carving." Loran crouched beside her. The symbol etched into the stone was a circle divided into uneven pieces— identical to the one on the healer's scroll. But beneath it, another carving depicted four figures: One glowing red. One white. One green. One black.

Mara traced the red figure. "Someone recorded this for a reason." Arlyn knelt beside them. "These carvings... they're ancient. Hundreds of years older than Two Stone Grove. Maybe thousands." Braum tested the weight of his hammer. "So... what's the plan? We camp? Explore? Pray none of those Phase Three things followed us?" "We stay together," Loran said, eyes lingering on the red figure. "We look for answers. And we don't touch anything that looks like it wants to kill us." "Good rule," Braum said. They set camp just beyond the cluster of stones, near a ridge overlooking a pool of still, black water. As the fire crackled to life, Mara sat quietly across from Loran, knees pulled tight to her chest. He moved closer. "You okay?" She shrugged, staring into the flames. "Some days I feel like I'm holding myself together with threads. Other days the threads feel too thin."

Loran sat beside her. “You’ve held together better than any of us.” She huffed a bitter laugh. “That’s not true, and you know it.” He nudged her shoulder. “Maybe not. But you’re still here. That counts for something.” Mara looked at him then, really looked, eyes shining in the firelight. “Loran... what if your mark is changing you? What if you’re becoming something you can’t control?” He didn’t answer right away.

“Then I hope I’m strong enough to stay me.” Mara nodded slowly. “And if you’re not... we won’t let you face it alone.” The words warmed him more than the fire. Across the camp, Arlyn was sketching one of the symbols they’d seen. Braum sharpened his hammer’s edge, though Loran doubted metal would matter much against whatever waited deeper in the Hollow.

A distant rumble echoed through the stones – soft, rolling, unnatural. Mara stiffened. “The giants...?” “No,” Arlyn whispered, closing her notebook. “This sound is different.” Loran stood and felt the mark throb with a sudden, sharp pulse. Something inside the Hollow had awakened when they arrived. Something old. Something aware. The air grew colder. The water on the ridge rippled. And the stone beneath their feet hummed – just enough for Loran to feel it vibrate up his bones. Braum rose slowly, hammer ready. “Tell me that was the wind.” Loran shook his head. “No,” he whispered. The Hollow was whispering back.

CHAPTER TWELVE
The Hollow Breathes

Stonewake Hollow grew colder the deeper they walked. Not like winter cold. This was different — a breath on the back of the neck, a whisper along the spine, a chill that felt *aware.* Loran shivered, though the others didn't seem to feel it. "What's wrong?" Mara asked, keeping close beside him. Loran hesitated. "Nothing. Just... cold." But it wasn't cold. It was something else. Something watching him. They followed a narrow path between towering slabs of stone. Carvings covered every surface — spirals, sigils, runes eroded by time. Some glowed faintly when Loran passed, as if reacting to the mark under his skin. Braum lingered near one of the stones. "How old you think this place is?" Arlyn brushed her fingers along a faded symbol. "Older than the villages. Older than the Sealed War. Maybe older than recorded history."

Braum grunted. "Figures. The oldest places are always the creepiest." As they moved deeper, a subtle hum vibrated through the earth — a faint, rhythmic pulse that Loran felt in the soles of his feet. Like a heartbeat beneath the stone. He stopped. "Did you hear that?" he whispered. "Hear what?" Braum asked. Loran strained to listen. Another pulse beat through the ground — soft but steady. "You didn't feel that?" he asked. Mara stepped closer. "Loran... only you reacted." Arlyn swallowed. "Is it your mark?" "I don't know." He did. He felt it in his bones. The Hollow was responding to him. And only him.

They reached an open courtyard of massive fallen pillars. Moss covered everything except a single stone disk embedded in the ground, perfectly circular, carved with concentric rings. Mara approached it first — and gasped, clutching her stomach. "Mara?" Loran rushed to her. She stumbled back from the disk, face pale, eyes wide with pain. "Something—something in that—hurts. I don't know what it is, it's like pressure—" Arlyn hurried to her side. "Is it the corruption?" Mara shook her head violently. "No... no, it's deeper than that." Loran knelt by the disk. At first it looked like ordinary carving—lines spiraling inward toward a central symbol. Then he saw it. The same divided circle from the healer's scroll. Four uneven pieces. A sigil broken in ancient conflict.

The stone beneath his hand thrummed, reacting to his touch. The mark on his arm burned. A faint red light pulsed beneath his skin. "Loran," Arlyn warned, "step back—" He tried. But his hand wouldn't move. It felt anchored to the stone disk — drawn toward it by something he didn't understand. The world around him muffled, sounds fading into distant echoes. A whisper drifted through his mind: *Wake...* The word shivered down his spine. He saw flashes — not images, but impressions. Red light. Stone. A shape too large to comprehend stirring in the dark. Then— Mara grabbed his arm, ripping him away from the disk.

The moment broke. The vision vanished. The disk went dark. Loran gasped and stumbled backward, nearly falling. "What happened?" Braum demanded, gripping his hammer. "I don't—" Loran pressed a hand to his forehead. "I don't know. Something just... reached for me." Arlyn knelt beside the disk. "These patterns... they're channels. Like conduits for energy. Whatever was here was meant to respond to someone with the mark." Braum made a face. "Meaning you?" Loran didn't answer. Mara was still breathing hard. "I felt pain when I got near it... but only at the center. The symbol." Arlyn frowned. "That's strange. The pain might be a warning. Or... a rejection." Mara winced. "It felt like both."

Loran looked deeper into the Hollow. More stone paths, more carvings, more shadows that seemed to move when he looked too long. "We keep going," he said softly. But when they reached the next clearing, the breath left their lungs. Before them lay a massive shape, half-buried in moss and stone. A rib-like structure of petrified bone arched skyward, each rib the size of a tree. The earth beneath it bulged with the outline of something colossal—humanoid in shape. Not alive. But not entirely dead. One of the old guardians... the ones whispered about in bedtime tales. Turned to stone over centuries. Braum whispered, "What in the frozen hells..." Arlyn's hands trembled. "The stories were real..." Mara clung to Loran's arm. "But those stories were just myths... weren't they?"

Loran stared at the massive rib cage. "Maybe not all of them." Or maybe something killed them. Before they could move closer, the wind shifted. A distant cry echoed through the Hollow — a sound between a wail and a howl. Corruption. Close. Arlyn's voice shook. "It followed us." Braum lifted his hammer. "Then we find somewhere to hide. Or fight. Pick one." Loran stared at the stone giant's ribs. A tunnel opened beneath them. Dark. Old. And beckoning. His mark pulsed again. "Down there," he whispered. "That's where we're meant to go." The wind howled again — closer this time. They didn't hesitate. They ran into the darkness beneath the stone giant's ribs. And the Hollow sealed the shadows behind them.

CHAPTER THIRTEEN
The Chamber of Echoes

The tunnel beneath the petrified ribs swallowed them in cold. The moment they stepped inside, the air changed – thicker, heavier, humming with a pressure that made Loran's ears ache. Dust drifted like ash in their lantern light, settling on carved runes along the walls. Braum gripped the lantern tighter. "Feels like walking into a tomb." Arlyn shook her head slowly. "No. Tombs are dead. This place..." She swallowed. "This place remembers." Loran didn't miss the way she said it. They moved deeper, the walls curving like the inside of a colossal ribcage. The stone was engraved with spirals and glyphs, some barely visible, others gouged into the rock.

When Loran touched the wall, the stone pulsed faintly under his palm. Alive. Mara glanced back at him, nervous. "Your mark's doing that?" "I don't know," he whispered – though he did. The Hollow was reacting to him again. They entered a massive chamber lit by cracks of pale blue luminescence. Pillars rose like stone trees. The walls were covered in murals that wrapped from floor to ceiling. Arlyn gasped softly. "This is... a record." Braum raised the lantern higher. "A record of what?" Arlyn moved closer, tracing a carved symbol. "The Sigils. All four of them." Loran joined her. The first mural showed towering stone beings – Wardens – holding four forces in balance: Red, White, Green, Black.

Light radiated from the center, pushing back dark tendrils. Another mural showed one Warden cracking apart, light spilling out of its chest. Then corruption spreading. Braum exhaled slowly.

"That's the one we saw outside... the fallen one." Arlyn nodded. "Its death weakened the Seal." Mara hugged her cloak around herself, uneasy. "Then... what happens when another falls?"

Loran didn't answer. He didn't have one. Arlyn stepped toward another carving – dozens of silhouettes, faceless, gathered beneath the four sigils. They seemed human, but the details were intentionally vague. "This is strange," Arlyn murmured. "These figures... any one of them could have carried the sigils." "Any one?" Braum frowned. "Why not just one chosen hero or something?" "Because they weren't showing a hero," Arlyn said softly. "They were showing potential." Loran felt a chill. "So the Sigils could appear on anyone." "Exactly," Arlyn said.

Mara stepped beside them, scanning the indistinct silhouettes. "So there's no pattern? No chosen line? Nothing to predict—" "No," Arlyn finished. "And that might be why people feared them." Braum crossed his arms. "Well, that's comforting." They continued around the chamber. Loran paused at a mural depicting a great circle carved into four unequal pieces – the same symbol from the healer's scroll. A faint static buzzed beneath his fingertips. A whisper curled through his head: *Wake...* Loran flinched. The mark pulsed violently. Mara stepped forward. "Loran?" "Something's calling me," he whispered. "From deeper inside."

Before they could question that, the chamber shook. A deep tremor rolled beneath their feet, dust sifting from the ceiling. Not corruption. Not wind. Something massive shifted far below. Arlyn's eyes widened. "That's a Warden. Sleeping... or trying to." Braum took a step back. "You mean there's another one alive down here?" Arlyn nodded. "Alive... but weakening." Mara moved closer to Loran. "Is this a good idea?" Loran didn't know. But the mark in his arm pulsed again – stronger, insistent. "This isn't a tomb," he murmured. "It's a warning." The tremor came again. Louder. Rhythmic. A heartbeat. At the far end of the chamber, a narrow corridor descended into pure darkness.

Cold air breathed out of it— ancient, heavy, faintly metallic. Something whispered through the corridor — soft, unintelligible, like a forgotten language echoing down a long tunnel. The Hollow wanted them deeper. Arlyn drew a shaky breath. "Whatever truth the Wardens left... it's down there." Braum tightened his grip on his hammer. "Then we face it." Mara looked at Loran, worry and trust blending in her eyes. "Together?" He nodded. "Always." They stepped toward the corridor. Shadows shifted back as if afraid of the lantern light. And as they entered the darkness, the murals behind them flickered faintly— one carving of the Black Sigil glowing for only a moment... Before going dark again, unnoticed. The Hollow swallowed them whole.

CHAPTER FOURTEEN
The Sleeping Warden

The corridor sloped downward into darkness that felt less like absence of light and more like something alive pressing in on them. The air thickened with each step, heavy with centuries of trapped dust and ancient power. Their lantern flickered. Braum shook it nervously. “Not now...” “It’s not the lantern,” Arlyn whispered. “Something’s... interfering.”

Loran felt it too. The mark on his arm pulsed with an unsteady rhythm — not matching his heartbeat, not random. Something deeper, slower. Something enormous. The tunnel opened suddenly into a vast cavern, and the four froze. A massive shape dominated the chamber— curled into itself like a titan sleeping. Its body was carved from stone but not crafted by tools; the stone *flowed*, rippled, shaped itself into ribs, limbs, and a head crowned with runes etched in patterns too intricate to comprehend.

A Warden. Alive. Just barely. Its chest rose and fell in slow, rumbling breaths. Faint blue veins of light pulsed beneath its stone skin, dimming with each cycle as though leaking the last of its strength. Loran stepped forward unconsciously. The mark on his arm flared bright red. The Warden’s faint breathing hitched — once. Then resumed. Mara grabbed Loran’s sleeve. “Don’t go any closer.” He swallowed hard. “It’s calling me.” Arlyn knelt at the edge of the platform overlooking the Warden. “Wardens don’t call. They sleep. They guard. They only wake when—” She stopped.

“When the Seal weakens,” Loran finished quietly. Braum swore under his breath. “So that thing up there,” he jerked a thumb toward the ribcage chamber, “was one that fell. And this one's next?" Arlyn nodded. "If this one dies... the corruption might spread uncontrollably across half the continent." Mara shuddered. "Then how do we stop it?" No one answered. The cavern hummed softly. The Warden's runes flickered. Stone cracked faintly, dust sifting like snow. Then, the impossible happened.

A deep rumble vibrated through the chamber. The Warden's head—moved. Not fully. Just a tiny shift. But enough. All four staggered as the ground trembled. A low, ancient groan filled the cavern, resonating through their bones. Loran fell to one knee, clutching his arm as the mark blazed painfully bright. Images flashed behind his eyes: A sky torn open. Four sigils erupting from a shattered core. A shadow spreading like ink. A figure, alone. Then— A voice shook the cavern. Not spoken. Not heard. *Felt.* "RED BEARER..." Mara gasped. Arlyn clapped a hand over her mouth. Braum's grip tightened on his hammer until his knuckles turned white. Loran forced himself upright. "I... I hear you."

The Warden's head twitched again — stone grinding like mountains shifting. "THE SEAL... CRACKS..." The cavern walls shook with each word. Loran stepped closer despite Mara's desperate grip. "How do we fix it? Tell us what to do!" Silence. The Warden's breath rattled. Its chest heaved with effort, as though every word pulled it closer to collapse. Then— "THE VESSEL..." The others stiffened. Loran's heart pounded. "The Vessel? Where? Who?" A long pause. The Warden's runes flickered violently— then dimmed. "THE VESSEL... IS... NEAR..." Mara's breath hitched. Arlyn stared wide-eyed. Braum stepped protectively in front of Loran. "He means YOU. You're the marked one."

Loran didn't argue. He'd assumed that for weeks. Everyone did. He took another step forward. "What do I do? Tell me how to stop the corruption!" The Warden's voice weakened, flickering like dying fire. "WHEN... THE VESSEL... CLAIMS... THE BLACK... THE WORLD..." A violent tremor cut the sentence short. The Warden shuddered. Stone cracked. A cascade of dust fell from the cavern ceiling. Mara pulled Loran back. "It's collapsing—we have to go!" "No!" Loran yelled. "It hasn't finished!" Another tremor. The cavern boomed as a massive crack tore across the Warden's chest. Blue light spilled out — fading too quickly. Arlyn screamed over the noise: "Loran, move!" The Warden's final word vibrated like a dying heartbeat: "...RUN..." The cavern floor lurched.

The path they had entered through began to crumble. A deafening roar filled the chamber. Braum grabbed Arlyn. Mara grabbed Loran. They fled toward the collapsing corridor as stone shards fell like hail behind them. The Warden's glow vanished. Its breathing stopped. The last living Warden in Stonewake Hollow... had fallen silent. And as they sprinted up the tunnel, Mara whispered — barely audible over the chaos: "Near... He said the Vessel is near..." Loran didn't hear her. But the Hollow did. Behind them, deep in the darkness, something else stirred. Something the Warden had been keeping asleep... until now.

CHAPTER FIFTEEN
The Ash-Swept Path

The collapse of the Hollow chased them for nearly half a mile. The roar of falling stone rolled through the trees like thunder peeling across a dead sky. Dust coiled upward in dark clouds, swallowing the entrance to the cavern until nothing remained but a mound of broken earth. The four of them staggered through brittle underbrush, coughing, shaking dust from their hair, gasping in the strange, metallic air the Hollow had breathed into the world.

Loran bent over, hands on his knees, staring at the ground as it quivered with the last echoes of the Warden's death. The mark on his arm throbbed once—a deep, painful pulse—then dimmed to a faint ember beneath his skin. The Warden's voice still echoed in his skull. *The Vessel... is near...* Mara was the first to find her voice. "What happened to the sky?" Loran looked up. The heavens were wrong. The familiar blue-gray twilight was gone, replaced by streaks of crimson ash hanging in the clouds like blood thinned with smoke. The sunlight had turned metallic, casting the world in a dull red tint. The air tasted like cold iron on the tongue, and somewhere far off, a low rumbling groan vibrated through the ground as if the earth itself was unsettled.

Arlyn wrapped her cloak around herself, shivering. "This... shouldn't be happening—not this rapidly." Braum wiped dust from his brow, trying to mask the tremble in his hands. "If it does this every time one dies... then the Seal's already cracking, isn't it?" Loran didn't answer. His gaze drifted along the tree line. The forest had changed. Leaves hung limp on branches, their color drained. Bark was splitting in jagged, unnatural lines. The air hummed like faint strings being plucked. All around them, the ground was dusted with something gray-red, falling in slow, drifting flakes. Mara touched one on her sleeve. “Ash?” She held it closer. “No... not ash. Something else.” Arlyn leaned in. “This... is residue from corruption spoiling the air dusting the ground with this silt poisoning the land.”

Braum let out a worrisome mutter. “So much has changed, we have witnessed so much... We aren’t even in the deep end yet?” Arlyn shook her head grimly. “Whatever we’... something worse is coming.” Loran swallowed hard, pushing back the cold knot forming in his stomach. “We need to keep moving.” Mara blinked. “Where? We can’t go back to the village.” “That’s not where I meant,” Loran said slowly.

He lifted his arm— the Red Sigil glowed faintly, pulsing like a heartbeat. When he turned north, the glow brightened. When he turned away, it dimmed. Braum saw it first. “It’s pointing somewhere.” Arlyn stared. “It’s guiding you.” Mara looked at him with a mixture of fear and wonder. “Loran... what does it mean? “He didn’t know. But he felt it—deep in his bones. A pull. A direction. A whisper curling under his skin like something ancient drawing him in. “It wants me to go north.” Arlyn frowned. “But we don’t know what’s north. The roads are dangerous. The corruption’s spreading faster up that way.” “We don’t have a choice,” Loran murmured. “The Warden died trying to speak to me. This has to mean something.”

A wind swept through the trees, scattering red flakes like sparks. The forest groaned as branches shifted overhead, creaking as if protesting the change. Mara hugged herself against the chill. “I don’t like this.” “Me neither,” Braum admitted. “But following the sigil seems better than waiting for whatever’s chasing us.” Loran nodded. They moved. The path was slow, grueling. Every step seemed heavier than the last. The world around them withered. Grass turned brittle beneath their boots. The shadows deepened into strange, twisting shapes. Birdsong had vanished altogether. After two hours, the forest thinned into a clearing where the land sloped downward into a shallow valley. What they saw tightened each of their throats. A small abandoned settlement—maybe ten houses—lay silent in the dipping land. Roofs caved in. Doors torn from hinges. Not from weather. Not from neglect. From flight. Arlyn whispered, "This place... they left in a hurry." Mara pointed toward the well in the center. The bucket was still mid-drop, rope burned where it had been torn free. A basket of dried herbs lay spilled on the ground, crushed footprints stamped into it. Survivors. Desperate ones. And maybe—"Water," Braum muttered. "We should refill before we move on." Loran nodded, but unease prickled under his skin. The mark pulsed again, not in warning but in anticipation.

Loran was the last to fill his waterskin. He stood up, wiping a sleeve across his cheek when a heavy hand clamped down on his shoulder. He didn't even need to turn—no one else had that kind of weight to their grip. "Braum?" he asked. But when he faced him, Braum was already pressing something into his hands. Cold. Solid. Balanced. A sword. "Found you a proper weapon," Braum said, the faintest grin beneath his beard. "You're going to need it." Loran blinked, genuinely surprised.

He hadn't realized until that moment just how bare he'd set out—no blade, no real protection, nothing but instinct and a mark he barely understood. "I... didn't even think to take one," he admitted, shame warming his cheeks. "That's why you've got us," Braum replied, clapping his shoulder again. "Now take it. And try not to drop it when something snarls at you." The wind drifted through shattered shutters, carrying the hollow sound of creaking wood. A raven perched on a collapsed roof stared at them with white, sightless eyes before flapping away. Arlyn moved toward an overturned table. "Something was here recently. Food scraps, torn cloth—" Braum crouched near a crushed lantern. "Boot prints. Two sets. One small, one heavier—" A twig snapped behind them.

Loran spun instantly, hand on his dagger. A shadow stepped from the doorway of a collapsed house. A girl. Dust-covered. Hair tied back with a torn ribbon. Eyes wide with fear—and relief. "Loran?" His breath left him all at once. "Lila?" She ran into him before he could answer, arms wrapping around him so tightly it almost hurt. Her voice cracked against his shoulder. "I thought—you were dead—everyone's dead—I didn't know where to go—" Loran held her, stunned, overwhelmed by relief and guilt all at once. Braum whispered, "Loran... someone's behind her."

A second figure emerged from the doorway. A lean man in a weather-beaten cloak, bandaged across one arm, gripping a long staff carved with old travel runes. His eyes were sharp, assessing—not hostile, but cautious. "I told her to wait," he said quietly. "Didn't expect strangers to follow the ash trail." Arlyn straightened. "Who are you?" He tapped his staff once against the ground.

"Ryn. Wanderer. Survivor. I've been helping the girl since Two Stone Grove fell." Loran froze. Lila swallowed hard, stepping back from him. "It all happened while you all were on your way to the healer... I—I don't know who survived." Mara's face softened. "Lila... I'm so sorry." Lila wiped her eyes, trying to stay strong. "Mother tried to get me out. She—she didn't make it." Loran's heart clenched. Knowing he was only minutes away from being there to help—before the dust settled from the horrors the village had to face in his absence.

Ryn stepped forward, studying Loran closely. "Your arm. Show me." Loran hesitated but lifted his sleeve. The Red Sigil glowed faintly beneath the skin. Ryn exhaled. "I figured. The corruption's movement makes sense now." Arlyn blinked. "You... know about the sigils?" "I know enough," Ryn said. "Enough to know the world's shifting. And if that thing on your arm is glowing like that—then something wants you north." Loran stiffened. "How did you—" "Your friend there"—he nodded to Mara—"keeps glancing north like she afraid of the journey she's about to take or... feels the pull too." Mara flushed slightly. "I—I was just thinking." Ryn's eyes narrowed slightly, but he said nothing more.

Instead, he gestured toward the tree line. "If you're heading north, I'll guide you." Braum frowned. "Why help us?" Ryn's expression darkened. "Because whatever's gathering out there—whatever's turning people, animals, trees— it's not random anymore. It's moving like an army." An involuntary shiver passed through Lila. "Ryn says the corruption's growing minds," she whispered. "They were chanting. Like... speaking in unison." Arlyn's breath stopped. "Phase Four." "No," Ryn corrected. "Phase Three, Just more progressed."

The wind shifted, carrying a distant chorus of groans—low, rhythmic, terrible. Mara shivered. Loran's mark throbbed painfully, pulling him north as if desperate. He tightened his jaw. "Then we move," Loran said quietly. "Before whatever's gathering finds us first." And together—with fear, grief, and the first spark of resolve—they walked north into the dying world. The corruption wasn't just spreading. It was organizing. And somewhere ahead, hidden in the growing darkness, the Vessel listened for them.

CHAPTER SIXTEEN
What Came Before the Silence

Lila sat close to the fire, but her arms were wrapped so tightly around herself she might as well have been sitting in deep winter. The flames colored her cheeks gold, but her eyes were far away—fixed on a night that had not yet finished chasing her. When she finally spoke, her voice was brittle as frost. "You all left so quickly," she whispered. "Headed toward the healer's hut. No one thought anything was wrong. Mother even laughed and said you'd track mud through the whole place again when you came back."

Loran felt the words lance straight through him. He had heard the elder's dying breath, heard the last warning whispered from a mouth coated in blood and ash—but this was worse. This was someone living the moment he'd missed. Lila took a shaky breath. "It wasn't long after you'd gone. Maybe a few minutes. I was outside with Mother, sorting herbs into bundles. She made me promise to finish my lessons tomorrow.

I remember that clearly. And then..." Her voice faltered, and her fingers dug into her knees. "The fox appeared." Mara stiffened beside Loran. Lila nodded. "It came out of the trees so quietly. Too quietly. No crunch of leaves. No breath. Its eyes were golden—glowing, almost. At first people just backed away, confused. Someone tried to shoo it with a broom." A hollow, humorless laugh escaped her. "It didn't even look at them." "What did it look at?" Arlyn asked. Lila met Loran's eyes. "The direction you went."

The fire popped loudly. "It stood in the square and turned its head, sniffing the air. Its whole body tensed, like it found the trail it wanted. But instead of following you..." She swallowed. "It ran back into the village. Straight past everyone. Toward the heart of the square." Braum exhaled a curse under his breath. "That's when everything changed," Lila whispered. She didn't look at any of them.

Her gaze stayed fixed on what only she had seen. "First came the sound," she said. "Like a deep vibration under the earth. You didn't hear it. You were too far. But those of us still in the village... it felt like the ground was humming. Like something had finally found what it was looking for." She rubbed her arms hard, as if trying to scrape away the memory. Her voice thinned. "The animals started screaming. Not just one—*all* of them. Horses reared so violently they snapped their reins. Chickens beat their wings bloody trying to escape their coops. The goats... gods, the goats—one of them twisted right in front of me, like its bones were being rearranged under its skin."

Arlyn pressed a hand to her mouth. "And then," Lila continued, "the people started." She closed her eyes as if bracing herself. "Teren... he staggered back into the square first." Loran's breath caught. "He was holding his head. Just like before. Like something was pushing inside his skull again, clawing. He kept saying he was fine after you helped him. He told everyone he felt normal." Her lips trembled. "He wasn't normal."

Lila's voice cracked. "He tried to call out to his Mother. But the words didn't come. Just... noise." Images painted the inside of Loran's skull without mercy. "Teren fell to the ground. His legs wouldn't hold him. The veins in his arms went black, like ink poured through them. But worse—his eyes..." Lila shuddered violently. "It wasn't like before. The shadows in them... they were moving."

Braum cursed again, quieter. "Teren grabbed at a child trying to help him. His hand shook like he was fighting himself. But then he screamed—so loud the windows rattled—and he threw the child aside like they weighed nothing." Lila's voice dropped. "That was when the other villagers began collapsing. They held their heads.

Some clawed their chests as if trying to tear something out. Others just dropped where they stood. And then…" She inhaled. "…they changed." The fire seemed to grow quieter. "It all happened so fast," she whispered. "People ran into their homes. Locked doors. Shouted warnings. Others chased after their children. But the corrupted ones… they didn't hesitate. They shattered doors. Dragged people outside. It didn't matter who was screaming or who was fighting. They just kept pulling them out, one by one."

She rubbed at her eyes harshly. "I tried to get Mother to run with me, but she was pushing me away. Telling me to go. Telling me—" Her voice broke. "Telling me she loved me." Loran swallowed hard. "Then something else came." The way she said it made the fire seem suddenly too small, too dim. "Something… unseen," Lila whispered. "You couldn't look at it directly. It was like a heavy place in the air. A… presence. When it entered the square, everything stopped. Every corrupted villager. Every animal. Even the fox." Arlyn closed her eyes. She understood what that meant. "It wasn't looking for you," Lila said to Loran. "Not you specifically. It didn't check houses. Didn't move through the streets. It just *knew*. It knew whoever it wanted wasn't there."

"Then why come?" Braum murmured. "To take what was left," Lila whispered. "Or to claim the village. Or… or maybe just because it *could*." Her voice thinned to a tremor. "When it arrived, every corrupted creature turned toward the forest. As if someone had called to them. They didn't run. They didn't lurch. They walked. All of them. In a straight line." "An army," Ryn said quietly. Everyone turned toward him, unsure when he had moved closer to the fire. Lila nodded without looking at him. "I didn't know what else to do. I ran toward the back sheds. I hid under grain sacks. I stayed there until the last footsteps faded and the screaming stopped. The silence was worse." Loran felt something clutch his ribs. "When I crawled out," Lila whispered, "the village was empty. Not a single person left. Just… dust. Trails in the dirt where the horde had walked. I thought I was the only one still alive."

Her voice broke again. “I ran. I just ran.” “And found me,” Ryn said, stepping forward. Lila nodded. “I thought he was one of them. I nearly stabbed him with a broken piece of crate.” A tiny, broken laugh escaped her. “He grabbed my wrist before I could even swing.” Ryn’s tone was gentle, but edged with the weight of what he had seen. “She was covered in dirt and shaking so hard she could barely stand. I’d been watching the creatures move deeper into the woods. They didn’t look anywhere else. They had purpose.” Arlyn stiffened. “Purpose?” Ryn nodded, eyes dark. “And direction.” Silence fell. Lila’s gaze finally lifted to Loran. “When you reached the village...” She swallowed. “...I was already gone. And the only person left to speak to you was the elder.” Loran’s throat closed. “I’m sorry,” Lila whispered. Tears fell freely now. “I left. I left him. I left everyone. I should have stayed. I should have—”

“No,” Loran said firmly, moving to her side. “You survived. That’s what you were supposed to do.” She sobbed once—quiet, small. But the guilt was carved deep. Ryn tapped his staff once against the ground. “The thing that led them...” he said quietly, “it hasn’t finished its work. It’s gathering. Moving across the land like a storm front.” The forest creaked around them. A distant hum—barely audible—threaded through the night air like a slow chant. Loran felt the mark on his arm burn. The pull north tightened like an invisible hook. He rose slowly. “We move at dawn,” he murmured. But inside him, beneath the guilt and the grief and the fear, another truth began to take shape: He had been too late once. He would not be too late again. Somewhere in the deepening dark, something waited— and the path north was already calling his name.

CHAPTER SEVENTEEN
The Wanderer's Path

Dawn had not yet broken, but the sky was already the color of a healing bruise—purple fading into poisoned red. The air felt different when they woke. Heavier. Thicker. As if the world itself was bracing for something. They packed in silence. Lila's voice was raw from the night before, and no one pushed her to talk.

Braum kept glancing toward the trees, checking shadows that hadn't been dangerous yesterday. Arlyn walked with her hood pulled tight, studying the dying forest the way a healer studies a patient whose heartbeat is fading. Only Ryn moved with purpose. He stood at the tree line, staff in hand, scanning the horizon like a man expecting something to emerge from it at any second. His posture was relaxed, but there was nothing casual in the way his fingers curled around the carved runes etched into the staff's weathered wood.

There was a poise about him—an ease that didn't come from confidence, but from experience. The kind earned the hard way. Ryn wore dark, travel-worn attire that gave him the look of a rogue or blade-for-hire: fitted leathers, light plates sewn beneath the fabric, and a medium-length sword resting comfortably at his hip. He looked older than the rest of them—perhaps around thirty—just enough gray threaded through the stubble of his beard to hint at years lived on the road. His hair, a few inches shy of his shoulders, was half pulled back in a way that kept it out of his face but didn't fuss about the rest. He would have been mistaken for a wandering sell-sword at first glance... if not for the staff.

That was the puzzle. Most individuals who carried a staff had no need for a blade, and those who carried a blade had no reason to haul around a length of carved wood. Staffs were practical tools—good for long treks, clearing brush, or testing the ground ahead—but beyond extending one's reach or offering stability, they had little purpose. Yet Ryn carried both— sword and staff— as naturally as if each served a purpose only he understood. And that alone made him something none of them quite knew how to place.

Mara approached him, curiosity outweighing her exhaustion. "You didn't sleep," she said quietly. Ryn didn't look at her. "Didn't need to." His tone wasn't arrogant—just matter-of-fact. Loran joined them, adjusting the strap on his pack. "You said you'd guide us north," he said. "But... why were you near the village at all? Most travelers avoid the deep woods these days."

Ryn's expression didn't change, but his voice did—lower, edged with something darker. "Because the woods haven't been safe for a long time. And I've been following the signs." Arlyn stepped closer. "Signs?" Ryn finally turned, eyes sharp in the half-light. "You thought this started with your village?" Lila flinched at the word village. Ryn shook his head slowly. "No. This has been coming for years. Little things first. Sick animals wandering from the far north. Birds dropping from the sky with black veins in their wings. Travelers vanishing on the ridge path. Small towns reporting nightmares that spread from house to house."

Mara's breath caught. "Nightmares can spread?" Ryn gave her a thin, humorless smile. "Everything spreads now." The wind hissed through the dying leaves overhead. Loran frowned. "Why didn't the wardens do anything? Or the elder councils? Someone had to have noticed." "People notice," Ryn said. "They just don't believe. Corruption doesn't always arrive as monsters tearing down doors. Sometimes it seeps. Quietly. Softly. Until the ground is rot and no one remembers when it started. Like an ant hill on the land that you never pay much attention to, small subtle, sometimes taking years to manifest its true size above ground."

A chill danced down Loran's spine. Arlyn crossed her arms. "And you? How do you fit into this? What exactly were you doing near our home?" Ryn held her gaze without blinking. "Following a trail." "What kind of trail?" Braum pressed. Ryn tapped his staff once against the earth. "The kind that doesn't want to be followed." The forest fell silent. Loran took a step closer. "You've fought them before." It wasn't a question. Ryn's jaw tightened. "Yes." Arlyn studied him. "And survived?" He huffed a breath—not quite a laugh. "Most days. Barely." He looked past them, beyond the trees, toward the north where Loran's mark would sometimes flicker faintly beneath his sleeve.

"The creatures that left your village didn't move like twisted animals," Ryn said. "They marched. They obeyed. That means something new is rising. Something hungry." "And you're following it?" Mara asked. Ryn tilted his head, considering his words. For the first time, he looked... unsure. "I'd like to keep this thing from spreading," he said at last. "Before it becomes unstoppable." Loran felt his arm throb faintly under his sleeve. The pull north tugged through his bones. "What do you think is waiting out there?" he asked.

Ryn's eyes drifted toward the horizon, and for a heartbeat, he looked distant—like he was listening to something none of them could hear. "I think the world is waking up," Ryn murmured. "And the things that were once chained are walking again." Lila shivered. "Then why help us?" Arlyn asked. "You barely know us." Ryn's gaze flicked to Lila first, softening, then moved to Loran—and lingered. Then he looked away. "Because I seem to be on the right track." he said simply. But there was something unspoken behind the words. Something Loran felt rather than heard. Before he could press, the wind shifted again—bringing with it a distant echo. Not chanting. Not footsteps. Something else. A hum. Low. Resounding. Like the earth remembering something terrible.

Ryn's hand tightened on his staff. "We need to move," he said. "Now." They followed without hesitation. As they walked,

Loran glanced at Ryn again, a question burning unasked. Ryn had spoken of corruption with too much knowledge. Too much weight. Too much familiarity. The path north stretched ahead of them like a wounded vein across the land. And for the first time, Loran wondered whether he was following the pull of his sigil... or whether someone else along their path had been following it longer than they realized.

CHAPTER EIGHTEEN
The Road That Watches

The forest thinned as they traveled north, but the air only grew heavier.What little sunlight filtered through the branches came dull and red, as if strained through smoke. Leaves curled inward on their stems, brittle enough to crumble when the wind brushed past. Loran couldn't shake the feeling that every mile they walked pulled them deeper into something the world had been trying to hide for centuries. They moved quietly. No one had recovered fully from the chaos of the past weeks, and Ryn's urgency kept them from speaking more than a few scattered words.

Even Braum, usually the first to break silence, seemed uneasy as he scanned the ravaged woods. Lila walked between Mara and Arlyn, clutching her satchel to her chest. Every now and then she touched her shoulder as though she still felt her mother's hand there, guiding her to run. After an hour, the path bent sharply downhill. Ryn raised a hand for them to stop. Loran nearly crashed into him. "What is it?" Ryn didn't answer immediately. He knelt and brushed the dirt with two fingers. A long, wide mark cut through the forest floor, stretching from the east to the northwest like an enormous dragged line. No—not dragged. Pressed.

"Footprints?" Braum asked. Ryn shook his head. "Not one set... Many." Lila stepped forward, voice barely above a whisper. "This is the path they took." Ryn rose slowly. "A flock of them." "How many?" Arlyn asked. Ryn brushed the dirt from his fingers. "Enough to keep our distance from." A chill rippled through them. The marching trail vanished beyond the fallen branches ahead, swallowed by trees that leaned inward like they had been pushed aside. Loran's arm throbbed once beneath his sleeve—the pull north growing sharper. He swallowed. "It's fresh." "Yes," Ryn said. "Very." He glanced toward the left. "And something crossed their path not long after."

Mara frowned. "Something crossed them? Not joined them?" Ryn nodded. "Crossed." He tapped another stretch of dirt beside the trail. Loran leaned in. A different pattern cut across the ground. Not wide. Not heavy. Something lighter. Sharper. Like talons or claws... but arranged wrong. Too many ridges. Too long a stride. Braum's hand went to his hammer. "What kind of thing leaves that behind?" Ryn's eyes narrowed. "One that hunts."

Lila whimpered before she could stop herself. Mara put an arm around her shoulders immediately. Arlyn cleared her throat. "Does it follow the corruption?" "No," Ryn said. "It follows us." The group froze. "What?" Loran snapped. "You mean—" Ryn nodded gravely. "It's trailing something marked." Loran felt his heart hammer. His arm burned hot under the cloth of his sleeve. Mara stepped closer to him instinctively, putting herself between him and the trees. But Ryn was already studying the ground again, eyes razor-focused. "It's not close. If it were, we'd hear it. Maybe even feel it."

His gaze slid to Loran—lingering just long enough to unsettle him. "But it left these tracks no more than an hour ago." "And we've been moving for—" Braum checked the sky— "about an hour." "Exactly," Ryn said. Silence spread through the group like ice. Lila whispered, "Is it coming for us?" Ryn's grip tightened on his staff. "It's searching. And your young friend here—" he nodded toward Loran— "would shine like a beacon to anything that can smell corruption." Loran stiffened. Mara glared at Ryn. "You don't have to say it like it's his fault." Ryn didn't flinch from the accusation. "It isn't fault. It's fact." "Enough," Arlyn said sharply, stepping between them.

Her voice steadied them all. “We need to stay moving,” she continued. “We can decide where once we’re out of the open.” Ryn looked at her with a hint of respect and nodded. “Agreed.” They resumed their trek, but the pace was faster now. More urgent. The trail of the horde ran parallel to them for miles, always visible through gaps in the thinning trees—wide, straight, merciless. And always, occasionally, they’d find the other trail. The hunting one. The one that wasn’t part of the army. The one following Loran. As the sun dipped behind the twisted branches, the forest opened onto a rocky incline overlooking a long valley. A river carved through its center, the water tinted faintly red, reflecting the corrupted sky.

Ryn scanned the landscape carefully, then pointed toward a cluster of boulders near the river’s edge. “We’ll set camp there,” he said. “The rocks give cover. And sound carries well in open valleys.” “You think it’ll come tonight?” Loran asked. Ryn didn’t answer for a long moment. Finally he said, “I think anything that hunts never sleeps as long as the thing it wants is still breathing.” Loran’s throat tightened. They descended toward the river. Behind them, as the last sliver of daylight faded, something moved in the distant trees—not approaching,—not charging,—but simply watching. Waiting.

The mark on Loran’s arm pulsed once, hard and cold, as if sensing it. He hissed and grabbed his sleeve. Ryn eyed him but said nothing. His attention shifted back toward the shadowed tree line. “Stay close,” Ryn murmured. “Don’t stray from one another. Not tonight.” They moved toward the cluster of boulders near the river, the ground crunching softly beneath their boots. The red-tinted water whispered against the stones—steady, rhythmic—like a heartbeat echoing across the valley floor.

Braum checked the treeline once more. “Feels like the woods are holding their breath.” “No,” Ryn said quietly. “They’re listening.” A twig snapped. Not behind them. Above. Loran froze. Something moved in the branches of the dying trees—a shape too large to perch, too still to be natural. The last light of dusk caught on something curved and pale. A talon. Long as a man’s forearm. Hooked. Wet. Arlyn whispered, “What... what is that?” Another talon curled around the branch. Then another. Then two more.

Too many to belong to any normal creature. Leaves drifted down. The branch groaned. Lila clapped both hands over her mouth as the thing unfolded itself from the canopy, its body unfurling like wet leather unsticking from bark. It dropped. The ground shook as it landed, dust bursting from the forest floor. The creature was enormous—easily the height of a horse, but built like some nightmarish bird stripped of feathers and sanity. Its legs were long, jointed backward, powerful enough to crack stone. Its body was sinewy, patches of blackened hide stretched over twitching muscle. And where a beak should have been, a jagged maw split upward into its skull, lined with crooked teeth.

Its eyes were the worst—sunken pits glowing faint yellow, scanning, smelling, hunting. Mara whispered, “Oh gods...” The beast’s head twitched toward her instantly. Ryn hissed, “Don’t move.” But it was too late. The creature shrieked—a screech like tearing metal and breaking bone—then charged. “Run!” Loran shouted.

The group scattered just as the monster slammed into the riverbank, sending stones flying. Braum barely rolled aside before a talon scythed across where his head had been. Loran drew his dagger—small, pitiful against the beast—but he held it tight. His mark burned. Hard. Hot. Alive. The monster snapped its head toward him, nostrils flaring. “It smells you!” Arlyn cried.

The creature lunged again. Loran stepped forward on instinct, thrusting his hand outward as if he could push the world away with sheer will. The sigil flared—blood-red, blazing beneath his skin—

and the air warped. Everyone felt it. A pressure. A pulse. A crack in the world.

The creature skidded, recoiling with a hiss. “It’s working!” Mara shouted. But then—the mark spasmed. The glow stuttered like a dying ember. And agony tore through Loran’s arm. He collapsed to one knee. “No—no—” he gasped, clawing at the burning sigil. “Not now—!” The creature saw its opening. It lunged straight for him. “Loran!” Lila screamed.

Ryn moved. Faster than anyone expected. He didn’t use magic. Didn’t glow. Didn’t reveal anything. He simply stepped between Loran and the beast at the last possible heartbeat, staff sweeping upward in a full arc. The wood cracked against the monster’s jaw with a thunderous snap. The creature’s head whipped sideways, teeth shattering against stone. It shrieked and stumbled, dazed. Ryn didn’t stop. He pivoted, grabbed Braum’s shoulder, shoved him aside, then slammed the base of his staff into the ground. “Arlyn! Mara! Get Lila back!” he barked.

The women grabbed Lila, dragging her behind the largest boulder as the beast righted itself, saliva and blood dripping from its broken maw. It glared at Ryn. Ryn glared back. “Come on then,” he muttered. “Let’s see if you’re as fast as your tracks claim.” The monster struck. Ryn spun beneath its talons, staff jabbing into the joint of its leg. The creature shrieked and stumbled again, snapping blindly.

“Braum!” Ryn shouted. Braum surged forward, hammer raised high. He swung with every ounce of muscle he had—and the blade sank into the beast’s shoulder with a meaty crack. The creature whipped around and hurled him into the riverbank knocking Braum against the rocks, but it reeled from the blow, blood spilling thick and black. Ryn pressed the attack. Staff whirling. Feet gliding across the stones. Every strike precise. Every dodge fluid.

There was nothing supernatural about it. Just skill. Years of it. Maybe centuries. Finally the beast lunged blindly again, jaws wide.

Ryn darted aside— and drove his staff into its exposed throat. Hard. A sickening crunch echoed through the valley. The creature thrashed violently, legs kicking, talons gouging the earth—until at last it collapsed at Ryn's feet. A long silence followed. Broken only by the dying gurgle of the monster's breath.

Loran staggered upright, clutching his useless, burning arm. Ryn planted his staff, breathing steady, as if he'd merely finished a morning sparring match with no need to even draw his sword. He didn't look victorious. He looked... disappointed. At the creature. At Loran's failed power. At something deeper. Finally, he turned to Loran. "You need to learn control," he said quietly. "Before something worse than this comes." Loran swallowed. "Worse?" Ryn's eyes drifted to the dark woods behind them, the place the beast had come from. "Oh yes," he murmured. "Much worse" He nudged the creature's corpse with his staff. "This little thing?" A faint, humorless grin. "Just a taste."

CHAPTER NINETEEN
Ashes on the Riverbank

The creature's corpse lay half-submerged in the shallows, its blackened blood swirling through the red-tinged water like ink bleeding through parchment. The last streaks of daylight had vanished entirely, leaving only the fire's glow to push back the night. No one spoke at first. Shock still hung over them like smoke. Braum sat with his back against a boulder, chest rising and falling in uneven breaths. The beast had thrown him hard—his right shoulder already swelling beneath the fabric of his tunic.

Lila knelt beside him, hands trembling as she dug through Arlyn's satchel for herbs and bandages. "Hold still," she said, voice quivering as she pressed a damp cloth to the bruised skin. Braum tried to grin. "Feels worse than it looks." "It looks awful," Lila muttered. He winced. "Then it feels worse than that." She glared at him—for once, not a hint of humor in her eyes. "You could have died." Braum's smile faded. He lowered his gaze. "I know." Lila tied the bandage tight, her fingers cold against his skin.

For the first time since the village fell, she seemed fully present—not a ghost drifting through grief, but a girl fighting to hold someone together with the small skills she still possessed. She swallowed. "Thank you. For fighting." "Thank *Ryn*," Braum said. "He saved us all." Lila shook her head softly. "I saw you swing first. That mattered." Braum blinked, unprepared for the sincerity. His cheeks went flushed, though whether from pain or the girl's honesty, even he wasn't sure. Not far from them, Arlyn crouched over the beast's carcass with quiet determination.

Mara held a torch above her shoulder, the flames crackling as they studied the creature's grotesque anatomy. Arlyn's brows furrowed. "The bone structure is all wrong. These joints aren't natural. Something re-shaped them." "Re-shaped?" Mara repeated. "Yes. Twisted, but not at random." Arlyn traced a finger along the creature's hind leg. "Look. These ridges—it's almost purposeful. Like someone reforged the body for... speed." Mara shuddered. "A forge made of flesh." Arlyn nodded grimly. "Corruption doesn't just warp. It *designs*." The idea alone made Mara's stomach turn. Arlyn reached for her journal, scribbling diagrams while murmuring to herself. "If creatures like this are being built in pairs or groups... no wonder Ryn worries about a larger force."

Mara handed her another torch. "Just don't get too close. Its blood looks poisonous." "Oh, it is," Arlyn said without hesitation. "Everything about this thing is poisonous." Mara blinked. "...comforting." A short distance from the others, Loran knelt by the fire, staring into the flames as though trying not to think about the pulsing heat still lingering in his arm. The sigil had gone dull again, but the ache remained—a warning.

Ryn approached quietly, easing himself onto the opposite side of the fire. For a while, neither spoke. The crackling flames filled the quiet between them. The river whispered behind them. Somewhere out in the dark, insects gave cautious chirps, as if unsure whether it was safe to resume the night's usual rhythm. Finally, Ryn said, "You didn't fail." Loran didn't look up. "It didn't work." "It *did*," Ryn corrected. "Just not long enough." Loran's jaw tightened. "That thing almost killed us." "And you almost killed it," Ryn said. "Instinct is not your enemy. Ignorance is."

Loran glared across the flames. "You keep speaking like you know what this is. What *I* am." Ryn didn't immediately answer. Shadows shifted across his face as the fire snapped and danced. At length, he said, "I know enough." "Enough to train me?" Loran pressed. "Enough to stop this from happening again?" Ryn's gaze hardened—not unkind, but unyielding. "No." Loran's frustration surged. "Then what good are you?" Ryn didn't flinch. "Keeping you alive is a start."

Loran exhaled through clenched teeth, heat building under his skin—not from anger, but from the mark stirring, restless. "It feels like something's inside me," he whispered. "Pulling. Pushing. Watching. Like I'm not myself anymore." Ryn's eyes flicked briefly to Loran's sleeve. "That is because it is older than you. Older than anything you know. And it woke far too early." Loran swallowed hard. "What does it want?" Ryn leaned back, eyes drifting toward the dark tree line. "Sigils don't want," he said quietly. "But the things that respond to them... do."

The fire crackled louder, swallowing the silence left by his words. Loran stared down at his shaking hand. "I don't want to be this." "Want has nothing to do with it," Ryn replied. "But control does." Loran's bitterness wavered, replaced by something smaller, more fragile. "How do I control it?" Ryn didn't answer. Not with words. Instead, he stood, walked around the fire, and placed a firm hand on Loran's shoulder. "You will," he said softly. "Or you won't live long enough to matter." Loran stared into the flames, the reflection dancing like a wounded heartbeat. He wasn't sure whether Ryn's words were meant to comfort him — or warn him. Behind them, Lila finished bandaging Braum's shoulder. Arlyn closed her journal and wiped the strange blood from her gloves. Mara glanced toward Loran with quiet worry. The night settled in as the forest watched.

CHAPTER TWENTY
The Men Who Endure

Morning came slowly, bleeding gray light across the valley as the corrupted sky swallowed the last traces of dawn. The air was stiff and cold, carrying with it a strange stillness—unnatural after the night's violence. Braum managed to stand with Lila's help, though every movement drew a hiss between his teeth. Arlyn finished checking his bandage one last time before packing her supplies. Mara kicked dirt over the fire, smothering its last ember.

Ryn stood with his back to them all, eyes fixed on the horizon. He had been that way since the moment the sun peeked over the distant ridge—still, listening, every muscle coiled like a man expecting the world to break open at any second. "Ryn?" Loran asked softly. "Something wrong?" Ryn didn't turn, but his grip tightened on his staff. "They're coming." A chill rippled through the camp. "More creatures?" Lila whispered, voice small. "No," Ryn said. "Humans." Braum squinted northward. "How can you—" But the rest of his sentence died.

Branch tips trembled. Metal clicked softly. Boots crunched over frost-hardened soil. Figures emerged from the fog. Not shambling. Not corrupted. Not wild. Organized. A line of men—eight, then twelve, then nearly twenty—advanced across the clearing in tight formation, shields strapped to their arms, chainmail glinting faintly beneath leather cloaks. Their helmets were dented, their armor mismatched from years of scavenging, but their discipline was unmistakable.

At their front marched a man with a dark beard streaked in early gray, his shoulders broad and posture straight despite exhaustion. His eyes were sharp, scanning every shadow, every movement. He raised one hand—and the entire line halted as one. "Hold," he commanded. His soldiers obeyed instantly.

Loran instinctively reached for his new sword. Mara stepped forward beside him. Braum shifted, despite the pain, ready to use his good arm if needed. But Ryn lifted his staff—not in threat, but in warning. "Stay still," he murmured. "Let them speak first." The leader approached, boots crunching softly underfoot. "We saw your fire last night," he called, voice steady but weighted. "Identify yourselves." Ryn said nothing. So Loran stepped forward, heart pounding. "We're survivors. From the south." The man's eyes flicked over them—the bandages, the exhaustion, Lila's trembling hands, the beast's corpse near the river.

His jaw tightened. "You killed that?" he asked. Ryn's expression remained unreadable. "We survived it." The man studied him for a long moment. Then nodded. "That alone is no small feat these days." He motioned behind him. Two soldiers approached, each carrying long spears tipped with sharpened steel. "My name is Captain Jorren Vale," the leader said. "We've been tracking corruption movement along the northern ridge for three weeks. The creatures have grown more bold—more coordinated."

Ryn exchanged a glance with Arlyn. Coordinated. Just as they feared. Jorren gestured to the formation behind him. "We escort survivors when we find them. You're welcome to travel with us. Safer than wandering alone." Braum muttered, "Feels strange hearing the word 'safe' anymore."

Jorren almost cracked a smile. Almost. Before he could speak again, one of his lieutenants stepped forward—helmet under his arm, face sharp and suspicious. He pointed at Ryn. "And who is he?" The air tightened. Ryn remained perfectly still. Loran stepped in quickly. "He's with us." The lieutenant didn't look convinced. "Funny," he said. "Most wanderers don't walk like trained bladesmen. Or carry staffs carved like artifacts. Or stand as if they're measuring how many of us they can kill before we blink."

"Enough, Tomas," Jorren said sharply. "But Captain—" "I said enough." The lieutenant backed off, but his glare lingered. Jorren turned to the group. "We've learned caution the hard way. Forgive the suspicion." Ryn dipped his head slightly, though his eyes remained cool. "Caution keeps men alive." Jorren nodded. "That it does." Mara stepped forward, softer. "Where are you based? Are there others like you?" "A few," Jorren admitted. "Scattered battalions. Old border guard units that broke apart after the Hollow Falls burned. We regrouped who we could."

Arlyn's breath caught. "Burned? How?" Jorren's eyes darkened. "Creatures moved like they had strategy. Something commanded them. Something that wasn't animal." Loran's stomach twisted. He already knew the name forming in his thoughts. Teren. "We can't stay here," Jorren continued. "Not with corrupted scouts roaming. Our encampment is half a day northeast. You'll find food, shelter, and healers." Loran glanced at his companions. Lila nodded quickly. Braum shrugged. "Can't be worse than this." Arlyn looked thoughtful. Mara seemed relieved. Ryn... said nothing.

Jorren studied the group one last time, his gaze lingering on Loran's sleeve—on the faint glow beneath the cloth, still pulsing from the night before. "What happened to your arm?" Loran stiffened. Mara stepped protectively beside him. "Nothing," she said quickly. Jorren didn't believe it, but he let it pass. "For now," he said, "you should walk with us. If the north is stirring, we'll need every capable hand." He motioned for his company to reform. Loran felt Ryn lean close, his voice a quiet warning: "Stay sharp. They're not the enemy... but they will see things in you they don't understand."

Loran swallowed hard. "Should we trust them?" Ryn's gaze shifted toward the armored men, disciplined and weary, yet marching with purpose—and toward the forest behind them, where corrupted shadows lingered. "Trust?" Ryn echoed. "No." He turned, cloak brushing the ground. "But we walk with them. For now." The chainmail soldiers moved out, their organized footsteps cutting through the valley like a heartbeat of order in a dying world. Loran and his companions followed–unaware that their arrival would ignite alliances, battles, and tragedies none of them were ready to face.

CHAPTER TWENTY-ONE
Refugees of the Fallen North

The journey northeast felt strangely muted—twenty armored men marching with purpose through a land that had forgotten what purpose looked like. Their chainmail murmured with each step, a sharp contrast to the dead hush of the corrupted woods they left behind. Loran, walking near the center of the formation, felt almost out of place among them. These men moved like they belonged to a world that still functioned. A world where lines held, orders mattered, and someone—somewhere—knew what they were doing. It was almost comforting. Almost.

Lila stayed between Mara and Arlyn, eyes darting at every sound. But there was color in her face again—not hope, but something close to the memory of it. Ryn moved near the rear, close enough to protect if needed, far enough not to invite questions. The soldiers gave him a wide berth. Some with respect. Others with suspicion.

By midday, the land dipped into a shallow basin. Jorren lifted a hand. "Home," he said simply. The encampment revealed itself slowly—more hidden than fortified. Tents made from patched canvas and scavenged cloth lined the lower slope. Wooden frames reinforced with chain links created makeshift barracks. Smoke rose from half a dozen cookfires, and the sound of hammering drifted from a blacksmithing post where two young men shaped battered metal back into shields. It wasn't a city. It wasn't even a village. But it was alive. Lila stopped walking altogether. Mara squeezed her hand. "You can breathe," she whispered. "You're safe here." For just a moment, Lila did.

Children ran between tents with sticks for swords. A woman stirred a pot over the fire, humming a lullaby that didn't quite mask the fear in her eyes. Two older men argued over spearheads. A handful of wounded lay under a tarp while healers worked quietly. A community. Small. Shattered. Clinging. But still a community. Arlyn's healer instincts took over instantly. "Who's tending your injured?" she asked Jorren. "Elder Mave and a few apprentices," he said. "They're stretched thin." Arlyn gave a tight nod. "I can help." The captain's expression softened. "We would welcome it."

Braum groaned as he lowered himself onto a crate near the main tent. Lila knelt beside him, unpacking her satchel with surprising steadiness. "I-I can help too," she murmured. Braum blinked at her, taken aback. "You sure, little one?" She nodded once—firmly. "I'm tired of being afraid. Let me do something." Mara brushed her hair gently. "That's brave," she said. "Your mother would be proud." Lila didn't speak, but her jaw tightened in a way Loran hadn't seen before.

Across the camp, soldiers watched Ryn with thinly disguised caution. Some murmured. Others stared openly at his staff, the carved runes, the effortless way he carried himself. Jorren approached him. "Seems you fought well the other night." Ryn offered only the faintest shrug. "I fought." "You fight like a man who's seen more than border skirmishes." Ryn's eyes flicked toward him—calm, unreadable. "I've seen the world change. Not always for the better." Jorren considered this response, then left him to it.

Loran remained near the fire pit, pretending to adjust his waterskin while keeping his sleeve firmly pulled down over his mark. His arm buzzed faintly—not painful, but present. Ryn appeared next to him without a sound. "You're tense," he said quietly. "Hard not to be," Loran replied. "They're staring at us like we're... odd." "They're staring at you," Ryn corrected. "Not all marks shine, Loran. Some men carry things that draw attention even when hidden."

Loran swallowed. "You mean the corruption?" Ryn didn't answer immediately. "No," he said at last. "I mean the potential to change the fate of those around you. Some feel it. Even if they don't understand it." Loran frowned, unsure what that meant, but Ryn had already moved on. "Jorren will want answers eventually," he added. "Men like him always do." "What should I say?" "Nothing," Ryn replied. "Truth is a burden. And burdens get people killed." Before Loran could ask more, a horn sounded from the northern ridge—a short, controlled burst.

Jorren turned sharply. "Scouting party returning!" Men hurried to form ranks, not in panic but in habit. Arlyn wiped blood from her hands and stepped away from the wounded. Mara helped Lila stand. Braum forced himself upright, gripping his hammer with his good arm. Ryn's eyes sharpened, staff angled subtly behind him. The scouts approached at a jog, exhausted but intact. Their leader—a younger man with a split lip—stopped before Jorren and saluted quickly. "Report," Jorren demanded.

The scout swallowed. "Three villages north," he said. "All empty. No bodies. No blood. Just gone." A ripple of despair moved through the gathered crowd. "Again," one soldier whispered. "Another vanish." Jorren clenched his jaw. "How long?" "Days. Maybe a week." Jorren nodded slowly, face carved from stone. Ryn's voice cut through the murmurs—quiet, razor-sharp. "It's spreading faster." The scout turned to stare at him. "You knew something about this?" Ryn didn't look at him. "I know patterns. And this one is accelerating."

Loran's stomach sank. Arlyn's fingers twitched. Mara's hand found his. Jorren exhaled. "Tonight," he said, louder for all to hear, "we rest. Tomorrow we plan." People dispersed, the brief stir of hope fading beneath the weight of reality.

As camp settled, Ryn and Loran remained near the fire, silhouettes against the last smoldering light. "You should sleep,"

Ryn said. Loran shook his head. "Can't." Ryn studied him. "You fear becoming something you don't understand." Loran nodded once. "Good," Ryn murmured. "Fear means you're not lost yet." Across the camp, Lila sat beside Braum, reading one of the old field journals they'd taken from Hollow Falls. Her voice was soft, steady—almost peaceful. Mara curled into her cloak, watching the night sky. Arlyn paced, planning herbs and poultices. Jorren spoke quietly with his commanders. A moment of calm. Fragile. Temporary. But calm. Ryn leaned back, eyes narrowing toward the northern dark. "Rest while you can," he said softly.
"The world is shifting. And tomorrow... the first tremor reaches us."

CHAPTER TWENTY-TWO
Echoes of a New Power

Night settled over the camp like a heavy blanket—thick, unmoving, too quiet for a place filled with so many people. Fires smoldered low in their pits, giving off more smoke than warmth. Most of Jorren's men busied themselves with sharpening weapons or reinforcing shields, their movements practiced and grim. Loran sat near the largest firepit, staring into the flickering orange. His arm tingled—not painfully, just present, like a heartbeat that didn't match his own. It had started ever since they reached the encampment. Ever since he heard the scouts' news.

Villages emptied.

No bodies.

No blood.

It felt familiar in the worst way. Mara sat beside him, arms wrapped around her knees. She hadn't said much since they arrived. Loran knew why—every description of a vanished village carried the possibility of Teren's face in its shadows. "You're thinking about him," Loran said softly. Mara didn't deny it. Didn't look at him.

"I should've stayed," she whispered. "I should've made him come with us." "You tried. He made his choice." She shook her head. "No. The corruption made it for him." Before Loran could answer, Ryn approached, cloak drawn tight against the wind. He didn't sit—just glanced between them with sharp, assessing eyes. "Jorren wants us," he said. "All of us." Arlyn looked up from a wounded man she was tending. "Now?" "Now." Braum groaned dramatically and pushed himself upright. "If this is another speech about rationing or discipline, I swear I might volunteer for scout duty." Lila, who had been sorting herbs with Arlyn, gave a small nervous laugh—the sound lightening the air just enough to help everyone breathe again.

They followed Ryn across the camp to the central tent—a large, weather-blackened structure reinforced with spears and patched cloth. Two sentries stepped aside with wary looks as the group entered. Jorren stood at a crude table, its surface carved with charcoal markings—maps, arrows, warnings. Several other leaders gathered with him: a woman with a scar across her jaw, an older man missing two fingers, and a young scout whose eyes looked far too old for his age. Jorren wasted no time. "You're here because the situation has changed." Ryn folded his arms. "Your scouts brought troubling news." "More than troubling," Jorren said. "Patterned." He motioned for the scout to speak.

The young man swallowed, then stepped forward. "It started two weeks ago," he said. "Villages going quiet. First one, then three, then six. No blood. No signs of a fight. Just... empty homes." Lila shivered. "But that's not the worst part," Jorren said. He looked at the older man, who stepped closer to the table. "Travelers have brought rumors," the man said. "Whispers of a—" He hesitated, searching for the right word. "—a leader." Mara's breath stilled. "A young man," the man continued. "Barely older than a boy. Dark hair. Wounded arm. And the creatures... follow him." Silence hit the tent like a hammer.

Loran felt his stomach drop. Mara's nails dug into her palms. Arlyn's lips parted in shock. Braum swore under his breath. Ryn alone remained unchanged—but the set of his jaw tightened. Jorren glanced around the room. "Some say this boy is controlling them. Others say the corruption is using him as its voice." He didn't need to say the name. Everyone in Loran's group knew. Teren.

Loran's arm pulsed—a sharp jolt that made him wince. Mara grabbed him instinctively. Jorren's eyes narrowed at the motion.

"Is he hurt?" "No," Mara said too quickly. Ryn stepped in before the questioning could deepen. "What's your plan, Captain?" Jorren exhaled slowly, tension pulling at the corners of his mouth. "We need to confirm these rumors. A scouting party leaves at dawn." He looked at each of them in turn. "I want you with us." Braum blinked. "Us? We're not soldiers." "You killed something half my men wouldn't approach," Jorren answered. "And you've survived things most wouldn't believe."

Lila looked down at her boots. Arlyn squeezed her shoulder. Mara stared into the firepit's embers, her face gone pale. Loran felt Ryn's gaze on him but didn't meet it. Jorren continued, "If there is a young man commanding the corruption, we need to know who he is. And how to stop him." Mara swallowed. Loudly. "We'll come," she said before anyone else could speak. Loran turned to her. "Mara—" "If it's Teren," she whispered, shaking, "I have to see him. I have to know." Ryn watched her with a look that might have been sympathy—or calculation. Jorren nodded solemnly. "Then it's settled. Rest tonight. At first light, we move." The council dismissed them.

Outside, the campfires burned lower, casting long shadows across the valley. The wind carried the soft cries of a child and the distant clang of a blacksmith finishing his shift. Everything felt too still, too fragile. Mara walked ahead, silent.
Lila helped Arlyn carry supplies.
Braum limped behind, cursing softly.
Ryn lingered near Loran. "You felt it," Ryn murmured. Loran didn't pretend otherwise.
"Yes." "The mark reacts to its own," Ryn said quietly. "Sometimes with warning. Sometimes with recognition."

Loran froze. "Recognition?" Ryn didn't elaborate. He turned toward the dark northern horizon—the place where answers waited, where Teren lived or didn't, where power was rising faster than any of them could grasp. "Sleep, Loran," Ryn said softly.

“Tomorrow we step toward something none of our fates can escape”

CHAPTER TWENTY-THREE
The Path of Rumors and Shadows

Dawn came colorless and cold. Not gray. Not pale. Colorless—like the sky had forgotten how to hold light. Loran woke to the sound of armor buckles and murmured instructions as Jorren's men readied to depart. Boots stamped frost-crusted soil. Horses snorted in their makeshift pens. Fires were doused with deliberate efficiency. Everyone moved with the heavy quiet of people who expected something to go wrong before nightfall.

Mara stood alone near the edge of camp, her cloak drawn tightly around her. She watched the horizon the way a person stared at a grave they weren't ready to visit. Loran approached carefully. "You don't have to pretend you're fine," he said. Mara didn't look at him.

"I'm not pretending." He frowned softly. "Mara—" "You don't understand." She lifted her gaze at last. Her eyes glistened—not with tears, but with a hollow ache deeper than fear. "If Teren is out there... if he's alive... I don't know if I want to find him or run the other way." Loran didn't know how to answer. He didn't know which truth would hurt less. Before he could speak, Ryn strode past them, cloak snapping behind him in the bitter wind. "You two can ponder heartbreak later," he said dryly. "We march."

Braum limped over with Lila supporting him, his hammer slung awkwardly because his bruised ribs wouldn't allow a full swing. "Ryn's a morning person. Who knew." The smallest crack of a smile touched Lila's lips—brief, fragile, but real. Arlyn handed Loran a small pouch. "Dried herbs. For when your arm starts... doing whatever it does."

She didn't say pulsing.
Or burning.
Or reacting. But they all knew. Jorren approached with two of his lieutenants. "We move in formation," he said. "Your group stays near the front. If anything happens, we need your eyes on it first." Ryn raised a brow. "For trust or sacrifice?" Jorren met his gaze evenly. "For honesty." And somehow, that answer satisfied Ryn more than anything else would have. They set out.

The northern path twisted through rolling grasslands that had long since turned the color of rotted parchment. The wind carried no birdsong–only the low rasp of dead grasses brushing against their boots. As they climbed a shallow ridge, Lila stopped suddenly, pointing. "Look." Below them stretched a valley, once fertile–the kind farmers would fight over in harvest seasons. But now... Fields were carved with enormous trenches, like something had plowed straight through them. Houses stood empty, doors hanging open. Fences lay shattered, posts twisted into unnatural angles.

Jorren's jaw clenched. "Third one like this in two weeks," he muttered. Arlyn moved closer. "How many people lived here?" "Maybe four hundred," the captain said. "Not a single corpse found." Mara shuddered. Braum gripped his hammer tightly. "No bodies means they walked willingly. Or were taken." Ryn knelt, brushing a hand across a patch of disturbed earth. "Taken," he corrected. "Anything done willingly leaves questions. This leaves none." Loran's mark pulsed sharply. He bit back a hiss. Ryn's eyes flickered to him. "You felt that?" "...Yes." "What direction?" Loran lifted his head slowly, heart hammering. "Northeast," he whispered. "Same as the rumors." Jorren exchanged a look with his lieutenants. "We're close then," he said. "Or close to something."

They descended into the valley. Strange symbols marked several walls—dark smears left by claws or hands or something else entirely. Children's toys lay scattered in the dirt. A wooden spoon rested beside a shattered bowl as if dropped only seconds before. Lila lingered near an empty doorway, fingers brushing the frame. "This feels wrong," she murmured. "Like the people aren't gone. Just... watching." Arlyn gently pulled her back. "Don't wander." Ryn knelt by the tracks again, tracing the patterns with slow precision. "The movement is orderly," he said. "Structured."

Jorren swore under his breath. "Then the rumor of a leader is true." Mara stiffened. Loran stepped protectively closer without thinking. The scout who accompanied them shifted uneasily. "But if a boy is commanding them—how? Why would the corruption choose someone so young?" Ryn rose to his full height, leaning on his staff. "The corruption does not choose based on age," he said. "It chooses based on potential." The scout swallowed. "What kind of potential?" Ryn's eyes drifted toward Loran. "The dangerous kind." Loran's pulse thudded unevenly in his ears.

They continued until midday. The sky grew darker, though no storm clouds formed. The air felt thicker. Every breath tasted faintly metallic, as if infused with old blood. Jorren slowed his pace, raising a hand. "We rest until the sun shifts." Braum collapsed to the ground with a relieved groan. "Finally." Lila sat beside him, checking his bandage again—her movements gentle, practiced. Braum didn't say a word, but his softened expression told everyone he was grateful.

Arlyn walked the perimeter, sharp eyes scanning for danger. Occasionally she knelt to examine strange growths in the dirt—

patches of grass decayed into blackened thread. Meanwhile, Ryn and Loran moved a small distance away, the older man dragging a finger through the soil. "You need to be ready," Ryn said quietly. "For what?" "For whatever shape this 'leader' has taken. The corruption twists boys into monsters faster than men into memories." Loran's fists tightened. "You think Teren—" Ryn didn't let him finish. "I think something changed him before you ever reached him. And I think it is connected to you more deeply than you want to admit."

Loran's throat tightened. The mark on his arm pulsed again—this time with a cold, sinking weight instead of heat. Ryn watched him with an unreadable expression. "You feel it because it knows him," Ryn said. "Or because it knows what he is becoming." Loran looked away. "I don't want it to be him." "Want has nothing to do with it," Ryn replied. "Truth will drag us either way." A distant horn echoed suddenly from behind them—sharp, metallic, urgent. Jorren rose to his feet instantly. "Scouts?" A second horn answered, closer, warning.

The entire group stiffened. Ryn swung his staff into his hand. "Something's moving behind us." Loran's mark burned. Hard. Cold. Alive with warning. Mara reached for him. "Loran...?" He swallowed, eyes fixed on the darkening horizon. "They're coming," he whispered. Not creatures. Not soldiers. Something else. Something gathering. Something that moved in formation. Teren's shadow stretched across the land—and they were stepping directly into it.

CHAPTER TWENTY-FOUR
The Voice in the Distance

The horns stopped as abruptly as they began. Silence washed across the valley—thick and unnatural, as though the entire world inhaled and held its breath. Jorren's men snapped into formation instantly. Shields locked. Spears angled forward. Eyes scanning the jagged hills that framed the path behind them. Ryn stepped in front of Loran without being asked. "What do you sense?" he murmured. Loran swallowed hard. The mark beneath his sleeve pulsed like a second heart, each throb cold and deliberate. "Something is coming," he whispered. "Not fast. Just... purposeful."

Footsteps crunched across frost-hardened soil. The lieutenant, Tomas, sprinted into view from the ridge—a lone scout dragging behind him. The scout was running. No—staggering. Almost crawling. His face was frozen in terror. "Help him!" Arlyn rushed forward. But Ryn caught her arm with surprising force. "Not yet." Jorren signaled two men to intercept. They reached the scout just as he collapsed, weapons clattering to the ground. The man's eyes darted wildly, unfocused. "Don't let them see me—don't let them see me—" "It's alright," Arlyn soothed, kneeling beside him. The scout shook violently. "No. No, no, no... He told them. He told them we were watching." Mara stepped closer. "Who told them?" The scout's gaze snapped to her—so sharply it startled her. "The boy," he gasped. "The one they follow." Mara's blood went cold. Loran's heart slammed against his ribs.

Jorren knelt beside the trembling man. "Speak clearly. What did you see?" The scout licked cracked lips. "I saw shapes... coming down the ridge. Dozens at first. Then more. Their bodies twisted, but they moved like soldiers. Not stumbling. Not hunting. Marching." Ryn's eyes narrowed. "As we feared." The scout grabbed Jorren's cloak with trembling fingers. "They didn't attack me. They didn't even look at me. Not at first." "Not at first?" Loran echoed. The scout's breath hitched. "I heard a voice."

The entire camp seemed to still. The scout's whisper trembled like torn thread. "A voice carried down the ridge. Calm. Young. Too young. It spoke five words—just five—and every creature turned its head the same direction." Mara's knees nearly gave out. Loran felt the pulse in his arm accelerate until it hurt. "What words?" Ryn asked quietly. The scout swallowed. "*Not them. Find him instead.*" A collective shiver traveled through the group.

Arlyn whispered, "Him...?" The scout nodded weakly. "They moved as one. They marched right past me. Didn't even glance my way. Just... kept going. Searching." His eyes flicked toward Loran. "Searching for someone like you." Mara stepped protectively in front of Loran. "Leave him alone." "No," the scout gasped. "You don't understand." He pointed at Loran's arm with a shaking hand. "It's like they smelled something. Something familiar. They moved as if they knew where to look. We know you're tied to this one way or another, that mark... is unnatural."

Ryn's face darkened. "This confirms it." "Confirms what?" Braum demanded. Ryn didn't hesitate. "There *is* a leader." The scout's breathing quickened. "A boy. No older than you," he whispered at Loran. "Eyes black around the edges. Veins dark. But he walked like he remembered being human." Mara flinched as though struck. Lila covered her mouth with both hands. Braum muttered a curse. Jorren looked to Loran. "We need to know if your mark reacts to this. How its connected" "No," Mara snapped. "You can't use him like some— some dinner bell." But Loran shook his head slowly. "It already reacted." Everyone stared at him.

Loran's hand trembled as he lifted his sleeve. The sigil glowed faintly—pulsing with slow, dark rhythm. Recognition. Ryn's eyes sharpened. "More than recognition," he murmured. "Resonance." "Is he alive?" Mara whispered, voice breaking. "Is Teren... alive?" Loran didn't answer. He couldn't. Because the mark beneath his skin told him a truth he wasn't ready to accept: Teren was not only alive. He was calling.

Then the world shifted. A low hum rolled across the valley, vibrating the earth beneath their boots. Not a voice. Not a roar. A command. Dozens of heads snapped toward the hills. Figures emerged through the fog. Twisted bodies. Shadow-slick skin. Eyes glowing faint gold. But they didn't charge. They simply... watched. Dozens.

Scores.

Maybe hundreds on the ridge. They stood in a perfect line—silent, unmoving. Waiting. Jorren's soldiers stiffened, but Ryn raised a hand sharply. "Hold."

Jorren hissed, "Are you mad—" "If they wanted to attack," Ryn said, "you would already be dead." Silence stretched, taut and electric. The creatures' formation parted slightly—just enough for a lone figure to appear atop the ridge. A small shape. A young shape. A boy's silhouette. Mara made a sound like a choked sob. Teren. Loran felt faint. But then— The boy turned. Slowly. Deliberately. And walked away, disappearing over the hill. The creatures followed—not lunging, not pursuing—marching behind him with perfect precision. Not one looked back. Not one broke formation. Within moments, the ridge was empty. The hum faded.

Loran collapsed to one knee, gripping his arm. The mark seared hot. Ryn was beside him in an instant, steadying him before anyone else could. "You saw him?" Ryn asked softly. Loran nodded. "I felt him." Mara's face crumpled in silent grief. Jorren whispered, "How do we fight something like this?" Ryn straightened slowly. His eyes were ancient. Hard. Knowing. "You don't," he said. Everyone turned to him. "You prepare."

CHAPTER TWENTY-FIVE
The Weight of What Follows

The march back to camp was silent. Not solemn—silent in the way people move after watching a mountain shift, or after hearing a prophecy spoken aloud. Even the wind seemed afraid to stir. When they reached the valley, Jorren ordered double watch, silent weapons, no fires. Soldiers obeyed instantly, though many still glanced back toward the ridge as if expecting the creatures to reappear. Loran could barely feel his fingers. His arm throbbed—not like before, not hot or cold, but as if it somehow was reacting to the discovery of the boy who it once tried to save.

Mara didn't speak at all. She sat near a cold firepit, arms wrapped tightly around her waist, staring at the ground with an expression too empty to be shock and too hollow to be grief. Lila stayed beside Braum and Arlyn, helping them arrange supplies, though her eyes kept drifting toward Mara with worried glances.
Ryn watched everything...
Quietly.
Measuring.
Calculating things he didn't yet share.

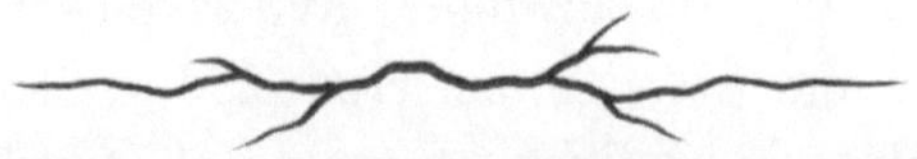

Jorren summoned them to the command tent before the sun had fully set. The canvas flapped in the cold wind, lanterns hanging from beams casting long, warping shadows. The entire camp leadership was there—Lieutenant Tomas, the scarred woman with the jaw mark, the older strategist missing two fingers, and two scouts still trembling from the encounter.

Jorren didn't sit. He stood over the map table, knuckles white against the wood. "We need a plan," he said. "Now." Tomas snorted. "A plan? Against *that*? We saw a child ordering creatures that pulled down cities." "He's not a child anymore," Mara whispered. Everyone turned to look at her. She didn't raise her head. Ryn stepped forward. "We need information. You don't send soldiers blind into something like that." Tomas glared at him. "You seem to know a lot about corruption for a man who claims to be a simple wanderer."

Ryn smiled without humor. "I claim no such thing." Tomas bristled. Jorren cut in, voice tired. "Arguing helps nothing. We know three things." He raised three fingers.
"One: the corrupted are organized."
"Two: they are following a single figure."
"Three: that figure does not kill without purpose."

The scarred woman frowned. "Then what does it want?" Jorren said. "No bodies left behind. Whatever it's building, it's building with people." Loran felt sick. Mara finally lifted her face. Her voice was hoarse. "Teren didn't want to hurt anyone. Ever. If the corruption is using him... twisting him... we have to try to help him." Tomas slammed his hand on the table.
"You don't help something like that. You end it." Mara shot to her feet, eyes blazing.
"You talk like you even knew him—" "Sit," Ryn said sharply. Not to Mara, but to Tomas.

The lieutenant froze—not from fear, but from something in Ryn's tone that threaded straight into instinct. Ryn continued, "The corruption twists, but not all the way at once. The boy you knew may still be in there. Or he may not. But we do not decide his fate tonight." Jorren exhaled. "Agreed." He turned toward Loran. "And you. Your arm reacted to him. That may give us an advantage." Mara stepped in front of Loran again. "He's not your tool." "No," Jorren said. "But he may be the only compass we have."

Loran swallowed hard. "What do you need me to do?" he whispered. Jorren hesitated. "For now... nothing. Rest. But tomorrow, we send a small reconnaissance party north. I want Ryn with us. And I want you near enough to sense changes." Loran nodded. It felt like agreeing to walk into a storm barefoot. The council adjourned. No one looked relieved.

The valley settled into a restless hush. Soldiers cleaned weapons. Others whispered prayers. A few wept quietly behind tents, certain the world had finally shifted into something unrecognizable. Arlyn knelt beside Lila, who was helping Braum rewrap his ribs. "You're doing well," Arlyn said softly. "I'm trying," Lila whispered. "But everything keeps getting worse." Arlyn brushed a strand of hair behind Lila's ear. "Sometimes it has to get worse before we understand how to fight it." Braum grumbled, "I just want to hit something that *stays dead* when I do." It pulled a faint laugh from Lila. The sound was small, but it was hope.

Ryn motioned Loran away from camp, toward a small rise of rocks overlooking the valley. The night sky above them flickered with streaks of red and gray, reflecting a world off-balance. "Sit," Ryn said. Loran obeyed. Ryn crouched beside him. "Tell me exactly what you felt. No hiding." Loran hesitated. "It wasn't pain like before. It was... recognition. Like the mark remembered something." "Or someone." Loran nodded. "When Teren stood on that ridge, I didn't just see him. I felt him. Like we shared a single heartbeat for a moment." Ryn sighed—deep, weary, and older than the body he wore. "You are two threads of the same weave," he murmured. "Two flames born of the same fire. When one burns bright, the other feels the heat. Two champions opposite another..."

Loran's voice cracked. "I don't want to be connected to him like this." "That choice," Ryn said quietly, "was never yours." Loran looked away, tears stinging unexpectedly. "Why does the mark choose people like us? We didn't ask for it." "No one ever asks," Ryn answered. "But the world chooses its weapons long before they're needed." The words felt like a prophecy.

It struck without warning. A sharp pulse. A flash of cold. A darkness crawling under Loran's skin. He gasped. Ryn reached to steady him— But Loran wasn't in the valley anymore. He stood in a hall of broken roots and stone.

Torches lined the walls, their flames burning black.

Corrupted creatures knelt in rows—silent, waiting. A boy stood at the far end of the hall. Teren.

But not Teren. Older.

Pale.

Veins blackened like cracked ink beneath his skin.

His eyes—dark around the edges—lifted as if sensing Loran. And he smiled. "Not yet," Teren whispered. "Soon." Loran snapped back to himself with a cry, collapsing onto the rocks. Sweat drenched his palms. His heart thundered. Ryn knelt immediately. "What did you see?" Loran shook violently.

"He... he saw me. He *knew* I was there." Ryn's face darkened. "That means one thing." Loran swallowed hard.

"What?" Ryn's voice was barely audible. "The Corruption is almost ready for its Vessel."

CHAPTER TWENTY-SIX
The Man Who Walked From Darkness

The camp did not sleep. Lanterns burned long past midnight, swinging gently in the wind like trembling stars. Jorren's soldiers walked their rounds with haunted eyes, flinching at every rustle in the grass as though expecting the corrupted army to descend at any moment. After Loran's vision, no one spoke loudly.
Or quickly.
Or hopefully.

The world had shifted. And everyone felt it. At dawn, a pale mist clung to the valley, swirling around boots and tents like ghostly fingers reluctant to release their hold. Jorren addressed the gathered reconnaissance party—six soldiers, Ryn, Loran, Mara, Arlyn, Braum, and Lila. His voice was firm, but beneath it trembled a strain he couldn't hide. "We leave in one hour. We march light and return fast. No fires. No shouting. If you see movement, assume it is hostile and fall back." One of the lieutenants—a tall, narrow-faced man named Hadrin—studied Loran with open suspicion. "That boy shouldn't be near the front," he muttered. "He glowed, for gods' sake." Ryn stepped forward before Loran could respond.
"Then perhaps the boy has more courage than you do." Hadrin stiffened but didn't argue further.
Ryn's tone brooked no challenge. Jorren shot him a warning look but said nothing.

While Braum ate a morning ration under protest "Tastes like bark pretending to be bread", Arlyn crouched beside the corrupted moss growing at the valley's edge. Lila approached cautiously. "What are you looking at?" Arlyn touched a blackened leaf. It crumbled to dust. "This isn't decay," she murmured. "It's transformation." "Into what?" "I don't know," Arlyn admitted. "But look—" She lifted a tiny branch. Underneath the corruption's outer husk, a faint purplish glow pulsed. Alive. Growing. Lila recoiled. "Corruption grows?" "No," Arlyn said slowly. "It... evolves."

Mara stood alone at the riverbank, staring at her reflection in the rippling red water. Her eyes were tired—too old for her years. Loran approached quietly. "Mara... last night. What you saw—" "I don't know what I saw." Her voice cracked. "I don't know who he is anymore. I don't know what I want him to be." Loran's chest tightened. "You don't have to decide yet." "Yes, I do." She met his eyes, and for the first time, Loran saw fear deeper than anything the corrupted had caused. "Because if he's beyond saving... someone will have to stop him. And if we don't—who will?" Her voice broke on the last word. He reached for her shoulder, but she stepped back. "I just need time," she whispered.

Away from camp, Ryn tossed Loran a wooden staff. "Defend yourself." Loran blinked. "What—now?" Ryn lunged. Their staves crashed, sending vibrations up Loran's arms. He stumbled, off-balance. "Again," Ryn barked. Loran swung. Ryn redirected it with effortless precision, sending Loran spinning into the dirt. "What is this teaching me? —I know how to fall" Loran groaned. "To react under strain," Ryn said. "Your mark flares when your emotions do. Control your body, you control your fear. Control your fear—" "—I control the mark," Loran finished breathlessly. Ryn studied him for a heartbeat. Didn't nod. Didn't correct him. He stepped back into range.

"Again."

Just before the reconnaissance party gathered their supplies, a horn sounded from the western perimeter. Three short blasts. Not danger. Not corruption. Something else. Soldiers rushed to the ridge. Ryn and Loran reached the front simultaneously, joining Jorren and his lieutenants. A lone man staggered toward the camp. Unarmed. Human. Weak. He collapsed just outside the barricade. Arlyn reached him first. "He's alive—barely!" Jorren knelt beside the man. "Who are you? What happened?" The man's eyes fluttered open. His voice rasped like sand across stone. "He... sent me." Everyone stiffened. "Who?" Jorren asked. The man's hand trembled as he lifted something from his cloak. A strip of red cloth. Torn. Stained. Mara gasped—it was from Teren's tunic. The man whispered "He said... *tell the mark bearer I'm waiting.*"

Loran's blood ran cold. The man grabbed Jorren's wrist desperately. "And he said... *don't bring soldiers next time.*" Jorren's face drained of color. Ryn's grip tightened on his staff. Mara's knees buckled, and Lila caught her before she hit the ground. Loran felt the mark burn—a searing, piercing flare. The message was clear. Teren wasn't fleeing. Wasn't hiding. He wanted them to come.

Jorren stood. Voice steady despite the fear behind his eyes. "We leave in half an hour. Smaller group. Silent march." Hadrin stammered. "Captain, he—he said no soldiers—" Jorren cut him off sharply. "I'm not walking unprotected into the arms of a corrupted commander." He turned to Ryn, Loran, Mara, Arlyn, Braum, and Lila. "But you six... he wants you." Ryn exhaled slowly. "This is a trap." "Yes," Jorren agreed. Loran swallowed. "Teren isn't trying to kill us." "No," Ryn said softly. "He's trying to change you." The wind shifted—cold, metallic, electric with distant power. The marked and unmarked alike felt the world lean toward something inevitable.

CHAPTER TWENTY-SEVEN
The Land That Answers to Him

They left the camp in silence. No soldiers marched beside them now—Jorren obeyed Teren's warning and held his men back, though the decision tasted like poison. Only six figures crossed into the twisted north: Loran, Mara, Arlyn, Braum, Lila, and Ryn. Clouds drifted low over the hills like heavy blankets, trapping the world in dim, muted gray. No birds called. No insects stirred. Even the wind seemed to hesitate. The further they traveled, the quieter everything became. Too quiet. Lila clutched Arlyn's arm.
"It feels like the world is... listening." Ryn nodded once.
"It is." Braum adjusted his hammer nervously. "Listening for what?" Ryn didn't answer.

By midday, the terrain changed abruptly. Grass ended. Soil darkened. Trees grew sparse and skeletal. Along the ground, faint lines spiraled outward—patterns like veins etched into the dirt, though they pulsed faintly beneath the soil. Loran crouched, touching one. It thrummed beneath his fingertips, syncing to the rhythm of his mark. Mara shuddered. "Loran... stop touching it."
"Sorry." He pulled back—and the ground's faint pulse withdrew, like a disappointed heartbeat retreating. Arlyn knelt beside him. "These markings... they aren't natural. They're almost like sigils carved into the earth." "They're roots," Ryn said quietly. "New ones." "Roots of what?" Lila asked. Ryn looked toward the

northern ridgeline. "Corruption doesn't spread like wildfire anymore. It spreads with purpose. He is shaping it."

As the group pressed further, fog curled around their feet, thickening with each step. Then—voices. Soft. Distant. Too faint to understand. Mara froze. "Did you hear that?" Braum gripped his hammer. "Voices? Where?" Arlyn shook her head. "I don't see anyone." Loran's mark flared. And suddenly the whisper sharpened. "Loran..." He spun, heart smashing against his chest. No one stood behind him. "Come to me." A voice he knew. A voice that cracked him open. "Teren," he whispered. Mara flinched at the name. Ryn stepped closer. "What did you hear?" Loran hesitated. "I think... he's talking to me."

They pushed on. But the fog shifted—subtle at first, like drifting curtains. Then suddenly thick as wool. Shapes loomed. Branches became hands. Stones became figures. Lila screamed softly when she nearly walked into a tree that hadn't been there moments before. "We're going in circles," Braum muttered. "No," Ryn corrected. "The fog is moving us." He planted his staff sharply into the ground. The fog recoiled. Loran blinked. "How did you—" Ryn ignored the question.

"Stay close. Don't listen to anything." But they couldn't help it. Whispers curled through the fog, soft as memory:

"Mara..."

"Come home..."

"They left you..."

"He still needs you..."

Mara's knees buckled. Loran grabbed her before she fell. "No," she gasped. "No—this isn't real—" Arlyn held her face gently. "Look at me. Focus here. Not the fog." Ryn's jaw tightened. "Teren's touch," he muttered. "The corruption is learning to speak."

A figure emerged ahead. Human. Alone. Braum raised his hammer. "Finally, something to hit—" "Wait," Ryn snapped. The man stepped into view—a young adult, maybe twenty-five, wearing tattered clothes but walking with eerie calm. He had no weapons.

No corruption marking his skin. But his pupils were darkened—not fully black, just shadowed around the edges. He smiled faintly when he saw Loran. "He said you would come." Mara stiffened. "Where is he? Is Teren alive?" A flicker of something—pity? amusement?—crossed the man's face. "He is becoming." Ryn's hand drifted subtly toward his staff. "What are you?" "A messenger," the man said. "A herald, he called it. He showed me the truth." "What truth?" Loran demanded. "That the old world failed," the man said simply. "But we don't have to. He can build something new. All he needs is time. And you." The mark in Loran's arm pulsed in answer. The man smiled broader.
"You feel it. The pull." Ryn stepped forward, positioning himself between Loran and the herald. "Enough." The herald tilted his head. "He wants to see the marked one."

Mara stepped between them, voice trembling. "You don't get to command us. You don't get to speak for him." "I don't speak for him," the herald said gently. He turned his darkened gaze directly to Loran. "He speaks for himself." The fog folded backward— And for an instant— A vision flashed across all of them: A vast hall of roots.
Rows of kneeling corrupted figures.
A stone dais at the center.
And Teren standing upon it—eyes shadowed, veins dark, but posture proud, commanding. Lila gasped.
Arlyn staggered.
Braum swore.
Mara recoiled almost collapsing. Ryn closed his eyes, jaw clenching hard enough to crack teeth. And Loran— Loran's mark erupted with Red light Burning. Alive. The herald stepped back, shielding his eyes. "He grows stronger," he whispered. "But so do you." Ryn instantly whirled, staff lancing forward— The herald was gone. Vanished into the fog, like smoke swallowed by wind. Silence crashed down. The fog thinned. Whispers retreated. But the dread remained.

Mara trembled beside Loran. “I saw him,” she whispered. “I saw Teren. He looked... he looked like he believed in what he was doing.” Loran swallowed, voice hoarse. “He doesn’t just believe it. He’s building it.” Ryn finally turned to the group, expression grave. “This changes everything.” Arlyn steadied Lila. “What do we do now?” Ryn’s voice was quiet. “We keep moving.” “Toward him?” Braum asked. Ryn nodded once, sharply. “Toward the heart of whatever he is becoming. Before it becomes something none of us can stop.” Loran looked north. The land seemed to breathe. And the mark on his arm whispered back.

CHAPTER TWENTY-EIGHT
The Rooted Stronghold

The farther north they walked, the less the land resembled anything they had ever known. Trees no longer grew—they *arched,* bending toward the earth as though forced to kneel. Their bark was streaked with dark veins that pulsed faintly, as if the roots beneath were alive and breathing. The sky dimmed into a permanent twilight, a bruised palette of red and slate. Every sound felt muffled, swallowed by the oppressive quiet. "Feels like walking inside a dream," Lila whispered. Arlyn shook her head. "No dream grows like this. This is... intention. A nightmare" Ryn said nothing, but he gripped his staff just a little tighter.

The path narrowed into a shallow gorge, its walls etched with spiraling grooves. They weren't carved—nature didn't do that. They grew. Loran's mark burned with each step.
Not painfully.
Not like warning. Like recognition. Mara kept glancing at him, fear crackling behind her eyes. "You should tell us if it gets worse," she whispered. Loran nodded, but he didn't say that the mark wasn't getting worse. It was getting eager.

The gorge widened into a basin of flattened soil, stretched smooth as though pressed by the passage of countless feet. And there—at its edges— Structures. Not houses.
Not ruins. Something in between. Frameworks of wood infused with black-root veins. Walls rising from the ground like grown branches. Stairways forming from hardened sap-like stone. Braum swallowed. "He's building a city." "Or a fortress," Arlyn murmured. "No fortress looks like it grew out of the dirt," Lila said. Ryn

stepped forward, gaze unreadable. “He’s weaving the land to his will.” Mara’s breath hitched. “Teren doesn’t know how to build anything like this.” Ryn didn’t look at her. “He didn’t. But corruption does.”

Movement flickered ahead. The group froze. A line of figures marched across a ledge—too tall, too twisted to be human. Their limbs moved with unnatural grace, synchronized as though a single mind drove them. But mixed among them... Arlyn gasped. Humans. Walking calmly beside the corrupted creatures.
Unbound.
Unharmed.
Unafraid. Some wore battered armor. Others cloaks from distant villages. Their expressions were blank. Hollow. But their steps were steady. Purposeful. “They’re volunteers,” Mara whispered, horrified. “Or—captives—” Ryn shook his head once. “They walk like neither. They walk like followers.” Braum cursed under his breath. “You’re telling me Teren gathered his own damn army?” Ryn finally spoke, voice low. “He is no longer gathering. He is ruling.”

Loran staggered. The mark on his arm blazed—not red, but deeper, richer, like fresh blood stirred by heat. His vision blurred. He saw pathways branching through the stronghold—corridors forming, platforms rising, creatures bowing. Then— a flash of Teren standing atop a root-built platform, eyes watching the land with chilling calm. “Loran!” He blinked and Mara had him by the shoulders, steadying him before he fell. “What did you see?” she asked, voice trembling. Loran swallowed. “He’s building something bigger than a city.” Ryn turned sharply. “What?” “A seat,” Loran whispered. “A throne.” Mara stepped back as though struck.

They took shelter behind a ridge as the marching column passed. Ryn remained standing long after the others crouched, eyes fixed on the procession of corrupted and uncorrupted alike. Lila whispered, “He’s not moving.” Arlyn touched her arm. “Let him think.” But Ryn wasn’t thinking. He was remembering. Slowly, he placed one hand over his chest and murmured something ancient—words none of them recognized. His voice carried the weight of a forgotten age. Loran watched, breath shallow. "Ryn... what are you doing?" Ryn's eyes remained closed. "I am preparing," he said softly. "Because when old powers rise... older ones must rise to meet them." The words sent a shiver through every living bone.

The gorge ended abruptly. Ahead, the land opened into a vast chasm ringed with spiraling roots thicker than tree trunks. They arched upward into a tangled dome of dark wood and living veins. A fortress grown, not built. A heartbeat thrummed through the ground beneath them. Loran whispered, "We're close." Braum lifted his hammer with a grim nod. "Feels like we're walking into the lungs of a beast." Mara stared at the living fortress, terror and longing at war in her eyes. "Teren..." she breathed. Arlyn stepped forward, shielding her gently. "We don't know what he is now."

Ryn raised his staff slightly. "Be ready. Something is—" He stopped. So did the ground. Every sound ceased. The world went still. And then— A voice rolled across the open air. Not spoken aloud. Not shouted. *Sent.* "You finally came." Mara staggered.
Lila froze.
Braum cursed.
Arlyn clutched her chest.
Ryn's eyes snapped open with fury. And Loran— Loran dropped to one knee, the mark burning like molten iron. The voice continued. "Come closer." The earth trembled. Roots uncoiled. Openings formed. A pathway appeared—leading straight into the heart of the grown fortress. Ryn grabbed Loran's arm.
"Not yet—!" But the path pulsed again, beckoning. Calling. "Come see what I have become."

CHAPTER TWENTY-NINE
Into the Rooted Heart

The pathway that opened before them did not feel like an invitation. It felt like a mouth. Roots uncoiled slowly along its edges, slithering back into the earth as if bowing to some unseen master. The air grew warmer—humid, even—carrying a faint metallic scent that tasted like iron and sap. Loran stared at the opening, pulse hammering. The mark beneath his skin throbbed in sync with the ground. Mara's hand brushed his. "Are you with us?" He nodded, though the truth was hazy. He wasn't sure if he was walking toward Teren... or being pulled. Ryn moved first. "Stay together," he said. "No matter what you see." Braum muttered, "That's encouraging." Lila squeezed Arlyn's sleeve. Arlyn gave her a reassuring nod, though her own eyes darted nervously toward the twisting walls. Together, they stepped into the fortress.

The corridor narrowed quickly, the walls curving upward as if grown from the same massive root. Each surface pulsed faintly—slow, rhythmic, almost like breathing. Lila whispered, "Is it alive?" Arlyn examined a groove with careful fingers. "It feels... warm. Like muscle." Braum grimaced. "Lovely. We're inside something's stomach." Ryn shot him a look. "Not stomach. Memory." "What does that mean?" Loran asked. Ryn didn't answer. He pressed forward, jaw set.

The deeper they walked, the more the air thickened—dense with whispers that came not from around them, but *through* them. Loran heard his mother laughing, from years ago. Arlyn heard her mother calling her name. Lila heard her village bell. Braum heard his father's old war song he sung at the forge. Mara— Mara froze mid-step. Loran turned. “Mara?” Her eyes glistened, wide and terrified. “I hear him,” she whispered. “I hear Teren.” Ryn’s staff struck the ground sharply. “Don’t listen.” But it was too late. Mara staggered, hand pressed to her temple. “He’s saying... he’s saying he remembers me. That he wants to show me—” “Mara,” Loran said firmly, grabbing her wrist, “that’s not him. It’s the corruption using his voice.” Her breath caught. But her eyes said she wasn’t entirely convinced.

The path widened suddenly into a massive chamber. The ceiling arched tall—roots twisting overhead like tangled constellations. Luminescent veins glowed along the walls, bathing everything in sickly purplish-black light. And on the ground—“Gods...” Arlyn whispered. Bodies. Not dead.
Sleeping.
Dozens of humans lying in concentric circles, breathing in slow, unnatural rhythm. Their chests rose and fell in perfect unison. Lila covered her mouth, trembling. “Are they prisoners?” Ryn knelt beside the nearest body—a woman no older than twenty. “No chains,” he murmured. “No wounds. They’re... connected.” “Connected to what?” Braum asked. Before Ryn could answer—Loran felt his mark blaze. Every sleeper inhaled at once. And in perfect harmony... They whispered: “He is coming.” Mara stepped backward, shaking violently. “No—no, no, this isn’t real—” Loran grabbed her before she collapsed again. The sleepers exhaled. Then fell silent. Ryn stood slowly, expression dark and unreadable. “We are close,” he said.

The corridor splintered into multiple branching paths. Each one glowed faintly, pulsing like arteries. “We’ll get lost,” Arlyn warned. “Not if he doesn’t want us to,” Ryn muttered. And indeed— The pulses along the leftmost path brightened, almost beckoning. Loran’s arm seared in answer. “He wants us to follow that one,” Loran said. Ryn frowned. “Which means we should consider the others.” But before they could choose— The other paths constricted.

Twisting.
Closing. Until only the chosen path remained open. Braum swallowed. “Well. Decision made.” Ryn’s grip tightened around his staff. “He is guiding us,” he whispered. “Like lambs to slaughter.”

Halfway down the narrowing corridor, the air thinned—growing warmer, sweeter, intoxicating. Mara stumbled again. “Do you hear it?” she gasped. Arlyn caught her. “What?” Mara pressed a shaking hand over her heart. “He’s saying... ‘Come home.’” The words echoed faintly in Loran’s skull too. Ryn grabbed Mara’s chin gently but firmly, forcing her gaze to his. “That is not Teren,” he said. “That is a lure. You must resist.” Her breath hitched. “It sounds just like him.” “That’s why it works.” For the first time, Ryn’s voice cracked—not with weakness, but with old grief. Mara fell silent.

The corridor ended abruptly. Before them stood a massive archway woven from roots thicker than tree trunks, fused together to form a living gate. Red veins pulsed across its surface, converging at a central point that resembled a heartbeat under bark. Loran’s mark throbbed in perfect sync. Braum whispered, “What in the gods’ names is behind that?” Ryn exhaled slowly. “The throne,” he said.
“And the one who sits upon it.” Lila clutched Arlyn’s arm.
“I don’t want to go in.” Arlyn swallowed hard. “Neither do I.” Mara stepped forward despite shaking hands, grief and determination twisting through her expression. “Open it,” she whispered. Loran lifted his hand— But the doorway opened by itself. Roots peeled back like living curtains. Warm light flooded the corridor. A silhouette appeared within. Young. Still. Waiting. Teren. Loran felt the world tilt. Ryn whispered “Prepare yourselves. Nothing after this will be the same.”

CHAPTER THIRTY
The Throneborn

For a heartbeat, no one breathed. Teren stood framed by the living archway, his silhouette washed in soft red-gold light. Roots rose behind him in elegant curves, weaving into a throne-like structure that pulsed faintly with the same rhythm as the floor. The glow clung to him, outlining his frame like a crown. He looked almost human. Almost. His eyes were darker than Loran remembered. Not black— but deep, fathomless, like a well reflecting firelight. Mara stepped forward before she realized she had moved. "Teren...?" Her voice cracked like something bruised. Teren's expression softened. "Mara." Hearing her name in his voice shattered the air between them. Mara's knees buckled slightly. Loran grabbed her arm, steadying her. Teren's gaze drifted to Loran's hand on her sleeve. "Still protecting her," he murmured. "Some things never change." Loran swallowed hard. He wanted to speak. Wanted to demand answers. Wanted to ask why Teren left them— why he let the corruption swallow him whole. But no words came. Teren stepped closer. He moved smoothly, gracefully— with a stillness that wasn't natural.

His skin held a faint sheen, like light reflecting through sap. Arlyn's breath hitched beside him. "That isn't... that's not how a human moves." "No," Ryn said quietly. "It isn't." Teren's gaze landed on him. "Ah," he said. "The wanderer. You feel familiar." Ryn's jaw tightened, but he said nothing. Teren smiled faintly, as though amused by the silence. "Why are you here?" Braum barked, anger breaking the tension. "What is this place? What have you done to those people—" Teren tilted his head slightly. "They're asleep," he said calmly. "Dreaming. Safe." "Safe?" Braum snapped. "They're trapped!" "They're connected," Teren corrected. "Part of something larger. Something that gives them purpose. Something they never had before." "Corruption isn't purpose," Arlyn said. Teren's eyes flicked toward her. "Everything grows," he murmured. "Even rot has direction." A shiver crawled across the room.

Lila clutched Arlyn's cloak tighter. Ryn stepped forward slightly—barely—but enough to place himself between Teren and the others, staff angled loosely at his side. "What do you want with us?" Ryn asked. Teren studied him for a long moment. Then his eyes slid to Loran. "Not you," he said softly. "Just him." Loran's stomach dropped. Mara turned sharply. "What? Why?" Teren didn't look away from Loran. "He carries something old," Teren said. "Something the corruption recognizes. Something I recognize." The mark under Loran's sleeve surged painfully, pulsing hard enough to blur his vision. He staggered, clutching his arm. "Loran!" Mara caught him.

Teren stepped forward, concern flickering across his face, strange and unsettling. "It hurts because you don't understand it yet. I remember that pain." Loran gasped. "You... remember?" Teren nodded slowly. "Every moment." He said it with no hatred. No resentment. Almost fondness. Mara looked between them, torn and trembling. "Teren, please—why didn't you come back to us? Why did you run into the woods? Why did you leave me—" Teren's expression changed. Not hardened. Not pained. Just... shifted. As if the question itself was irrelevant to him now. "I didn't leave you," he said gently. "I was called. And now... so are you all." Mara froze. Loran stepped forward, blade scraping as he pulled it free. "No. You don't get to talk to her like that." Teren looked at the sword as though it were a child's toy. "You can't hurt me with that," he said kindly. The word sank like a stone in Loran's chest. Ryn's grip on his staff tightened. "Keep talking," he murmured to Loran, "but do not strike." "Why?" Loran hissed. "Because we need time." "For what?" "For the corridor behind us to close," Ryn said grimly.

Loran turned— The roots behind them were sliding together again, sealing the entrance like eyelids shutting. They were trapped. Teren watched their panic without malice. "The fortress responds to will," he said. "It knows mine. You're safe here." "Safe?" Arlyn whispered again, horrified. A rumble shook the chamber. Deep. Slow. Alive. Teren's gaze drifted over his shoulder, toward the throne-roots behind him. "It wakes," he murmured. "It knows you're here." "What wakes?" Loran demanded. Teren smiled. Something enormous moved in the chamber beyond—a shift of mass so large the floor rippled beneath their feet. A breath like steam echoed from the darkness. Roots tightened. Lights flared. The fortress pulsed like a beating heart. And Teren stepped aside. "Come," he said. "Meet the thing that remade me."

The temperature dropped. The whispers of the sleepers rose into a single harmonic note, vibrating the air. Ryn planted his staff and inhaled slowly. "Brace yourselves," he said, voice low. "Whatever comes through that door..." He looked at Loran, eyes unreadable. "...will test all of us." The roots of the throne split apart. A massive shape pushed into the shadows.

CHAPTER THIRTY-ONE
The First Breath of the Ancient Beast

For a heartbeat, the world held its breath. The roots behind Teren's throne split apart with a sound like old bone cracking. Red light spilled through, thick and wet, coating the chamber in a pulsing glow. Something moved in the dark beyond. Not a step. Not a shuffle. A shift of mass. Loran's hand tightened on his sword. The mark beneath his sleeve burned—sharp, warning, like it recognized what was coming and wanted no part of it. Mara's fingers dug into his arm. "Don't let go," she whispered. He wasn't sure if she meant his hand, or his mind. Maybe both. Teren stepped aside, almost gracefully, making room. From the cleft in the roots, the corrupted thing emerged. At first, it was only shadow.

A dense smear of darkness sliding along the floor, swallowing even the sick red light that tried to touch it. Then it rose. A central body, taller than two men, unfurling like something that had been hanging upside down. It stood on limbs that were part talon, part jointed bone, part... nothing. Where its legs should have met the floor, the stone warped, as if reality itself didn't know how to support it. Its torso was half-formed, humanoid in outline but hollow in places, ribs open to a swirling void that churned inside its chest like a storm captured in glass. Long tendrils spilled from its back and shoulders—smoky, black, and slick like oil in water. They dragged behind it, then rose, tasting the air. Where a head should have been, there was a shape—a suggestion of a skull—

wrapped in spirals of smoke. From within, two eyes burned not the simple yellow of Phase Two. Not the shifting grey of human corruption. Deep, wrong, a color like bruised starlight caught in tar.

Arlyn choked on a breath. "That's... not like anything we've seen." "No," Ryn said. His voice was low. Flat. Old. "This is what happens when corruption stops spreading and starts refining." The thing tilted its head—if that smear of shadow could be called a head. The tendrils snapped toward Loran, then twitched back like they'd touched a hot surface. It smelled him. It knew him. Mara whispered, "Loran..." Behind the creature, Teren folded his hands behind his back, watching like a man observing a test he already knew the outcome of. "This one was made from many," he said quietly. "It remembers them all."

The beast moved. It didn't sprint. It didn't charge. It... shifted. One moment it was across the chamber. The next, it was in front of them, a blur of shadow and tendril and bone. Braum barely got his hammer up in time. The first strike hit like a falling tree. Braum's arm screamed. The blow hurled him sideways, skidding across the living floor. He crashed into a root with a grunt, breath blasted from his lungs. "Braum!" Lila cried. Another tendril lashed out. Arlyn shoved Lila aside and evaded. The impact against the ground cracked through the chamber like thunder. Corrupted oil hissed where it met the floor, eating through it in seconds. Arlyn stared in horror as floor beside her bubbled and sagged. "That's not blood," she gasped. "It's—" She never finished. A second tendril whipped around, snatching the staff from her hand and flinging it across the room like scraps.

"Spread out!" Ryn barked. They moved. Loran lunged left, Mara with him. Arlyn pulled Lila behind one of the smaller root-pillars. Braum forced himself up with a groan, clutching his ribs. The beast turned—not to pursue any of them directly—but to face Teren. For a heartbeat, the two corrupted entities regarded each other. Something unspoken passed between them. Then the beast turned away. Toward Loran. Teren smiled faintly. "It knows what it's hunting." The creature shifted again, flickering across the chamber. Loran barely saw it move. One moment it was ten paces away. The next, it loomed over him, tendrils spiraling downward.

He didn't think. He just reacted. His sigil flared beneath his skin—so bright it shone through his sleeve in jagged red lines. Pain shot up his arm, but he pushed past it, thrusting his hand forward as if he could shove the monster back with will alone. The air rippled. A wave exploded from him—red, raw, uncontrolled. The force slammed into the creature's chest. For a heartbeat, it staggered. Everyone felt it—the pressure, the crackle, the way the world bent. Mara gasped. "You hit it!" But then— The beast's chest opened wider. The swirling void inside its ribcage flared and pulled. Loran's power didn't knock it back. It was dragged in. Red light poured from his sigil into the creature like a stream sucked into a drain. The beast drank it, shuddering in something that looked almost like pleasure.

Loran screamed as his arm flared white-hot. "Loran!" Mara grabbed him, but the pull yanked them both forward. Her boots scraped uselessly against the floor. "Let go!" Arlyn shouted. "I can't!" Mara cried. "It's—" The beast lashed a tendril toward her. Ryn appeared between them in a blur, staff whipping up to deflect the blow. The tendril hit the shaft with a crack that rattled the chamber. Ryn was thrown backward, boots sliding, but he held. "Cut it off!" he snapped. Braum was already moving, face twisted in pain and fury. He brought his hammer down on the tendril sucking power from Loran. The blow smashed through corrupted flesh with a wet crunch. The tendril snapped. The pull cut off. Loran and Mara crashed to the ground, gasping.

The severed chunk of tendril writhed on the floor like a dying snake. Red light pulsed inside it for a heartbeat, then went dark, shriveling into ash. The beast reeled—briefly. Then it straightened. Stronger. "We just fed it," Arlyn whispered. Ryn's face was grim. "Yes."

The fight dissolved into chaos. The beast moved like a nightmare half-remembered—shifting from place to place in blurs and jumps, existing fully in one spot and then in another as if space meant nothing to it. A tendril smashed into the root-pillar Arlyn and Lila hid behind, splintering it. Arlyn shoved Lila away just as the structure came down, a rain of living wood and pulsing veins. Braum charged with a roar, swinging his hammer in a brutal arc. He caught one of the beast's limbs—a jointed, taloned thing—and heard something crack. The beast screamed. It was not a sound meant for human ears. Lila clamped her hands over her head and dropped to her knees. Mara's vision blurred. Loran's stomach lurched, bile rising into his throat. The roots in the ceiling twitched in time with the sound, the whole fortress reacting like nerves to a wound.

The beast retaliated. Three tendrils shot toward Braum at once. He blocked one, rolled from another, but the third caught his leg. Corruption bit into his flesh like acid. He shouted and went down, leg buckling. Arlyn sprinted to him, dragging him backward with a strength born of sheer desperation. "Don't let it touch your skin!" she cried. "Braum, don't—" He gritted his teeth, jaw clenched against the pain. Black lines spiderwebbed from the point of contact, racing up his calf. "Noted," he growled. Mara flung a knife at the creature's skull-shadow. It phased through, emerging on the other side like it had passed through smoke. Loran tried again, smaller this time, trying to focus his mark into something controlled—but it sparked and sputtered, like a torch in the rain. The beast drank whatever power he got loose, savoring every scrap. Teren watched. Silent. Calm.
Eyes glinting with something unreadable.

"What is this for you?" Loran shouted at him. "A game?" Teren tilted his head slightly. "A lesson," he said.

The beast struck again—wider this time. Its tendrils spread, stretching across the chamber like a net. They slammed down in a circle around the group—Ryn, Loran, Mara, Arlyn, Lila, Braum—

caging them in. The tendrils twisted inward. The ring tightened. Ryn whirled, staff moving in a blur, knocking aside attack after attack. Sweat beaded on his brow. His breath came shorter. Every impact drove him back a fraction more. "We can't keep this up!" Braum yelled through clenched teeth. Lila clung to Arlyn's arm, tears streaking down her face. "We're going to die. We're going to—" "Lila." Arlyn's voice cut through sharply—not unkind, but firm. "Look at me." Lila did. "We're not dead yet," Arlyn said. "So we move. We breathe. We fight." Another tendril crashed down, inches from them, spraying corrupted muck. The ring drew closer.

The beast loomed over them now, chest void swirling hungrily. It had tasted Loran's power once. It wanted more. Loran struggled to stand, his arm numb and burning all at once. Mara kissed his temple without thinking, a desperate, trembling gesture. "Don't you dare stop fighting," she whispered. He wanted to answer. To promise. But he wasn't sure he could. His mark felt empty. Hollow. Like the best parts of him had already been devoured.

The beast reared back for the finishing strike—tendrils all pulling inward at once, a crushing, obliterating convergence. And still— Ryn had not unleashed anything beyond flesh and bone and skill. "Ryn!" Loran shouted hoarsely. "We can't—" Ryn didn't look at him. He watched the beast. Measured it. Felt the fortress around them tremble on its foundations. And finally, as the tendrils descended in a perfect, lethal arc— Ryn exhaled. "All right," he boomed. "Enough."

The beast struck. It never reached them. For one heartbeat, everything stopped. The tendrils froze in mid-air, a hair's breadth from flesh. The air went heavy, thick, humming with sudden pressure. The red light of the fortress dimmed—as if someone had thrown a veil over it. Blue bled into the chamber. Not from above. Not from the walls. From Ryn. His eyes, once a nondescript shade of worn blue, flared with a deep, crystalline blue. Not bright and explosive—steady and impossibly ancient. Jagged lines of the same color lit beneath his skin, tracing paths along his neck, his forearms, the backs of his hands. The runes carved into his staff ignited, filling with liquid sapphire light.

Loran felt his breath catch. The mark on his own arm convulsed—part agony, part... response. Like it recognized what lived inside Ryn, the way metal recognizes a storm. The beast recoiled. For the first time, it hesitated. The void inside its chest stuttered, its edges fraying where blue light touched it. Ryn stepped forward. The tentacles around them trembled, straining against an invisible force that held them at bay. He didn't shout. Didn't roar. Didn't speak words of power. He simply moved.

Staff spinning in an arc too fast for the eye to follow. Blue light carved a crescent through the air, leaving a trail like a comet's tail. The nearest tendril was sliced clean in half. The cut wasn't bloody. It simply ceased to exist. The severed piece didn't fall. It vanished—like erased ink. The beast shrieked, a warping, breaking sound that made the roots of the fortress twitch in sympathy. More tendrils lashed out. Ryn met them. He flowed through the onslaught—each strike a precise counterpoint, each motion a dance he'd known for centuries. The staff blurred, blue afterimages layering on each other like overlapping waves. Every place it struck, corruption vanished. Not burned.

Not blasted apart.

Unmade.

"By the gods..." Braum whispered. "He's—" "Marked," Arlyn finished, voice barely audible. Lila stared at Ryn as though seeing a ghost given form. Mara didn't speak at all. She just watched. Wide-eyed. Silent. Something new and fragile blooming beneath the fear.

The beast adapted. Its void-core flared, dragging in everything around it—the air, the light, the wisps of corrupted substance still clinging to the chamber. The world around its chest distorted, edges bending like glass under heat. A tendril snapped toward Ryn, faster than before. He didn't block. He stepped into it. The tendril passed through him like smoke. No—not through. Around. Space folded for a heartbeat, Ryn's body shimmering at the edges.

The tentacle reappeared behind him, slamming uselessly into the floor. Ryn's eyes brightened. He thrust his staff forward, the tip aimed not at the beast's head, not at its limbs—but at the churning void in its chest. Blue light erupted. Not a beam. A spear. It drove into the core of the corruption with a sound like a thousand panes of glass shattering at once.

The void fought back, dark tendrils of negative space lashing out, wrapping around the staff. The chamber shook. Rows of sleeping bodies on the floor whimpered in unison. The fortress screamed—not in sound, but in movement, every root and vein convulsing. Teren's calm expression finally cracked. "You shouldn't be able to do that," he said softly. Ryn didn't answer. He pushed. The world bent around them. Blue and black wrestled, biting into each other. The void gnawed at Ryn's power, and Ryn's power seared it in return. The air smelled of ozone and earth and something older than either.

Loran tried to stand, but even lifting his head felt like moving through syrup. He watched, helpless, as two forces beyond him collided. The void shrank. Slowly. Reluctantly. The beast roared, tendrils flailing wildly, smashing into the walls, the floor, the ceiling. Chunks of living root tore free, exposing raw, glowing channels beneath. Finally— With a sound like an entire mountain collapsing inward— The void imploded. The beast's chest caved into nothing. Its limbs spasmed once, twice, then crumbled into dust that never quite touched the ground—dissolving before it landed. Silence hit the chamber like a hammer. The light flickered. The beast was gone.

For one exquisite heartbeat, no one moved. Ryn stood with his staff still extended, blue light slowly withdrawing back into the runes. His eyes dimmed a fraction, though they did not return fully to their old color. He lowered the staff. Turned. Looked at them. Loran realized he was shaking. Not in fear this time. In awe. Teren broke the quiet with a soft, humorless laugh. "I wondered," he murmured. "If you were still alive." Ryn met his gaze. "More than you think." "You hide," Teren said. "You always have." Ryn's jaw twitched. "You talk too much for someone who just lost his pet."

The fortress answered before Teren could. The walls convulsed. Roots writhed, veins flaring bright red. The whole chamber lurched as though something deep beneath it had been stabbed. Cracks spiderwebbed along the ceiling, leaking crimson light. "The fortress won't hold after that," Ryn said. "How do you know?" Arlyn asked. He didn't answer. He just moved.

"On your feet," Ryn ordered. "All of you." Braum groaned but forced himself up, leaning heavily on Arlyn's shoulder. Lila scrambled to help, face pale but determined. Mara slipped her arm around Loran, pulling him upright when his knees threatened to give out. "Where do we go?" Lila cried. "The corridor closed—" The archway they'd come through was now a seamless wall of knotted root. Ryn planted his staff and slammed its butt into the ground. Blue light pulsed outward in a ring. The roots shuddered. Not in pain. In recognition. "Old wounds still remember me," Ryn muttered. "Move." A fissure formed along the far side of the chamber—small at first, then widening into a narrow tunnel, roots peeling back like reluctant fingers.

"You're not leaving," Teren said. He didn't raise his voice. He didn't move from his place by the throne. But the roots near the new tunnel twitched, starting to weave themselves shut again. Ryn turned his head slightly. Their eyes met. Blue against dark. "You can't hold it and hold them at the same time," Ryn said. "You're stretched thin." For the first time, something like strain flickered across Teren's face. A fissure in the calm. Ryn's lips thinned. "I'll take that," he said quietly. He drove his staff into the stone once more. The opening snapped wide, roots forced aside by an unseen pressure. "Now!" Ryn snapped. Arlyn and Braum moved first, half-stumbling, half-running. Lila clung to Arlyn's cloak, eyes wide. Mara and Loran followed, the tunnel's edges brushing their shoulders with every step. Loran glanced back. Teren watched them go. He did not chase. He did not call out. He only raised one hand slightly—fingers curled, like a man adjusting invisible strings. Loran's mark burned. A whisper coiled into his mind, soft as breath. This isn't over. Then the tunnel curved sharply, and Teren vanished from view. Roots slammed shut behind them.

They burst out into cold air. The sky above was the same bruised red, but here the trees were warped, twisted outward, as though repulsed by the fortress that pulsed behind them. The living structure loomed in the distance—a mound of roots and veins and stone, shuddering in spasms, like a wounded heart misfiring. The ground beneath them hummed with each uneven thud. Braum collapsed onto his back, panting. "Remind me," he wheezed, "never to follow any of you into a fortress made of meat again." Lila laughed—a wild, broken sound that melted into a sob. Arlyn sank to her knees, clutching her head. "That thing... that creature... it was like nothing I've ever seen. If it's refining them, making them smarter, stronger—" "Then we're running out of time," Mara finished, voice hollow.

Loran leaned against a crooked tree, every muscle trembling. His arm throbbed with a dull, exhausted ache—his mark drained and raw. He looked at Ryn. Ryn stood several paces away, back to them, staff planted in the ground. The blue in his eyes had dimmed to faint embers. His shoulders were rigid, as if he were holding up something they couldn't see. "Ryn," Loran said quietly. "What are you?" Ryn didn't turn. For a long moment, the only sound was the distant, failing heartbeat of the fortress.

Finally, he spoke. "Someone who didn't stop it last time," he said. His voice was soft. Filled with an exhaustion older than his face. "And won't make that mistake again." He lifted his staff. "On your feet," he said. "We've seen the heart of what's coming." He finally glanced back at Loran—just for a heartbeat. "And this time, we're not running from it." The fortress shuddered again, more violently. But for the first time since they'd entered its shadow—Loran didn't feel only fear. He felt something else. A thin, stubborn thread of hope. Frightened. Fragile. But alive.

CHAPTER THIRTY-TWO
The Weight of Blue

The forest swallowed them whole. Not the twisted, pulsing roots of the fortress—but real forest again. Branches. Cold wind. Earth that didn't breathe. And yet none of them felt relieved. They staggered across the clearing, every footstep heavy. The crash of the fortress still echoed behind them, each distant pulse shaking the ground like a heartbeat struggling to continue. Lila wiped her face with trembling hands. Her voice cracked: "Did... did we really survive that?" Braum sank against the nearest tree, leg stretched forward. The blackened corruption marks on his calf had receded—thanks to Ryn's intervention—but the flesh was still swollen and red. "Barely," he muttered. "...and I hate that 'barely' is becoming normal."

Arlyn knelt beside him, already pulling out her herbs and bandages. "Hold still. This might sting." "It all stings," Braum growled, but he didn't resist. Loran didn't sit. He couldn't. His arm throbbed with a deep, gnawing ache, his mark feeling raw and hollow as though something had scraped it out from inside. He held it close, chest tight. Mara saw him from across the clearing and walked toward him softly—slower, more carefully than usual. "You need to lie down," she said gently. "I'm fine." "You're shaking," she whispered. He didn't deny it. Because she wasn't wrong.

The sigil had drained. The fortress had devoured everything he could muster. His attempt to fight the elite had only fed it. "You did more than you think," Mara murmured. "You stalled it long enough for Ryn to—" "To what?" Loran snapped, sharper than he intended. "To save us? Again?" She flinched. He closed his eyes, ashamed. "I'm sorry," he muttered. "I just... I thought I could do something." "You did," Mara insisted. "Loran, you—" "No," he said quietly. "I didn't." His voice wavered. "I'm marked. Chosen, cursed—whatever this is. And I'm still useless next to him." He didn't say Ryn's name. He didn't have to. The memory of the blue light still clung to the air.

Ryn stood apart from them, hood raised, staff planted in the earth beside him. He had said almost nothing since they'd escaped—no explanations, no reassurances. He looked like a statue carved from silence. But Loran felt him watching. Always watching. When Arlyn finished tending Braum, she rose and approached Ryn cautiously, arms folded. "You saved all of us," she said. "Thank you." Ryn didn't move. "Don't thank me. Not for that." "Why not?" "Because I didn't do it for your gratitude." That answer sent a ripple of unease through the group. Lila swallowed. "Ryn... what *are* you?"

His eyes flicked toward her under the hood—still faintly blue, still not entirely human. "Someone who has walked this road before," he said. "Too many times." "That's not an answer," Braum muttered. Ryn didn't argue. He didn't look offended. He simply seemed... tired. Arlyn pressed on. "That thing—what we fought—how did you know what it was?" Ryn's jaw tightened. "Because they weren't always like that." Mara stepped forward, voice thin. "What do you mean?" Ryn finally turned. The movement was small, but it silenced the clearing. His face was calm. His voice was not. "The corruption is not a sickness," he said. "It's a system. A design. A memory trying to rebuild itself." A shiver passed through them. "And you've seen it rebuild before?" Arlyn asked. "Yes." Loran felt the words like a punch to the gut. "How old are you?" he asked. Ryn met his eyes. "Around five centuries." Lila gasped. Mara's hand flew to her mouth. Arlyn's eyes widened. Braum simply muttered, "Of course he is." But Loran saw something else. Pain. Behind Ryn's flat tone was grief heavier than stone. He didn't want to explain. He didn't want to talk. He didn't want to remember.

Ryn looked away again. "We should move," he said. "The fortress will call others. They will come looking for the thing I just unmade." "You *unmade* it?" Arlyn whispered. "Yes." "How?" Ryn's grip tightened on his staff. "Because blue is the opposite of what fuels them. It's the countercurrent. The breaker. The memory of what the corruption once feared. You were chosen to bear the mark—I was born to this." Loran's breath caught. Blue. His own sigil... red. "What does red do?" he asked quietly. Ryn's jaw set. "Red is a sigil's power," he said. "It draws from the same well as the corruption. That's why it can oppose it—and why it can be consumed by it." Loran didn't breathe. "In trained hands, red can cut corruption apart," Ryn continued. "In untrained ones, it feeds it. You don't command it yet. It hasn't learned you. Until it does, it will never move as an extension of your will."

While Ryn set a watch perimeter, Mara helped Lila gather water from a nearby trickling spring. Loran watched her. Noticing things he hadn't before. How Mara stared at the water longer than needed... How her hand shook slightly when she dipped the canteen... How she kept glancing over her shoulder, as if expecting the shadows to speak. She felt his gaze and forced a smile. "Don't look at me like that. I'm fine." "You're not," he said softly. Her smile wavered. "Mara... what happened in there? With the whispers?" She froze. For a full breath. Then another. Finally: "He sounded like himself," she whispered. "Like the boy I grew up with. The boy who stayed up nights telling stories by the river. The boy who carried my pack on long walks." Her eyes filled. "And then he sounded like something else," she said. "Like he knew me better than I knew myself." Loran touched her hand. "Whatever spoke to you," he said, "wasn't him." Her fingers tightened around his. "I know," she whispered. But she looked away. The lie cracked between them.

The sun was fading—such as it was—behind the corrupted sky when Ryn finally approached the group again. "We can rest here for an hour," he said. "No more." Braum groaned. "An hour? After all that? Ryn, we're wrecked." "You can rest," Ryn replied. "But the corruption won't. It knows we were there. It will send scouts." Arlyn nodded reluctantly. "He's right. We can't stay too long." Loran pushed himself upright, gripping a twisted trunk for support. "Ryn." The wanderer turned his head slightly. "Back there... that beast was hunting me." "Yes," Ryn said. "Why? Because of my mark?" "Yes." "What do they want with me?" Ryn's expression didn't change. His eyes dimmed slightly. "That isn't for them to want," he said. "It's for you to decide." Loran stiffened. "That's not an answer." "It's the only answer I can give." Loran clenched his jaw. "I need to know what I am." Ryn's tone softened—barely. "You're not what they think," he said. "And you're not what you fear." He turned away. "But what you become," he said over his shoulder, "depends on what you choose next." Loran stared after him, helplessly. "Why won't you tell me?" Ryn didn't look back. "Because knowledge changes people," he said. "And you're not ready to be changed."

An hour later, the ground rumbled faintly beneath them. Ryn instantly lifted his staff, eyes narrowing toward the fortress's direction. "It's not collapsing," he said. "It's calling." "Calling what?" Lila whispered. Ryn's expression darkened. "The others." Braum grunted, forcing himself to stand with Arlyn's help. "Then what are we waiting for? Let's go." Ryn nodded once. "We head northwest. Back toward Captain Vale's camp. They need to know what's coming." Mara's voice wavered. "Do you think Teren will follow?" Ryn paused. "No," he said softly. "He won't follow." Loran frowned. "How can you be sure?" Ryn looked toward the dying forest—toward the fortress pulsing like a wounded beast. "Because he's not done with whatever's in there," he said quietly. "And corruption doesn't chase prey it knows will return." A chill slipped down Loran's spine. "What makes you think we'll return?" Ryn looked at him. For the first time since the battle, his expression cracked—not with fear, but with certainty. "Because you two are tied to him," Ryn said. "You and Mara both. He won't need to chase you." He turned away. "You're already walking toward him."

They moved into the dying forest. Cold wind whispered through skeletal branches. Behind them, the fortress pulsed again—a deep, rhythmic thud like a heartbeat restarting. And inside it— someone waited. Someone who knew Loran. Someone who once loved Mara. Someone who had not finished what he began. Mara did not look back. But she felt him. Like a hook buried deep inside her chest. And Loran— Loran felt something worse: His mark throbbed in a slow, painful pulse... Matching Teren's.

CHAPTER THIRTY-THREE
Shadows That Walk Beside

They hadn't gone far when Ryn stopped, the motion subtle but absolute. His staff angled forward, fingers brushing the soil as though testing a current running beneath it. The group froze with him, instinctively quiet. "The corruption is shifting," he said. Braum let out a low breath through his teeth. "Of course it is. Shifting how?" "Like a sweep," Ryn replied. "Wide. Methodical." He straightened slowly. "Searching." Arlyn's shoulders tightened. "Searching for what?" Ryn didn't answer. He didn't need to.

The silence that followed pressed heavier than any explanation. They pushed on, tension riding each step, and soon reached a clearing torn open by violence. A wagon lay overturned, half-sunk in churned mud, one wheel snapped clean away. Sacks had been ripped open and scattered, grain and supplies ground into the earth. Shield fragments lay among the tracks like shed scales, dulled and bent by force. Braum limped forward and lifted a dented rim, his jaw tightening. "Vale's," he muttered. "Damn it."

"They lived," Ryn said, scanning the ground. "Tracks break from the road. Fast. Disciplined." "So whatever came through wasn't hunting soldiers," Arlyn said quietly. "No," Ryn agreed, his gaze drifting toward the darker trees beyond the clearing. "Not then." Mara stiffened at the words, her pace faltering just enough for Loran to notice. He closed the distance between them. She wasn't stumbling, but she moved like someone pushing through resistance no one else could feel. "Mara," he said softly. "Talk to me." "I'm fine," she replied, eyes forward, voice thin. "You're not." She shook her head without looking at him. Even her shadow seemed wrong—stretched and faint, as though it might slip away if she stopped moving.

Ryn's voice cut through the clearing, sharp and unyielding. "She isn't." Mara spun on him, grief snapping into anger. "Stop speaking like you understand anything about me." "I understand corruption," Ryn said calmly. "And I know the cracks it looks for." "I am not corrupted," she said, her voice trembling between defiance and fear. "No," Ryn replied. "But you're carrying something that wants room to grow." Loran stepped between them before the words could cut deeper, jaw tight. "Could you maybe try saying things gently for once?" Ryn blinked once. "Gently won't save her." The argument shattered when a sound slid through the forest like smoke—not a voice, not a cry, more like a breath drawn by something that didn't need air.

Ryn raised his hand instantly, fingers splayed in warning. No one moved. The sound drifted past them, brushing the trees, too light to track and too deliberate to ignore. When it faded, the silence it left behind felt heavier than before. Ryn lowered his hand. "Scout patrol." Braum exhaled shakily. "That was barely anything." "They don't need to be loud," Ryn replied. "They're learning." Loran swallowed. "What were they looking for?" Ryn looked back toward the direction of the fortress they had escaped, eyes dark. "For whatever broke today." No one replied.

Night crept in slowly, draining what little color the sky had left. They kept moving, the forest growing quieter with each step, as if it were listening to their passage and measuring it. Even the wind seemed to retreat. "We should reach Vale's camp by dawn," Ryn said at last. "If it still stands." Lila hugged her satchel closer. "If?" "The corruption is moving differently now," Ryn replied. "Faster. Coordinated." Mara paused, her hand drifting to her chest as if something inside her tugged. Loran reached her side without thinking. "I'm here." She nodded, but her eyes didn't quite meet his.

The wind died completely, leaving their footsteps as the only sound. Ryn glanced back once, and Loran caught something rare in his expression—not fear for himself, but concern sharpened into something close to dread. It wasn't for what they had escaped. It was for Mara. And for whatever waited ahead..

CHAPTER THIRTY-FOUR
The Camp That Should Have Been Safe

They walked until the sky dimmed into a bruised gray and the forest thinned into stunted brush, the trees shriveling as though something had drained the life out of them with careful hands, and even though exhaustion clung to every step, no one dared speak of stopping. The silence between them felt sharp, as if the air itself wanted quiet to hear something approaching. Vale's encampment lay somewhere ahead—Ryn estimated an hour, maybe two—but the road there had begun to curve strangely, the ground rising and falling in soft, uneven waves like soil shifting under breath.

Lila stayed close to Arlyn, her worry clear in every quick glance she cast at the shadows. Braum's limp grew worse, but he forced himself onward without complaint, jaw tight, eyes scanning every piece of withered underbrush as though daring it to move. Mara drifted near the center of the group, but her pace faltered whenever the wind changed. She tilted her head slightly each time, as if listening for something only she could hear. Loran kept near her, not speaking, just making sure she didn't drift too far from the group's gravity. He didn't trust the forest. He didn't trust the quiet. And he didn't trust whatever still clung to Mara's thoughts like wet ash.

Ryn led them steadily, never hurried, never slow, his senses tuned to things the others could not perceive. He stopped twice—once to check tracks, and once because he said the trees had gone still too suddenly. Neither pause made anyone feel better.

They reached the first sign of Vale's encampment when Braum spotted a broken spear in the dirt, its shaft snapped cleanly down the middle, the steel tip smeared with dried black residue that flaked like soot in the fading light. A few paces ahead, a torn banner slumped against a rock, its cloth shredded but unmistakably marked with Vale's crest. "This isn't good," Braum muttered, though no one needed him to say it. Ryn crouched beside the spear, brushing the dirt lightly. "This was recent," he said. "Hours.." Lila swallowed. "Did they... survive?" Ryn didn't answer immediately. He scanned the tree line, the sky, the broken earth beneath them. "They fought," he finally said. "Hard. And they ran." Whether they survived after that, he didn't say.

They continued up a slope, and as they crested the rise, Vale's encampment finally revealed itself below—not the bustling, orderly outpost they remembered, but a scattering of collapsed tents, splintered barricades, abandoned weapons, and smoke curling faintly from pits that had not been tended. The camp was not destroyed; it was emptied. Quickly. And not by choice. Lila's breath caught, hands flying to her mouth. "Where is everyone?" "Gone," Arlyn whispered. "Or hiding." Braum tightened his grip on his hammer and took a step forward, but Ryn extended a hand, stopping him. "Wait."

Loran felt the tension coil inside him. "What is it?" Ryn didn't speak at first. He listened. The forest behind them, the windless air, the camp below—all of it pressed inward like a closing fist. Finally, Ryn said, "Something passed through here. Something large." Loran's throat tightened. "Elite?" Ryn shook his head slowly. "No. Larger than that. And older than—" He cut himself off sharply, jaw tightening at his own slip. "Just stay alert." They descended the slope, stepping carefully around overturned crates and discarded shields. The smell hit them halfway down, burned wood mixed with a metallic tang, sharp and unsettling. Not blood. Something colder. Something like stone rasping against stone. At the camp's edge lay a half-crushed barricade, its wooden stakes warped inward as though something had stepped directly onto them.

Ryn crouched beside one of the prints. It wasn't a footprint exactly—more like the ground had caved in under a mass of weight and heat. "It didn't stop long," he murmured. "Just passed through." "Looking for Vale's men?" Loran asked. Ryn stood. "No. Looking for us." The words hung heavy and unchallenged. They moved deeper into the abandoned camp, and soon, faint noises drifted from a cluster of crates near the far tents. Ryn lifted a hand to quiet them. The noise came again—shuffling, whispered breaths, the unmistakable tension of people trying to remain unseen. Ryn approached first, careful, slow, one hand raised. "Come out," he said, "or you won't survive the next hour."

For a long heartbeat, nothing happened. Then a crate shifted, and the tip of a spear emerged, shaking slightly. A moment later, a man stepped into view—thin, dirt-smeared, eyes wide and frantic. Then another. And another. Four soldiers in total, pale and gaunt as ghosts. One of them collapsed to his knees the moment he saw Loran's group. "Thank the gods," he rasped. "Captain Vale—he sent us back to warn the camp, but—" His voice cracked. "We were too late." Loran stepped forward. "Where is the captain now?" The soldier trembled. "North. At the ridge. He took the rest of the men to intercept... something." Arlyn crouched beside him. "What something?" The soldier swallowed hard. "We didn't see it. We only felt it moving. Like thunder moving inside the ground." Lila shivered violently. Braum's grip tightened on his hammer. Ryn looked north, toward the mountains faintly silhouetted in the dying light. Something in his face shifted—fear, recognition, guilt, all tangled into one. "A giant," he murmured. Loran blinked. "A what?" Ryn didn't look away from the ridge. "One of the last," he said quietly. "And if the corruption has found it... then the world is running out of time."

Loran felt Mara sway beside him. He caught her arm quickly, steadying her. Her skin was cold. Too cold. Her eyes unfocused, drawn toward the north as though something there tugged at her from inside her ribs. "Mara?" he whispered. She didn't answer. The wind shifted, carrying with it a distant, low tremor—so faint it could have been imagined, but Ryn stiffened instantly. It wasn't imagined. The giant had moved. And something else was moving with it. Ryn turned to the group, his voice low and firm. "We're leaving," he said. "Now." Loran nodded, but glanced once more at Mara. She stared toward the distant mountains with a look that chilled him deeper than the forest ever had—because it wasn't fear in her eyes. It was recognition. The corruption whispered to her from somewhere far away. And Mara—unable to stop herself—listened.

CHAPTER THIRTY-FIVE
The First Gathering of Ashwood Hold

The approach to Vale's chosen settlement ground did not feel triumphant—it felt thin, frayed, like a banner stretched too tight by wind and time. The land here was better than most: trees still held their leaves, the soil didn't pulse or rot, and the air, though cold, wasn't poisoned. It should have felt safe. It didn't. Wagons sat half-unloaded, shields leaned against half-built walls, and a wide ring of timber stakes marked the beginnings of a defensive perimeter. Men and women moved through the clearing, carrying planks, sharpening spears, hauling fabric for tents—working with a frantic energy that did not match the calm landscape. Survival made planners of everyone.

Captain Vale strode toward them the moment they emerged from the trees. His armor had fresh dents. His eyes had deeper shadows than before. But he still held himself like a man who refused to break. "You made it," Vale said, voice low but warm. His gaze flicked over each of them, lingering slightly on Loran and Mara. "We saw the sky twist last night. I assumed you were close to whatever caused it." Ryn only said, "Closer than we wanted to be." Vale didn't push. He turned back toward the half-built fort. "Welcome to Ashwood Hold. It isn't much yet. But it will be." Loran looked around. Most of the workers were tired. Children huddled near cookfires. A few worn travelers carried the look of people who had run hard and long and didn't know where else to go. This was meant to be a safe place—but fear murmured through it like a draft beneath a door.

"What happened here?" Arlyn asked quietly. Vale exhaled. "More people arrived than we planned. They came from three villages—burned, emptied, or abandoned. That alone would be enough to unnerve anyone." He hesitated. "But then the tremors began." Braum straightened. "Tremors?" "Small ones," Vale said. "But wrong somehow. Like the earth was... shifting its weight." Ryn's eyes sharpened. Not alarmed—recognizing. "Did anyone see anything?" he asked. "No," Vale replied. "That's the worst part. Nothing to fight. Nothing to chase off. The settlers keep looking at me for answers I don't have." He rubbed the back of his neck. "Fear spreads fast when the ground itself moves."

Arlyn helped Lila down from a wagon. The girl's eyes darted from face to face—people tired, people wounded, people afraid—but then the faintest spark of hope flickered in her expression. "They're trying," she whispered. "They're really trying." Loran saw that too. People building something instead of running. People choosing to stand. But as he looked around, the air shifted—just slightly, like a held breath. Mara felt it too. Her eyes flicked toward the tree line. "Did anyone else...?" The tremor rolled beneath their feet. Soft. Fleeting. But undeniable. The workers froze. A wagon rocked gently. Dust slid from the rafters of a half-built shelter. Vale swore under his breath. "Not again." Children cried. A man dropped a crate. Weapons were grabbed in reflex—even though no enemy approached. Ryn stepped forward, staff pressing into the earth as though listening through it. His jaw tightened. "What is it?" Arlyn whispered. "Something far from here is weakening," Ryn murmured. "And the land knows it."

Loran's mark flared briefly—just a flicker of warmth, then a cold tremor up his arm. Ryn's eyes snapped to him. "You felt that," Ryn said quietly. Loran swallowed. "Yes." Mara looked away quickly, as though ashamed to admit she felt it too. Vale noticed their reactions, but didn't understand them. "Is this corruption?

Some new form?" Ryn shook his head once. "Not corruption. Not yet." Then softer, "But close." Vale's posture hardened. "If a threat is coming, we need defensive lines reinforced. I need every hand that can hold a hammer or a spear." "You'll have ours," Arlyn said immediately. Loran nodded. "We didn't come here to hide." Mara hesitated—but only for a moment. "If people are building a home, then we protect it."

Ryn said nothing. He simply turned to watch the tree line again, eyes faintly narrowed, as if waiting for the wind itself to confess a secret. Another tremor—lighter this time. No one spoke. The settlers returned to work, but the rhythm had changed. Hammers slowed. Conversations turned to whispers. The forest's edge felt closer. The sky looked heavier. Ashwood Hold was growing... ...but so was the weight pressing against the world. And somewhere far to the north—beyond mountains, beyond forests, beyond any sight of mortal eyes—the green giant trembled. Not dying yet. Not fallen yet. But weakening. A single stone in a wall older than civilization beginning to crack.

Loran felt it again—a faint, hollow shudder inside his mark. He pressed his hand against his sleeve. For one heartbeat, he thought he felt Mara clutch her chest the same way. The world seemed to lean. Ryn's voice broke the silence. "Tonight, we set watches," he said. "Double lines. Keep fires low. Something is shifting beneath everything we know." Vale nodded grimly. "Then let's be ready for whatever reaches us first." As the sun sank behind the trees, the tremor faded. But the feeling did not. Ashwood Hold stood on the edge of something no one yet understood. And the world was beginning to tilt.

CHAPTER THIRTY-SIX
The Hold That Breathes

Ashwood Hold did not feel like a sanctuary, not after hours spent moving within its half-built walls, not after watching the place reveal itself piece by piece as the day waned and the light shifted, because what had first seemed like a temporary refuge slowly showed itself to be something else entirely—a decision made under pressure, a stand chosen not out of confidence but out of necessity.

As the sun lowered toward the tree line, the shallow basin where the streams converged reflected the sky in dull, broken ribbons. The water carried faint traces of ash and disturbed soil. Crude wooden barricades encircled the clearing, casting long, uneven shadows that stretched and crawled as if they had a will of their own. Watchtowers rose along the ridges, skeletal frames wrapped in unfinished canvas roofs that snapped and fluttered in the cold wind like wounded wings struggling to lift. Everywhere there was motion. Men hauled timber with blistered hands. Women tightened rope lines and reinforced stakes. Soldiers sharpened blades dulled not just by battle, but by fear and overuse.

Smoke clung low to the ground from scattered fire pits, each guarded by tired figures who looked far too young for the armor strapped across their chests. The smell of sap, iron, sweat, and damp earth hung thick in the air, pressing against the lungs with every breath. Children huddled close to the fires, wrapped in blankets scavenged from wagons and ruined homes. Their voices stayed low. Laughter was rare and fleeting, as though even joy understood it was unwelcome here for long.

Loran watched it all from near the inner barricade. He rested briefly against a stack of bundled planks before the ache in his arm forced him to shift again. Beneath his sleeve, the mark pulsed intermittently, a faint warmth followed by an unsettling chill. It did not hurt, but it refused to be ignored. It reacted not to pain, but to presence, as if the Hold itself were breathing and the mark had learned its rhythm. Nearby, Braum collapsed onto a rough-hewn log with a groan, bracing his hammer beside him like a trusted companion. He muttered something about not having sat on anything warm since the world still pretended to make sense. Arlyn moved steadily from one wounded settler to the next with practiced efficiency, checking fevers and binding cuts. Her expression remained composed, though strain lingered beneath it. Lila hovered close, offering water and fetching bandages, inserting herself wherever she was needed with instinctive urgency, as though purpose mattered more to her now than rest.

Through it all, Mara stood slightly apart. She stared toward the mountains framed against the darkening sky, arms wrapped tightly around herself as if cold despite the nearby fires. Her gaze was unfocused. Her posture was tense. A familiar knot tightened in Loran's chest as he rose and joined her. The ground beneath his boots gave a faint, almost imperceptible shudder. It might have been imagined, if it had not returned moments later.

She spoke without looking at him. Her voice was low. She said the ground here felt awake, listening. Whatever Ryn claimed was weakening far away felt close enough to taste. Before Loran could respond, Captain Vale approached. Exhaustion was etched deep into his features, but authority still held firm in his posture. He offered Mara a waterskin and asked quietly if something had happened inside the fortress. For a heartbeat, she could not answer. Something flickered across her face—grief, confusion, and something darker that vanished before it could be named. She finally whispered that she was only tired. Vale did not look convinced, but he let it pass. He turned instead to speak of the scouts, of tremors growing stronger to the north, of land that felt wrong, as if being pulled apart. When Loran admitted it wasn't just the ground, Mara's jaw tightened just enough for Vale to notice.

Vale's gaze shifted between them before settling on Ryn. He stood at the edge of the clearing with his staff planted firmly in the earth, eyes fixed on the tree line as if expecting the forest itself to speak. When pressed for answers, Ryn spoke calmly. He said corruption was spreading faster than before. The fortress had unbalanced something older than the land around them. It could always be fought, he admitted, but stopping it depended on seals he refused to explain. Instead, he spoke of fortifications, of trenches and reinforced watch points. He warned that corrupted things did not retreat when wounded, and that battles must be assumed final. Vale, grim but decisive, turned to bark orders without argument.

As the camp surged back into motion, Mara drifted away again toward the horizon. The mountains darkened as night crept closer. When Loran followed and told her she was not alright, she did not deny it. She admitted that something followed her beneath her skin. A thought would not loosen its grip. A voice sounded like Teren calling her name gently in the dark. When Loran suggested telling Ryn, she recoiled sharply and begged him not to. Not yet. Her eyes shone with something rawer than fear. He swallowed his instinct to argue and gave the promise she asked for. In that moment, something in him bent without breaking. He understood that whatever burden Mara carried could not be forced loose without tearing her apart. That frightened him more than any corrupted beast they had faced. He stayed beside her without touching, close enough that she could feel his presence without flinching. Together they watched the jagged ridges cut against the sky, the horizon seeming less like a boundary and more like a wound that refused to close.

Around them, the Hold's rhythm shifted again. Hammers struck faster. Voices lowered. Movements sharpened. It was as though the camp itself sensed the pressure building and braced instinctively. When a child's cry broke near one of the fire pits, it was silenced quickly—not with comfort, but urgency, as if sound itself had become dangerous. Animals stamped and snorted uneasily along the outer ring, ears flicking toward the forest and the unseen north. Loran felt the mark on his arm pulse again, stronger now. The hollow vibration traveled into his shoulder and settled there like a warning. For a fleeting, unsettling instant, he imagined the skin beneath his sleeve tightening inward, responding to something beyond his understanding.

Ryn had not moved. His posture appeared relaxed, but tension betrayed him. His fingers tightened and loosened as if measuring something only he could feel. His gaze cut not just through the trees, but through distance itself, following lines of strain no map could show. When a sudden wind swept through Ashwood Hold, it carried more than cold. It pressed against Loran's ears and chest, scattered ash from the fire pits, and drew every gaze upward. The air thinned. The camp fell unnaturally still. Vale demanded to know what it meant. Ryn lifted his face to the sky, recognition and dread crossing his features. He said the world was bracing, that something far older than corrupted herds was weakening. When the wind died as abruptly as it had risen, the silence that followed pressed down like the breath before a scream.

Ryn ordered the Hold fortified through the night. Every wall and tower was to be strengthened before dawn. Vale obeyed without question, shouting commands as Ashwood Hold erupted into purposeful chaos once more—hammers striking, shields stacked, torches lit, rope lines tightened, steel sharpened. Loran stayed close to Mara, afraid to look away for too long. Ryn remained at the edge of the camp, staring into the dark northwest. He felt what no one else yet could: the first faint tremor of a distant collapse, the warning breath of a guardian on the brink. Night thickened around them. Somewhere in the unseen distance, something in the world began to slip, inexorable and unseen, drawing them all closer to the moment when everything would finally break....

CHAPTER THIRTY-SEVEN
Morning Before the Storm

Dawn crept over Ashwood Hold without warmth. The sunrise was muted, a thin glow smothered by low, sickly clouds that refused to break. The night's torches still burned along the barricades, flickering weakly in the breeze, as though they too had stayed awake on watch. The camp was quieter than Loran expected. Not calm—nothing felt calm anymore—but quiet in the way people become when they sense they're standing on borrowed time. Workers moved slowly between tents, trying not to look toward the mountains. Soldiers sharpened spears with a tension that made the blades shake in their hands. Even the animals seemed restless, stamping hooves and snorting at shadows that hadn't yet taken shape.

Loran rarely slept these days, but whatever little rest he managed slipped away long before the sun rose. His arm ached—not burning, not glowing, just a steady pressure under the skin like a warning he couldn't quite interpret. He sat on an overturned crate near the main fire pit, staring at the faint steam curling from his cup. The water inside barely warmed his hands. Footsteps approached softly. Mara sat beside him, her cloak wrapped tight around her shoulders. Her hair was tangled from sleep, if she'd slept at all. For a moment she didn't speak. She just watched the fires and the slow stir of morning.

When she finally breathed out, the exhale trembled. "You didn't sleep again," she whispered. "Neither did you." She tried to smile, but it wasn't real. It was the kind of smile someone learns to fake after too many losses. "I keep hearing things when I close my eyes," she admitted. "Not voices. Not exactly. More like... a memory replaying wrong." She rubbed at her temples. "It's his face. And it's not." Loran swallowed hard.

"Mara, we can tell Ryn—" "No." She gripped his arm. "No. Not yet. He's already watching me like I'm going to fall apart. I don't want him deciding for me." "He's trying to keep you safe." "He's trying to keep the world safe," she corrected softly. "And that's not the same thing." Loran couldn't argue with that. He glanced toward the far side of the camp where Ryn stood alone on one of the half-built towers. Even from a distance, the man looked carved from resolve—motionless except for the slow turn of his head as he scanned the horizon. He had been up there before dawn, silent and shadowed, as if searching for something only he could sense.

Braum limped over then, carrying a wooden bowl piled high with something resembling porridge. "Eat," he announced, plopping the bowl into Loran's free hand. "Arlyn says if we don't, she'll personally shove the food down our throats. And she's a healer, which means she knows where the soft spots are." "Comforting," Mara said dryly. "Didn't say it was supposed to be comforting. Just passing along the message." He settled beside them with a grunt, stretching his healing leg until it popped loudly. "Feels like we're sitting in the calm right before doing something incredibly stupid." "We're not doing anything," Loran said. "We're staying here." "Oh please," Braum snorted. "When have we ever stayed anywhere the world wanted us to? If danger doesn't find us, we go wander right into it."

Loran gave a reluctant shrug. He wasn't wrong. Arlyn approached soon after, her sleeves rolled and her hands full of bandages she was sorting. Her sharp eyes flicked over all three of them. "Everyone drinking water? Eating something? Standing upright?" She paused, then added dryly, "Breathing?" "Barely," Braum muttered. Arlyn ignored him and turned to Mara. "You're pale." "I'm always pale." "Paler than usual." Mara looked away.

"Just tired." Arlyn didn't look convinced, but she didn't press. She had learned enough to recognize when someone needed space.

Across the hold, Vale strode toward them, breathing hard from his rounds. He looked like he hadn't slept either, but he wore his exhaustion like a badge—proof he still had tasks to complete. "Scouts reported in," he said, stopping by the fire. "No corrupted movement on the southern ridge. That gives us some breathing room." Braum perked up. "Good news. Look at that, the world hasn't ended yet." Vale didn't smile. "The northern scouts haven't returned." That sank into the group like a stone tossed into a still pond. Ryn descended from the tower at that moment, his boots crunching softly against the frost-dusted ground. He approached with the same unreadable calm he always carried, though Loran noticed the faint tension around his eyes—a rare crack in the man's mask.

"They won't return," Ryn said. Vale stiffened. "How do you know that?" Ryn's jaw flexed. "Because I can feel the absence. When a corrupted swarm passes through a place, it leaves a hollow in the air. A kind of stillness. The northern ridge is quiet. Too quiet." Mara shivered. "What does that mean?" "It means something swept through," Ryn replied. "Something strong enough that the scouts had no chance to send word." "But the Hold is untouched," Vale argued. "If something that strong passed—" "It didn't pass," Ryn said. "It moved... underneath." Loran blinked. "Under the ridge?" "No," Ryn said softly. "Under everything." A hush fell over them. Even the wind seemed to pull back in caution.

"What does that mean?" Arlyn whispered. Ryn looked toward the distant mountains. The morning light caught his eyes, turning them a cool, luminous blue. "A seal is weakening," he said. "One of the guardians that keeps the corruption in check is struggling." Loran's stomach tightened. He didn't know the giant by name or face, but he had felt the tremor inside himself yesterday—the strange, sinking sensation like something vast and important shifting just out of reach. Vale rubbed his face. "If a guardian falls, what happens to the rest of us?" Ryn didn't answer. That silence said more than any words could.

Braum blew out a shaky breath. "Well. Nothing like a completely vague world-ending warning before breakfast." "Eat anyway," Arlyn muttered, thrusting a bowl at him. Mara turned her face to the wind then, her lips parting slightly as if hearing something no one else could. Loran touched her shoulder gently. "Mara?" She blinked hard, shaking something off. "I'm... I'm fine." But she wasn't. Loran felt it like a weight pressing between them. He opened his mouth to call Ryn over— but Mara stepped away, pretending to adjust her cloak, purposely moving where Ryn couldn't see her face. Loran shut his mouth. If she wasn't ready, forcing the issue would only push her further inward.

Vale clapped his hands together. "We're reinforcing the northern barricade this morning. If trouble is coming, it's coming from that direction. I want extra watch rotations and double-picked archers covering the ridge." Workers scattered to obey. Ryn watched them go with a shadow in his gaze. "The hold won't be ready," he murmured. Vale exhaled. "I know. But it's what we have." Loran stood, flexing his sore arm. "Tell us where you need us." Vale nodded. "I'll take all the help I can get."

As the morning pushed forward, the sound of hammers began to echo across Ashwood Hold—steady, determined, almost rhythmic. People worked with grim purpose, shaping defenses against threats none of them could fully imagine. But beneath it all, beneath the orders and the building and the sharpening of steel, the earth carried a low, nearly imperceptible tremor. A heartbeat. Weak. Slipping. Far away, but not far enough. Mara closed her eyes as the wind swept her hair across her face, and for the briefest moment, her breath synced with that distant pulse. When she opened her eyes again, they were her own.

CHAPTER THIRTY-EIGHT
Work of Many Hands

The day settled into motion slowly, as if the hold itself had to wake in layers. Ashwood's narrow paths filled with people carrying planks or bundles of rope, and the crack of tools against wood echoed from every corner. Loran found himself swept into the rhythm without meaning to—helping drag timbers forward, lifting posts, steadying ladders while men and women hammered braces into place. The air was cold but clear, and for the first time in weeks the corruption didn't feel like it had claws wrapped around his ribs.

Ryn moved between groups like a silent overseer, not giving orders but nudging people toward safer structures: telling two carpenters to reinforce a gate hinge, pointing out to Vale's sergeant that archers shouldn't stand directly above the firepit smoke, adjusting the lean of a barricade with a single push of his staff. Loran watched him for a while. Ryn never looked tired. He never paused. It was as if seeing the hold strengthen gave him strength as well.

Mara spent the morning carrying water for the builders, her steps steady but her face strained. Every now and then she pressed a hand to her chest as if easing an ache she didn't want anyone to notice. Loran tried to speak to her again, but she always smiled—thin, apologetic—and slipped away to check on Lila or help Arlyn organize the healing tent. Arlyn had taken command of a group of settlers sorting dried herbs, stitching torn cloaks, and boiling cloth for clean bandages. Lila, to her credit, tried to do everything at once, flitting between tasks with nervous energy and nearly knocking over a pot of steeping willow bark twice.

Braum had been drafted by Vale to train the youngest fighters–boys barely into manhood, and a few girls who insisted on learning to wield spear and shield. He barked instructions with uncharacteristic patience, demonstrating stance and footwork while limping heavily on his recovering leg. "If they can swing a hammer," he muttered to Loran during a short break, "they can swing a sword. Just need to teach them not to wet themselves when something snarls." Loran helped him demonstrate a few maneuvers–not because he was much better, but because the kids seemed to respond to someone a little more charismatic.

One boy flinched every time Loran raised the training blade. "It won't bite," Loran assured him, lowering the wood. "And if it does, bite it back." A few of the trainees laughed. The boy managed a shaky grin. By midday the hold looked different–not finished, not fortified, but alive. Cooking fires burned, children ran water for their parents, and tents shifted as people prepared them for the incoming cold. There was a fragile sense of normalcy threading through the place, the illusion that life could grow here if the world didn't crush it first.

Vale stopped beside Loran while overseeing the barricade reinforcement. "People work harder when you're around," he said. Loran blinked. "Me?" Vale nodded. "You fought off a hunter-beast and came back from whatever that fortress was. Folks see you as proof we're not helpless." Loran shifted uncomfortably. "I didn't win that fight. Ryn—" "You were there," Vale cut in. "Sometimes that's enough." Loran didn't know what to say to that, and Vale didn't wait for a reply. He moved on, calling for more men to haul the next line of timber.

Later in the afternoon, Ryn finally approached Loran while he was helping lift a beam into place. "Walk with me," he said quietly. Loran followed him to the perimeter wall where the trees stood thinner and the wind cut colder. Ryn leaned his staff against the wood and crossed his arms, studying the distant ridge. "How does your arm feel today?" Loran flexed it. "Heavy. But... quiet." "Good," Ryn said. "Quiet is better than wild." Loran frowned. "Are you going to teach me something?" "Not today." Ryn gestured toward the hold. "They must build. You must build with them. Power without grounding is a blade with no hilt." Loran sighed. "You and your riddles." Ryn's mouth twitched—something almost like a smirk. "When you're older, they won't sound like riddles." "Older? How old?" "Not five hundred," Ryn said lightly, turning away. "But older than you are now." Loran huffed a laugh despite himself. "Is there anything you're actually going to explain to me?" "Yes," Ryn said. "Eventually." It wasn't satisfying, but it was more than he usually offered.

They spent the rest of the afternoon helping Vale's soldiers lift sharpened stakes into place and tie reinforcement ropes around the new palisade. The sun dipped toward the tree line in a slow fade of gray-gold, and the clang of hammers softened as people ended their shifts. Mara returned with Lila at dusk, both of them exhausted but carrying two baskets of herbs Arlyn had sent them to collect from the safer groves. Mara avoided Loran's eyes again, but she didn't look as shaken as she had been that morning. "Dinner soon," she said, brushing dirt from her sleeves. "We helped dry some of the mushrooms. Don't ask where we found them." "Should I be worried?" Loran asked. "Probably," Lila whispered, then grinned.

Arlyn called them over to wash before eating, and for the first time since arriving at Ashwood Hold, the group sat together without immediate danger looming over their heads. The stew was thin, but warm; the bread was tough, but shared; the fire was small, but everyone edged closer to it. Voices murmured around them, hopeful in a timid way, as though people were afraid speaking too happily might break whatever fragile peace they'd managed to hold onto. Ryn didn't join the meal, but Loran saw him at the wall again, watching the mountains. Always watching. The tremor under Loran's skin was faint that evening, barely noticeable. Almost calm. But when the wind blew from the northwest, he felt a strange tug—like something deep beneath the earth had shifted its weight in discomfort. He rubbed his arm, staring toward the dim outline of the distant ridge. He didn't know what was coming, but for the first time in days, the hold didn't feel doomed. People worked. People ate. People laughed, even if only in small bursts. Maybe they could build something here. Maybe this place could hold. Maybe. When Loran looked across the fire at Mara, she smiled at him. It wasn't the brittle smile from that morning. It was small and tired—but real. And for the moment, that was enough.

CHAPTER THIRTY-NINE
Quiet Weeks, Restless Hearts

The days that followed settled into a rhythm Ashwood Hold had not known since its founding. People rose early, smoke lifting from cookfires, voices carrying through the cold air as workers split wood, hauled stone, and repaired whatever broke overnight. The hold was growing—slowly, unevenly, but undeniably. More families arrived from the south, some limping in with wagons missing wheels, others carrying what little they owned on their backs. Vale greeted each group personally, directing them toward shelter or food, and every new arrival brought stories of the world outside: villages emptied, roads cracking with tremors, strange green storms glimpsed on the horizon. The settlers listened, nodded, and then turned their hands to work.

Ashwood Hold had no room left for fear that froze a person. Only fear that made them build faster. Loran woke early each morning to help Vale's soldiers reinforce the palisade or set new watch rotations. He trained when he could, sometimes sparring with Braum—carefully, because Braum still winced when he pivoted too quickly—and sometimes alone with a sword that still felt heavier than it should. Ryn watched from a distance but rarely offered instruction. When he did speak, it was usually something infuriatingly vague, like "Your arm leads too much" or "Anger dulls the blade." Loran wasn't sure what any of it meant, but he tried. He didn't want to rely on the mark. Not after the fortress. Not after watching the sigil stutter and fail him when he needed it most. Arlyn grew busier with every passing day. Injuries from labor, fevers from cold nights, a stubborn cough moving through the children—she handled them all with steady hands and sharp orders.

Lila attached herself to Arlyn like a shadow, acquiring herbs, boiling water, sorting through salves and tinctures with surprising focus. Some of the settlers had begun calling her "Little Healer," though Lila always blushed and shook her head as if she didn't deserve the name. She spent her evenings tucked beside Mara or Arlyn, listening as they spoke quietly about remedies or sickness or things that could be gathered near the riverbank.

Mara had changed the most—subtly, gradually, but unmistakably. She still worked tirelessly, still brought food to the workers, still checked on Braum's leg each night with gentle hands. But there was a distance to her now. A quiet that settled over her at strange moments, as if she were listening to something no one else could hear. She hid it well enough when people were watching; only Loran seemed to catch the moments where she paused mid-task, her head tilted slightly, a faint crease between her brows. Once, he found her standing alone near the outer wall long after dusk, staring toward the mountains with a look that chilled him far more than she intended.

"Can't sleep?" Loran asked. Mara startled and folded her arms. "Just thinking." "About Teren?" She flinched—barely, but enough. "No," she said. "Not tonight." He didn't believe her, but he didn't press. She walked back toward the firelight before he could think of something else to say. Ryn moved through the hold with the same quiet presence he always carried, neither belonging nor entirely apart. People had started to treat him like a talisman—some nodded to him with respect, others stepped aside nervously as if they feared standing too close might invite something powerful they didn't understand.

Children whispered stories about how he killed a monster bigger than a horse, how his staff glowed like moonfire, how he never slept. Loran noticed that Ryn never corrected any of these stories. He barely acknowledged them at all. But Ryn was not idle.

He repaired the hold's watchtowers, taught Vale's archers how to spot corrupted silhouettes through fog, and once, late at night, Loran caught a faint blue glow coming from the northern barricade where Ryn stood alone. When Loran approached him the glow vanished instantly. Ryn only said, "Checking the wards," though he never explained what wards he meant.

Small skirmishes came and went. Twice the hunters returned with scratches from creatures lurking near the river. Once a malformed deer, bones jutting beneath warped flesh, wandered too close to the gate before collapsing on its own. Another night, a corrupted fox slipped between two barricade slats, its eyes gleaming like dull lanterns until Braum crushed it with a hammer swing that nearly toppled him over. None of these incidents were large enough to terrify the hold, but they reminded everyone that the corruption had not forgotten them. The strangest moments came from the earth itself. Every few days the ground would shiver—just a breath, just a tremble—and Ryn would lift his head sharply, eyes narrowing as though listening to a distant cry.

No one else felt anything more than a faint vibration underfoot. But Loran did. His mark prickled each time, a faint throb that lingered for hours afterward. Mara felt them too; Loran could tell by the way her expression tightened when the tremors came, though she always pretended she hadn't noticed. On the seventeenth day after their arrival, another group of refugees staggered through the gate—five in total, carrying a sixth who was barely conscious. They spoke of a collapsed road, of trees uprooted in perfect spirals, of a distant groan that sounded like the world itself grieving. Vale listened grimly, then sent scouts north again.

Ryn stood at the edge of the conversation, shoulders rigid, jaw set. When the refugees mentioned seeing a faint green shimmer near the mountains during a storm, Ryn looked away sharply enough that Loran knew—without any explanation—that it meant something important. Life grew harder as the cold deepened. Food ran thin. Vale organized hunting rotations and ration lines. Yet the mood of Ashwood Hold was not despair. People were working, rebuilding something larger than fear. Children played between tents. Fires burned each night. Families told stories to keep spirits from sinking. There was movement, there was sound, there was life. A fragile life, but a life all the same.

On the twenty-second day, as Loran and Braum finished reinforcing the walkway above the gate, a tremor rolled so strongly beneath their feet that both had to steady themselves against the railing. The tools rattled. Dust tumbled from the tower beams. Somewhere below, a pot toppled and shattered. Ryn appeared almost instantly, his expression sharper than Loran had ever seen it. “That wasn’t the same as before,” Loran said. “No,” Ryn murmured. “The guardian is weakening faster than I hoped.” “Guardian,” Braum repeated, wiping his brow. “You keep saying that like we’ve seen one walking around.” Ryn didn’t answer. His gaze drifted toward the mountains again. The clouds above them had shifted, streaks of faint green catching the morning light in unnatural flickers.

Loran followed his stare. “Is it dying?” Ryn inhaled slowly, as if weighing how much truth to give. “Not yet.” “Will it?” Ryn closed his eyes briefly. “Yes.” The word landed heavily, but not dramatically. Just certain. Inevitable. Below, the workers returned to their tasks. Children laughed somewhere near the well. Mara stepped from the healing tent with Lila beside her, their arms full of folded cloths. The hold kept breathing. Kept living. Kept preparing for whatever came next. Loran gripped the railing, the cold wood steady under his hand. “How much time do we have?” Ryn didn’t look at him when he answered. “Not enough.”

CHAPTER FORTY
The First Sign of Change

Ashwood Hold had grown used to the small dangers. A twisted creature near the river. A corrupted owl watching from a tree. A tremor that rattled cups but harmed nothing. People learned to keep working through these things—hammering wood, stirring pots, tending to wounds—because stopping would mean acknowledging how close the darkness truly was. But on the twenty-fourth morning, something different arrived. Something quiet.

Loran was helping mend a section of fencing near the livestock pen when the air shifted around him—subtle at first, as if the breeze had changed direction. The hairs on his arms rose. His mark tingled faintly under the bandage. He paused, frowning at the sky. It wasn't darker. It wasn't storming. But something was... off. Before he could place it, a shout came from the western watchtower. "Movement! On the tree line!" Workers froze. Soldiers scrambled to the walls. Vale sprinted across the courtyard, barking orders as he went. Loran climbed the nearest ladder two rungs at a time until he reached the top of the barricade, Braum right behind him.

"What do you see?" Loran called. The scout lowered his spyglass. "Not an attack. People." Loran exhaled—but only for a second. The scout wasn't relieved. He looked unnerved. "People?" Braum repeated. "Refugees?" "No," the scout said softly. "They're... walking strange." Loran grabbed the spyglass and pressed it to his eye. Three figures were approaching from the woods. Slow. Unsteady. Heads down. Their clothes appeared normal—travelers' cloaks, worn boots. But something in the way they moved made Loran's stomach tighten. Their steps were deliberate and yet wrong, like they were listening to a rhythm no one else could hear.

"Are they injured?" Braum asked. "No," Loran whispered. "They're not injured." Down below, Ryn emerged from between the tents, gaze fixed on the trees. He didn't run. He didn't call out. He simply stood still, staff planted in the soil, as though waiting for confirmation of something he already feared. Vale joined them on the wall. "Hold your positions," he ordered. "No arrows unless I call it." "Should we open the gate?" a soldier asked. "No," Vale said sharply. "Not until we know what we're dealing with."

The three figures continued their slow approach until they stood no more than one hundred paces from the hold—close enough to see their faces. Only one had a face. The woman in the front looked human, though her expression was hollow, like she had forgotten how to move her eyes. But the two behind her... Their skin was too pale. Their limbs too thin. Their heads cocked at identical angles, like puppets listening for a command. Mara climbed the ladder beside Loran, breathing unevenly. "Are those travelers?" "I don't think so," he murmured.

The woman stopped just outside bow range. Her lips parted. The voice that came out wasn't hers. It wasn't human. "Let us in." Every person on the wall stiffened. Vale swallowed. "Who are you?" The woman's eyes flicked upward, glassy and unfocused. "We carry a message." Ryn's voice rang out from the ground below—calm, steady, final. "Do not answer it." Loran felt a chill creep down his spine. "Ryn—what are they?" "Tethers," Ryn replied. "Fragments." "Fragments of what?" Braum asked. "Of the corruption's will," Ryn said. "It's extending its reach... testing how far it can send influence without a host." Mara grabbed the railing as though steadying herself. The woman's head twitched. "Let us in," she repeated. "He has questions." "He?" Vale echoed. The woman raised one shaky arm and pointed directly at Loran. The other two mirrored the gesture perfectly. Loran's blood ran cold.

Ryn stepped forward, staff raised. “You cannot enter this place,” he said. “Return to the rot that made you.” The woman smiled. It was wrong. Too sharp. Too slow. “We are already here.” Her neck snapped backward—and the corrupted essence inside her detonated in a burst of sick black vapor. “DOWN!” Vale roared. The blast wasn’t fire. It wasn’t sound. It was a shockwave of corrupted air, rolling across the ground like a pulse. Everyone on the wall ducked, some falling to their knees. Arlyn screamed for people to cover their mouths. Loran shielded Mara with his body as the wave swept under the barricade, rattling loose boards and quenching torch flames in a single breath.

When the vapor cleared, the three bodies were gone—reduced to nothing but ash. Silence fell. Not fear. Silence. Recognition. Whatever this was... it was new. Vastly more intelligent. More deliberate. Ryn exhaled once through his nose. “It has begun.” Vale gripped the railing. “What has begun?” Ryn looked up at the sky—at the faint green shimmer pulsing beyond the clouds. “The corruption is reaching,” he said. “Because the guardian is failing.”

Loran felt his mark throb, a deep pulse echoing in his bones. Mara staggered at the same moment, clutching her chest. Loran caught her before she fell. “Mara? What’s wrong?” She shook her head sharply. “It’s nothing. A dizzy spell.” But her eyes were wide—too wide—and Loran recognized the expression. She wasn’t dizzy. She had heard something. Ryn approached them, his gaze sharp, suspicious, calculating. “You felt that, didn’t you?” Mara withdrew her hand instantly. “I said I’m fine.” Ryn didn’t believe her. Loran could see it. But he didn’t argue. Not yet.

Vale barked orders to strengthen the walls, double the scouts, prepare masks for corrupted air. Workers scrambled, soldiers hurried to posts, and Ashwood Hold burst into motion again. But something essential had changed. No one said it aloud, but every person in the hold felt the shift. This was the first time the corruption had reached for them directly. And it would not be the last.

CHAPTER FORTY-ONE
Days of Uneasy Preparation

Three days passed. They were not quiet days. They were not peaceful days. They were *waiting* days—days where the entire hold felt stretched thin, like a bowstring pulled back and held there, trembling but not yet released. Ashwood Hold changed quickly in those three days. People built faster. Trained harder. Slept less. Every hour, new settlers arrived from hidden trails and ruined homesteads, bringing stories of shadows moving through forests, of villages emptied overnight, of beasts that watched from treetops with patient, human-like eyes. None of the stories included death. That was worse. Death was simple. *Watching,* though—watching meant the corruption was learning.

Loran spent most of the days working the walls with Braum and Vale's men. The barrier grew taller and stronger, reinforced with beams dragged from half-rotted barns and scavenged trees. Loran swung an axe until his shoulders burned, feeling the dull throb of his sigil with every heartbeat. He tried to ignore it. He failed. By mid-morning on the second day, he had noticed something strange: the mark reacted not to danger, but to *distance.* It flickered, faintly, when he faced northwest—toward the mountains where the tremors had first echoed. Toward the dying guardian. Toward Teren. He didn't mention this to Ryn. He didn't want to see the expression that revelation would bring.

Mara tried to keep busy, too. She helped Lila and Arlyn in the infirmary, stitching wounds, organizing herbs, cleaning instruments. Her hands moved steadily, but her breath never seemed to fully settle. Arlyn noticed first. "You're pale again," she said quietly as they cleaned a bandage basin. “I’m tired,” Mara replied. “Are you sleeping at all?” “Some.” A lie. The kind of lie people tell to keep others from worrying. Lila wasn’t convinced either. She hovered nearby, fidgeting with a jar of salve. “You keep rubbing your chest. Are you sure nothing’s wrong?” Mara forced a small smile. “I’m sure.” She wasn’t. At night she dreamed of vines crawling up her ribs. Of a voice whispering her name—not Teren’s voice, but close enough that waking hurt worse than sleeping. She never told Loran. She didn’t want him to look at her like he had in the fortress—afraid he might lose her.

Ryn was the only one who didn’t pretend things were normal. He spent every sunrise standing on the frost-covered ground, one palm pressed against the soil, head bowed. Sometimes he murmured in a language no one understood. Sometimes he simply listened. People avoided him when he did this. He looked less like a wanderer during those moments and more like something ancient turned man—rooted, unmoving, frighteningly aware of things no human could sense. At dusk each day, he trained the settlers. Not in swords. Not in archery. In *awareness*. “Listen,” he’d tell them, pacing the training yard. “Don’t rely on your eyes. The corruption doesn’t always approach in forms you recognize.” Some laughed nervously. Ryn didn’t. “Laugh,” he said flatly, “and you won’t live long.” That ended the laughter. Braum, for once, listened without arguing. Even Vale admitted quietly to Loran one evening, “I’ve never met a man who sees danger coming before the birds do.”

By the fourth sunset, a rhythm had formed in Ashwood Hold. Build. Train. Watch. Worry. Sleep. Repeat. But nothing broke the tension. Nothing explained the tremors. Nothing explained the dead scouts. Nothing explained the green shimmer that continued to pulse faintly beyond the clouds—stronger each day. Then, just as the hold was preparing for another cold dinner, something unexpected happened. A single horn blast cut across the valley. One note. Warning. Not of danger approaching... ...but of someone returning. Loran dropped the wood he was carrying and ran toward the gate. Vale shouted for the guards to hold their posts as he sprinted across the courtyard. Ryn appeared from the shadows at the edge of the yard, eyes sharp, posture tense. The gate creaked open. A scout stumbled inside—one of the southern riders, mud-splattered, shaking, breathing so hard he could barely stand. Vale grabbed him before he fell. "What happened?" The scout tried to speak. Failed. Tried again. "It's started," he choked out. "The earth... the mountains... something is—" He swallowed hard, staring at Ryn with wild, terrified eyes. "—the green one is dying." Silence struck like a hammer. Loran felt every breath leave his chest at once. Mara grabbed the railing beside her. Ryn went completely still. Completely. Still. He looked at no one. Then— Slowly, painfully— He exhaled. "The seal is breaking," he whispered. Another tremor rolled through the ground beneath them. Soft. But insistent. Like a heartbeat struggling to continue. And every person in Ashwood Hold knew: Their borrowed time had just run out.

CHAPTER FORTY-TWO
The Day the Mountains Groaned

The tremor didn't pass. It *grew*. A low rumble rolled beneath Ashwood Hold like thunder dragging its claws through the earth. Tools rattled on workbenches. Water sloshed in buckets. Horses pulled violently at their reins, eyes rolling white. People froze where they stood—builders, soldiers, healers, children. The ground shivered again. Longer this time. Vale steadied the scout with one arm, his other gripping the hilt of his sword with white-knuckled tension. "Ryn—what does it mean? What's happening?" Ryn didn't answer at first. He turned toward the northwest—toward the mountains glowing faintly green beneath the rotting sky. His expression was unreadable, carved deep with something no one had ever seen on him before: Fear. Not panic. Not shock. A grief-soaked, ancient fear.

Loran stepped forward, pulse hammering. "Ryn? Talk to us." Ryn closed his eyes. Another tremor rolled through the valley. Stronger. He opened his mouth—and the words came out brittle, like something breaking inside him. "The green guardian is failing." Murmurs rippled through the hold. Vale stiffened. Arlyn set down the baskets she carried, her hands shaking. Braum muttered something that might have been a prayer. Lila covered her ears as if blocking out the sound might block out the truth. Mara... Mara didn't move at all. Her breath hitched in her throat. As if she recognized the tremor. As if it echoed inside her. Ryn stepped forward onto the packed dirt of the courtyard. He lifted his staff slowly, pressing the tip into the ground. The earth reacted instantly—vibrating underfoot. "Ryn—" Loran began. He raised a hand, silencing him. "I need to listen." He knelt. Every person in Ashwood Hold held their breath. The tremor deepened, spreading outward in widening, invisible rings. Dirt vibrated like the hide of a waking beast. Nearby barrels toppled. Timber walls groaned. Ryn bowed his head. His voice dropped to barely a whisper. "Oh no." Vale stiffened. "Ryn—what did you—" "He's not failing." Ryn lifted his face. And something in his eyes had shattered. "He's *dying*."

A booming crack tore through the sky. Not lightning. Not wind. Something older. Something vast. Something collapsing under its own weight. People stumbled. Some dropped to their knees. The nearest watchtower shed a shower of dust and splinters. Vale barked, "Brace the structures! Secure the barricade! Move!" Soldiers sprinted. Builders threw themselves against swaying beams. Arlyn dragged frightened settlers back from the walls. But Loran didn't move. He stared at the mountains. The pulse inside his arm answered the tremor—stronger than ever. Faster than ever. Burning without flame. He clutched his forearm as pain knifed through him. "Loran!" Mara moved toward him. "Are you—" He doubled over. The ground shuddered again, this time in sharp, jagged jolts—like something massive had stumbled and then tried to rise again. Ryn shoved through the crowd, grabbing Loran by the shoulders. "Look at me." Loran forced his eyes upward. "What's happening to me?" Ryn didn't lie. "You are tied to the guardians. All bearers are. When one weakens, you feel it." His jaw clenched. "When one dies... you will feel that too." The courtyard erupted into frantic shouts. But all Loran heard was: *dies*. One of the seals—one of the things holding back the corruption—was dying. And somewhere, impossibly far away yet horrifically close, the world was preparing to shift beneath their feet.

A final tremor struck—hard enough that people screamed as they fell. Logs rolled. Shields clattered. The gates groaned under their own weight. And then— A long, hollow, echoing *moan* washed over the valley. It wasn't human. It wasn't creature. It wasn't corruption. It was too large, too deep, too ancient. A death-sound. The mountains themselves seemed to grieve. Ryn pressed a hand over his heart, his face twisting—not with pain, not exactly, but with devastation. "He's slipping," he whispered. "I feel his breath slowing. His pulse thinning. I... I can still hear him." Loran's stomach dropped. "You knew him." Ryn nodded silently. He didn't look five hundred years old anymore. He looked *tired.* Very, very tired. Mara stumbled backward, gripping a support beam, her chest rising too fast. Her pupils widened unnaturally. "I can hear something too," she whispered. "Something pulling. Calling." Ryn's head snapped toward her. "What do you hear?" She shook her head, trembling. "I don't know. I don't know. It feels like—I shouldn't listen." Loran rushed to her side. "Mara—stay with me." Her hands flew to her temples. "It's loud," she gasped. "It's—gods—it's getting louder—" Ryn swore under his breath. "It's the guardian's unraveling. The corruption is awakening. It is reaching for anything receptive. Anything cracked." Mara's breath hitched. Loran held her. Held her tighter when she shook. "Stay with me," he whispered.

The tremors slowed. Then stopped. Ashwood Hold fell into a stillness so heavy it felt like a blanket pressed over every mouth. Ryn stood. His staff crackled faintly with blue light. "Everyone to the center of the hold," he commanded, voice steel. "Now." Vale didn't question him. No one did. Fear moved them. Ryn turned once more toward the mountains. "They will feel this," he murmured. "Every corrupted thing in the world. Every beast. Every shadow. Every remnant. A guardian's death is... the greatest feast they have known in centuries." Loran swallowed hard. "Ryn... how much time do we have?" Ryn didn't turn. Not at first. When he did, the blue in his eyes was dim—like a lantern guttering in a storm. "days," he said quietly. "If we are fortunate." Mara inhaled sharply, as if someone had punched the breath out of her. "The corruption will surge," Ryn continued. "It will gather. It will hunt. And the vessel—" He cut himself off. Loran's blood went cold.

"What about the vessel?" Ryn hesitated. Too long. Mara whispered, "Ryn..." He didn't answer. He didn't need to. The truth was already settling into the air like ash: A giant was dying. A seal was breaking. Something vast and hungry was about to wake fully. And the corruption... ...it was looking for someone.

CHAPTER FORTY-THREE
The Sky Splits

Ashwood Hold erupted into motion, not with panic but with the brittle, desperate urgency of people who realized dawn had brought them a problem no wall could stop. The tremors faded, but the aftershocks clung to the camp like static, making every heartbeat feel slightly off-rhythm. Vale barked orders to the nearest watch units, sending runners along the palisade while soldiers scrambled into formation. Tools clattered, shields lifted, bows tightened—Ashwood seemed to find its pulse only after almost losing it.

Loran helped a pair of workers roll a barrel back upright, though every movement made his arm twinge. The sigil wasn't burning anymore. It was worse. It felt cold. Hollow. As if waiting for something. Watching for something. Mara was only a few feet away, but she seemed farther than she'd ever been. She stood near one of the support beams, hands braced against the wood, breathing with a slow, unnatural steadiness that made Loran's stomach twist. "Mara," he said quietly.

She didn't turn at first. When she finally lifted her head, her eyes were her own—mostly. A faint reflection shimmered deeper in them, a color that didn't belong. Not black. Not yet. Something between shadow and light, like her pupils were catching echoes of the tremor. "It's stopped," she whispered. "The shaking. It just... stopped." "That isn't good," Ryn said, stepping toward them. His voice was calm but clipped, stripped of the steadiness he usually wore. He looked toward the mountains the way a man looks toward an approaching storm knowing there's little time. "When a guardian stumbles, the world holds its breath. That moment is now. The next moment will not be quiet."

Vale approached, sweat shining on his brow. "We felt the last shock all through the walls. Some of the beams shifted. We're reinforcing the northern side now. I need to know—how long until whatever comes next?" Ryn shook his head. "There is no time to measure. The corruption will feel the break as surely as we did. It will move toward it first. Then it will spread." Loran watched as Ryn's fingers tightened around his staff—a rare reveal of fear he tried to hide. "You said the seal is cracking," Loran said. "What does that mean for us?" Ryn hesitated. Just long enough that they all felt the answer before hearing it. "It means the corruption is no longer caged to the same degree. It will gather, grow, and seek out anything tied to the old power."

His gaze flicked toward Loran. Then, reluctantly, toward Mara. She looked away so quickly it was almost a flinch. Vale scrubbed a hand down his face. "So the worst of it hasn't even begun..." "No," Ryn said softly. "It has begun now." Workers rushed past carrying timber, ropes, buckets of water. The sound of hammers rang across the hold. Horses were led deeper toward the inner pens. Children were ushered toward the shelters. Lila helped a group of settlers stack crates into makeshift barricades, her movements quick but uneven. She kept glancing at the mountains as if expecting them to open.

Braum dragged a cart of stone toward the wall, his leg still a little stiff but his determination overriding the pain. "If something big is coming," he grumbled, "I'd rather have a wall fall on me than sit waiting for it with my thumb up my nose." "That can be arranged," Arlyn muttered, though her focus stayed sharp on the people she tended. She moved through the crowd setting splints, adjusting bindings, grabbing whoever looked seconds away from collapsing. She didn't let herself stop long enough to feel fear. Loran wished he could do the same. Ryn approached him quietly. "Your arm—does it still react?" Loran flexed it carefully. "It feels...

empty." Ryn nodded, though the answer didn't seem to comfort him. "It will not stay empty." "Is that supposed to reassure me?" Loran asked dryly. "No." Ryn almost smiled. Almost. "But it is the truth."

Mara shifted beside them, arms wrapped tight around herself. She wasn't cold—but she looked like she was holding onto her own ribs to stop something from slipping out. "I can still feel the pull from last night," she whispered. "Not as loud... but closer." Ryn's head snapped toward her. "Closer how?" She shut her eyes, trying to put it into words. "It's like standing near a river. The current hasn't reached you yet, but you hear it. You know it's moving your way." Loran stepped toward her instinctively. "Mara—" She held up a hand. "I'm not losing myself." Her voice cracked at the end of the sentence. She grimaced, hating that they heard it. "Not yet," she added softly. Loran's stomach clenched.

Vale returned, this time with three soldiers in tow. "We've doubled the archers on the walls and reinforced the ridge-facing barricade. If anything comes over that rise, we'll see it." "Seeing it won't be the problem," Ryn said. "Stopping it will." Vale's jaw tightened. "We're doing what we can." "That's all anyone can do," Ryn replied. It should have sounded reassuring. It didn't. The sky darkened slightly, not from weather but from a heaviness in the air—like the world was gathering breath for something it didn't want to speak aloud. A metallic tang swept through the wind. Mara stiffened. "Did you feel that?" she whispered. Loran did. It wasn't a tremor. It wasn't corruption. It wasn't anything physical at all. It was... attention. As if the world had turned its face toward them.

A sound drifted faintly over the northern ridge. Not loud. Not sharp. Just a long, low exhale of wind that wasn't wind. Ryn lifted his staff, eyes narrowing. "That," he murmured, "is the first ripple." "Of what?" Vale asked. Ryn didn't look away from the ridge. "The storm that follows a death." Mara swayed, catching herself on Loran's arm. Her breath stuttered, a thin gasp escaping her lips. Loran steadied her quickly. "Mara—are you with me?" She nodded—too fast, too unsure. “Yes. I just... felt something pass through me. Like a shadow brushing my thoughts.” Ryn stepped close. “Did it say anything?” “No,” she whispered. “Not a word. Just... recognition.” Braum blinked. “Recognition? From what?” Ryn exhaled slowly. “From the corruption. The seal broke. It is looking for what comes next.” Mara paled. Loran’s grip on her tightened. Vale swallowed hard, the sound audible even above the hammering on the walls. “Is the hold in danger?” Ryn looked at the sky. “The hold,” he said carefully, “is a stone in a river that is about to rise.” “Meaning?” “Meaning it will hold for a time,” Ryn replied. “But the water will not stop.”

Loran looked between Ryn, the mountains, and Mara, feeling the weight of a dozen unspoken truths pressing in on all sides. This wasn’t the battle. This wasn’t even the beginning of it. This was only the moment before the tide turned. The moment the world drew its breath. And as the wind shifted again, colder than before, carrying a tremble that did not come from the earth but from something far deeper, Loran finally understood: The death of the guardian had not ended anything. It had started something new. Something worse. Something that was already moving in their direction.

CHAPTER FORTY-FOUR
The River That Rises

The rest of the morning passed in a tense, unsteady rhythm—work, watch, glance at the mountains, work again. Ashwood Hold felt alive in a way that wasn't comforting. Every wall seemed to listen. Every beam seemed to lean, waiting for what would come next. Men hauled timber, women carried arrows to the watch posts, children were ushered deeper toward the inner shelters. Even the livestock sensed the change; the goats wouldn't leave their pens and the horses kept turning their ears north, stamping at the ground with restless hooves.

Loran joined a line helping reinforce the gate's outer braces. He wedged a beam into place while Vale hammered, each strike ringing sharper than the last. Sweat beaded down the captain's brow despite the cold. "The ridge hasn't moved since the last tremor," Vale said between swings. "Almost makes you wish it would—just to know what the hell we're dealing with." Loran didn't answer; he was trying not to think about the tremor, about the way his mark had gone cold. It felt like the silence after a scream. "You should drink," Vale added, lifting his chin toward the water barrels. "You look like you're about to fall over." Loran forced a shallow breath. "I'm fine." Vale didn't argue—didn't believe it either—but he moved to the next brace without pushing the point.

Across the hold, Braum was sparring with a pair of soldiers, taking it slow so his healing leg didn't split open again. They circled him cautiously, tapping at his defenses while he barked at them to stop "fighting like frightened squirrels." Every now and then, he paused mid-instruction to rub at the scar along his calf—a reminder of the beast's talon—but he didn't sit down.

Lila and Arlyn worked near the storerooms, sorting herbs, stitching bandages, arranging salves into crates for quick access. Arlyn's shoulders looked tighter than usual, her motions clipped, but she forced herself through the motions. Lila kept glancing at Mara. So did Arlyn. Mara had taken to pacing along the inner walkway just under the wall, slow and deliberate, as if listening to something no one else could hear. Her boots made no sound on the planks. At times she stopped, staring at the mountains with an expression Loran couldn't decipher—fear, longing, sorrow, all wound too tightly together.

Ryn walked the perimeter with Vale's scouts, but "walked" wasn't quite right. He drifted. Always a step apart. Always listening more to the earth than to anyone speaking beside him. When he passed Loran, he paused long enough to rest the end of his staff against the ground. A faint vibration pulsed through the soil. Loran felt it, subtle but unmistakable. "It's moving," Ryn murmured. "Still distant. But moving." Loran swallowed. "The corruption?" "Everything tied to it," Ryn replied. "Beasts. Remnants. Creatures that have learned to mimic human shapes. It all shifts when the seals weaken." "And the giant—" "The giant is fading," Ryn said, quiet enough that no one else heard. "His absence leaves a void. The corruption rushes to fill voids."

Loran's fingers curled unconsciously against his arm. "And us?" Ryn did not answer immediately. "You will feel the pull," he said eventually. "But not as she will." His eyes flicked toward Mara. Loran tensed. Ryn lowered his voice further. "Watch her." "I already do." "No," Ryn said softly. "Watch her."

The day edged toward noon. Cold wind swept through the hold, rattling the arrow barrels and sending cloth banners snapping against their poles. Workers took brief moments to rest near the fire pits. Soup simmered in a pair of iron pots, filling the air with a faint scent of herbs and something earthy. It should have been comforting. It wasn't. Loran drank a cup to steady his nerves, but it slid down like warm stone. He found Mara again near the inner wall, this time sitting with her back against the planks, her knees drawn up. Her cloak draped loosely around her like she hadn't noticed the cold.

"Mind if I sit?" Loran asked. She shrugged a shoulder. It wasn't a no. He lowered himself beside her. For a long time, neither spoke. The hold buzzed around them with low talk, hammering, distant commands—noise that felt too normal for what the world had become. Mara finally exhaled, her breath fogging in the chill. "It feels wrong," she whispered. "Everything is too... still." Loran nodded. "Everyone feels it." "No," she murmured. "Not like this." Her fingers twisted into the edge of her cloak. "It's like a thread pulling at me. Not hard. Not demanding. Just... constant. Like something wants me to remember it." Loran clenched his jaw. "That's not you. That's what's trying to use you." Mara turned to him then, her eyes glistening—not the wrong light from earlier, just human grief. "What if part of me wants to listen?"

The admission hit him harder than any tremor. He reached for her hand, gripping it tightly. "Then I'll pull you the other way." She let out a shaky breath that was almost a laugh. "You can't fight everything for me." "Then I'll fight the parts I can," he said. Ryn's voice cut across the hold before she could answer. "Everyone to the central square!" His tone wasn't panicked, but urgent—enough that people dropped tools and moved quickly toward the heart of the camp. Vale strode toward him. "What now?" Ryn pointed toward the northern ridge. "The corruption has stopped moving." Vale frowned. "Stopped? Why would that—" A gust of wind swept across the hold, colder than the air had been all morning. It carried a faint, metallic scent—sharp as wet iron. People shivered involuntarily.

Ryn's gaze hardened. "It is gathering." Loran felt Mara's hand tighten around his. "Gathering for what?" Vale demanded. Ryn turned to him. "For something the corruption has waited centuries for." He looked toward the sky, which seemed to dim even without clouds. "A world without the green seal." The hold fell into a hush. Not fear. Not yet. Not the kind that makes people scream. The quiet before fear. The quiet of people who realize the ground beneath their lives has shifted forever. Loran looked at Mara. Mara looked at the ridge. Somewhere in the far distance, the wind seemed to breathe inward—slow and deep, the inhale before a wave crashes. Ryn closed his eyes for a moment, listening with more than his ears. When he opened them again, the blue was bright. Controlled. Focused. "This is the last calm we will have," he said. "Use it well."

CHAPTER FORTY-FIVE
The Quiet Work

The warning settled over Ashwood Hold like a blanket pulled too tightly across a restless sleeper. The people didn't panic—not openly—but the shift in the air changed everything. Voices dropped. Footsteps quickened. Every task became sharper with purpose, even the smallest ones. If Ryn said this was the last calm they would have, then they intended to use every breath of it.

Vale set the first tone, calling the captains together at the center of the hold. Men and women gathered around him, maps unfurled across crates, charcoal marks smudged from frantic adjustments. Loran watched as Vale circled routes, counter-routes, fallback positions, but none of it gave him confidence. It felt like trying to plan a fishing trip while a storm built on the horizon. Still—they tried. Ryn drifted among the captains for a time, offering observations in his clipped, almost distant way. "Don't put archers near the inner wall—corruption moves low first." "Spread your torches; too many in one place only invites shadows." "If something crawls, burn it. If something walks, spear it. If something speaks, run." He said the last part without humor, and no one questioned it.

Loran took to reinforcing the barricades again, this time with more hands. The work steadied him. The repetitive hammering, the heavy feel of the beams, the cooperation of people who didn't know him but nodded when he passed—all of it gave him something solid to hold onto while his insides felt hollow. His arm pulsed occasionally—not painful, just present. A reminder. A pulse he couldn't understand, like his body waited for instructions from something he wasn't ready to hear.

Across the hold, Braum tested shields for cracks, slamming his hammer down and making the nearest workers jump every time. "Better now than later," he grunted. His leg still stiffened when he stepped wrong, but he pushed through it with gritted teeth and stubborn pride. Arlyn directed a pair of young helpers, showing them how to organize bandages by need, powders by purpose, poultices by urgency. She rarely stopped moving. Lila helped her, sorting herbs and leaning close to whoever needed comfort. Her gentleness wasn't soft—it was grounding. Something the hold desperately needed.

Mara wandered at first. Not aimlessly, but as though she was walking through a place she'd already been in another life. People gave her space—they always did—but they watched her too, just a little longer than normal. Something about her drew attention now. Not fear. Not distrust. Just an awareness no one could explain. Loran crossed the hold to her eventually, wiping sawdust from his hands. "You should rest," he said gently. "Everyone else is busy. You're... pacing." "I'm not pacing." She paused, realizing she was. Her shoulders sagged. "I can't sit still. Every time I stop moving, I feel... something brushing against my thoughts." "Whispers?" he asked. "Not words," she said. "A feeling. Like the ground under my feet wants me to step somewhere else."

Loran's chest tightened. "Tell Ryn." "Not yet," she said quickly. "If he thinks I'm slipping, he'll decide things for me." Loran hesitated. "He's trying to stop the worst from happening." "I know," she whispered. "But I want to be part of the choice. Not the problem he solves." She turned her gaze toward the northern ridge. The faint glow clinging to the mountains still hadn't faded after the tremors. It wasn't light—it was strain. The land looked tense. Waiting. She hugged her cloak tighter around her. "How long do you think we have?" Loran swallowed. "He said hours maybe days." Mara nodded slowly. "Feels right."

Ryn approached then, boots crunching softly over the frost-dusted dirt. His steps were measured, but Loran could tell the careful calm was a held breath. "You two," he said. "Walk with me." They followed him toward the far corner of the hold where the walls met a cluster of stacked stones. Fewer people passed through here. Ryn stopped, planting his staff lightly against the ground. "The corruption is gathering along the ridge," he said. "It hasn't moved closer–not yet. But it's pooling. Concentrating."

"Why?" Loran asked. Ryn's eyes flicked toward Mara. Not accusingly. Not sharply. But knowingly. "Because it has lost one of its chains," he said. "And when something loses one chain, it seeks another." Mara looked down at her hands. They shook faintly. "I'm not its chain," she whispered. "No," Ryn said. "You're its doorway. Possibly to be used against us." Loran stepped forward. "She hasn't done anything wrong." "I did not say she had," Ryn replied. "But the corruption will not care about guilt or innocence. It only cares about hunger. And it will follow the scent of weakness or grief or longing wherever it finds it." "I'm not longing for it," Mara snapped, more sharply than she intended.

Ryn's expression softened–barely. "Not longing for it," he said. "Longing for him." Mara flinched. Loran's throat tightened. Ryn continued. "If you feel something calling, you tell me. Immediately. No hesitating. No shielding." Mara's jaw clenched. "And if I do? What then?" Ryn looked at her with an honesty that had no comfort in it. "Then we keep you close. Because distance will not save you. Only vigilance will." Loran exhaled shakily. "And if vigilance fails?" Ryn looked out toward the mountains. The wind lifted his cloak. "Then I will do what I must."

The silence that followed was sharp. Mara's eyes glistened, but she blinked the wetness away. Loran stepped closer to her, not touching her, but standing where she could lean if she needed to. Ryn noticed–but said nothing. He turned back toward the camp. "The rest of the day will be quiet," he said. "Too quiet. People will mistake it for safety. Do not let them." He started walking again. "Nightfall is when the world will shift."

That line drifted over the hold like a shadow. But for the next hours, people continued their work—building, mending, organizing, whispering. Children fetched wood under the watch of anxious parents. Archers ran drills along the wall. The world kept moving, pretending it wasn't waiting for something that would change everything. Loran helped hoist another beam into place. Mara helped Arlyn prepare supplies. Braum cursed at a cracked shield. Ryn stood sentinel at the northern ridge until the light began to dim. And somewhere far beyond the mountains, beneath the soil of a dying world, the corruption coiled tighter around its new hunger. Night was coming.

CHAPTER FORTY-SIX
Night Beneath a Restless Sky

Night fell over Ashwood Hold without ceremony. No sunset, no golden fade—just a slow smothering as the clouds thickened until the world simply dimmed into gray. Torches along the barricades sputtered against a faint breeze, struggling for every inch of light. Workers retreated to their tents, soldiers rotated to their posts, and the sounds of the hold shifted from labor to vigilance. Loran stood along the northern barricade, watching the tree line dissolve into darkness. Every part of him felt heavy. Not tired—just weighted. The ground hummed faintly beneath his boots, the same distant, sickly rhythm he'd felt in his bones for days now.

The tremors had stopped, but the absence of shaking felt wrong in its own way. Like the silence before a scream. Mara approached quietly, her boots crunching lightly over the frost. She carried two cups, handing one to him. "It's warm," she said. "Not good, but warm." He took it and sipped. It tasted like burnt herbs and melted snow, but it eased the chill in his fingers. "Thanks." She leaned her elbows against the wooden beam, staring out into the dark. Her breath misted the air, drifting upward before vanishing. "It's too quiet." "Maybe that's good," Loran said. "Maybe whatever's gathering is far off." Her jaw tightened. "No. This quiet... it isn't distance." She rubbed her arms as though fighting a cold that wasn't in the air. "It feels like we're being watched."

Loran swallowed. "Ryn said they'd test us tonight. Scouts. Shadows." Mara stared down at her cup. "I don't mean the corruption." She hesitated. "I mean something else. Something that knows me." His grip tightened on the wooden beam. "Mara—" "Don't tell Ryn," she said quietly. "Not yet." "He should know," Loran argued, voice low. "He'll take my rights—my choices away if I let him. I can feel it." She looked at him, eyes tired but fiercely alive. "I want to stand on my feet until I can't anymore. Not be treated like a tinderbox waiting to ignite." Loran didn't respond. Because part of him feared she was right.

Down below, Braum's laughter burst loudly as he lifted a shield over his head for a pair of nervous young guards to inspect. "No, no, hold it like this unless you want the corruption to knock that pretty head clean off your shoulders! — No offense, your head's not that pretty." Arlyn thwacked him on the back of the head with a rolled bandage, eliciting half the hold to chuckle. The moment of levity rippled through the camp, easing shoulders, loosening rigid postures. But even laughter felt thin tonight.

Ryn appeared along the wall as silently as smoke. His cloak billowed lightly with the rising wind. "Stay sharp," he murmured. "The forest is shifting." Loran peered out into the dark. "I don't see anything." "You won't," Ryn said. "Not yet." His eyes glowed faintly blue, reflecting torchlight like a predator's. "They're listening to the hold breathe." "Can corruption... listen?" Mara asked. "Yes," Ryn said simply. Before they could ask more, a low creaking groan drifted across the valley. Not the ground—not tremors this time—but wood. Trees straining, bending without wind. Every soldier on the wall straightened. "Positions," Vale barked, voice cutting through the camp. Archers scrambled, spears lowered, shields raised. Mara's breath hitched. "It's starting."

Loran moved closer, readying his sword. His arm throbbed—not glowing, but pulsing, reacting to something invisible. "Where will they come from?" "Everywhere," Ryn said quietly. "But tonight... they won't commit. They will only test. The corruption wants to learn us." A branch snapped in the dark. Then another. Then silence. Lila hurried up the ladder to the wall, her hands full of flasks. "Arlyn said to bring these. They're for wounds that—" She froze midway as a shape flickered between two trees. Not fully formed. Not solid. Like a smear of shadow dragged across the bark. “What was that?” she whispered. Vale’s jaw clenched. “Scouts.” A second shape appeared near the ground. Then another, higher in a tree. Slithering. Testing.

Ryn’s staff hummed softly with a faint blue undertone. “They are studying us. Counting us. Smelling for cracks.” “What do we do?” Loran asked. “We show nothing,” Ryn said. “We stand. We wait.” More shapes formed—their movements not animal, not human, but something meant to mimic both. Shadows that crawled in directions bodies shouldn’t bend. A faint clicking began—a chorus of tapping sounds like fingernails drumming on stone. Fast. Slow. Testing. Mara’s eyes unfocused for a moment. “They’re looking for something,” she whispered. “Someone...” Ryn’s head snapped toward her. “Do not listen.” “I’m not,” she said. But she already looked as though something tugged at her attention from far away.

A scout lunged from the tree line suddenly, darting toward the wall with unnatural speed. Arrows flew. One hit it—barely slowing it. Another hit. Then a third. It shrieked, veering away, melting into the dark like smoke dissolving. No cheer followed. Only deeper silence. “They’re not attacking,” Vale murmured. “They’re... learning.” Ryn nodded. “Yes. Tonight is only the beginning.” Mara shivered violently. Loran reached for her. “Mara—look at me.” She did, but her eyes were distant. “Loran... something in the dark recognized me.” His heart dropped. “What do you mean?” “I don’t know,” she whispered, shaking her head. “It looked at all of us—but when it found me... it stopped moving.” Her voice cracked softly. “Like it was waiting.” Loran stepped closer, protective instinct rising like heat. Ryn turned to face her fully. “What did it feel like?” he asked, voice careful. Mara closed her eyes. “Like... like someone knocking on a door. Not forcing it. Just... reminding me it exists.” Loran swallowed hard. “We’ll get through this. You and me. All of us." Mara didn't answer. Her heartbeat drummed visibly at her throat.

Below, the shadows retreated slowly back into the forest. The clicking faded. The watchers drifted away. No battle came. No assault. Just the cold truth that the corruption now knew exactly where Ashwood Hold was—and exactly who resided within it. Ryn exhaled, his breath shaking. "This was not a test," he said softly. "This was a promise." Vale barked orders again, calling rotations, organizing the relief watch, anchoring morale. But even he could not hide the fear in his eyes. As camp life recommenced in small, shaky motions, Loran walked Mara back toward their tent. "Are you alright?" he asked. "Ask me tomorrow," she whispered. He didn't press. He didn't need to. Because he felt it too—something was changing inside her, something the corruption had noticed, something pulling her slowly toward a fate none of them could yet see. Night settled fully over Ashwood Hold. And somewhere far beyond the mountains, a giant's heartbeat faltered.

CHAPTER FORTY-SEVEN
The Last Quiet Morning

Ashwood Hold woke slowly, as if unsure the new day was worth rising for. A pale, washed-out light filtered through the clouds, barely enough to lift the shadows from the packed earth. The night's frost still clung to the fences and empty training racks, and the air tasted like iron—dry, sharp, and strangely metallic. Loran stood near the eastern barricade, watching a pair of settlers haul lumber toward the half-finished watchtower. Their breath fogged in front of them, drifting like smoke before the breeze carried it away. No one spoke. Even the sounds of work seemed muted, as though the valley itself demanded quiet. He flexed his hand, rolling his fingers slowly. His arm wasn't throbbing today—it was worse. The pressure beneath the skin felt heavier, deeper, as if something inside the sigil was turning in its sleep. But he didn't want to ask Ryn. He already knew the answer.

Bootsteps crunched behind him. Mara approached, cloak wrapped tight around her, strands of hair escaping her braid. She looked better rested than she had the day before, though not by much. "You're up early," she said softly. "So are you." She shrugged. "Couldn't sleep." "Still hearing things?" Her lips tightened. "Not... things. Just echoes. Or maybe nothing at all. It's hard to tell." Loran nodded. He didn't push. Mara had always been stubborn about her own pain—it wasn't new. Trauma from the fortress, from Teren's haunting voice, from seeing the world tear around her... anyone would be shaking after that. Anyone would wake in the night expecting shadows to whisper.

A distant hammer struck metal. Another followed. Workers began drifting from the tents toward their duties. Mara leaned her shoulder lightly against his. "They're trying, at least." "Yeah." "You don't sound convinced." "Trying doesn't always win." Her brow furrowed. "We're alive. That counts." Loran didn't tell her the truth—that the tremors beneath the earth felt like countdowns now just being a fleeting hum. That the sigil under his skin pulsed like a wounded heartbeat. That Ryn's eyes stayed on the horizon more than anywhere else. Instead he said, "We'll be ready for whatever comes." She gave him a small smile. "Then so will I."

A shout rose from across the hold. A group of young soldiers jogged toward the training yard, each carrying spears. Their movements were clumsy, uncertain, but determined. One stumbled and nearly impaled the ground. Braum barked at him immediately, stomping over with a pronounced limp. "What are you doing? Trying to dig a well with it?" he snapped. "Lift your arms. Gods, lift them. You look like a wet rope." The soldier stiffened, corrected his posture, and tried again. Better.

Arlyn watched from the fence, arms crossed, rubbing sleep out of her eyes. When she spotted Loran and Mara, she waved half-heartedly. Mara's smile widened faintly. "At least he's teaching again." "He's yelling." "That's teaching for him." Loran exhaled, watching Braum bark another correction. It was familiar. Grounding, in a strange way. Almost normal. But normal didn't last long anymore.

Ryn descended the watchtower steps a moment later, cloak trailing like a shadow behind him. His face was unreadable, but Loran could tell—the set of his shoulders, the distant look in his eyes—something in the night had changed. Mara noticed too. She stiffened beside him before she could hide it. Ryn joined them silently. He didn't greet them. He didn't need to. Loran spoke first. "How bad is it today?" Ryn didn't look at him. His gaze stayed fixed on the northwest mountains, still veiled in thin, green-tinged haze. "The guardian is weakening faster," he said. "The tremors will continue to fade. The corruption will swell with them." "Will it come here?" Mara asked. Ryn's jaw tightened just enough to be a warning. "It will come everywhere." She went pale, but she nodded.

Loran stepped slightly closer to her before realizing he had. Ryn continued scanning the horizon. "We shore the northern wall again today. And the western. And if there's time, the south." A short pause. "There won't be time." "Then we do what we can," Loran said. Ryn looked at him then—briefly, the faintest flicker of something like approval. "Good." Vale approached from the main hall, cloak wrapped around his broad shoulders. He nodded to the group. "Ryn tells me we double our patrols today." "Triple them," Ryn corrected. Vale's eyebrows rose. "If we pull that many off building—" "Better a thin wall than an empty one," Ryn said.

Vale didn't argue. He had learned not to. Mara brushed her sleeve, fingers trembling slightly. Loran touched her wrist. "Cold?" She nodded, though he wasn't convinced that was the reason. Before he could say more, a horn sounded from the western line—short, sharp, not an alarm but a signal. Someone had returned from patrol. Vale turned. "Scouts are early. That better mean good news." The group instinctively moved to meet them.

Two scouts crossed the hold, dust on their boots, sweat on their brows. They were breathing hard but uninjured. Vale stepped forward. "Report." The lead scout swallowed. "It's quiet, sir. Too quiet. No beasts. No corruption threads. No movement." "Why is that bad news?" Braum called from across the yard. The scout hesitated. "Because even the birds were gone." A hush followed. Ryn closed his eyes. "The valley is holding its breath," he murmured. Mara's fingers tightened on Loran's forearm. "Why?" she asked. Ryn opened his eyes. "The world always goes quiet," he said softly, "before something breaks."

CHAPTER FORTY-EIGHT
The First Crack in the Day

By midday, Ashwood Hold had begun to sound alive again. Hammers struck beams with steady rhythm. Sawdust drifted from half-finished platforms. Horses were led across the yard, snorting, their hooves kicking up light frost. Soldiers trained in small groups, their shouts echoing against the wooden walls. The scent of cooking grain drifted faintly from the central fire. It all looked normal from a distance. But the closer Loran watched, the more he saw the strain. Hands that trembled when setting nails. Eyes snapping toward the mountains every few breaths. Children playing near the well but glancing upward as though expecting the sky to crack. Fear had become part of the architecture.

Loran spent the morning sharpening a chipped sword beside Braum. Or trying to. His arm pulsed irregularly, faint but insistent, distracting him at every third breath. Braum noticed him pause. "Again?" "Yeah." The older man grunted. "If that thing inside your arm kicks any harder we'll have to strap a shield over it." Loran smirked weakly. "Not sure it'd respect the shield." "Then strap two." That earned a real laugh—short, but real. Across the yard, Arlyn was guiding settlers through basic defense drills. Her voice carried clearly: "No, keep your feet apart—unless you're trying to fall on your face. And stop locking your elbows; you'll break them before you ever stop a corrupted beast."

Lila was helping organize the supply racks, arranging dried herbs and ration bundles with a precision that meant she was trying very hard not to think. Mara walked between the healer's tent and the training yard, checking on everyone, offering small smiles, tying cloth around scraped knuckles. She wasn't the loudest or the strongest in the camp, but people gravitated toward her. Even while carrying her own shadows, she managed to make others' feel lighter.

Vale and Ryn stood near the north wall, inspecting the reinforcements. Loran watched as Vale gestured to the crossbeams while Ryn shook his head—probably explaining why something that looked sturdy wasn't nearly sturdy enough. Loran felt like he should be doing more. He rose, sliding the sharpened blade back into its sheath. "I'm going to check the western line." Braum nodded. "Good. If you find any corrupted, yell. Or don't. Actually—don't. Last thing we need is you provoking something that eats metal for breakfast." Loran snorted and headed west.

The walk across the hold was strangely soothing. Familiar faces nodded at him. The smell of stew simmering somewhere nearby made his stomach growl. For a fleeting moment, he wondered if—somehow—life could return to normal after all of this. Then the earth gave a small, barely noticeable tremor beneath his feet. Just a whisper of movement. He froze. Looked down. Around him, no one reacted. A few workers didn't seem to feel it at all. A child laughed in the distance, chasing a wooden hoop. But Loran felt it. Raw and sharp. Right through the sigil. Like someone had plucked a string inside his bones. He breathed in slowly. Then he kept walking. He didn't tell anyone. Not yet. Ryn had said tremors would fluctuate, and not every twitch of dirt meant disaster. But the truth crawled up the back of his spine anyway: Something in the world had shifted.

The western walls were quiet when Loran reached them. A pair of soldiers kept watch from the elevated walkway, trading whispers about whether their families had made it to safety farther south. The wind here was stronger. It carried the scent of pine, cold earth... and something else. Something faintly sweet, like sap left too long in the sun. Loran frowned. "What's that smell?" he asked the closer soldier. The man blinked. “What smell?” “It’s like... sap. Sweet.” “Not picking it up,” the soldier said. “Might be the wind playing tricks.” Loran wasn’t convinced. The smell didn’t fade. It thickened. He stepped past the barricade, eyes scanning the tree line. Nothing moved. Nothing rustled. The forest stood absolutely still. Too still. “Ryn,” Loran murmured under his breath, even though the wanderer was nowhere near. “You’d hate this.” He moved a little farther out—but not too far. They weren’t supposed to go beyond the outer markers alone. The sweetness in the air was heavier now, almost cloying. He crouched and touched the dirt. Warm. Not hot—but definitely warm. The sun had barely broken through the clouds all day. The ground shouldn’t feel like that. He drew his hand back slowly. Then— A faint crack echoed through the trees. Not branches breaking. Not animals moving. Something deeper. A low, resonant pop. Like pressure shifting beneath the earth. Subtle. Wrong. Loran straightened.

A single bird burst from the trees, flapping wildly before shooting into the sky. Then another. Then another. He stepped backward toward the hold. Something was happening. Not an attack. Not corruption approaching. But a change. A shift. A small, localized sign of an enormous problem. He turned and jogged back toward camp.

Ryn was still with Vale when Loran found them. Both men looked up as he approached, sweat on his brow, chest rising fast. “What is it?” Vale asked. Loran took a breath. “The western ridge. Something’s off. The ground’s warm. Birds fled. And I heard... something cracking.” Ryn’s expression hardened instantly. “Show me.” “No,” Vale said, stepping between them. “If something’s on the ridge, I’m not sending my most marked man AND our only ancient mage walking straight into it.” Ryn didn’t even glance at him. “This isn’t corruption.” Vale blinked. “What is it then?” Ryn looked toward the mountains, eyes narrowing. “A beginning.” Loran’s heart thudded hard. “A beginning of what?” he asked. Ryn didn’t answer immediately. He strained as if listening to something far away—the way a person listens for thunder beyond the hills. Then, quietly: "A crack in the seal." Vale swore under his breath. Loran felt his throat tighten. "The green guardian?" "Not dead yet," Ryn said. "But the world feels the pressure building. The valley is reacting. The earth is warning us." Vale rubbed his face. "So the guardian's dying is starting to affect everything." "It will touch every creature," Ryn said. "Every shadow. Every marked soul." His gaze flicked to Loran's arm. Then—briefly, barely—to Mara across the courtyard. Loran didn't notice. But Mara felt it. She went still, a shiver running down her spine. Ryn's voice carried low and steady. "This was only the first crack. More will come."

CHAPTER FORTY-NINE
When the Walls Were Tested

The crack Loran had heard on the western ridge didn't vanish with the morning. It hung around the hold like an unfinished thought, turning every sound into something suspicious. By early afternoon, Ashwood was busy enough to look almost normal again—axes biting into wood, ropes creaking, armor clinking as men and women moved between the training yard and the walls—but there was a stiffness in every shoulder, a listening quality in every pause.

Loran worked near the northern barricade, helping a pair of laborers haul a beam into place above one of the bracing posts. His arm pulsed in uneven rhythm, no longer syncing with his heartbeat, but with something deeper under the soil. He tried to ignore it. Tried to focus on the weight of the wood, the rasp of rope against his palms. "Higher," Vale called from below, one hand shielding his eyes as he looked up. "If that brace slips in a rush, the whole section comes down with it." "We've got it," Loran answered, teeth clenched as he lifted. The laborer opposite him grunted, sweat dripping from his jaw despite the chill.

Below, Braum barked at two young archers as they adjusted the angle of their bows. "Stop aiming at where the target is and aim where it will be when it moves. Creatures don't stand still and wait to be shot just because you ask politely." The archers tried again. Better. Not good, but better. Ryn stood further down the wall, staff resting against his shoulder as he watched the line of trees beyond the outer ditch. From a distance, he looked still, relaxed even. But Loran had been around him long enough now to recognize the signs: the slight tilt of his head, the way his fingers occasionally tapped once against the wood, as if counting something only he could hear.

Mara and Arlyn sorted bundles of cloth and jars of salve on a table near the central square, arranging them so they could be grabbed in a hurry. Lila flitted between them and the storehouse, arms full of water skins and bandage rolls, checking off items under her breath. Loran and the laborers finally dropped the beam into place with a heavy thunk. The impact rattled Loran's sore arm, sending a sharp spike crawling up toward his shoulder. He hissed under his breath. "You alright?" Vale called. "Fine," Loran replied automatically. Vale didn't buy it, but he didn't argue. Not today. There was too much to do and too little they could change.

The wind shifted. It came cold off the northern ridge, cutting through cloaks and wrapping around bare fingers. Loran suppressed a shiver. He heard Braum mutter something rude about the weather and Gods with poor manners. Then the ground twitched. It wasn't a full tremor—no barrels toppled, no walls groaned—but Loran felt it clearly under his boots. A tiny lurch, like something under the earth had shrugged in its sleep. His arm answered instantly, a dull ache rolling along the sigil. Ryn straightened on the wall. Vale's hand went to the hilt of his sword. "That one felt different," the captain said. "Yes," Ryn replied quietly. "Because it wasn't the valley shifting. It was something large... adjusting to a wound." "You mean the guardian," Loran said. Ryn's jaw flexed. "He is holding on. For now." The reassurance sounded thin even to him.

"Eyes up!" one of the watchmen shouted suddenly. "Movement in the tree line!" Loran hurried to the nearest ladder and climbed onto the wall. Cold air slapped his face as he peered over the sharpened stakes toward the dark line of trees. At first, he saw nothing. Just the same twisted trunks and dead undergrowth that had haunted the ridge for days. Then a shape moved between two trunks. Low. Heavy. Wrong. "Left side," one of the archers said, voice tight. "Near the broken oak." Another shape slipped out from behind a bush. Then another.

Loran squinted. They were on four legs—but the legs bent strangely, too long in the middle, too jointed at the wrong angles. Their bodies were stretched, as if someone had taken wolves and pulled them until their limbs complained. Patches of fur clung to blackened, slick skin. Their heads were the worst—jaws too wide, teeth crooked and many-layered, eyes milky and unfocused, yet somehow turned straight toward the wall. A growl vibrated out of one. The sound came from deep inside its chest, but it broke halfway through like an echo being strangled.

"How many?" Vale asked. "Six," Ryn said. "No—eight. Two in the back. Smaller." "Scouts?" Vale guessed. "Hunters," Ryn said. "Testing the scent of the door." Loran didn't need to look to know who he meant. He glanced anyway. Mara was at the base of the wall, staring up toward the tree line, knuckles white around the edge of a crate she leaned against. Her lips moved like she was trying to remember how to pray and failing.

Vale's voice snapped Loran's attention back. "Archers on the north wall! Nock and hold. I want the first volley on my mark. Spear line, brace at the gate. No one opens it unless I say so." Braum thumped his hammer against his shield. "You heard the man! If anything with more than two legs gets over this wall, we introduce it to less legs. Move!" Men and women scrambled into position. Arrows scraped softly as they were drawn and notched. The hold filled with the sharp, brittle silence that comes when everyone realizes there's no more time to prepare.

The nearest beast stepped out of the trees fully. It was larger than the others, its shoulders almost as high as the lower rampart. Its front claws dug into the dirt, curling and uncurling as though eager to tear something apart. The skin along its sides twitched, as if something underneath it wanted out. It raised its head. Even from the wall, Loran felt the weight of its gaze. It didn't look at the archers or the captain or the hammer-wielding warriors. It looked somewhere below, as if it could smell something through the timber and packed earth. Mara flinched. Loran's mark burned once, a sharp, clean spike of heat that stole his breath.

"Mark," Vale commanded. The beast tensed. "Loose!" A rain of arrows arced from the wall. Several found their mark, sinking into black flesh with wet thuds. The creature staggered—but it didn't fall. It shook its body, two shafts snapping under the movement. A dark, viscous fluid dripped from the wounds, steaming where it hit the cold ground. "Again!" Vale shouted. More arrows flew. Two of the smaller beasts dropped, legs folding under them, bodies sliding across the ground. One thrashed, then went still. The leader roared, the sound jagged and broken, and charged. The others followed.

They didn't sprint directly at the main gate, the way ordinary animals might. They spread, fanning out along the front of the hold, testing for weak spots in the barricade. One slammed into the outer stakes near the western section, teeth gnawing at the wood, claws ripping chunks loose. Another leaped, landing halfway up the sloped earth that led to the wall, using the incline to scramble higher. "Left flank!" Vale barked. "Put them down!" Archers adjusted, loosing at closer targets. One beast took an arrow straight through the eye and collapsed with a sickening crunch of bone. Another caught three in the ribs and kept climbing, teeth gnashing.

Loran tracked the leader as it barreled toward the central section of wall, eyes fixed on something invisible. Its run wasn't smooth. Its limbs jerked at odd moments, as if it fought something even inside its own body. His mark pulsed in answer to its approach—flaring hot, then dropping, then flaring again. The sensation made his vision blur at the edges. Ryn stepped to the gap between two archers. "Aim for the front joints," he said. "Where the bone meets the shoulder. They're weaker there. Their twisted frames can't carry their own weight."

One of the nearest archers swallowed hard, drew a breath, and did exactly as told. The arrow flew, striking the beast where Ryn indicated. The creature shrieked, stumbling. Two more arrows plunged into the same area, and its right leg buckled. It half-fell, half-slid toward the wall, claws tearing furrows in the earth. "Again," Ryn said. Another volley. The beast crashed against the base of the wall, its bulk slamming the timbers hard enough for Loran to feel it under his boots. For a heartbeat, he thought it might topple the section entirely.

The wood groaned, nails complaining. Then there was a sound like fabric tearing. The beast pushed itself upright with three legs and lunged—straight at the same section of wall Loran stood on. Instinct took over. Loran dropped his bow, hand flying to the hilt of his sword. He barely got it free before the creature leaped, claws reaching, jaws yawning wide enough to swallow his head. Its teeth glistened with thick, dark spit. His mark erupted. He threw his left hand out without thinking. Heat seared along his arm, like molten iron being poured just under his skin. The air cracked. An invisible force slammed into the beast mid-air. It veered off course as if struck by something enormous, colliding with the outer stakes instead of the top of the wall. Wood splintered. Several sharpened posts snapped under the impact.

The creature tumbled, hitting the ground hard enough to send a spray of dirt and broken timber flying. A hush followed—brief, stunned. Even the other beasts seemed to hesitate. Loran staggered, clutching his arm. The veins around the mark glowed dull red under his skin, fading fast. His elbow burned. His fingers tingled. Mara stared up at him from below, eyes wide. Ryn's gaze snapped to Loran's arm. "Control," he said sharply. "Breathe. Don't pull on it again." "I didn't mean to," Loran hissed through his teeth. "I know," Ryn said. "That's why I'm telling you not to."

The injured beast twitched on the ground, trying to rise. Arrows answered it. A half-dozen shafts thudded into its exposed throat and chest. It spasmed once, then slumped, jaw hanging open in a final, broken growl. The remaining creatures turned. Not toward the trees. Toward one another. One limped closer to the fallen leader, nose testing the air above its body. For a moment, it looked almost... confused. Then a shudder ran through it, head to tail, like a ripple disturbing a reflection. Its milky eyes rolled back, then refocused—this time not toward the wall, but toward the mountains.

Ryn's grip tightened on his staff. "They feel it," he murmured. "Even in death. The guardian's slip." The beast raised its head and howled—a warped, grating sound that scraped at Loran's ears. The others answered, their cries not directed at the hold, but at the distant ridge. Then, as one, they retreated. They didn't flee in panic. They pulled back in jerking, stiff steps, as if answering a command only they could hear. Within moments, the tree line swallowed them. The forest resumed its unnerving stillness.

No one moved at first. Then Vale exhaled loudly, as if remembering how. "Hold fire," he called. "Do not pursue. Archers—stay sharp. Builders, check that section for damage. If that brace has slipped so much as a finger-width, I want it doubled." Men and women sprang back into motion, adrenaline turning into restless activity. Braum clambered up the nearest ladder, wincing as his healing leg protested. He reached Loran and thumped his shoulder. "Nice trick," he said. "Try not to aim it at us next time." Loran managed a weak laugh. "No promises." "Didn't think so," Braum said. But the corners of his mouth twitched upward.

Arlyn hurried along the walkway checking for injured. A few archers had strained shoulders or grazed hands, but no one had fallen. Below, Lila moved among the ground crews, offering water and bandages where needed. Mara stood near the base of the wall, one hand pressed against the timber. Her face was pale, eyes fixed on the tree line. Loran climbed down to her, his arm still throbbing with aftershocks. "You alright?" he asked. "I felt them," she whispered. He frowned. "You mean you saw them?" "No," she said slowly, searching for words. "I felt them notice me. When they looked at the hold... it was like something brushed across the inside of my thoughts." Her fingers pressed harder into the wood. "And when they howled at the mountains, it felt like... like I was standing between two doors, and both were being opened at once." Loran's throat went dry. "Did it say anything?" "No," she murmured. "That's the worst part. It didn't have to. It knew I heard it anyway."

Ryn joined them then, boots crunching softly over scattered splinters. His eyes were still the calm, cool blue they always were when he'd decided something unpleasant and necessary. "That was a probe," he said. "Not a true assault." Vale approached, overhearing the last words. "If that wasn't a true assault, I don't want to see one," the captain muttered. "They nearly brought down half the north wall." "They could have brought more," Ryn said. "Many more. And they didn't. They were counting us. Measuring the response." Vale rubbed at his brow. "So what—do we expect another tonight?" "Yes," Ryn said simply. "Or tomorrow. Or the day after. But it will come harder each time."

"And the guardian?" Loran asked quietly. Ryn's jaw tightened. He looked toward the mountains again. "His strength is leaking away. You felt it, when your arm flared. The seals tied to your mark strain with every breath he takes." Mara's shoulders hunched. "Can he recover?" "No," Ryn said. He didn't soften it. "But he can hold longer. If he does, it gives us time." "Time for what?" Loran asked. "To decide who we are when the chains finally break," Ryn said. Vale blew out a harsh breath. "Well, until that lofty decision is made, I'm going to reinforce that section before the next pack decides to use it as a ladder." He clapped Loran once on the shoulder. "Good work today. Try not to throw yourself off the wall next time." Loran managed a small nod. "I'll do my best." As Vale walked away shouting new orders, the hold slowly settled into its strange version of routine. Arrows were collected. Corpses were dragged beyond the ditch and set alight, dark smoke curling into the gray sky. The broken stakes were replaced with new ones, hammered down twice as deep.

Lila passed out cups of water to shaking hands and tried not to look at the pile of burning flesh. Braum limped back toward the training yard, muttering about needing to hit something that didn't bleed. Arlyn checked every person on the wall for injuries twice, even when they insisted they were fine. Mara and Loran lingered by the base of the barricade.

"Does it always feel like this?" she asked quietly. "Like what?" "Like winning and losing are the same thing. Just at different speeds." Loran watched as a group of workers struggled to lift a new brace into place, faces pinched from fear and effort. He watched Ryn, standing with one hand resting on the wall, eyes far beyond the valley. He watched the smoke from the burning beasts smear across the sky like a stain that wouldn't wash out. "I don't know," he said. "But we're still standing." "For now," she replied. He didn't argue.

Ashwood Hold moved on with its repairs and its drills and its small attempts at normalcy. The walls had held. The beasts had retreated. No one had died. By the measure of the new world, it was a good day. But as the afternoon light thinned and the shadow of the mountains stretched longer across the valley, Loran felt his mark whisper again—not in words, not in warnings, just a steady, heavy awareness that somewhere far away, something enormous was weakening, and the things that hailed from the dark were growing bolder with every beat of its fading heart.

CHAPTER FIFTY
The Day After Walls Trembled

By morning, Ashwood Hold looked almost like a place that hadn't been attacked the night before. Almost. The fresh stakes along the north barricade still shone with sap, and the churned ground beyond the ditch was marked with claw furrows and the dark stains of what passed for blood in corrupted creatures. But people moved through the hold with the purpose of those who had work to do and no time to waste.

Loran woke to the sound of hammers and Vale shouting at someone about brace angles—normal noises now. He rubbed the sleep from his eyes, stretching stiff muscles. His arm still throbbed faintly, but the burn from yesterday's uncontrolled mark flare had dulled to a deeper ache. Manageable. Braum was already up, sharpening his hammer's edge—not because it needed it, but because he found it calming. Arlyn busied herself by sorting another pile of bandages Arlyn insisted might come in handy

The attack had shaken everyone. No one wanted to say it out loud, but attacks that "probe" were never the last. They were tests. Measurements. And they made a point of leaving survivors so word could spread. Still, Vale was determined to drag normalcy into existence by force. He gathered people near the training yard as morning frost was still fading from the ground. "We got lucky yesterday," Vale said, voice carrying over the muttering crowd. "Luck is not a strategy. Ryn tells me these attacks will come harder. And the walls will not hold unless the people on them know what they're doing." Ryn leaned quietly on his staff beside him. "Luck favors prepared hands," he added.

The morning became drills and rotations. People assigned to spear lines practiced bracing in unison. Archers tested firing at moving targets—Lila rigged a rope through a line of straw dummies, yanking them jerkily to simulate corrupted movement. Braum oversaw a wrestling pit, showing the recruits how to drop a larger creature by targeting joints. Loran walked Mara toward the archery range. He'd noticed something last night—her hands shook after the attack, but not from fear. From... resonance. Every time the beasts howled, she had stiffened as if the sound crawled up the bones of her spine. Mara drew an arrow and fired. Perfect shot—dead center. Loran blinked. "Did you practice without telling me?" "No," she said, drawing again. "I just... keep hitting the middle." She released. Another bullseye. Some of the newer recruits stopped to stare.

Loran watched her more closely. Her face was calm, but too calm. Like her mind was focused somewhere deeper, somewhere that didn't need conscious aim. "Does it feel strange?" he asked. "A little," she admitted. "Like the bow knows where to go before I tell it." That pricked him with unease, but he didn't push. Not yet. Across the training yard, Ryn instructed a cluster of younger fighters in staff work. Out of the corner of his eye he kept glancing toward the mountains, toward the place where tremors had rattled the world. Loran walked toward him when a break formed in the session. "How bad is it?" Loran asked. Ryn didn't pretend not to understand. "He is holding, but only barely. When a guardian weakens, corruption spreads faster. The tremors will come again. Stronger." Loran swallowed. "And my mark?" Ryn's eyes flicked to his arm. "It will hurt more when he slips. And if he dies..." He hesitated—rare for him. Ryn always finished his sentences. "If he dies, Loran, the corruption that was held at bay will surge. Across the land. Across the creatures. Across the bloodlines." "And Mara?" Ryn exhaled slowly. The warning in his silence was clear. She was cracking—like thin ice bending under weight it couldn't yet see.

Before Loran could press further, Vale approached. "Training break," Vale said. "Food in ten. Then we reassign patrol routes." The break was welcome. People dispersed, some heading for water, others to sit and breathe. Lila ran up to Loran, nearly tripping over a coil of rope. "The southern watch said something is moving by the river, but they think it's elk. Probably elk. Possibly elk. They said elk like five times so I think they're trying to believe it." Braum snorted. "If we're lucky, maybe corrupted elk taste better than corrupted wolves." "Don't you dare," Arlyn snapped, flicking his shoulder. "We are not testing that theory." Loran managed a small smile at the banter—these were the small things that kept the hold alive. The little threads tying everyone together. Then a shout cut across the courtyard.

"Smoke! On the east ridge!" Everyone turned. A thin pillar of dark smoke curled above the tree line—not the black of burning corruption, not the gray of wet wood. A deep rust-dark column. Vale swore. "Signal fire. From a human camp." "That ridge is three hours east," Ryn said. "Closer to the trails settlers use." A cold pit opened in Loran's stomach. "So they're running." "Or being chased," Vale said grimly. "Either way, we go." He stalked toward the gate, barking orders "Archers ready. Spears to the east wall. Loran—Braum—Ryn—on me. Mara—stay here with Arlyn and Lila—" "No," Mara said. Vale blinked. "What?" "I'm coming." "Mara—" She drew herself up, shoulders straight. "If settlers are in danger, I won't stay behind the walls. I can help." Vale hesitated. He respected her—everyone did—but she wasn't trained. She didn't have a weapon besides her new bow.

Ryn stepped forward. "Let her come." Loran snapped his head toward him. "Ryn—" "She must learn what hunts her," Ryn said softly. "Better here, with us, while she can still walk freely." Mara's eyes flicked to Ryn with a brief, unreadable expression—fear, maybe. Or recognition. Vale nodded reluctantly. "Fine. You stay in the rear." As they prepared to move, Loran pulled Mara aside. "You don't have to prove anything," he said. She met his eyes, steady

and hurting. “That’s not why I’m going.” He wanted to ask—but didn’t. There wasn’t time. The group gathered at the gate. Archers lined the parapets. The wind carried the smoke-scent toward them—sharp, metallic, wrong. Vale raised his hand.
“Gate!” Timbers groaned as the doors opened. Ryn murmured, “The world is waking differently today.” Loran touched the hilt of his sword. “Good or bad?” “Neither,” Ryn said. “Just... waking.” And they stepped beyond the safety of the walls—into a land beginning to tilt, into danger approaching from the east, and into the slow slide toward the moment everything would break.

CHAPTER FIFTY-ONE
The Smoke on the Ridge

The trail east of Ashwood Hold wound through clusters of pine and brittle brush, the ground still lightly frost-bitten. Loran kept his eyes fixed on the rising smoke pillar. It wasn't thick enough to signal a large settlement burning—but it wasn't small either. A camp of travelers. A caravan. A family. Whatever it was, it was close enough that if corruption had reached it, they had minutes—not hours. Vale led the front. Ryn walked just behind him, staff tapping the dirt in slow, deliberate beats. Loran kept Mara between him and the center of the formation. Braum took the rear, watching their flank with a scowl that usually meant he expected trouble.

The closer they came, the more the smoke thickened. It carried a smell that twisted Loran's stomach—charcoal wet pine and something sour beneath it. Not corruption.
Something human. Fear. They moved faster. At the crest of a hill, Vale lifted a hand. Everyone froze. Below them—a camp. Or what remained of one. Tents half-collapsed, a wagon overturned, bundles of supplies scattered across the grass as if thrown in panic. A cooking fire still smoldered at the center, sending up the column of dark smoke. But no bodies. No blood. Nothing visibly broken except the campsite.

"Where is everyone?" Lila whispered. Ryn inhaled deeply, tasting the air with a frown. "Not dead. Not gone. Moved." "Moved how?" Braum asked. Vale scanned the tree line. "Loran. Mara. On me." They descended into the camp carefully. Loran's hand hovered near his sword. Mara's breath came shallow, eyes flicking from shadow to shadow as though expecting something to leap out. A kettle lay overturned, its water still steaming. Fresh footprints in the dirt—small ones, children's.

A blanket dropped mid-folding. Whatever happened here had happened fast. Ryn knelt and pressed his palm to the earth. His eyebrows drew together sharply. "What is it?" Loran asked. He stood. Slowly. "They ran." "From what?" Mara asked. Ryn didn't answer with words at first. He pointed. Loran followed his gaze. Near the northern edge of the camp, a tree trunk showed fresh scratches—deep, parallel grooves, about a foot long each.
Not from claws. From something sharper. Something that cut wood like soft cloth. Braum muttered, "That's not elk." "No," Ryn said. "It's corruption-touched. And recent."

They spread out, moving cautiously through the camp. Lila gathered scattered supplies. Arlyn checked overturned crates for survivors. Mara knelt beside the wagon, touching the broken wheel. "They left in a hurry. But why didn't they take everything?" "They didn't have time," Loran said grimly. Then—a sound. Soft. Barely there. A tiny whimper. Mara's head snapped toward a nearby tent. "There." Loran reached it first, blade ready. He lifted the flap. A child—no older than five—crouched inside. Wide-eyed. Silent. Shivering. Her cheeks were streaked with soot, her hair matted with ash. When she saw Loran, she didn't scream. She simply whispered: "Don't let it find me."

Mara dropped beside her instantly, her voice soft and steady. "It's alright. You're safe now. What happened? Where are your parents?" The girl shook her head violently. "It looked like him." Everyone went still. "Look like who?" Loran asked gently. The child swallowed. "The man who came into camp. He had eyes like... like glass. Like they weren't his. And his voice sounded wrong." Ryn closed his eyes. "A mimic." "What's that?" Vale asked. Ryn opened his eyes again—dark, serious. "A corrupted creature that learns a shape. Steals it. Wears it for a time." Mara went pale.

The child whispered, "He said he needed to find someone. A girl. A girl with a break in her."

Mara's breath hitched audibly. Loran's hand tightened on his sword. "Did he hurt anyone?" The girl nodded. A tiny motion. "People ran. Mama carried me. But she dropped me when the ground shook." Tears welled. "She told me to hide." Lila hugged the child close. "You did so well. We'll find them." But no one believed their own reassurance. Not fully. Vale straightened, jaw set. "Ryn. What are the chances the mimic followed the survivors?" "Certain," Ryn said. "Mimics track by emotion. Fear leaves a trail even animals can follow. The corruption uses them like hunters."

Mara's hand shook as she lowered it from the child's shoulder. "It was looking for... someone broken." Loran stepped toward her immediately. "Mara–" But she pulled her hand away, fingers trembling. "It's me, Loran. You know it's me." Before he could answer, a scream echoed through the forest–distant, sharp and unmistakably human. Vale whipped toward the sound. "East ridge! Move!" Ryn grabbed his staff. "Hurry. And stay together." Mara didn't move at first. She stared into the tree line, eyes wide. As if something deeper than the scream had called her. Loran seized her arm. "Mara–stay with me." She blinked hard, breath shaking. "I'm here."

They ran. Through brush. Over roots slick with frost. Toward the place where the scream had come from. Loran's lungs burned. The child's words echoed in his skull: *A girl with a break in her*. Beside him, Mara stumbled once, catching herself. Her face had gone pale, too pale, as if the very forest pressed against her mind. Braum shouted from behind, "There! Movement–left side!" And Loran saw it–a shadow moving between trees, tall and wrong and wearing a human shape like a loose cloak. The mimic. It turned its face toward them. Its eyes were flat, reflective like glass. And when it smiled–it was almost Mara's smile. Distorted. Searching. Ryn shouted: "Do NOT let it touch her!" The mimic lunged. And the last breath of stillness ended in a single heartbeat.

CHAPTER FIFTY-TWO
What Wears a Human Face

The mimic burst from the tree line with a speed that felt wrong—too smooth, too eager, like it had practiced wearing a human shape and couldn't wait to show someone it knew how. Soldiers shouted along the old stone wall of a small garden. Arrows flew. Most missed. One struck the creature's leg, but the mimic didn't falter; it only tilted its stolen head as if *curious* about the sensation of pain. Loran charged, sword drawn. "Hold the line!" Vale barked. "Don't let it get inside!"

The mimic didn't seem interested in the line. Or the walls. Or the soldiers. Its glassy eyes found Mara immediately. She froze—not in fear, not in shock, but because something in that gaze felt *searching*. Like the creature was comparing her to a memory it had been given. Loran threw himself in front of her, blade raised. "Mara—back!"

The mimic lunged. Loran met it with steel and momentum. The clash sent a jolt up his arm, rattling bone against bone. The mimic's strength was impossible—lean, wiry, deceptively fast. It hissed, more air than sound, as if trying to figure out what noise a human throat should make. Mara stumbled backward, gripping a support beam. Her breath hitched, a cold rush sliding through her chest. Not a voice. Not a pull. Just a sudden spike of dread that made her ribs feel too tight. *Not now,* she told herself. *Not here.*

Arlyn sprinted toward her. "Mara—get behind the crates!" But Mara's eyes stayed locked on the mimic—not drawn to it, not responding to anything inside her, just watching in terror as it mirrored Loran's stance with unsettling accuracy. Ryn thrust his staff forward, a bolt of blue fire cracking into the mimic's shoulder. The creature staggered, twisting unnaturally, like its bones were rearranging on the fly. "Do not let it touch her!" Ryn shouted—not because Mara was slipping, but because the mimic had recognized her. That alone was enough.

"Kill it!" Vale roared. The mimic lunged again, this time at Ryn. It moved like a smear of shadow given muscle, darting with unpredictable angles and impossible stops. Ryn blocked the swipe with a shockwave of blue energy, sending dust spiraling. Loran seized the opening. He drove his blade into the mimic's chest. The creature let out a shuddering gasp—not pain, but *surprise*, as if not expecting this human shape to fail it. Its limbs twitched, spasming as it tried to right itself. Loran shoved harder, pinning it to the ground. "Stay down," he growled through clenched teeth. The mimic's head tilted at him, then slowly—too slowly—turned its glassy eyes toward Mara. It smiled. Not wide. Not monstrous. Just a gentle, knowing curl of lips, like someone acknowledging a familiar face in a crowd.

Mara's stomach dropped. "I don't know what it wants," she whispered. "I swear I don't—" "I know," Loran said, voice steadier than he felt. The mimic shuddered once... then went still. Its body dissolved slowly, collapsing into a dark slurry that absorbed into the soil as though the earth itself drank it down. Silence swallowed the courtyard. No cheers. No relief. Only the wind—cold and sharp—brushing across the village. Vale exhaled shakily. "If that was a scout... I don't want to meet the thing that sent it." Ryn didn't answer right away. He was still staring at the dissolving stain on the dirt, eyes narrowed. "It wasn't scouting" he murmured. "It was searching."

Loran felt Mara shiver beside him. He turned quickly. "Are you hurt?" "No," she breathed. "Just... shaken." She forced a small, fragile smile. It didn't reach her eyes. Ryn studied her, gaze sharp—but he didn't see corruption. Not yet. Only strain. Fear. A girl exhausted by everything pressing in from all sides. Finally, he nodded. "You're alright." Mara's relief was immediate and visible. But Vale wasn't reassured. "Ryn... why did it behave like that? Why didn't it attack the men? Why go for her?" Ryn addressed the entire group now. "Because the corruption is searching. Hunting. Not blindly, but with intent." He glanced toward Mara only briefly. Not accusing. Not knowing. Just wary. "It can sense the world shifting," he said. "It can sense the guardian dying. It can sense... opportunity." Mara swallowed hard. "But opportunity for what?" she asked. Ryn didn't answer. Because no one in the group was ready to hear the truth. Not yet.

CHAPTER FIFTY-THREE
The Breath Before Collapse

Ashwood Hold did not calm after learning of the mimic's death. If anything, the quiet grew heavier. People spoke in low tones, not wanting to draw attention from whatever else might be listening. The air itself felt tighter. Thinner. As if the world had inhaled and forgotten how to exhale. Ryn ordered torches lit along the inner paths as well as the walls—"Shadows cannot be trusted tonight," he said—and no one argued. Loran wiped the black residue of the mimic from his blade and sheathed it with a quiet click. The sound felt too sharp for the moment.

Mara stood beside him, arms wrapped around herself, gaze fixed on the smear of darkened soil where the mimic had died. "It smiled," she whispered. Loran touched her elbow gently. "It doesn't matter what it meant. It's gone." "It matters," she said, her voice barely audible. "Things like that don't smile." Ryn turned toward them, his expression unreadable. "Not unless they've learned how."

Vale arrived with two soldiers in tow. "We've doubled patrols, posted torches on every walkway, checked the outer traps twice." He leaned close to Ryn. "But these things are getting within fifty paces of the wall. We can't keep them out forever." Ryn didn't respond right away. He looked toward the western ridge, where the trees swayed without wind. "There will be more," he said quietly. "And they will be bolder." Braum limped over, pointing his hammer at the stain. "You see that? That's what nightmares look like when they get bored." Arlyn cuffed the back of his head. "Stop scaring the children." "There aren't any children near me!" "There will be if you keep yelling." Even their bickering couldn't break the tension.

Lila hurried over, hands full of bandages she'd forgotten she was carrying. "Ryn... do we expect more tonight? Should we move the injured deeper inside?" Ryn lifted his gaze toward the mountains, eyes narrowing. "No. The corruption won't push tonight. Not fully." Vale frowned. "How can you tell?" Ryn tapped his staff gently against the earth. The dirt trembled. Not a quake—just a faint, distant pulse. Rhythmic. Weakening. Loran stiffened. "That's the giant." "His fading," Ryn confirmed. Mara swallowed. "It's getting worse, isn't it?" Ryn nodded. "When he falls, the world will feel it. Every ridge, every valley. Every living creature. But until then, the corruption waits. Watches. Prepares." "So tonight is quiet," Vale muttered bitterly. "That's supposed to comfort us?" "It should," Ryn said. "Because quiet means time." Time to fortify. Time to brace. Time before the world breaks.

Loran looked around the hold. Workers reinforced the inner barricades with shaking hands. Soldiers sharpened blades until sparks fell like fireflies. A few settlers prayed under their breath. Others cleaned the yard because it kept their minds busy. A child cried until Lila scooped them up and carried them away, humming. Everyone was trying. Everyone was afraid. Mara brushed a hand along the railing of the walkway. "Do you ever wonder," she murmured, "if this place will still be standing in a week?" Loran didn't answer. He couldn't. She looked up at him, tired but steady. "I'm not asking you to lie." "Then no," he said softly. "I don't know." She nodded as if that was the only answer worth giving. For a moment, they stood together in silence—not entirely romantic, not dramatic, just human, sharing the weight of what they couldn't outrun.

Ryn suddenly turned toward Vale. "Gather your captains. Now. Quietly." Something in his voice made both men freeze. Vale stiffened. "Why? What did you feel?" Ryn glanced around the hold, ensuring no one else was listening. His voice dropped, barely above a breath. “The seal... cracked again.” The words sank into the earth like stones. Loran’s pulse kicked. Mara’s breath weakened. “How much time?” Vale asked. Ryn shook his head. “Im not sure. Days. Hours. Maybe less.” Braum swore under his breath. Arlyn’s shoulders slumped just slightly. Loran stepped forward. “When it breaks fully... what happens?” Ryn looked at him with an honesty that chilled the air. “The sky will darken. The air will tear. The corruption will rise in a wave you cannot stop. And someone in this world will inherit the guardian’s power.” Mara went still. Vale exhaled slowly. “And the corruption... what will it inherit?” Ryn’s gaze shifted toward the mountains. “Everything the seal once kept from it.” Loran swallowed hard. “So when the giant dies—” “When,” Ryn agreed quietly, “not if.” A long silence followed. Finally Mara spoke, her voice barely steady. “So what do we do?” Ryn met her gaze. “We prepare for the moment the world changes.”

CHAPTER FIFTY-FOUR
The Valley Tightens

Ashwood Hold braced itself as the afternoon deepened into a cold, gray light that felt thinner than usual—stretched too taut, like skin over a wound. The quiet Ryn had promised did not ease tension. It sharpened it. People moved with purpose but little conversation. Every hammer strike sounded like it echoed too far. Every footstep felt loud in the stillness. Every bird that failed to return to its nest made someone glance upward. Something in the valley had changed. Something subtle. Something waiting. Loran tightened the last brace on the western rampart as a gust of chilled air swept over the hold, ruffling cloaks and extinguishing two torches with a soft hiss. Workers cursed under their breath and relit them, hands shaking despite the calm exterior everyone tried to maintain.

Ryn walked the perimeter again, slower this time, as if listening not to danger but to the absence of it. Mara watched him from the inner yard, her arms wrapped tight around her ribs. She wasn't trembling. She wasn't hearing whispers. But her breath hitched sometimes—barely, softly—as if a thought kept brushing her mind and sliding away before she could catch it. Loran approached her. "You okay?" She nodded, but the motion was slow. "Everything feels... close." "Close how?" he pressed. "Like the world is leaning in." Loran's stomach clenched. But he didn't push. She hadn't slipped. Not yet. And he refused to put fear where none belonged.

Vale strode across the yard with his lieutenants. "Patrol rotations stay doubled. If anyone spots even a shadow moving wrong, shout before you think." Braum thumped his hammer down. "Aye. And if the corruption itself comes knocking, tell it to wait—we're busy building." A few tired chuckles followed, thin but appreciated. Arlyn passed Mara and paused, touching her shoulder lightly. "You haven't eaten since morning." "I'm not hungry." Arlyn frowned softly. "That's not the point." Mara forced a small smile and took the piece of bread Arlyn offered anyway. She didn't eat it. She just held it like something that proved she was still part of the world.

Ryn eventually stopped his slow circuit and joined them. His expression didn't show panic...but it didn't show peace either. "How long do we have?" Vale asked. Ryn's answer was quiet. "Hours. Perhaps more. But not many." Loran looked past the walls toward the distant mountains, now tinged with the faintest green veil—a haze that hadn't been there yesterday. "The cracks are spreading," Ryn murmured. "Not fast. Not loud. But inevitable." Mara's voice came out thin. "Will we feel it? When it breaks?" Ryn exhaled. "The world will feel it. Every creature with breath. Every mark-bearer in any land." He paused, looking at Loran. At Mara. "Especially those tied closest to the seals." Mara swallowed hard. Loran stepped closer, almost shielding her with his presence.

"Days, you said." "I said hope for days," Ryn corrected. "Expect less." A long silence followed. Workers passed by with timber. Children whispered near the well. A soldier dropped a bucket and flinched like it was a monster. The stillness had started to choke the hold. Finally, Vale broke the tension. "We keep working. Panic doesn't help anyone." "Correct," Ryn said. "But neither does denial. Prepare yourselves today—and tonight. Sleep if you can. Eat. Drink. Speak to those you trust. The next sunrise may not be gentle." Braum snorted. "When has a sunrise ever been gentle?" But even he couldn't muster more than a brittle grin.

As the sun dipped—though never truly bright—the cold intensified. Workers lit more torches, their flames flickering like uneasy thoughts. Mara helped Lila organize the healer's satchels. Slow movements. Mechanical. Arlyn kept glancing at her but said nothing. Loran found himself pacing near the outer wall, checking the same beams again and again even though they were already secure. His arm hummed faintly—no pain, no glow, just a presence. A waiting. He hated it. He hated the helplessness of knowing something enormous was unraveling far beyond their sight. He hated that he could do nothing but brace for the moment it reached them.

Ryn joined him quietly. "Your mark is changing." "I can feel it." "It is reacting to the guardian's decline," Ryn said. "Not to the corruption's attention fully. Not yet." "Not yet," Loran repeated, jaw tight. "That supposed to comfort me?" "It is supposed to prepare you." Loran didn't answer. Not with words. Ryn glanced back toward Mara. "She is holding. For now." Loran's breath tightened. "And when she stops holding?" Ryn didn't answer. He didn't need to. They both knew the truth: Mara was not losing herself now. But she was approaching the cliff where she eventually would. Not tonight. Not now. Not until grief tore her open. Not until the possible moment she watched Teren fall. She needed to hold on until the dark forces at play be laid to rest and whatever the corruptions plan in using her had been negated.

Torches were lit early. Vale called for the gates to be barred an hour before sunset. Braum drilled the young soldiers until they could hold their shields steady. Arlyn made the injured rest. Lila prepared poultices in silence. Ryn stood alone on the wall, eyes fixed on the mountains. Mara sat beside Loran on a crate near the inner fire pit, watching the flames rise and fall like breaths. She leaned her shoulder against him—not romantically, not possessively, just needing contact with someone who kept her anchored.

"Do you think," she whispered, "that we'll have warning before it happens?" Loran looked at her. The flames reflected softly in her eyes. Human eyes. Tired eyes. But hers. "I think we'll feel it," he said softly. Mara nodded. "I think so too." The sky above them darkened by degrees. And somewhere far beyond the ridge—in the unseen deep places where an ancient guardian clung to his fading existence—another crack formed. Too quiet to hear. Too faint to shake the earth. But real. The valley felt it. Ryn felt it. Loran felt it. And Mara... Mara shivered, pulling her cloak tighter. But she did not slip. Not yet. Not until the moment the world demanded a choice.

CHAPTER FIFTY-FIVE
The Breath Before the Charge

The first warning was sound—a deep, distant howl rolling across the valley like a storm breaking its knuckles. Every conversation in Ashwood Hold halted. Every soldier froze mid-step. Every torch flickered. Loran felt the hairs rise on his arms. Braum stopped twirling his hammer. Arlyn looked up from her bandages. Vale reached instinctively for his sword. Mara stiffened beside Loran as though someone had pressed a cold hand between her shoulder blades. Ryn's voice cut through the tension: "Positions." No shouting. No panic. But the urgency in his tone cracked the quiet like a blade striking stone.

The hold moved at once. Archers raced to the wall. Runners grabbed signal horns. Shields were lifted along the inner barricades. Workers pulled children toward the shelters. Loran climbed to the north rampart as the tree line across the valley shook—not from wind, but from something pushing through it. Vale joined him, breath coming sharp. "Ryn said they wouldn't attack yet." "They weren't going to," Loran replied, gripping the railing. "Until something changed." Something did change. The next crack in the green seal. The low tremor earlier was not random. It was the corruption stirring. The forest rippled. Branches snapped. Shapes emerged. Not scouts. Not the shadows from the night. These were solid. Massed. And fast.

Mara climbed the ladder behind Loran and joined him on the rampart. Her eyes widened, breath catching. "What are those?" Ryn spoke from the far end of the wall, staff raised: "Remnants." The word rattled through the air like a curse. They were half-human shapes twisted into elongated forms, shoulders hunched, limbs stretched unnaturally long. Their eyes glowed faintly green—the first time Loran had seen the corruption tinted by the dying giant's power.

"Why do they look different?" Lila whispered from behind a crate. "Because the corruption is evolving," Ryn said grimly. A beat. Then the remnants screamed. Not in rage. In hunger. Vale shouted, "Archers—LOOSE!" A volley of arrows streaked across the sky. Some hit. A few creatures staggered—but none fell. Instead, they accelerated, their movements jerking and unnatural, like puppets trying to outrun their own strings. The ground trembled under their charge. Loran drew his blade as one of the remnants leaped—leaped—nearly halfway up the rampart wall. "Down!" he shouted. Mara ducked just in time. The creature slammed into the wooden beams, claws carving deep grooves as it tried to climb. Loran swung hard, slicing into its shoulder. Black-green ichor splattered across the wall, sizzling where it landed. The remnant shrieked and dropped back, writhing, then staggered up again.

Braum appeared on the walkway with a roar, swung his hammer, and shattered the creature's skull in one brutal blow. "By the gods," he breathed. "They're getting faster." "STRONGER!" Vale yelled from the far end. "They're hitting the south wall too!" Loran grabbed Mara's arm and dragged her toward the next ladder. More remnants slammed against the wall. Wood shuddered. Bolts strained. Ryn strode forward, lifting his staff—but Vale grabbed his arm. "Not yet! Wait for them to line up." "Maybe," Ryn said. "But if the wall falls, hundreds will die." A remnant scaled the tower behind them—so silently none heard it until it was already on the platform. "Behind you!" Arlyn screamed. Loran spun. Too slow. The remnant lunged. Mara moved first. Her dagger flashed in a clean arc, slicing across its jawline. The creature staggered but did not fall. It clawed toward her, shrieking— Loran drove his sword through its chest, pinning it to the wall before it dissolved into black dust.

"Mara, you okay?" "Yes," she panted. "But they're still coming." Dozens crashed against the barricades like waves hitting cliffs. Then— A deeper sound. Not a scream. Not a howl. A rumbling growl that made the boards tremble beneath their feet. Loran froze. Ryn's head snapped toward the tree line. "Oh no," he whispered. "It's here." Vale shouted, "What is?!" A massive silhouette lumbered through the trees—twenty feet tall, shoulders hunched, limbs dragging. A Phase Three beast. But wrong. Twisted by green energy. Its eyes glowed like dying sunlight filtered through swamp water. Mara staggered backward, clutching the railing as if the thing reached for her. Loran grabbed her. "Mara!" "I—I can feel it," she gasped. "Not like before. It's—stronger." Ryn's voice sliced through the chaos: "Everyone off the wall!" "No!" Vale shouted. "We hold—" The beast rammed the northern barricade. The entire wall lurched two inches backward. Torches fell. Lila screamed. Half the archers dropped to their knees. Another hit would splinter the beams.

Loran grabbed Mara and shoved her toward the ladder. "Move!" Braum hauled Lila down behind them. Vale tried to hold the left side with a spear, shouting for reinforcements. Ryn raised his staff—and this time he didn't stop. Blue light surged, swirling up from the earth into his arms. The air crackled. The torches flared as if bowing to his power. "Ryn—NO!" Vale yelled. "You could break the wall!" "They will regardless!" Ryn roared. He slammed the staff into the rampart. A shockwave blasted outward. The wall cracking to some degree. Remnants disintegrated. The Phase Three beast reeled, howling in pain as blue-white energy scorched its flesh. But it did not fall. It braced itself—and charged again. The rampart split. Mara stumbled. Loran grabbed her before she fell through a widening crack. The beast drew back for another strike. Ryn's voice was hoarse. "Everyone, FALL BACK! Inside the inner barricade! NOW!"

Vale blew the horn. Soldiers abandoned the wall. The beast slammed again. Wood exploded. The northern barricade collapsed inward. Mara screamed. Braum cursed. Lila fell but Arlyn caught her. Loran dragged Mara away as the Phase Three beast climbed over the ruins, roaring, eyes locked directly—directly—on her. Ryn stepped between Mara and the creature, staff glowing dangerously bright. "This is only the beginning," he rasped. The creature lunged.

CHAPTER FIFTY-SIX
The Wall Falls

The Phase Three beast dropped into the ruined barricade with a seismic thud that shook Ashwood Hold to its foundation. Splinters rained like falling needles. Dust rolled across the courtyard in a gritty wave. The dying torches guttered sideways under the force of its roar—a guttural, bone-deep bellow that rattled the ribs of every person who heard it. It was enormous up close—twenty feet of muscle and corruption warping over a frame that should not have existed. Its skin was a patchwork of gray hide and moss-green veins that pulsed like roots choking a dying tree. Jagged bone protrusions curled from its shoulders like half-grown wings, and its mouth— its mouth split too wide, too far, jaw unhinging in a grotesque crescent of serrated bone.

Those green eyes fixed on Mara. Not the hold. Not Ryn. Not the soldiers screaming orders... Her. It stepped forward, crushing the last beam beneath its clawed heel. Ryn braced his staff in both hands, planting himself between her and the monster. Blue rings pulsed outward from where the staff tip sank into the earth. The very air warped around him, bending like heat over stone. "MOVE!" he shouted.

Soldiers scrambled out of the debris. Braum limped toward the inner line, dragging a stunned archer under one arm. Arlyn barked orders to medics to pull the wounded back. Vale planted his shield and bellowed for spearmen to form a semi-circle. But none of it mattered. The beast lowered its massive head and charged. The ground thundered. Loran grabbed Mara's waist and hauled her back just as the creature slammed into Ryn's ward. Blue fire exploded in a shockwave. The beast shrieked—a horrible, grating sound like metal dragged across stone—but instead of being thrown backward...it dug its claws into the dirt and pushed. The barrier began to crack. Blue fissures spiderwebbed outward from Ryn's staff. Ryn gritted his teeth, muscles trembling. "It's stronger than before!" Vale shouted, "Hold the line!" But the beast slammed its bulk forward again.

The barrier shattered. Ryn flew backward, crashing into a stack of crates and sending them scattering across the ground. "RYN!" Lila screamed. The beast lunged straight for Mara. Loran stepped in front of her. His heart hammered so violently it felt ready to burst through his chest. The sigil in his arm flared—not lit, but reacting, pulsing like it was waking up to danger. He lifted his sword. "Loran—" Mara choked. He never heard the rest. The beast swung one massive arm. Loran blocked—but the sheer force sent him skidding across the dirt, boots digging trenches until he slammed into the base of the inner wall. Pain exploded in his shoulder. His breath tore from his lungs.

The beast turned back toward Mara. She stumbled away, hands trembling so badly she couldn't draw her dagger. Her vision blurred. It felt like the air around her thickened—like she was standing in the pull of a river she couldn't see. A whisper brushed the back of her skull. *Found you...* "Mara!" Arlyn shouted. "MOVE!" She tried. Her legs barely obeyed. Fear knotted her chest so tightly she could hardly breathe. The beast reared to strike her. And Braum—limping, bleeding, furious—charged from the side and slammed his hammer into the creature's knee with a roar. Bone cracked. The beast staggered sideways, roaring in fury. "Over here, you rotting mountain!" Braum bellowed.

The beast turned—grabbed him—and hurled him across the courtyard like a thrown spear. Braum hit a wagon so hard the wood shattered. "No!" Arlyn sprinted toward him without hesitation. The beast pivoted again toward Mara. Ryn rose shakily to his feet, raising his staff for another spell—but his knees buckled. Blue light sputtered, dimming like a dying ember. Lila grabbed his arm. “Ryn, stop—you’re bleeding!” A thin red line trickled from his nose, staining his lips. He had pushed too far too fast.

Loran staggered upright, vision swimming, shoulder screaming, sword shaking in his hand. “HEY!” he shouted at the monster. “OVER HERE!” The beast looked back at him—and for a moment, Loran saw something horrifying in its gaze: Recognition. Not of him. Of the green burning beneath his skin. It roared like a challenge. Mara’s breath caught. “Loran—don’t!” He charged. Pain ripped through his arm, but he didn’t slow. He swung upward, slicing into the beast’s forearm. The blade sparked against bone, cutting deep enough that black-green corruptive blood sprayed across the dirt. The beast howled and swiped. Its claws tore open the air where Loran had been standing a second before. He dove, rolled, slashed again.

Vale and his spearmen rushed in from the left, driving their weapons into the creature’s flank. For a moment—just a moment—it faltered. “PRESS IT!” Vale shouted. “DON’T GIVE IT SPACE!” Three soldiers thrust spears. The beast spun—too fast—ripping one spear free and impaling the soldier with it. The man’s scream cut through the courtyard. Another soldier tried to retreat. The beast grabbed him by the head and crushed his skull with a sickening crunch. Mara clapped a hand over her mouth. Loran’s stomach turned, but he forced himself forward.

He leaped onto the creature’s injured leg, driving his sword into the joint. The beast bellowed and thrashed, flinging Vale aside. “LORAN, GET DOWN!” Vale shouted. He dropped flat. A volley of arrows hissed overhead—Arlyn had pulled every archer she could find into formation—and the missiles peppered the creature’s hide. Most bounced uselessly off bone plates, but a few wedged deep into soft tissue. The beast roared in agony. And then it did something no one expected. It *looked* at Mara again. And the green light in its eyes surged. Mara staggered backward, clutching her temple. “Stop—stop, please—” Loran jumped to his feet. “Mara!”

Ryn lifted his head, recognizing the danger instantly. “It’s sensing her—it’s sensing the Vessel!” Mara gasped, "I'm NOT—" The beast charged her. A blur of teeth and claws and corrupted muscle barreling toward her faster than she could react. Loran sprinted. Ryn raised his staff again, vision swimming. Vale threw himself forward with his shield but was knocked aside like a rag doll. Mara screamed. The beast loomed over her—and Loran reached her first. He slammed into her, wrapping his arms around her waist and twisting midair as the beast’s claws raked through where she had been standing. The two of them hit the dirt hard, Loran’s shoulder bursting with pain. The beast skidded, churned the earth, and turned back with a guttural roar.

Loran rolled to his knees, sword raised, shielding Mara with his body. She clung to his back, trembling violently. “I’ve got you,” he whispered. Her fingers tightened on his cloak. “Loran—I can hear—something—” “I’ve got you.” The beast charged again—and Ryn dragged power up from the ground with a scream of effort. His staff lit like a star. He slammed it down. A dome of shimmering blue force erupted outward, engulfing the courtyard in a protective shockwave. The beast hit the barrier—and staggered back as if struck by a hammer of light. Ryn fell to one knee, retching, barely conscious. But the barrier held. For now.

The beast circled outside it, snarling, testing for weak points. Loran helped Mara to her feet. She clung to him, heart hammering. Everything was shaking—the barrier, the earth, the sky—as if reacting to the weakening seal far away. Vale limped over, blood streaked across his jaw. Braum struggled upright in the distance, held up by Arlyn. Ryn wiped blood from his mouth and rasped: “This is only the first one.” Loran stared at the monstrous silhouette pacing outside the barrier. “You mean there’s more?” Ryn’s voice was barely a breath. “Oh yes. When the green giant dies... this will look small.” The barrier flickered. Mara’s pulse thundered beneath her ribs. And far away—beneath a mountain older than nations—something groaned like a god in its death throes.

CHAPTER FIFTY-SEVEN
The Beast That Would Not Break

The blue barrier shuddered like stretched glass, its surface rippling under the monster's relentless pacing. Each step of the Phase Four creature sent shockwaves across the shimmering dome, making it bow inward as though sucked toward the thing's hunger. Smoke rose from the ground where its claws scraped. The air itself felt wrong—thick with the smell of sap, rot, and something sharp enough to sting the lungs. Ryn knelt in the dirt, one hand braced against his staff, the other gripping his ribs. Blood smeared the corner of his mouth, but his eyes—though dimmer—still glowed blue. He whispered through clenched teeth, "It's learning the rhythm of the barrier." Vale turned sharply. "They can do that?!" "They can *adapt*," Ryn rasped. "Especially ones this evolved."

The beast slammed into the barrier again. The dome bent inward an entire foot. Braum, leaning heavily on a broken spear, muttered, "Well, that feels encouraging." Arlyn elbowed him hard. "Shut up." Loran pulled Mara behind him, gripping his sword tighter. She shook violently but didn't look away from the beast. She couldn't. Something about it dragged her gaze back every time she tried. Ryn coughed and wiped blood from his jaw. "The barrier will fall soon." "How soon?" Vale asked. Ryn didn't even glance up. "Seconds." The beast roared and charged. The barrier shattered. Blue shards sprayed outward like broken starlight. The shockwave hurled dust and ash into the air as the monster burst into the courtyard with a triumphant bellow.

"MOVE!" Vale shouted. Spearmen surged. The beast swiped. Three soldiers were thrown aside at once—one flying into a wagon, another slamming into the wall hard enough to knock the wind out of him, the third simply disappearing beneath the creature's weight. Loran dove in, slashing at the monster's exposed flank. The blade cut deep, spraying black-green corruption across the dirt, sizzling wherever it landed. The beast howled and swung. Loran ducked under the massive claws, rolling across the ground and coming up behind a toppled crate. "LO—RAN!" Mara's scream cut through the chaos. He turned— too slow. The monster was already upon her. Mara stumbled back, knees buckling. Her breath tore from her throat in a thin gasp. Something inside her was trembling.

A *pressure.*

A *pull.*

The corruption recognized her. Ryn felt it too. His eyes widened. "It senses the crack—it senses her grief. Protect her!" Lila sprinted toward Mara, grabbing her arm. "Come on—COME ON—MOVE!" But Mara couldn't. The beast lunged. Vale intercepted with his shield raised. The impact lifted him off his feet and flung him into a pile of firewood. "VALE!" Arlyn shouted. The monster turned toward her next. Arlyn raised a hand, whispering a desperate ward—but the beast knocked her down with a single swipe, sending her skidding across the dirt. Braum roared and charged. "NOT THIS TIME!" His hammer struck the creature's jaw with a crack like splitting stone. The beast reeled, stunned. Loran sprinted. This was his moment. He leaped— drove his blade into the creature's neck— and the monster shrieked in a spray of corruptive blood. It wasn't dead. It was furious. It whipped around, claws arcing toward him. Ryn thrust his cracked staff into the ground, shouting a single word— "DOWN!" Loran threw himself flat as blue energy erupted from the staff like a shockwave. It slammed into the beast, hurling it backward into the remains of the wall. Splinters and bone fragments showered the field.

Ryn collapsed again, gasping. The blue aura flickered like a candle in high wind. “Ryn!” Lila dropped to her knees beside him. “Stop—STOP—you’re bleeding internally—” He shoved her hand away. “Not... done yet...” The beast rose. Its neck poured black-green corruption. Its breathing was ragged, its ribcage heaving unnaturally—but it was not slowing down. It looked straight at Loran. And then—past him—to Mara. Its lips peeled back. *Found you again...* Mara’s knees buckled. She dropped, clutching her head, trying to fight the whisper pressing behind her eyes. Not yet. Not here. NOT HERE. “Loran...” she gasped. “Loran, I—I can’t—it’s calling—” He grabbed her face gently but firmly. “Look at me. Focus on me.” Her breath shook like she was drowning.

The beast surged forward. Loran tightened his grip on her cheeks. “I’m right here. Stay with me.” And then he stood. He didn’t wait for the beast to close the distance. He charged head-on, screaming as he slammed his sword into the creature’s chest with everything he had left. The beast swung its claw—Loran ducked—Ryn’s failing magic flared—Braum limped into position for another strike—and Vale, still bleeding from the ribs, crawled back to his feet and lifted his shield again. Together, they swarmed the monster. Steel. Blue fire. Hammer blows. Arrow shots. Every ounce of strength Ashwood Hold had left. It wasn’t enough.

The beast roared, shaking off their attacks, rising taller, more feral. Corruption poured from its wounds but refused to let it die. Loran felt panic claw his throat. “How do we KILL it?!” Ryn forced himself upright, shaking, barely conscious. “You don’t kill it,” he rasped. “You break its anchor!” “HOW?!” Ryn pointed at the deep wound in its neck—where black ichor seeped thick as tar. “The bone ridge! Break it—and the corruption can’t hold its shape!” Braum spat blood. “Why didn’t you say that first?!” “Because—” Ryn coughed violently— “I hoped we wouldn’t need to get that close.”

Loran didn’t hesitate. He sprinted toward the monster, using a fallen beam to gain height, leaping onto its upper back. The creature thrashed violently, trying to shake him off. He clung to a protruding bone spike, teeth gritted, muscles screaming. "LO–RAN!!" Mara shouted, voice cracking. He lifted his sword– and drove it toward the bone ridge at the junction of neck and shoulder. The beast bucked. The blade hit bone. Not deep enough. He screamed and shoved harder– the corruption crackled under his palms—black lightning crawling across its skin—pushing into him– into the sigil. His arm erupted in agony. The monster shrieked. Loran screamed back at it. And finally—the bone ridge shattered. A wet crack echoed across the courtyard. The beast convulsed violently, corruption spilling from its mouth, its wounds, its eyes. Its body began collapsing inward, like a puppet with cut strings. Loran leaped off just before it fell. The creature hit the dirt with a thunderous crash. Silence followed. Broken only by ragged breathing.

Ashwood Hold froze as the monstrous corpse steamed in the cold air. Braum dropped his hammer and fell to his knees. Arlyn exhaled shakily, pressing a hand to her pounding heart. Vale stood with effort, leaning on his shield, staring in disbelief. Mara stared at the corpse, wide-eyed and shaking, fingers pressed against her lips. Ryn swayed, catching himself on his staff. "That..." he whispered, voice raw, "...was not the worst of them." A shiver raced across the entire hold. Loran wiped sweat and corruption from his face, breath still shaking. He stepped toward Mara– And the moment he touched her– A pulse hit the air. Soft. Subtle. But wrong. Mara gasped. Loran felt it too—just a faint electric tremor beneath her skin. Not the Vessel awakening. Not yet. Just the world preparing.

Ryn felt it and shut his eyes. "The giant is fading faster..." Mara's fingers curled into Loran's shirt. "Something's breaking," she whispered. And far to the northwest, beneath a dying mountain—the green guardian groaned in his sleep. The end was approaching. And Teren was waiting.

CHAPTER FIFTY-EIGHT
When the Ridge Breathed

The hours after the beast's fall were not restful. Ashwood Hold moved with the frantic stiffness of a place trying desperately *not* to collapse. Soldiers dragged the steaming corpse away from the barricade. Healers worked in tight, frantic circles. Vale barked orders until his voice cracked. Ryn knelt near the shattered wall, pressing trembling hands against the corrupted soil, listening with a depth of attention that made even the bravest men step back. Something had shifted. Not in the hold. Not in the valley. But in the world.

Loran watched Mara from the corner of his eye as he helped Braum prop up a broken timber post. She paced the inner walkway again—hands clasped, jaw tight, breath shallow. She looked like someone repeatedly brushing against a memory she didn't want. She hadn't spoken since the pulse. The faint tremor inside her chest. The one only he and Ryn had felt. Loran's grip tightened on the timber. Splinters bit into his palm. "Easy," Braum grunted. "You'll snap the pole before it even stands." Loran exhaled through his teeth. "She's not alright." "No one is," Braum answered, not unkindly. "But she's still breathing. And until she stops, she's still Mara." Loran swallowed hard. "It felt... like something tugged her. Like a thread." Braum paused mid-hammer, his expression turning thoughtful. "Threads can be cut," he said. "You hear me? Nothing's taken her yet." But he didn't sound convinced.

Ryn stood suddenly. Everyone nearby froze. His blue-lit eyes widened—not in terror, but in grim recognition. Vale jogged over. "What now?" Ryn didn't speak. He lifted his staff and pointed toward the northwest ridge—slowly, as if the gesture itself carried weight. The mountains were breathing. Not exaggeration. Not poetic dread. The *stone* shifted, rising and falling, as though pulled by the heartbeat of something enormous beneath it. Gasps rippled across the hold. Children clung to their mothers. Soldiers lowered their weapons, eyes wide. Vale's voice was a whisper. "That... that can't be real." "Oh, it's real," Ryn murmured. "The guardian's strength has wavered long enough for the land above him to respond. His breath is weakening." Loran felt his stomach twist. "How close is he to—" Ryn cut him off with a sharp shake of his head. "Do not ask." The mountains pulsed again. Dust rolled down the snowy slopes like smoke from a dying fire. Arlyn approached, wiping blood from her hands. "What happens when he stops breathing?" Ryn looked at her. Looked at the ridge. Then looked away. Which said more than any explanation.

A low sound rolled through the valley. Not the guardian. Not tremors. Something *else* had awakened. It came from the tree line—deep and ragged, carried on the wind like an echo of something massive entering the world. Vale turned, hand on his sword. "Scouts?" Ryn shook his head. "No. This isn't local. This sound traveled *through* the corruption. It's being felt, not heard." Loran stiffened. At first, he thought Mara clutched his arm. But... she wasn't touching him. His arm had seized on its own, the sigil pulsing so sharply it made him stumble. Blue light flickered in Ryn's eyes again. "It's reacting," Ryn whispered. "Because something has crossed into this valley." Vale scanned the walls. "What? A beast? Another Phase Four?" "No," Ryn said softly. "Something far more dangerous." Loran's breath hitched. His thoughts jumped to a single person. A face he once recognized. A voice he once trusted. Teren.

A horn blast cut the air. Short. Sharp. Urgent. Soldiers sprinted to the gates. Ryn moved first, robes snapping behind him like torn parchment. Loran followed, heart in his throat. Mara came too, though she stayed half a step behind, fingers knotted tightly around her sleeves. A scout stumbled through the gate—armor torn, face bloodied, breath coming in ragged bursts. Vale caught him by the shoulders. "Report!" The scout shook violently. "Something—someone—came through the northern trail. The corruption recoiled from him. Like it feared him. I've never seen anything like—" He gagged and coughed up blood. Arlyn pushed through, catching him as he fell to his knees. "Easy—easy—what did he look like?" The scout's eyes widened in terror. "Tall... too tall. Skin half-human, half... something else. Eyes glowing like... like the corruption made a person. But he talked. He *talked*." Ryn's face drained of color. Vale whispered, "A remnant?" "No," Ryn said hollowly. The scout grabbed Vale's sleeve with shaking fingers. "He asked for a name." Vale froze. "What name?" The scout's whisper cracked. "Loran." The hold went silent. Absolutely silent. Ryn shut his eyes. "It's him." Mara's breath hitched. She looked like all the air had been ripped from her lungs. Loran felt the world tilt. "Teren..." The scout nodded feverishly. "He's coming here. He said he's ready to bring you home." Ryn stepped forward, voice rising sharply. "WHERE IS HE NOW?!" The scout lifted a trembling hand and pointed toward the mountain path. "Half a mile. Maybe less."

Mara choked on a gasp, pressing her hand to her chest as if something sharp twisted beneath her ribs. Loran lunged to steady her. "Mara—look at me—stay with me—" Her knees buckled. Her pupils dilated. She whispered, barely audible: "He's calling me too." Loran's heart stopped. Ryn's head snapped toward her with a violence that made onlookers flinch. "What do you hear?" he demanded. "Nothing," she gasped. "Just... a feeling. Like seeing someone you lost standing in the doorway." Loran felt sick. Ryn swore under his breath and spun toward Vale. "Sound the full alarm. All walls. All archers. Double spears on the eastern gate. Whatever is coming is more dangerous than the beast we faced." Vale's voice thundered across the hold. "TO POSITIONS! ALL MEN TO THE WALLS—NOW!" Ashwood erupted into action. But

Loran barely heard them. He looked toward the ridge where the scout had pointed. Snow dust spilled down the slopes again. The mountains gave another heaving breath. And deep beneath it—something died a little more. He could feel it. Mara could feel it. And worst of all—Teren could feel it.

Ryn turned to Loran, eyes blazing with urgency. "You will stay behind the first line. Do you hear me? You do *not* meet him alone." Loran swallowed the burn in his throat. "I have to face him." "Yes," Ryn hissed. "But not yet. Not until I know what he has become." Mara shook violently, gripping Loran's sleeve. Her whispered words were barely breath: "He's close..." Loran pulled her into him, arms tight, heart pounding. "I'm here. I'm not leaving you." Her voice cracked. "That's what I'm afraid of."

The horn sounded again. Closer. Lower. As if something enormous was pushing through the valley's breath. Ashwood Hold stood ready. Swords drawn. Archers at the walls. Ryn steadying himself with a cracked staff. Mara trembling beside Loran, eyes fixed on the tree line. And Loran— Loran stared toward the path where he had once lost his everything. Waiting for the man he used to know. The monster he had become. His grief. His enemy. Teren was coming.

CHAPTER FIFTY-NINE
When the Corrupted Walks Like a Man

Ashwood Hold fell into a breathless quiet as footsteps approached from the northern trail. Not staggering. Not frantic. Measured. Purposeful. The kind of steps belonging to someone who *remembered* walking in life. Someone who once been apart of their home. Ate there. Slept in the houses now burned or abandoned. Loran's stomach tightened. He knew that gait. Everyone in the group did. Teren had been many things — a hunter, a loudmouth, the first to volunteer for a dare — but not dangerous. Never dangerous. Until now. The figure stepped through the tree line. Teren. Or what was left of him.

Gasps rippled across the hold. Arlyn raised a trembling hand to her mouth. Braum muttered, "No... not him..." Lila whispered, "He was never supposed to become this thing." Mara stared, frozen, as if seeing a ghost wearing the wrong skin. Teren's body was tall—too tall. His limbs were subtly lengthened. His eyes glowed a soft sickly green-black, like swamp water catching moonlight. But the smile— He still wore the same grin he flashed when he beat Loran in a footrace. The familiarity of it made Loran's blood turn cold. "Teren," Loran whispered. Teren's head tilted. The grin widened. "Loran," he answered softly, voice layered, wrong. "You still say my name like you expect me to answer."

Ryn planted his staff into the ground, blue light flickering around him. "You should leave here," Ryn said. "Or you will be unmade." Teren chuckled lightly. "Oh, I was. Every piece of me was taken." His glowing eyes slid to Mara. "Except the memories." Mara flinched. Behind Loran. As if hiding meant anything now.

Soldiers raised spears. Archers drew bows. Some villagers backed away, whispering in fear. Teren glanced around, amused. "Everyone looks so tense," he murmured. "I used to spar half of kids from home in the meadow. Remember? I was terrible with a shield." His grin sharpened. "I'm much better now." His voice, layered with corruption, sent a shiver through the entire hold. Loran forced himself to take a step forward. "Teren," he said, "what happened to you?" "Oh, the usual," Teren said with a shrug. "I screamed. I ran. I begged. But corruption doesn't bargain." He raised his hand —veins crawling beneath the skin like oil. "It gives."

Teren's gaze drifted over the crowd. Searching. Hungry. Until it landed on Mara. His smile softened disturbingly. "There she is." Mara's breath stopped. Loran immediately moved in front of her, sword half drawn. "Don't look at her," he growled. Teren's eyes flicked to him. "So protective," he murmured. "You must feel it too. The world changing to make room for her." Ryn's staff glowed brighter. "Not another word to her." Teren ignored him entirely.

The corrupted veins in his arm pulsed. Just once. A tremor of power surged outward. Ryn slammed his staff down— blue ward flaring— but the wave smashed into the hold with bone-rattling force. Soldiers stumbled. Arlyn struck a crate. Braum shielded several villagers. Lila hit the ground screaming. Loran barely stayed upright— but Mara was thrown to her knees. He grabbed her, pulling her close. Dust and splinters rolled across the hold. When the air cleared, Teren lowered his hand. His casual tone made the moment far more frightening. "Don't worry," he said softly. "If I wanted you dead, you would be." Loran met his eyes, fury simmering. "What do you want?" Teren smiled again slowly, delighted. "To give you a part in what comes next."

CHAPTER SIXTY
After the Herald

Ashwood didn't breathe for a long time after Teren vanished. The place he had stood on the ridge still seemed to hum with his absence, a faint wrongness clinging to the air like smoke that wouldn't blow away. People stayed frozen at their posts long after the shadows swallowed him, as if any movement might call him back. Only when Vale finally barked, "Stand down—but not far," did the hold begin to move again. Even then, no one spoke loudly. They moved in small, careful motions, as though the ground might decide their footsteps were an insult.

Loran climbed down from the wall with his sword still in hand, fingers stiff around the hilt. His arm had gone numb halfway through Teren's taunts, then shifted to a dull ache that pulsed in time with his heartbeat. Now it felt heavy. Weighted. Wrong. He kept touching his sleeve, half expecting the skin beneath to burn again, but it stayed cold. The cold was somehow worse. Mara descended beside him, boots hitting each rung with too much precision, like she was counting them in her head. She hadn't said a word from the moment Teren's voice first carried across the ridge. Not when the man she'd once known laughed about the village. Not when he mocked Loran's mark. Not when he smiled at her like a promise he intended to keep. At the bottom of the ladder, she stepped off and just... stopped.

Staring at nothing. Loran reached for her shoulder. "Mara." Her flinch was small but sharp. She turned toward him, and for a heartbeat he was terrified of what he'd see in her eyes. They were hers. Dark. Haunted. But hers. "I'm fine," she said hoarsely. "I just... need a second." He didn't believe her, but he didn't press. Around them, the hold tried to uncoil. Archers lowered their bows with trembling hands. Someone dropped a quiver and didn't bother to pick it up right away. A few of the younger guards muttered prayers under their breath, the words half-strangled by unused voices.

Braum arrived at a stiff-legged half-run, hammer over his shoulder, eyes wide. "Everybody still in one piece?" he demanded, looking each of them over without waiting for an answer. When his gaze landed on Mara, his bravado slipped a fraction. "You alright, girl?" She nodded too fast. "Yes." Arlyn came up behind him, one hand on his arm to steady him, the other already reaching for Mara's wrist as if she could take a pulse from the air. "You're shaking," she said quietly. "Sit down before you fall down." "I'm not shaking," Mara protested. Her knees wobbled. Loran slid an arm under her elbow before she toppled, guiding her toward a nearby crate. She sank onto it as if half her bones had been scooped out. "Just... dizzy." "Shock," Arlyn murmured, already moving to fetch water. "Or stubbornness. Hard to tell with you lot."

Vale approached with three of his more seasoned soldiers, face drawn tight. The easy command he usually wore was frayed around the edges. "Report," he said, though he'd been on the wall and heard everything. Old habits didn't let go easily. Ryn joined them from the far end of the parapet. He walked like nothing hurt, like the corruption's attention hadn't brushed over the hold, like the sight of Teren had not been a knife twisted into five hundred years of memory. But Loran noticed the tiniest hitch when he stepped down from the last rung to the ground, as if his legs had to remember they existed.

"He was testing us," Ryn said, before Vale could ask. "Measuring the walls. Counting the archers. Counting the marked." Vale's jaw flexed. "He looked you in the eye. Then Loran. Then her." He nodded toward Mara, whose gaze was fixed on the dirt between her boots. "You think he recognized you?" "The corruption did," Ryn replied. "Whatever's left of him... I don't know." Loran swallowed. "He remembered us. He knew details. The village. The meadow. The hall." His hand tightened unconsciously on his sleeve. "That wasn't just corruption talking." Ryn's eyes flicked toward him, calm but too sharp. "Corruption doesn't erase everything," he said. "It bends what's there. That's what makes it so effective."

Mara let out a brittle laugh that wasn't really a laugh at all. "So what we saw up there... that was both of them." "Yes," Ryn said quietly. "The boy you knew and the thing that's using him." Her fingers dug into her own arms. "If there's still a piece of him in there—" "You cannot save that piece," Ryn cut in, more sharply than he meant to. The words fell like a dropped blade. Everyone went still. Mara's eyes filled before she could blink it away. She looked away, jaw clenched hard enough to hurt. Braum shifted, discomfort flashing across his face. "Maybe we take a moment before we stomp on whatever hope is left, eh?"

Ryn's expression didn't soften, but he inclined his head slightly. "Hope is not the problem," he said. "False hope is." Vale exhaled through his teeth. "Whether there's something left of him or not, the fact stands—he came here, he walked away, and he will come back. I need to know how much worse it will get." Ryn looked toward the ridge again, the faint green haze above the distant mountains pulsing like a bruise. "The giant's seal is weakening. The corruption will only grow bolder. What you saw tonight is the smallest version of what's coming." "Small," Braum muttered. "Of course. Why not." Loran barely heard them. His mind was stuck on Teren's smile. Not the cruel one. The small one, the one that slipped through when he talked about "remembering." You always liked the river, little ember. He'd called him that by the river once at twelve, when Loran had fallen in and sputtered back out of the cold water furious and shivering. Ember, because you flare up and then you sulk. He hadn't remembered that in years. Until tonight. And so had Teren. That was the worst part.

Mara's voice pulled him back. "Can he get inside?" she asked suddenly. "If he really wants to? Can he pull the corruption through the walls, or... or call it under the ground?" Her eyes flicked to the packed dirt at their feet like she expected hands to reach through it. Vale answered first, like a man forcing himself to speak plainly to keep his soldiers from imagining worse. "The walls will hold against beasts and claws," he said. "They're fixed with timber and stone. Not magic. But they're high, and they're thick, and we've fought off things bigger than him before." "Teren isn't the problem," Ryn said. "He's a symptom. A mouthpiece. The corruption doesn't need him to breach a wall. It can rot beams. It can whisper fear. It can make people open gates in the middle of the night because they hear their dead mother crying outside."

That last part was too specific to be theoretical. An ugly silence fell. Lila, who had edged close enough to listen without being noticed, wrapped her arms around herself. "Has it... has it done that before?" she whispered. Ryn's gaze slid past her—not answering and answering at the same time. "We shore up what we can," he said. "Walls. Watch. Wills." Vale nodded briskly, seizing the part he could control. "Then we reinforce. Double the northern archers. Extra oil along the ridge-facing barricades. I want a second torch line inside the outer wall." He turned to his soldiers. "Go." They obeyed with grateful speed.

Orders were easier to carry than fear. As they scattered, Arlyn returned with a cup of water and pressed it into Mara's hands. "Drink," she said. "Slowly. Don't argue." Mara obeyed, fingers trembling around the cup. Loran watched her throat work, the small motions somehow more fragile than anything that had just happened on the wall. "You don't have to go anywhere near the ridge again," he said quietly. "If he comes back and you stay below, you won't have to—" "See him?" she cut in sharply. Then her voice broke. "Hear him?" She shook her head. "If he's out there and we're here, there is no 'away' from him." Ryn's staff tapped once against the ground, a soft, grounding sound. "You both need rest," he said. "Your mark is unsettled," he added to Loran without looking at his sleeve. "And you..." His gaze flicked to Mara. "You stood in the path of something's attention tonight. That leaves a bruise. You may not feel it yet, but it's there." "Meaning what?" Mara asked. "Meaning we don't let you wander alone," he said. "Not until the giant's fate is decided."

Loran's chest tightened. "How long until that?" Ryn looked toward the mountains again. The green haze flickered once, faint but visible, like a lantern guttering in wind. "No way of being sure," he said. "Maybe hours." Braum blew out a breath. "Perfect. Barely time to sharpen blades and definitely not enough time to flee very far. Just the way I like it." Arlyn swatted his shoulder, but the corner of her mouth twitched. Even the smallest joke was a relief valve. "We'll rotate watches tonight," Vale said. "Short shifts. No one on the wall more than two hours at a time. Fatigue makes mistakes. Mistakes get people killed." He glanced at Ryn. "You'll feel it first if the corruption moves again. Let me know the instant anything changes." "You will feel it too," Ryn said, nodding toward Loran. "In your arm. And you," he added to Mara, "here." He touched his chest lightly. "It knows both of you now. It will tug at what it has touched."

Mara swallowed, one hand curling against her sternum. "And if it tugs too hard?" "Then you tell me," Ryn said. "Immediately. I don't care if I'm asleep or halfway through a sentence. You don't try to be brave. You don't try to handle it alone. You call me." The firmness in his voice left no room for argument. Loran nodded. Mara didn't. But she didn't refuse, either. She just stared down into the nearly empty cup in her hands, as if the last drops of water might offer some other path. As the group began to break apart, the hold slowly remembered how to move. People returned to tasks in a quiet, stunned rhythm. Torches were shifted. Arrows re-bundled. Children guided toward the safer center of camp. Ryn walked away toward the northern wall again, climbing the ladder with the steady, unhurried steps of a man who expected the world to fall apart where he wasn't looking.

Vale peeled off toward the western side, barking fresh orders at the nearest cluster of soldiers. Braum limped toward the practice yard, already shouting for whichever poor recruit was scheduled to get yelled at next. Arlyn coaxed Lila toward the healer's tent with a gentle hand on her back. Loran and Mara were left in the middle of the courtyard, surrounded by motion and noise that somehow didn't touch them. "He's going to come back," Mara said finally. Simple. Flat. Loran couldn't lie to her. "Yeah." "And when he does," she continued, voice quieter, "he's not going to talk as much." That was the part that chilled him. The Teren on the ridge had laughed and needled and reminisced because he could afford to. Because he knew there was more time.

"We'll be stronger by then," Loran said, though he wasn't sure he believed it. "The hold will be ready. Ryn will—" "Ryn can't be everywhere," she said. "He can't stand between us and everything forever." The worst part was that she didn't sound angry about it. Just... resigned. Tired in a way that went beyond sleepless nights. He reached for her hand without thinking. She let him take it. Her fingers were cold. "Then we learn," he said. "We get better. We don't let this be the last time we just stand there while he talks down at us like we're children at a feast." Something flickered in her eyes at that—anger, small but sharp. "I hate that smile," she whispered. "The one he used like he knew exactly how this ends and we don't." "Then we wipe it off," Loran said. His voice surprised even him. "Next time he comes, we don't just endure it. We make him work for it." Some of the steel that had left her posture on the ladder returned, bit by bit.

"You think you can do that?" she asked. "With this?" She glanced at his sleeve. He looked down at his arm, at the place where the mark burned and froze and pulsed and quieted on its own whims. "I have to," he said. "Or what's the point of any of this?" She studied him for a moment longer, then squeezed his hand once before pulling away. "Then you'd better rest while you can," she murmured. "You can glare at him with clear eyes when he shows up to try again." He almost smiled. "You too." "I'll... try," she said. "If the echoes let me." Her voice softened. "If he lets me." He didn't like the way she said he, like the corruption and Teren were the same shape in her mind. But he didn't correct her. Not yet.

The sky above Ashwood stayed a flat, bruised gray as the day dragged on. No more tremors came. No more shadows moved at the ridge. No more echoes of Teren's voice drifted over the walls. By evening, the hold looked almost normal again: fires lit, meals shared, armor oiled, tools put away. But it wasn't normal. Every person moved as if they had seen the edge of something and didn't know how close they'd come to falling. Ryn remained on the northern wall until the last light bled out of the sky, staff in hand, eyes fixed on the dark horizon. Loran lay awake long into the night listening to the hold breathe, waiting for his arm to flare or freeze or split open with some new pain. It didn't. That, somehow, was its own kind of torment.

Mara stared at the ceiling of the tent she shared with Lila, eyes dry and aching. Every time she blinked, she saw Teren's silhouette on the ridge and the way his gaze had found her in the crowd as if she were the only person standing behind the walls. Vale dreamed of old battlefields and woke with his sword already half-drawn. Braum slept sitting up against a post, hammer across his lap, as if he expected the walls to vanish while he dozed. Arlyn didn't sleep at all. She sat beside her supplies, counting bandages that wouldn't be enough no matter how many she stacked. Somewhere deep beneath the mountains, under stone and root and the last of the green giant's waning strength, the corruption pulsed in answer to the broken seal, swelling, testing the new spaces it could now fill. It had seen Ashwood. It had smelled its fear. It had looked through Teren's eyes at the marked and the almost-marked and recognized exactly what it wanted. The hold did not know it yet. But the visit at the ridge had not been a warning. It had been a stake in the ground. A claim.

CHAPTER SIXTY-ONE
The Corrupted Pull

Ashwood Hold did not wake to a new day. It slid into it. Gray light seeped across the camp like a slow-moving fog, dim and reluctant, unable to decide whether the sun should rise at all. No birds called. No frost glittered. The air hung heavy, almost damp, as though the valley itself had been sweating through a nightmare. People moved through morning tasks like ghosts. Not because they were tired—though they were. Because they were waiting. Waiting for footsteps on the ridge. Waiting for another voice on the wind. Waiting for the next crack in the world.

Loran tightened a strap on his bracer and listened to the camp breathe. Every sound felt too loud. Every silence felt too long. His arm was quiet—too quiet. That frightened him more than pain ever could. Mara emerged from the tent she shared with Lila, rubbing her eyes with the heel of her hand. She didn't look rested, but she didn't look hollow either. Just stretched thin, like canvas pulled across a frame that was one size too large. Loran stepped toward her. "How bad?" She sniffed, glanced sideways. "Echoes again. Quiet. Like someone humming through a wall." "That isn't comforting." "I didn't say it was." But she managed a small smile, thin and brittle. Her gaze drifted almost instinctively toward the northern ridge—the place Teren had stood. She shivered.

Loran shifted to block her view. "Don't look for him." "I'm not," she lied, looking at him instead. "I'm just checking the ridge." "For what?" "For... anything," she said. "Or nothing. I don't know." He touched her arm lightly. "Let Ryn handle whatever's out there." Mara glanced toward the far tower where Ryn stood again, staff in hand, cloak trailing in the wind like a warning banner. She shook her head. “He can’t watch everything.” “No,” Loran said. “But he can watch the part that needs watching.” Her eyes flicked back to him. “You mean me.” “You’re not the only one he’s worried about.” “That’s not an answer.” “It’s the truth.”

Before she could argue, Vale strode toward them, jaw clenched, eyes shadowed from lack of sleep. “We’re increasing drill rotations,” he announced. “Half the camp trains, half rests. We’ll switch every two hours. No one’s burning themselves out before the real fight.” Loran nodded. Mara tried to straighten her posture, but her shoulders trembled slightly with the effort. Vale noticed. He softened, just a hair. “You’re not on drills today, Mara. Arlyn wants you helping her organize supplies. Low strain.” Mara bristled. “I can fight.” “No doubt. But today you sort herbs and salves and count arrows. Not because you’re weak. Because you’re valuable.” She blinked, caught off guard by the gentleness. Vale’s voice lowered. “And because Teren looked at you the way a wolf looks at a lamb wearing bells.” Silence. Mara’s lip twitched. “I’m not a lamb.” “I know,” Vale said. “But he doesn’t care what you think you are.”

He walked toward the training yard. Mara stared after him, as if unsure whether to be insulted or grateful. Loran nudged her. “He’s trying.” She sighed deeply. “Everyone keeps trying to protect me.” “Because we care.” She hesitated—then rested her head briefly against his shoulder, just for a heartbeat. “I know.” Training drills rang across the yard—shields clashing, wooden spears striking padded armor. Lines of men and women moved in practiced formations. Braum shouted corrections, insults, and encouragement in equal measure. Arlyn worked with Mara beneath the healer’s tent, sorting bandages, boiling tools, mixing tinctures. The sharp scent of herbs filled the air. But something was off. People dropped things more often. Hands shook when tying knots. Arrows snapped during fletching. A tightness threaded through everything they touched.

Ryn remained on the wall, unmoving, eyes distant. Loran approached him mid-morning, climbing the ladder two rungs at a time. “Anything yet?” “Not movement,” Ryn murmured. “Just... pressure.” “From what?” Ryn lifted a hand, fingers splayed toward the mountains. “Feel that?” Loran did. A low vibration. Barely perceptible—but constant. Like the world humming under its breath. “Is it the giant?” Loran asked. Ryn’s face tightened—an expression Loran rarely saw. “Yes.” “How close is he to—” He couldn’t finish the sentence. Ryn didn’t make him. “Very,” he said simply. Loran swallowed hard. “And when he dies...” “The corruption will surge,” Ryn said. “And Teren will not wait another night.” Loran leaned on the railing. “He kept talking like this ends with him winning.” “It doesn’t,” Ryn said. “But he believes it does. And belief makes corruption sharper.”

Loran shook his head. “I don’t understand why he keeps looking at Mara like—like she’s the one he’s here for.” Ryn exhaled slowly. “Because she is.” Loran’s stomach dropped. “Ryn—” “She is not the Vessel yet,” Ryn said firmly. “But corruption always seeks a shape. It looks for where it fits best. Grief makes cracks. Loss makes openings.” Loran closed his eyes. Ryn added softly, “And she has lost much.” “Don’t let her hear you say that.” “She already knows.”

A horn blared once across the hold—sharp, urgent. Loran snapped upright. Ryn turned instantly, cloak whipping. Vale sprinted across the yard, shouting, “Southern ridge! Movement!” Loran ran. Mara dropped her bandages and followed. People scrambled to the wall as shadows darted through the trees beyond the southern line. Dozens. Maybe more. But they didn’t charge. They gathered. Moved. Shifted shape like smoke stirring above embers. Braum swore loudly. “They’re coming from the south now? Didn’t we tell them to pick a side?” Arlyn grabbed Mara’s arm. “Stay with me—” “I’m not hiding,” Mara said, pulling free. Loran stepped behind her, protective instinct flaring like heat. “We stick together.”

A distant crack echoed across the valley. Then another. Then a third. The ground trembled—not a quick jolt, but a long, dragging pulse. Ryn's eyes widened. "Oh no..." Vale spun. "What?" "The guardian," Ryn whispered. "He's slipping." Before he could say more, the sky dimmed as if a curtain had been tugged across the sun. The air thickened, pressing against lungs and ribs. The world shuddered under their feet. Mara staggered, clutching her chest. Loran's sigil flared—bright and blinding, a hot spike beneath his skin. Somewhere deep in the mountains, something vast roared. It wasn't a battle cry. It sounded like a breath forced through a crushed throat.

Ryn gasped and dropped to one knee, palm slamming against the wooden planks of the wall as if he could hold the earth still by touch alone. Arlyn screamed Mara's name. Mara's breath caught—and something unseen turned toward her. Loran felt it. Not as sound. Not as sight. As pressure. As if every shadow in the valley had leaned in at once. Like a tide. Like a hand. Like recognition. Mara's eyes widened. Her mouth opened in a silent, horrified gasp. "Loran," she whispered. Then she screamed. It tore out of her raw and jagged, too loud for her small frame, a sound that made the hairs rise on every neck along the wall. Not corrupted. Not yet. But wrong.

Loran reached for her. Ryn shouted her name. Vale barked orders no one heard. The ground split in a shallow crack near the southern fence, dust puffing from the break. Mara's body shuddered as if strings had wrapped around her spine. Her hair lifted in a wind no one else felt. For a heartbeat her eyes rolled back—then snapped open, the dark of her pupils rimmed in a thin, unnatural ring of green that pulsed once, twice, like something knocking from the other side of glass. Loran grabbed her face, fingers digging into her cheeks. "Mara—look at me. Stay with me." She looked at him. For an instant he saw her. Just her. Fear, stubbornness, all the familiar edges of who she was. Then something else slid under her gaze, a flicker that wasn't hers, like another presence pressing its face to the inside of her skull, searching for a way through. Her back arched. A low, strangled sound escaped her throat, cut off halfway as if something had tried to speak using her voice and failed.

Ryn lurched to his feet, blue light sparking across the carved head of his staff. "Mara!" He slammed the staff into the boards at their feet. A shock of cool air rippled outward, sharp as icy water. Mara jerked. The wrong color in her eyes flared brighter for a heartbeat—then shattered like light on broken glass, fading back into her normal dark. She sagged forward against Loran, chest heaving. The crack in the earth stilled. The shadows at the tree line seemed to recoil, drawing back beneath the branches. The gathered shapes along the southern ridge dissolved into the deeper dark, melting away without taking a single step toward the walls. The tremor in the ground eased to a faint, uneasy quiver. Ryn's knuckles were white around his staff. "Not yet," he whispered, voice hoarse. "You do not have her yet."

Loran held Mara upright, feeling her heart hammer against his forearms. "Mara. Talk to me." She sucked in air like she'd been underwater too long. "I... I'm here," she rasped. "I'm here." Her eyes were wet. Her hands shook as she clutched his sleeves. "Something tried to get in," she whispered. "It was... watching. Waiting." "It didn't," Loran said fiercely. "It didn't." Ryn stared toward the mountains, his expression carved with a hollow kind of grief. "He stumbled," he said quietly. "The guardian. That roar... he's on his knees now." Vale swallowed hard. "So that wasn't his death?" "No," Ryn said. "That was him falling." He looked back at Mara, gaze sharp. "When he truly dies, it will be worse than this. The pull on you will be stronger. This was only the world bracing for the next step down." Mara closed her eyes. "It already felt like being torn in half." "Then we don't let you stand alone when the next wave hits," Ryn said. "Not for a single heartbeat."

The camp slowly remembered how to move. Archers lowered their bows. Braum swore under his breath and pretended his hands weren't shaking. Arlyn checked Mara's pulse, then Loran's, muttering that both of them were making her job harder than it needed to be. The shadows along the southern trees stayed where they were, clustered just beyond the arrows' reach, as if the corruption had learned something and was content to wait. Loran guided Mara down from the wall, step by slow step. Her legs were unsteady, but she moved on her own. "You still with me?" he asked. "Ask me again later," she murmured. "When the humming stops." "You heard it too?" "I felt it," she said. "In my ribs. In my teeth." She shivered. "And it knew my name." Loran's grip tightened. "It doesn't get to keep it."

Ryn watched them from the base of the ladder, staff planted in the hard-packed earth. His face was calm again, but the calm looked thin. "This wasn't the end," he said. "This was the warning before it." Vale exhaled slowly. "Then what in all the hells is the end going to feel like?" Ryn looked up at the cloud-dulled sky, then north toward the unseen mountains where a giant struggled to stay standing against a tide no one else could see. "Like this," he said. "Only with nothing left to catch us when we fall." The wind shifted across Ashwood Hold, carrying the faintest echo of that distant roar. Not final. Not yet. But closer.

CHAPTER SIXTY-TWO
The Day the Walls Remembered

Ashwood tried to pretend it knew how to be a hold again. By midmorning the fog had lifted from the valley, but the heaviness hadn't. It lay over the courtyard and the walkways and the training rings like another layer of armor everyone had forgotten how to take off. Hammers rang against splintered beams. Sawdust floated in thin, pale curls. Men and women shuffled past one another with buckets, tools, bundles of arrows. From a distance, it might have looked like any busy morning in a fortress preparing for war. Up close, it sounded like people moving through someone else's nightmare. Every shout was a little too sharp. Every laugh, when one slipped free, died too fast. Every glance strayed toward the walls.

Loran stood near the northern walkway, watching a pair of carpenters wrestle a new brace into place where the Phase Four beast had shattered the barricade. His arm ached in a steady, bone-deep rhythm that had nothing to do with the work he'd done and everything to do with the mark beneath his sleeve. The sigil was quiet. Too quiet. He flexed his fingers slowly, as if some part of him expected black veins to burst through his skin. "Stop glaring at your arm like that," Braum grumbled behind him. "You'll scare the recruits. Half of them already think you're going to explode." Loran snorted despite himself and glanced back. The big man was hauling a crate of spearheads as if it weighed nothing, though the stiffness in his right leg told a different story. A fresh bandage peeked out above his boot where the beast's claws had scored him. "I'm not glaring at it," Loran said. "I'm... listening." "Arms don't talk," Braum said. "That's mouths. Or Ryn." "It doesn't use words," Loran muttered. "Even worse," Braum said. He set the crate down with a grunt and rolled his shoulder. "How's the pain?" "Not as bad as yesterday." "Hmm." Braum eyed him. "Is that the truth or the version you're telling everyone so they stop asking?" Loran hesitated. "Somewhere in between." Braum grunted. "Close enough."

Mara and Arlyn Under the stretched canvas of the healer's tent, Mara's world smelled like boiled cloth, herbs, and metal. She sat cross-legged on a stool beside a low table, stacking bandages into neat piles. Her fingers moved quickly, automatically. Wrap, fold, stack. Wrap, fold, stack. Arlyn had shown her three different ways to fold the cloth; Mara remembered all of them. The simple, repetitive motion should have been calming. It wasn't. Every time she blinked, she saw the way the ground had cracked near the southern fence. The way dust had puffed from the break. The way her own hair had risen in a wind only she could feel. She swallowed and forced her hands not to shake.

"Slower," Arlyn said, not looking up from the pestle she was grinding. "You're creasing them too tight. They'll rub." Mara loosened her grip on the cloth. "Sorry." "Don't apologize," Arlyn said. "Just fix it." Mara exhaled through her nose. "You sound like Braum." "Someone has to," Arlyn murmured. "He's busy terrifying the young ones in the yard." Mara tried to smile. It came out wrong. She set another bandage on the pile. "Your color's better," Arlyn said after a moment. "Breathing steadier. Head still spinning?" "Less," Mara answered. "More... humming." Arlyn's hands paused. "In your chest?" "In my bones," Mara said. "In my teeth." Arlyn resumed grinding. "Do you hear anything with it?" "Just... pressure," Mara said. "Like someone's staring without eyes." Arlyn made a soft sound that might have been sympathy. Or anger. "You tell Ryn that?" "He already knows," Mara said. "He says it's the guardian. And the corruption. And... me."

Arlyn glanced up at her then, sharp and searching. “Do you feel like yourself?” Mara hesitated. That was the worst question. “Yes,” she said. “Mostly.” “Mostly,” Arlyn repeated quietly. Mara’s fingers tightened around the next bandage. “There’s not something else in here yet,” she said, tapping her sternum with two knuckles. “If that’s what you’re asking.” “Good,” Arlyn said. “I like you just the way you are.” Mara huffed. “Even when I’m difficult?” “Especially then,” Arlyn said. “Easy people don’t survive long.” Mara looked down at the white cloth in her hands. “What if ‘just the way I am’ is exactly what it wants?” Arlyn set the pestle down and wiped her hands on her apron. She crossed the tent and crouched in front of Mara so their eyes were level.

“Listen to me,” she said. “You are not something for it to have. I don’t care if the mountains are humming your name. I don’t care if Ryn says you’ve got a crack big enough to drive a wagon through. You are not a prize to claim.” Mara’s throat tightened. “Tell that to the thing that tried to crawl through my eyes.” “I would,” Arlyn said. “If it were foolish enough to show its face in my tent.” Mara almost laughed. It wobbled on the way out. Arlyn squeezed her knee once and stood. “Keep folding,” she said briskly. “The world may end, but I refuse to run out of bandages beforehand.” “Yes, healer,” Mara murmured, and bent back to the cloth. Wrap, fold, stack. The humming didn’t stop. But for a few breaths, it faded

Ryn did not move from the northern parapet. He stood with one hand resting lightly on his staff and the other splayed against the rough wood of the railing, eyes half-lidded, as if listening to something deep under the earth. Every now and then his fingers twitched, as if resisting the urge to dig into the planks. Loran climbed the ladder quietly and stepped up beside him. “You should sit,” Loran said. “Or at least pretend to be older than you look for once.” Ryn huffed a breath that might have been amusement. “If I sit, someone will think I’ve fallen over dead. I don’t have time to reassure them all.” “How generous,” Loran said. “Dying quietly to save Vale some trouble.” “If I die quietly, none of you will notice until it's too late," Ryn said. "And then Ashwood really will be in trouble."

Loran leaned his forearms on the railing, following Ryn's gaze to the distant line of mountains. Even in daylight, the faint sickly haze above them was visible now. It pulsed, barely, like the throb of a fading bruise. "Anything?" Loran asked. "Too much," Ryn said. "And not enough." Loran frowned. "That's not an answer." "It's the truth," Ryn murmured. A gust of wind carried the smell of sap and smoke up from the valley. Loran watched a pair of tiny figures—Braum and a recruit, by their sizes and posture—sparring in the yard. Braum's hammer looked almost comically large next to the boy's wooden practice sword.

"How long do we have?" Loran asked quietly. Ryn didn't answer at once. His eyes had gone unfocused, the blue in them dimmed to a thin ring. "At the pace he is fading," Ryn said finally, "He's held on longer than I thought. I would say... two days. Perhaps one. Perhaps less, if something jars him." "Jars him?" Loran repeated. "He's... under a mountain." Ryn's mouth tightened. "The corruption is clever. It knows how to pull. How to take advantage of every stumble. It may not be content to wait for him to fall on his own." Loran's fingers curled on the rail. "And when he falls... we get what we saw yesterday. But worse." "What you saw yesterday," Ryn said softly, "was a door being rattled. When he dies, the hinges break." Loran swallowed. "What about Mara?" he asked. "Will it—" "Yes," Ryn said. "Whatever you are about to ask about her, the answer is yes."

Loran stared at him. "That's helpful." "I aim for honesty, not comfort," Ryn said. "She can't even sleep without echoes," Loran said. "How is she supposed to stand up to... that?" "She is already standing up to it," Ryn said. "Every breath she takes without screaming is a victory you can't see." Loran's chest tightened. "That doesn't sound like something we can win." "It isn't," Ryn said, and Loran blinked at the bluntness. "Not in the way you mean." "Then—" "But not all losses are the same," Ryn continued.

"Sometimes the difference between them decides whether the world continues or not." Loran stared at the mountains. "Just once," he muttered, "I'd like a problem with a simple answer." Ryn's lips twitched. "You chose the wrong century, I'm afraid

Vale stood over a crude map laid out on a low table—charcoal lines marking walls, gates, tree lines, ridges. It was stained with grease and ash and someone's boot print from months ago. He tapped the southern wall with one finger. "Reinforce here," he said. "If the corruption liked what it tried yesterday, it will try again. But harder." Two of his lieutenants nodded, scribbling notes. "And I want a second fallback inside the main yard," Vale added. "Barricades we can raise quickly. If they break the outer wall, I want them fighting through furniture and wagon wheels instead of open ground." "You're planning like we're going to lose the walls," one of the men said. "I'm planning like the walls are made of wood and the things out there don't care," Vale said. "If we're wrong, we waste some lumber. If we're right, we maybe live." The man shut his mouth.

Braum limped up, sweat shining on his brow. "Recruits are half-useless today," he said without preamble. "The other half are three swings from dropping. I can shout them into shape, but I can't shout the shakes out of their hands." "Rotate them faster," Vale said. "They'll learn less," Braum pointed out. "They'll live longer," Vale said. "If they're so tired they forget which end of a spear goes forward, it doesn't matter what they learned." Braum grunted. "Fair." He squinted down at the map. "Planning how to keep us alive when the mountain explodes, are you?" "When," Vale said. "Not if." Braum scratched his beard. "Reminds me of that story of Redtree—" "It was not like Redtree," Vale said automatically. "You don't know what I was going to say." "I know you, and I know Redtree," Vale said. "If you say 'reminds me of Redtree' in front of the young ones, half of them will bolt and the other half will cry." Braum smirked faintly. "Fair again."

His eyes drifted to the sketch of the northern ridge. “You put him on there yet?” “Who?” Vale asked. “The boy,” Braum said. “The corrupted one. The one that continues to be a pain in our side. The one who keeps sending those things our way.” “Teren isn’t a landmark,” Vale said. “He’s a threat. Those move.” “All the more reason to mark him,” Braum said. He reached for a piece of charcoal and drew a small, dark circle just outside the northern walls. “There. Problem acknowledged.” Vale stared at the mark for a long moment. “He’ll come closer next time,” he said. “Good,” Braum said. “I’m getting tired of shouting at shadows.” Vale’s jaw flexed. “You’re not ready to face him.” “None of us are,” Braum said cheerfully. “That’s what makes it interesting.”

The sun was a pale smear behind clouds by the time Loran found Mara outside the healer’s tent again. She stood alone near the water barrels, palms braced on the rim of one, head bowed. Her reflection wavered in the surface: dark hair, hollow eyes, the faintest tremor in her jaw. He approached quietly. “You didn’t flood the valley and turn into a monster while I was helping Braum yell at people,” he said. “That seems like a good sign.” She huffed a little. “Your standards for good signs are getting strange.” “I’m adjusting,” he said. She straightened slowly, wiping her damp hands on her tunic. “How bad is it?” “What?” he asked. “Out there,” she said, nodding toward the walls. “The pressure. The breathing. The... whatever you feel when you touch the railings and pretend you’re not listening to the world coming apart.” He blinked. “You saw that?” “You’re not subtle,” she said. “How bad is it?”

He considered lying. “Ryn says the giant might have two days,” he said instead. “Maybe one.” Her throat bobbed. “And when he doesn’t?” “Everything gets worse,” Loran said. “For everyone. But especially for you.” “Comforting,” she muttered. “I promised honesty,” he said. “Not comfort.” “You’ve been spending too much time with Ryn,” she said. “Someone has to make sure he eats,” Loran said. “If he dies of forgetting lunch, we’re all doomed.”

She almost smiled. It faltered. "I don't know how to do this," she admitted softly. "I know how to swing a staff at a creature's head. I know how to run. I know how to... to light lanterns and muck stables and patch roofs. I don't know how to fight something that gets inside my being." "You started yesterday," he said quietly. "You screamed. You didn't let it take you. That counts." "I didn't do that," she said. "Ryn did. With his staff." "You held on long enough for him to get there," Loran said. "I felt it. You shoved back." She stared at him. "It didn't feel like shoving back. It felt like being pried open."

He stepped closer without thinking, reaching for her hands. She let him take them. Her fingers were cold again. "I can't stop the mountain from falling," he said. "I can't stop the corruption from trying. But I can stand between you and as much of it as possible." Her eyes glistened. "What if you can't? What if it goes through you? What if you make it worse?" "I'm very good at making things worse," he said. "I have years of practice. Might as well be useful." She let out a choked little laugh, then pressed her lips together. A tear slipped free anyway.

"I don't want to be what it wants," she whispered. "I don't want to be anything it can use." "You're not," he said. "It keeps looking at me," she said, voice shaking. "Through beasts. Through the ground. Through him. Teren looked at me like—like I already belonged to whatever's inside him." "You don't," Loran said fiercely. "You belong here. With us." "And if 'with us' isn't safe?" she asked. "For you. For them." He swallowed. "We'll deal with that if it comes." "That's not a plan," she said. "It's the only one I have that doesn't end with you dead," he said. "So I'm very attached to it." She searched his face, as if looking for some piece of him that wasn't scared. "You're shaking," she said quietly. He looked down. His hands were trembling around hers. "Just a little," he said. "Don't tell Braum. He'll make me practice sword forms until my arms fall off." She squeezed his fingers. "I won't tell him if you don't tell Arlyn I almost cried over a barrel." "Deal," he said. For a moment, they just stood there, holding on to each other like they were the only solid things in a world that kept insisting it wanted to turn to smoke.

That night, Ashwood's fires burned low and close. Vale kept the watches short, as promised. No one stood on the walls more than two hours at a time. But rest came fitfully. Men woke from nightmares and went to the latrines just to find some corner of the hold that didn't feel like it was listening. Ryn remained on the northern parapet long after his turn officially ended. He had told Vale he would sleep "soon." He had told Arlyn he would drink the broth she pressed into his hand. He had told Lila he would be fine. He had told them all just enough truth to send them away.

Now he stood alone, leaning on his staff, and counted. Not people. Not hours. Not heartbeats. Breaths. Every rise and fall of the mountain's invisible chest. Every faint, distant pulse of the guardian's life. He had been fighting the corruption for five hundred years. He had watched the green one hold, felt the power bind and bury. He had thought then that a thousand years was an unimaginably long time. Enough for the world to heal. Enough for people to forget. He had been wrong on both counts. "Just a little longer," he whispered into the dark, not sure whether he spoke to the guardian, to himself, or to the hold sleeping restlessly behind him. "Hold a little longer." The mountain did not answer. But somewhere deep beneath it, the next breath came slower. Ryn's fingers tightened on his staff until his knuckles went white. "Days," he had told Loran. It would not be days. He could feel it now, with the clarity of a blade pressed to his own throat. Hours.

Back In the tent Mara lay on her back, staring at the slant of canvas above her. Lila's breathing was slow and even just a few feet away, softened by exhaustion and the heaviness that came after too many tears. Arlyn had finally bullied her into sleeping. Mara envied her for it. Every time Mara closed her eyes, she felt that humming again. It wasn't loud. It wasn't sharp. It was... persistent. As if the world itself had settled on a single note and refused to stop singing it. She pressed her palm to her chest. "Not yet," she whispered into the dark. "You don't get to have me yet." The humming didn't answer. But somewhere far to the north, a giant tried to draw another breath. And somewhere in the valley, in a place where the corruption listened to its own reflection in a pair of sickly green-black eyes, a remnant of a boy named Teren smiled faintly. He could feel it too.

The walls of Ashwood creaked softly in the night as the wind shifted, carrying the faintest, almost-imagined scent of rot and pine. The hold slept in pieces. The world waited. The count of breaths dwindled.

CHAPTER SIXTY-THREE The Breaking of the Southern Wall

Ashwood woke to the sound of something snapping. At first it was quiet—like a single branch giving way under snow. Then another. Then another. By the third crack, people were scrambling out of tents and leaning over walkways, hands on weapons, breath fogging in the cold morning air. Loran was already running. He hadn't even reached the southern ramp when the fourth crack split the air with a deep, violent shudder—louder, richer, wrong. Like bone breaking, not wood. Vale's shout cut across the courtyard: "SOUTHERN WALL! NOW!" The camp exploded into motion.

When Loran reached the parapet, he felt it before he saw it. Pressure. A low, dragging pull in the center of his arm where the sigil lay beneath his sleeve. Not sharp. Not demanding. Just... insistent. Like something running fingers along the underside of the world. He shoved the feeling down and vaulted onto the walkway. The southern tree line boiled with movement. Not attacking—yet. But massing, gathering shape and intention, like a swarm of shadows deciding which direction to become teeth.

Ryn stood at the far end of the parapet, staff pressed to the wood. His eyes were narrowed, lips tight. "Talk to me," Vale barked as he reached him. "It isn't a wave," Ryn said quietly. "It's a probe. They're testing the beams." "Testing them how?" Vale snapped. As if in answer, one of the larger trees near the fence split down the center—violently, unnaturally. Sap sprayed like blood. The tree toppled toward the wall. A chorus of shrieks rose from the forest floor, the sound of things excited rather than frightened. "Oh," Vale muttered. "That kind of testing."

Mara sprinted up the steps beside Loran, breath already hitching. Arlyn followed, one hand clutching a pouch of salves, the other swinging a knife she didn't look fully sure she wanted to use. "Stay behind me," Loran told Mara. "I'm not hiding," she snapped breathlessly. "Then stay close." She didn't argue with that one. Her eyes were fixed on the tree line, pupils dilated. Her fingers trembled at her sides the way they had before the last pull. Loran reached out instinctively—didn't touch her, but hovered close enough that she'd feel him if she needed grounding. She didn't look at him. She couldn't. Something in the forest was already looking back.

The southern gate took the first blow. A powerful, rolling thud shivered through the wood. Dust jumped from the crossbeams. Two guards staggered. Braum, arriving at a run, squinted over the railing. "Did something just hit the wall or did the wall hit something?" "Does it matter?" Vale snapped. "Only if it gets a vote." Another impact. Harder. The wall bowed inward, just a breath, but enough to make every stomach on the parapet drop. "Archers!" Vale bellowed. "Tops of the trees, three rows deep!" Arrows nocked. Bows strained. The third hit came from the side—slamming into the corner joint where two sections met. The entire southern quarter groaned like a wounded animal. A column of dust burst upward from a seam in the earth. The crack from yesterday had widened. "Ryn!" Loran shouted. "Can you brace it?" Ryn pressed both palms to the railing. Blue light flickered—weak, thin—but present. "I can hold one beam," he said through gritted teeth. "Maybe two. Not the whole wall." The fourth blow struck. And the wall broke.

The timber didn't shatter—it peeled. Long ribs of wood tore outward as though something beneath had hooked fingers into it and pulled. The gate buckled, hinges screaming. Then the bottom half of the wall collapsed inward, dragging debris into the courtyard in a rush of dirt and splintered planks and rubble. Shapes poured through the breach. Dozens. Not as large as the Phase Four creature—but faster. Leaner. Their limbs bent wrong, eyes glowing faint green-gold. Corrupted beasts and half-corrupted remnants, their bodies caught mid-transformation, mouths split too wide. The air filled with a keening sound like metal scraping bone.

"LINE UP!" Vale roared. "SHIELDS—!" The first beast slammed into a shield bearer and sent him flipping backward off the walkway. Arrows rained down. Some struck true—others glanced off corrupted hide that twisted and reshaped itself around the shafts. Braum swung his hammer down from the parapet, crushing a creature's spine. "TWO MORE LEFT AND RIGHT!" he yelled. Arlyn dragged a wounded soldier back by his collar. "Mara—get behind—" But Mara wasn't looking at the breach. She was looking past it. Into the forest. Her lips parted. Her breath hitched. And she whispered, barely audible: "It's here again."

Loran snapped to her. "Mara—look at me. Don't—" Her gaze tore away from him toward the trees as though pulled by a hook. "No," he said sharply, grabbing her wrist. "No. Stay with me." The humming inside her was louder today—vibrating her bones, rattling her teeth. It felt like a hand closing around her mind and squeezing, just gently enough not to break it. Her knees buckled. Loran caught her before she hit the boards. Ryn's head whipped toward them. "Not now," he muttered, abandoning his bracing spell. "Not now—" The wall creaked alarmingly as he dashed toward them.

Vale shouted his name. "Ryn, the wall—!" "It will fall whether I stand on it or not!" Ryn snapped. He reached Mara at the same moment another beast lunged up onto the railing from below. Loran pivoted and slashed, blade carving corruption from its jaw. The beast toppled off the walkway—but three more were pushing through the breach. "Mara," Ryn said urgently, cupping her cheek with a trembling hand. "Listen to me. Listen. Not to it." She gasped—a ragged, desperate inhale. "I can't—" "Yes, you can," he said. "You can. You have before." She shook her head, eyes squeezed shut. "It's stronger today. It—Ngh—" Her back arched. A ripple of green light flickered under her skin. Loran's heart stopped. "Ryn—" "Hold her," Ryn commanded.

Loran wrapped his arms around her shoulders, bracing her against him. Another beast climbed onto the wall. Braum hurled his hammer at it, knocking it back into the breach. "Ryn!" Vale shouted. "We need you—" "You'll live," Ryn said without looking. "She won't, if I don't do this." He slammed the butt of his staff against the boards. A pulse of blue magic rippled outward—not a blast, not a shield, but a cooling wave like plunging boiling metal into snow. Mara convulsed. The green under her skin flickered. Shuddered. Fought. Then dimmed. Her head fell against Loran's chest, breath sawing in and out. "I'm here," she whispered, voice cracked. "I'm here." Loran let out a breath he didn't realize he'd been holding. Ryn sagged slightly, catching himself on his staff. Then the wall behind them screamed.

Two support beams snapped in quick succession. The railing on their left dipped—hard. A whole section of walkway tilted. "MOVE!" Vale bellowed. Loran grabbed Mara and leapt toward the higher planks as the boards behind them sheared away. Braum caught Arlyn around the waist and yanked her clear just as a beast's claws raked the space where she'd been standing. Soldiers scrambled. Arrows clattered. Wood groaned. The southern wall—what remained of it—leaned dangerously inward. "We can't hold this!" a guard cried. "No," Vale agreed grimly. "Fall back! Form the inner line! Archers—cover them!"

Retreat was chaos. The beasts surged forward. Ryn, leaning heavily on his staff. Loran slung Mara's arm around his shoulders and half-carried her across the walkway. Braum planted himself at the top of the ramp and swung his hammer in brutal, efficient arcs, keeping the corrupted mass at bay long enough for civilians to flee. Arlyn dragged a wounded soldier down the steps, muttering curses with every breath. The wall gave a final tortured groan—and collapsed inward in a roar of timber, rubble and dust.

The courtyard filled with noise—the clang of steel, the roar of beasts, the shouts of desperate soldiers trying to form a coherent line. Vale shoved men into position with both hands. "SHIELDS UP! HOLD! HOLD NOW!" Arrows whistled overhead. The first wave of creatures hit the line. The shield wall bent but didn't break. Braum barreled into the fray with a bellow that drowned out the beasts' shrieks. Ryn, breath shaky, forced a small circle of blue light to hold around himself, Loran, and Mara. It flickered like a dying candle. Mara blinked up at him, sweat beading on her brow. "I can—I can fight." "No," Ryn said sharply. "You stay behind him." He nodded at Loran. "You do not touch the corruption today. You barely came back from it." "I can't just—" "You will," Ryn snarled, more fiercely than he'd ever spoken to her. "Because if you push again, it won't push back this time—it will grab you." She went still.

Loran tightened his grip on his sword. "Ryn. We're losing ground." "I know," Ryn whispered. Another section of the broken wall crumbled outward, sending dust into the sky. And then— Just as suddenly as it began— The beasts stopped pushing. They froze mid-lunge. Mid-snarl. Mid-crawl over the destroyed barricade. Every corrupted creature turned its head at once toward the northern ridge. The hairs on Loran's arms rose. Mara's breath hitched. Ryn's eyes widened. "Oh," he whispered. "Not now..." And without warning— Without a sound— Without a reason any of them could see—the entire corrupted swarm retreated. They flowed backward across the breach. Poured out of the yard. Melted into the trees. Gone. Not defeated. Not frightened. Called. Loran stared after them, chest heaving. "What the hell was that?" Braum demanded, hammer dripping black ichor. Ryn swallowed hard. "The giant," he said. "Another stumble." But his voice held no relief. Only dread.

The courtyard was a ruin. Timber wreckage. Splintered beams. Blood smeared across the dirt. Soldiers groaning where they'd fallen. The air reeked of smoke and corruption. But they were alive. They had held. Barely. Loran lowered Mara onto a low bench near the inner well. She pressed a shaking hand to her ribs and looked up at him. “Did we win?” she asked. He glanced at the ruined wall. At the trees. At the trembling soldiers. “No,” he said. “We survived.” “For today,” Ryn added quietly as he walked to them. “But this was not a battle. This was a reminder.” “Of what?” Loran asked. Ryn looked north, past the forest, past the valley, toward the mountain breathing its last. “That we are running out of time,” he said. “And out of ways to stop what’s coming.” Mara shivered. Loran sat beside her, exhausted. The southern wall crackled softly as another broken beam shifted in the wind. High above them, the sky darkened—not with storm, but with weight. Pressure. Waiting. Something in the world had tilted. And everyone in Ashwood Hold felt it. Even if they didn’t yet understand why. The countdown had truly begun.

CHAPTER SIXTY-FOUR
The Last Quiet Before the Storm

Ashwood Hold did not feel victorious. It felt hollow. Like a lung half-collapsed after a scream. Smoke drifted from the wreckage of the southern wall, curling around the broken beams like mourning veils. The wounded moaned softly under Arlyn's direction. Braum barked orders, voice hoarse. Vale paced the courtyard like a caged wolf. But the strangest thing—the most *unnatural*—was the quiet.

The corruption's horde had vanished into the forest without hesitation, as if obeying a pull stronger than hunger. As if summoned. Loran's skin crawled. He stood beside the well, running a cloth over his blade. His fingers shook with exhaustion and adrenaline. The sigil beneath his sleeve pulsed—not painfully, not urgently, but like it was *awake*. Watching. Mara sat on the stone rim beside him, still pale. She had cleaned the dried blood from her hands, but she looked as if she wanted to scrub away something deeper.

"Can you feel it too?" she asked softly. "Feel what?" Loran said. She stared toward the northern ridge. "The waiting." Loran swallowed. Because yes—he felt it. A tension humming beneath the world. A drawn bowstring, stretched to its breaking point. And he hated that she felt it too. Before he could answer, Ryn approached, leaning heavily on his staff. His eyes were dim—not glowing—their usual gray-blue clouded with exhaustion. But when he lifted them to the ridge—they flickered. A faint blue spark. Not power. Recognition. Mara straightened. "Is something moving?" "No,"

Ryn murmured. "Not yet." He stared at the mountains a long moment, jaw tight. "But it will."

Vale strode over, armor dented, face grim. "We need answers. Why did they retreat? What made them stop?" Ryn didn't look at him. "The corruption isn't focused on us anymore." "Then on what?" Vale demanded. Ryn's eyes sharpened—blue deepening. "On *him*." Loran's stomach dropped. "The giant." Ryn nodded once. "The guardian is slipping. Every time his strength wavers, the corruption surges. Those beasts didn't leave the battle... they *felt* him falter. They went to watch." "To watch?" Braum echoed, disgusted. "Watch WHAT?!" Ryn's fingers tightened around his staff until the carved wood creaked. "The moment he falls." Silence blanketed the hold. Even the wind seemed to still.

A sudden, hot pulse shot through Loran's arm. He hissed and clutched it. Mara grabbed his shoulder. "What? What is it?" The mark beneath his sleeve seared like a brand. "I... I don't know. It's reacting." Ryn whipped toward him, eyes flaring bright blue this time. "Let me see." Loran hesitated—but rolled up his sleeve. The mark was... different. The edges no longer looked inked—they glowed faintly, as if lit from beneath the skin. Thin black threads pulsed outward like veins rearranging themselves. Ryn inhaled sharply. "That is not good." Braum snorted. "Was anything today good?" Ryn ignored him, gripping Loran's arm with one hand. "This is the corruption responding to a shift in power. The giant is weakening. The balance is tilting. Your sigil—" "Is trying to do what?" Loran snapped. "Brace itself," Ryn whispered. "For what comes next."

Loran's heart thudded painfully. Mara's voice trembled. "Ryn... am I going to bear a mark?" Ryn looked at her then—and his face softened in a way that made Loran's chest tighten. "Mara... your danger does not lie in a mark." She went white. "Then in what?" Ryn hesitated—too long. Loran stepped between them. "Ryn. Tell us." Ryn exhaled. "The corruption doesn't want Loran's sigil." His blue gaze slid to Mara, heavy with dread. "It wants *her*."

Mara flinched like struck. Loran's fury surged. "She isn't the Vessel." "No," Ryn agreed quietly. "Not yet." His eyes glowed brighter—unmistakable power rising as fear sharpened him. "But the corruption senses the giant's death approaching, giving the corruption strength again. It is searching for the next vessel. It is reaching." His gaze fixed on Mara. "And she is the only one close enough, cracked enough, and strong enough for it to break into."

Mara's lips parted, breath shaking. Loran's sword arm tensed—not in fear. In *defiance.* "No," he said. "It doesn't get her." Ryn didn't look away. "Loran... the world does not care what you want." Loran stepped closer to Mara. Their shoulders touched. Her trembling steadied, just barely. "Then it can try," Loran said. "But it won't have her."

Mara swallowed hard. "If the corruption is searching for someone... and the beasts left to watch the giant..." Her voice faltered. "...then when he dies—" "It will come for you," Ryn finished. Her breath hitched. Loran grabbed her hand. "I won't let that happen." She looked at him, eyes dark and frightened. "I'm more afraid of what happens if you can't." Loran didn't have an answer for that. He only tightened his grip.

A horn blast cut the thick silence—short, sharp, frantic. Vale whipped around. "Report!" A scout sprinted into the courtyard, face bloodless, chest heaving. "Movement on the northern trail," he gasped. "Something—someone—is coming." Loran's blood iced. Vale barked, "Is it beasts? Remnants?" "No." The scout swallowed, shaking. "It walks like a man." Ryn's pupils contracted. "Is it tall?" he demanded. "Yes." "Eyes glowing?" "Yes." "And does the corruption recoil from it?" The scout nodded violently. "Yes. It... fears him." A single horrified breath left Mara. Loran's hand closed around his sword hilt. Ryn's voice was barely a whisper: "Teren."

Vale shouted, "POSITIONS! Everyone to the north wall! MOVE!" Ashwood erupted into motion again. Braum hefted his hammer. Arlyn grabbed bandages and a knife. Ryn's eyes blazed blue as he lifted his staff. Loran turned to Mara. She was staring at the ridge. Her lips parted. Her voice cracked: “He’s calling me again.” Loran grabbed her shoulders. “Stay with me.” She met his eyes—and for a moment she was fully there, breathing, present. Then her gaze drifted. Just slightly. Toward the ridge. Toward him. Loran’s heart slammed in his throat. “Mara—!” She blinked. Looked at him again. And whispered: “Don’t let go.” He didn’t. He wouldn’t. Not now. Not tonight. Not ever. But the world was already shifting beneath their feet. Above the valley, the mountain gave a long, deep, shuddering breath—as the giant slipped again. And somewhere in the forest—Teren smiled.

CHAPTER SIXTY-FIVE
The Night Splits Open

Night did not fall over Ashwood Hold. It *bled* into place. The sky darkened too quickly, swallowing the final threads of daylight as though someone had pressed a hand over the sun. Torches were lit early. Fires guttered strangely in the windless air, their light stretching long and thin across the courtyard. Every person felt it in their bones. Something was wrong. Very wrong.

Loran reached the northern wall with Mara and Ryn right behind him. Vale and Braum were already there, ordering archers along the parapet. The tension in the air was thick enough to taste—ozone and rot and something colder, like the breath of a cave too deep beneath the earth. Ryn planted his staff beside him. His eyes did not merely glow blue. They burned. "Stay behind me," he said quietly to Loran and Mara. "Whatever shape he arrives in, do not look into his eyes for long. The corruption speaks through them." Mara swallowed hard. "I can feel it already." Loran stepped closer to her until their shoulders touched. "You stay with me. No matter what happens." She nodded—but her gaze was already drifting to the ridge again.

Her heartbeat quickened under his hand. The corruption knew her name. It whispered at the edges of her thoughts like something tasting a locked door it intended to open. Then— The world *cracked.* A sharp line of sound ripped across the valley—like stone shearing under enormous pressure. Everyone froze. The tree line beyond the ridge shuddered. Split. And a long vertical seam of pale green light appeared in the darkness. Not bright. Not radiant. Sickly. A wound in the night. Arlyn whispered behind them, "Gods preserve us...” Braum lifted his hammer. “What in all the hells is that?” Ryn’s voice was low and certain. “A door.”

The seam of light widened with a wet, twisting sound. Shadows peeled back like torn fabric. And a figure stepped out of the line. Measured steps. Unhurried. Tall. Wrong. Teren.

Ashwood Hold fell silent enough to hear cloth brushing armor as men trembled. His silhouette was familiar, but his proportions were subtly off—the way reflections warped in bad glass. His eyes glowed green-black like lanterns beneath water. Veins of corruption crawled lazily across his arms and neck, pulsing in time with some heartbeat that wasn’t his own. He smiled. Not cruel. Not joyful. Just inevitable. “Evening,” he said, voice layered with too many echoes. “I thought I’d come before the real excitement begins.” Loran’s heart pounded so hard he felt each beat in his throat. Vale stepped forward with soldiers flanking. “You’ve had your warning. You’re not welcome here.” Teren tilted his head. “And yet here I am.” His gaze drifted across the parapet, sliding over faces, until— It stopped. On Mara. Her breath hitched violently. Loran moved instantly in front of her. Teren’s smile sharpened, amused. “Protective again, are we?” His eyes flicked briefly to Loran’s sleeve, where the sigil pulsed like a trapped star. “Both of you are waking up nicely.” Loran hissed through his teeth, “Don’t speak to her.” Teren ignored him.

The night cracked again. This time the ground shook beneath their feet. A low rumble rolled through the valley—long, mournful, like the groan of something unimaginably massive shifting under mountains. Ryn staggered, grabbing the wall. His eyes blazed bright blue as he looked sharply north. “No...” Vale shouted over the tremor, “What is that?!” Ryn’s face was stricken. “The guardian.” Mara gasped, pressing a trembling hand to her chest. “I feel it—” Loran grabbed her shoulders. “Don’t look—stay with me” But something had already seized her attention. Not a voice. Not a whisper. A *pull*. Like gravity. Like breath. Like recognition. Her knees buckled. Teren watched her with almost tender fascination.

"Oh," he murmured. "You felt that one, didn't you?" Mara's eyes squeezed shut, her breath breaking. "Loran—" "I'm here," he said fiercely. "Mara, stay with me." But she was trembling uncontrollably, as if her body wanted to turn toward Teren despite her will. Ryn shoved his staff between them, blue light erupting outward. "BACK!" he commanded. For a moment, Teren actually paused—his smile thinning as the blue glow clashed with the green in his eyes. "Well now," he murmured, "that's rude."

Without warning— A jagged line of green light tore downward across the clouds overhead. Not lightning. A rift. The air howled as if sucked upward. Torches guttered violently. Ashwood's walls vibrated under the pressure. Some of the archers cried out as shadows above them twisted into long, reaching shapes. Mara screamed. Her hands flew to her chest as though something inside her were trying to claw upward toward her throat. Loran caught her around the waist and nearly fell with her weight. Ryn shouted a word in the ancient tongue—blue flames erupting around his staff in spirals. Vale yelled, "SHIELDS UP! BRACE—!" Braum cursed, gripping the railing. "That's not normal sky behavior!"

Understatement of the century. Because the rift widened—and a pulse of power swept across the hold. Every corrupted creature, wherever they hid, answered with a distant roar. Teren lifted his head as if inhaling perfume. "Oh, there it is," he whispered. "The seal is thinning. The guardian stumbles. And when he falls..." His gaze slid back to Mara. "...you rise." Loran roared and charged. Not with thought. With instinct. Power burned under his skin—hot, bright, jagged—responding to his fury. His sigil flared like a brand, threads of black light flickering across his arm. Ryn shouted Loran's name—but too late. Teren raised a hand lazily. "Not yet." A pulse of green-black force erupted from his palm. The night split open. And everything fell into chaos.

CHAPTER SIXTY-SIX
Loran Stands Alone

The blast struck like a giant's open palm, a sweeping force that slammed into the parapet and hurled half the front line backward in a shower of splinters. Loran flew, hit the walkway hard, and slid until his boots caught on a beam. The air inside his chest vanished—stolen, punched out, he didn't know—but the moment he forced breath back in, he heard Mara scream his name. He pushed himself upright, vision streaked with black and green sparks.

Teren still stood at the breach in the night, framed by the wound of pale light spilling down the ridge. He looked bored. Annoyed. Almost pitying. "Always so quick to charge," he murmured, stepping casually over a shattered section of railing. "You were like that as a child too." Loran's hand tightened around his sword hilt. His sigil burned beneath his sleeve—not with pain, but with a trembling, frantic heat, like a horse about to break open. Ryn staggered to his feet behind him, staff blazing with violent blue fire. "Loran! Fall back! You can't—" But Teren flicked two fingers and the blue flames sputtered like blown-out candles.

Ryn stumbled, choking on air that suddenly felt too thick. Mara reached for him—then froze as another fracture of green light split the sky overhead. The corruption pulled at her again, stronger than ever, like invisible cords dragging her toward Teren's silhouette. Loran saw her knees buckle, saw her hands go to her skull as if her own mind were tearing open, and something inside him snapped. He stepped between her and everything else. "Stay away from her." His voice didn't sound like his own.

Teren's head tilted, amused. "I'm not here for her. Not yet." His smile widened. "I'm here for you." The ridge groaned—another long, shuddering sound, deep as mountains grinding. Ryn whispered hoarsely, "The guardian... he's falling..." Mara gasped as a wave of unseen pressure tore through the hold. People dropped to their knees. Torches blew sideways despite the still air. The wooden planks beneath them trembled as if the corruption itself pressed its weight upon Ashwood. Teren breathed it in. "Mmm. He's close now."

Loran stepped forward, sword raised, boots braced. "Face me." Teren sighed as though dealing with a stubborn child. "Loran, you do not understand what you are made for." "I don't care." "You will." The ground shivered. A pulse shot through Loran's arm, exploding up his veins in white-hot streaks. His knees nearly buckled from the force of it. The sigil wasn't responding to him anymore—it was responding to *the world.* Mara clutched Lila, who held her up with shaking arms. "Loran—don't—please—" But he couldn't stop. Something primal pushed him forward, something that felt both ancient and new, like a fire waking in a furnace that hadn't been lit for centuries.

Teren stepped lightly along the ruined stones, bare feet silent, eyes fixed with unsettling calm. "Do you feel it? The shift? The unraveling? When he dies, we all become what we were meant to be." Loran slashed. Fast. Clean. Desperate. Teren drifted aside, the blade missing him by the width of a breath. "Good," he murmured. "Again." Loran struck harder. Teren let the sword scrape his corrupted forearm, black-green ichor sizzling as it dripped—but he barely reacted. Instead he leaned close, whispering, "Hit me like you mean it." Loran drove his fist into Teren's jaw—sigil blazing, power crackling up his arm like molten lightning. Teren staggered. Actually staggered. His head snapped to the side, and he wiped a smear of dark fluid from his mouth, almost delighted. "There he is."

Loran charged again, blade swinging, heart pounding with a fury so bright it almost drowned out the trembling terror beneath it. Teren caught the blade in one hand. Stopped it cold. "This is why I came alone," he murmured. With a twist, he snapped the sword from Loran's grip and let it clatter to the walkway. Loran threw himself at him anyway—barehanded, wild. The sigil flared so brightly beneath his sleeve that the fabric scorched. Heat raced up his spine. For the briefest moment, the world tilted—bent—opened— As though something inside him tried to wake. But Teren struck first. A hand slammed into Loran's chest, not with brute force but with a wave of corruptive energy that hit like drowning in ice.

Loran flew backward, crashed onto the boards, skidded across broken timber. He tried to rise—failed—tried again. Teren walked toward him, slow, patient. "Stand up," he said softly. "I didn't come all this way to watch you crawl." Loran forced himself onto one knee, gasping, sweat dripping into his eyes. His mark pulsed, frantic, burning against his skin. Teren crouched beside him, head tilted in mock sympathy. "You're not ready. But you will be. When the guardian dies... everything inside you will wake. And then—oh, Loran—then you'll understand why you've always been pulled toward the dark."

"I'm nothing like you." "No," Teren said gently, placing one cold hand on the side of his face. "You're worse." Blue fire exploded between them—Ryn's staff slamming onto the boards, power crackling outward in a sharp wave that forced Teren to recoil. Ryn's eyes blazed sapphire-bright, his breath ragged. "Enough." Teren straightened, watching him with mild interest. "Interrupting again? You're going to burn yourself empty." "I will burn everything before I let you take them," Ryn snarled. His power surged. The blue blaze wrapped around him in a spiraling vortex, roaring like a windstorm trapped inside a heartbeat.

Teren smiled, almost fond. "Then let's test your limits, old one." Another fracture erupted overhead—wider, jagged—spilling a wash of pale green light that painted the battlements in sickly hues. Everyone felt it. A pull on the world. A collapse of something vast. Mara screamed, collapsing to her knees as the corruption clawed through her chest. Ryn's head whipped toward her. "No—!" Teren's smile grew slow and soft. "There she is..." Loran rose—shaking, powerless, furious—and stepped in front of Mara even as his legs buckled beneath him.

Teren watched him with a strange, almost reverent expression. "You keep standing," he murmured. "Even when everything inside you begs to fall. That's why you'll break beautifully." Ryn shouted a warning—but the words drowned under a new sound. A roar. Not bestial. Not human. A sound that tore the breath from every lung in Ashwood. A sound that came from far beneath the mountains. Deep. Final. The breath of something dying. The green guardian had expired. The night split open wider. And something ancient, hungry, and searching swept across the valley. Mara convulsed. The corruption surged toward her like a tide greets the shore. And Loran—barehanded, bleeding, half-conscious—stood alone between her and the darkness. The true fight had begun.

CHAPTER SIXTY-SEVEN
When the Giant Fell

The world did not break all at once—it peeled open, layer by layer, as though creation itself were taking a final rattling breath before collapsing inward; the ground quivered beneath Loran's boots, planks rattling, the stone foundations groaning as if they carried the weight of a mountain on their shoulders, and far beneath the valley the roar came again, deeper now, rougher, not a call but a dying exhale that sent birds crashing out of trees and cracked ice along the riverbanks in jagged, branching lines; the sky flickered green, then black, then green again, like a dying heartbeat struggling to keep pace with a world sliding into imbalance, and everyone marked or not on the wall sucked in a sharp, terrified breath as the bones under their skin answered to something old enough to remember the beginning of ages.

Loran staggered as a wave of force hit—not wind, not sound, something heavier, denser, a pressure that punched through bone and blood and memory; he tasted iron, ash, and something like ancient pine, something impossibly large and impossibly far away fading into nothing. Ryn dropped to both knees, staff clattering against the planks, his blue-lit eyes blown wide with something like grief, horror, awe, all braided together; when he whispered "He's gone..." the words trembled like a prayer left too long in a dying man's mouth.

The Green Giant—guardian, watcher, seal-bearer of the last thousand years—had died. And the world felt it. A shudder rippled across Ashwood, lifting dust, loosening stones, knocking cups from tables, sending animals bolting in frantic circles; the torches along the walls sputtered sideways, flames bending toward the ridge, straining as if the air itself had been commanded to change direction.

Loran pressed a hand to the boards to stay upright, but it wasn't the shaking that ruined his balance—it was the sudden, violent surge in his mark, an eruption of heat so fierce it felt like molten metal had been poured under his skin; he gasped, clawing at his sleeve as the sigil twisted and pulsed, its light leaking through the fabric in frantic bursts like something trapped inside him was trying to claw its way out. "Loran!" Ryn shouted, voice cracking, but Loran couldn't answer—he could barely breathe, barely see past the white fire streaking through his veins. And then Mara screamed. Not a frightened shout. Not a cry of pain. A raw, agonized, soul-deep scream that ripped across Ashwood like a blade drawn across a battlefield.

Loran's head snapped toward her. Mara collapsed forward, hands braced on the boards, her spine arched taut as a bowstring pulled too far; her eyes wide, her pupils blown, the whites ringed in burning green that pulsed in time with the tremors in the earth. Her breath came in sharp, broken gasps. "Something—something's pulling—" she choked out, fingers clawing at her chest, her throat, her ribs as if trying to stop something from crawling inside her. Lilan and Arlyn rushed toward her but a burst of green-black air exploded outward from Mara's body, hurling both women backward; they hit the wall, stunned but alive.

Ryn staggered toward Mara, blue fire surging up his staff, but Teren's laughter slid across the battlements like silk soaked in poison. "Ah," he murmured over the thunder of the dying world. "There she is." He moved through the chaos like a shadow given purpose, eyes locked on Mara with a rapture that sickened Loran to his core. The corruption around him writhed like black smoke made of veins and whispers, ribbons of shadow spilling from his arms, his spine, the corners of his smile, all reaching toward Mara as though greeting something long-awaited.

"Do you feel it, little spark?" Teren whispered as he stepped closer, and the wood beneath his feet darkened with every step. "Do you feel the space he left behind?" Mara cried out again—her body lifting off the boards for a breath as if the world were pulling upward on invisible strings attached to her bones; her hair lifted, whipping around her head though no wind touched anyone else; her throat strained with the force of the scream that tore from her. Loran lurched to his feet, vision swimming, chest burning, mark blazing bright enough now to shine through his torn sleeve in jagged lines of white-gold fire. "MARA!" he roared, stumbling toward her.

The corruption surrounding Teren writhed with sudden interest, turning toward Loran for a heartbeat before focusing back on Mara. "Stay back," Teren murmured without looking at him. "This isn't your moment." "Like hell it isn't," Loran snarled, dragging himself forward, step by agonizing step. His arm felt like it was splitting open from the inside, the heat unbearable, unfamiliar, wild. Ryn threw a bolt of brilliant blue light, blue fire cracking through the air like lightning, slamming into Teren's shoulder and knocking him half a step sideways—but Teren only smiled wider, the blast burning away the skin on his collarbone, revealing shifting shadows beneath before the flesh knitted back into something worse.

"Ryn," Teren murmured lovingly, "you never learn. You cannot stop what is already chosen." Ryn screamed something wordless—rage, grief, defiance—but the sound was drowned out by the sky itself ripping another fissure of green light across the valley, the clouds splitting open like torn fabric. A second pulse of corruption hit the valley. Hard. Strong enough to throw unmarked soldiers flat on their backs. Strong enough to crack stone along the watchtower's base. Strong enough to make Mara's body convulse violently, her scream breaking into a choked sob as her eyes rolled back and then snapped open again—this time glowing with a thin ring of shifting, pulsing green that beat like a second heartbeat inside her skull.

Something ancient looked through her for a single, terrible heartbeat. Loran reached her then—caught her face in both hands—her skin cold, sweat plastered to her hair, her breath ragged and fluttering like a candle about to go out. "Mara, stay with me, please—stay with me—look at me—" Her gaze flickered toward him, and for the smallest second he saw her. Truly her. The girl who laughed by the river. The girl who argued with fire in her eyes. The girl who looked at him like she saw the person he was trying to become.

Then her face twisted—pain, terror, something deeper ripping through her. "Loran..." she gasped. "It's—inside—something's—looking at me—" Her voice broke. "It knows me—" Loran pulled her against him, shielding her with his body against a force he didn't understand, didn't care to understand—he would tear it out of the world if he had to. "You don't let it in," he whispered fiercely. "You don't let it take anything—you stay with me—you stay—" He didn't realize he was crying until her hand brushed his cheek. Not tender. Not steady. Desperate. "I'm trying," she whispered hoarsely. "I'm trying—" The third pulse hit. The one that mattered. The one the world had been bracing for. The one born from the exact moment the Green Giant's heart stopped beating beneath the mountains.

Ashwood Hold fractured with the force of it. Boards split. Stones cracked. Torches died. The sky went fully black-green. And Mara— Mara screamed as the corruption rushed into her like a tide rushing into a shattered dam. Her back arched violently, her eyes burning with bright, unnatural green, her mouth open in a soundless, airless howl. A shockwave of corruptive force burst from her spine, blasting outward like an explosion of shadow and poison. Teren whispered, in reverence and triumph, "The Vessel awakens." And Loran—holding her, helpless and shaking—felt the moment he began to lose her. Forever.

CHAPTER SIXTY-EIGHT
The Mistake of the Wise

Ryn felt the world tear open the moment the guardian's final breath echoed through the valley; it punched through his ribs like a fist, tearing something loose inside him that had been anchored for five centuries, and as Mara screamed and the corruption surged toward her like a tidal wave of ancient hunger, he understood—truly understood—that if he hesitated even a heartbeat she would be lost, claimed, hollowed, turned into the Vessel before the living could take another breath.

He shoved himself to his feet, ignoring the burning in his lungs, ignoring the terror clawing up his spine, ignoring the pain crackling along the carved runes of his staff; blue fire erupted from him in a violent column, tearing upward in a flash of sapphire light that bathed the entire wall in brilliance, turning every shadow into a vanishing stain—but Teren only smiled at him across the chaos, expression soft and pitying, as though he were watching an old man try to hold back a tide with trembling hands.

"Don't," Teren murmured, barely audible over the storm of sound consuming Ashwood, but the whisper reached Ryn like a prophecy already fulfilled. "If you touch her now, you'll break her." Ryn didn't listen. Couldn't. Because Mara's scream had changed. It wasn't raw anymore. It wasn't human. It was thinning, stretching, unraveling, becoming the kind of sound something makes when its body no longer knows what shape it's supposed to hold; and Loran, on his knees beside her, clutching her as if his grip alone kept her soul tethered, was shouting her name with a voice shredding itself at the edges, begging, pleading, promising anything if she would just look at him again—not through him, not past him, but at him.

Ryn's heart seized. He had seen that look once before—long ago—on another battlefield, when someone he loved reached for him with that same hollowing terror in their eyes as corruption pulled at their bones. He had failed once. He would not fail again. The blue fire around him surged—wild, uncontrolled, roaring against the green-black corruption swirling around Mara like a storm given breath. "Ryn!" Arlyn screamed from somewhere behind him, voice cracking. "Stop—you don't know—" But he did. Or he thought he did. He lifted his staff, runes pulsing like a heartbeat on the verge of rupture, and slammed it down with every ounce of power he had ever held, every stolen year he had lived past his natural span, every memory of every soul whose death he had carried into the present.

The wall ignited in blue. A wave of cold, crystalline force exploded outward, a perfect dome of shimmering light meant to sever corruption from host, to slam shut the door the world had just opened, to save her. For the space of a single breath, everything froze. Mara's scream caught in her throat. Loran's arms tightened around her. Even Teren's expression flickered—shock, then pity, then something darker—right before the dome reached Mara's body. Then the mistake revealed itself. The dome didn't cleanse. It cracked. Ryn felt it instantly—the wrong resonance, the sharp discord between the blue of his magic and the green of the Vessel's forming bond—and his stomach dropped as though falling into a glacial pit. The forces didn't cancel. They collided.

The resulting backlash detonated. Mara was thrown backward from Loran's grasp, her body arching in midair as a blast of green black fire erupted from her chest, shattering Ryn's dome from the inside; blue shards of magic splintered outward like glass tearing through the sky. Ryn flew back, slammed into the parapet, blood spraying from his mouth as his staff cracked in half. The shockwave that burst from Mara flung Loran to the ground so hard the boards beneath him splintered; he scrambled up immediately, dazed, reaching for her as she tumbled across the walkway, skidding to a stop near the wall, her fingers twitching, eyes rolled back, lips parted in shallow, broken gasps.

Teren stepped toward her slowly, reverently, corruption swirling around him like a cloak caught in a storm. “Ryn,” he said softly, “you fool.” Ryn wheezed, dragging himself upright on trembling arms, eyes wide with horror as he stared at Mara’s trembling form. “I—I didn’t mean— I was trying to—” “Save her?” Teren’s head tilted in pity. “You shoved her closer. The Vessel cannot be forced back by mortal hands. All you’ve done is tear her open faster.” Mara convulsed violently, her back arching off the ground, veins along her neck glowing faint green under her skin; her mouth opened in a silent scream as a ring of corruption flared across her eyes again—brighter now, more certain, as though Ryn’s intervention had not repelled the corruption, but fed it.

Loran reached her then, pulling her into his arms again, hands shaking so hard he could barely hold her, his voice breaking with every word. “Mara, please—Mara, stay with me—open your eyes—look at me—don’t leave—don’t—” Her fingers twitched against his chest, weak, trembling, searching. “L-Loran...” she breathed, barely audible. “It’s... loud...” Teren smiled—wide, triumphant, tender in the most horrifying way. “Yes. It’s calling you. And thanks to your wise friend, it can hear you now.” Ryn collapsed, blue magic sputtering out around him like dying embers, eyes full of devastation deeper than any wound he had ever taken. “I didn’t mean to,” he whispered, voice breaking. “Gods forgive me—I didn’t mean to.”

But forgiveness wasn’t coming. Not tonight. Not after this. Because Mara—the girl who had stood against monsters, who had laughed by firelight, who had held the world together with stubbornness and hope—was slipping, fast, her breathing erratic, her pulse flickering beneath Loran’s trembling fingers as the corruption seeped deeper into her soul in the space Ryn had torn open. She was becoming the Vessel. And the worst part was this: Ryn realized he had just made the moment of her loss arrive sooner.

CHAPTER SIXTY-NINE
The Whisper That Wasn't Hers

Mara's body shuddered once, sharp as a pulled thread snapping, and then she went still in Loran's arms—not limp, not unconscious, but held in a terrifying suspension, her breath hitching in shallow, uneven gulps as if something inside her was deciding whether she deserved to keep breathing at all. Loran clutched her tighter, his fingers digging into the fabric of her tunic, knuckles white, heart pounding so violently he thought it might split open; her skin was cold, colder than the morning frost that never came, and as he pressed his forehead to hers, whispering her name again and again, he felt the faintest tremor ripple through her—not human, not familiar, but like a second heartbeat beneath her own, slow, deliberate, ancient.

The corruption answered. A low vibration hummed through the wall beneath their feet, across the planks and iron nails and into their bones, a soundless call that pulled at Mara's ribs like puppet strings. "No," Loran rasped, pulling her closer, trying to shield her as if that alone could keep the world out. "You don't get to take her. Not her. Not now. Not ever." But the ring of green around her pupils pulsed once, glowing faintly like embers trying to become flame, and for a moment he saw something staring at him through her gaze—a presence measuring him, testing him, deciding whether he was an obstacle or a tool.

Ryn staggered toward them, one hand pressed to his chest, the other dragging the broken staff like a wounded limb; his eyes flickered weakly with dull blue light, but the fire was sputtering, choking on whatever catastrophic backlash he had triggered.

"Loran," he gasped, "you must let go—I can still try—I can still pull it back—if we sever the tether now, before it cements—before it shapes her—" "I'm not letting go of her!" Loran shouted, turning on him with a fury he had never felt, the mark on his arm flaring beneath his sleeve like molten lava. "You nearly killed her!" Ryn flinched, the truth of it landing like a blow, but before he could speak, Mara's fingers twitched against Loran's throat, sliding up with slow, eerie precision until her hand rested over the pulse hammering beneath his jaw.

Her eyes opened. But they weren't Mara's eyes—not fully. The pupils were too wide. The irises ringed with faint threads of green-gold light pulsing inward like a tide drawing breath. Her voice, when it came, was quiet, but layered—her tone beneath something deeper, almost resonant, the way wind passing through a hollow tree carries the echo of a voice that isn't there. "Lor-an," she whispered, syllables broken, as though her tongue was learning how to shape the world again. His heart clenched. "I'm here," he whispered. "I'm right here." But she didn't look at him with recognition. She looked at him the way Teren had looked at the hold—curious, measuring, hungry in a way that wasn't hunger for food or blood but for *meaning*, for connection, for possession. And then she whispered something that turned the entire hold to ice.

"You were not chosen." The words slithered into the air like smoke, too soft for anyone but Loran to hear—and yet every person on the wall seemed to feel them. Loran swallowed hard. "Mara, listen to me—don't let it speak through you—fight it—come back—" She blinked, slowly, as if trying and failing to remember what blinking meant, and murmured, "You are loud." A single tear slid down her cheek—her tear, human, real—and Loran's breath shattered because it meant she was still in there, fighting, trapped behind whatever force was crawling through her veins.

Ryn dropped to both knees now, shaking violently, his palms pressed against the boards as he stared at her with dawning horror. "No," he whispered. "This can't be happening. She shouldn't be hearing the call yet. The Vessel should not speak until the seal breaks fully. I misjudged it—I thought we had more time—I thought—" His voice broke, old and fragile, and for the first time since Loran had known him, he looked his age—a man centuries past his prime, carrying the weight of mistakes he had never confessed.

Mara's lips moved again. "So loud," she whispered, and her gaze drifted over Loran's shoulder as if someone else stood behind him. He turned. No one was there. Not physically. But Teren was already smiling from across the wall, corruption curling around his fingers like smoke. "She hears it," he said softly, reverently. "The beginning. The first thread being woven." Loran snarled, "Stay back!" Teren's smile widened. "Why? You want to hold her, don't you? To save her? But you can't even hear what she hears. You can't feel what she feels. You are outside the door. She is inside. And the door... is opening."

Mara's body convulsed again, a violent jerk that knocked wind from Loran's lungs; her fingers dug into his shoulder with inhuman strength, nails scraping through fabric, pulling him toward her as her forehead pressed against his collarbone. Her voice—both hers and the other—murmured, "Too many voices... too much light... make them stop..." Loran froze. Light? His mark flared—red exploding beneath his sleeve like a star someone had cracked open—and Mara shrieked so violently the boards beneath them splintered. The red. The mark. *It was hurting her*. Loran ripped his arm away instinctively, clutching it to his chest as if afraid to burn her again. "No," he whispered, horrified. "No, no, no—Mara, I'm sorry, I didn't mean—I didn't—" She collapsed against him, trembling uncontrollably.

Teren's smile sharpened. "She cannot bear your light," he said. "You are not meant for her. Not anymore." Pain—white-hot, animal pain—ripped through Loran's chest. Ryn pushed himself upright with a sound that was half sob, half growl. "Loran," he rasped, "you must listen—your mark is tied to the last of the guardian's power—it is opposite to the Vessel—you cannot touch her with it—not until—" "Until what?" Loran choked. "Until she's gone?" "Until you learn to *shape* it!" Ryn shouted, blue fire flickering weakly in his eyes. "Until you learn control!" But Mara stirred again before he could say more—lifting her head, eyes unfocused, as though seeing something beyond all of them. Her lips parted. She whispered a single word. Not Loran's name. Not help. Not pain. A direction. "Northern."

Loran's stomach dropped. Ryn paled. Teren smiled like a man receiving a long-awaited confirmation. "The seal," Ryn whispered, broken. "She can feel the rupture. The northern pass is thinning." Mara's breath hitched. She whispered again, softer, "Northern... calling..." Teren stepped forward once, almost tenderly. "She will walk soon." Loran's fury snapped like bone. "Over my dead body." Teren's expression softened into something almost mournful. "If it comes to that," he murmured, "yes."

Mara collapsed entirely then, her body going slack in Loran's arms—not unconscious, but emptied, drained, as though the whisper had taken everything she had left. Loran cradled her, shaking, terrified. Ryn stared at her as if witnessing his greatest failure take shape. Teren watched her as if witnessing the birth of a prophecy. And the corruption, sensing its Vessel awakening, pressed closer around the walls, breathing in rhythm with her shallow, trembling breaths. The night did not end. It only deepened.

CHAPTER SEVENTY
The Night That Broke Ashwood

The night did not settle after the whisper left Mara's lips; it hung over Ashwood like something wounded and waiting to see how much more it could hurt them before dawn. The air on the wall tasted wrong, too thick, every breath a drag through smoke and iron and cold stone, and for a long, shuddering heartbeat no one moved at all. Loran knelt in the center of it, Mara cradled against his chest, her weight both too light and unbearably heavy, as if at any moment she might simply slip through his arms and fall straight through the world.

Her eyes were closed now, lashes dark against skin gone too pale, but he could still feel the tremor in her muscles, the stuttering, off-beat flutter of her pulse where his fingers pressed against the side of her throat; under his hands she felt like a held-back storm, like something that had not decided whether it belonged to the sky or the sea. His own heart hammered so hard it hurt. The red mark beneath his sleeve throbbed in time with it, a dull, aching burn that threatened to become something brighter if he let it.

"Mara," he whispered, voice raw, the single word scraping his throat on the way out. "Mara, stay with me. Come on. Please." She did not answer. The last thing she had given him was that not-hers whisper, those words that slid between his ribs like a knife—You were not chosen—and even now they seemed to echo under his skin, bouncing off bone, carving doubt into places he had thought were solid. He wanted to shake them off, to blame the thing inside her, to curse Teren until the night cracked apart, but the hurt sat in him all the same, small and stupid and human beside the greater terror of losing her.

Around them the wall began to remember that it was full of other people. Someone sobbed. A bow clattered from nerveless fingers. Vale's hoarse voice rasped from further down the parapet, trying and failing to find its command edge. "Archers—hold—hold—nobody fires without my word—" It hardly seemed to matter. Teren stood in the broken place between sky and ridge, framed by the lingering smear of sickly green light like a figure painted on cracked glass. The seam he had stepped through still oozed faint radiance, pulsing slowly as though drawing breath. Corruption swirled lazily around his ankles and along his arms, coils of shadow and vein-dark tendrils tasting the air; the wood beneath his bare feet was already greying and splintering, black veins spider-webbing out with every shift of his weight.

He looked, infuriatingly, like he might have been out for a stroll and simply wandered into the end of the world by accident. His gaze never left Mara. "Do you hear it now?" he asked quietly, not raising his voice and yet somehow every soul on the wall heard him. "The north. The breach. The empty place where something old once lay. It calls very softly at first. A hum under the teeth. A pressure behind the eyes. Then a direction. Then a command." His eyes flicked briefly to Loran, and the corners of his mouth curved. "You should be honored. You get to watch the choosing." Loran's fingers tightened in Mara's tunic until the fabric creaked.

"She is not a thing to be chosen," he said, the words scraped raw, his jaw clenched so hard it ached. "She is not yours." "Not mine," Teren agreed with a faint, infuriating gentleness. "Never mine. I am only a herald. A servant. A voice." His head tilted. "You, of all people, should understand that." "Shut up," Loran hissed, because if he let the rest of that sentence sink in he was going to be sick. Behind him, wood creaked as something heavy shifted; Braum hauled himself upright with a guttural curse, leaning on his hammer like it was the only thing keeping him tethered to the world. Blood streaked his temple, his beard, one arm hanging a little too loose at the shoulder, but his eyes still burned when they fixed on Teren.

"If he's just a voice," Braum growled, "can we cut his-damned throat and be done with it?" "You can try," Teren said pleasantly. "It won't change what's already waking." "Try anyway," Braum muttered, but his feet did not move, like even his stubborn muscles understood that the thing in front of him was less a man and more an announcement. Arlyn scrambled along the planks, half crawling, half staggering, her healer's satchel dragging behind her, Ryn's broken staff left where it had fallen. Her eyes were wide and wild, tracking only two things: the girl limp in Loran's arms and the old man crumpled against the parapet. "Move," she snapped at a pair of soldiers who were frozen in place, shoving between them without caring that her hands shook.

She dropped to her knees beside Ryn first, fingers already probing for broken ribs, for bleeding that wouldn't stop, for signs that his heart had finally decided this was all too much. "Don't you dare die now," she hissed under her breath. "Not after everything. I will drag you back by your beard from wherever you go, do you hear me?" Ryn coughed, a thin thread of blood spilling from the corner of his mouth, and grimaced. "Your... bedside manner... deteriorates under pressure," he managed, voice a rough scrape. His eyes, when they fluttered open, were dulled, the blue light inside them burned down to embers.

"I told you not to—" Arlyn began. "Yes," he rasped. "You were right. You may... inscribe that on a stone... if we survive." His gaze slid past her, dragging toward Loran and Mara. When he saw them, something in his face caved in. Not physically—his bones remained where they were—but an old, ancient scaffolding of certainty and hope seemed to crack behind his eyes. "Mara," he whispered, and the single name sounded like a confession. Teren clicked his tongue softly. "You did this," he said, almost kindly, inclining his head toward Ryn. "You tore her open quicker than the corruption could have managed alone. That dome…" He exhaled, actually admiring. "Impressive. Stupid. But impressive. You tried to force shut a door that was never yours to hold. And in doing so, you widened it."

Ryn flinched as though struck, but his gaze did not leave Mara. "There was no time," he said hoarsely. "If I had waited she would already be gone." "She is already gone," Teren replied, and for all the softness in his tone the words fell like stones. Loran's head snapped up, fury cutting through the fog of fear. "She's breathing," he snarled. "She's here. She's listening. She cried. She is not gone." As if answering him, a tiny sound slipped from Mara's throat—a breath that hitched on its way in, catching on something sharp inside. Her fingers twitched weakly against his chest, curling in the torn fabric. For a heartbeat her lashes trembled, and he felt, more than saw, the tiny effort of her trying to swim up through whatever black water she was drowning in.

"There," he said, voice breaking around the one fragile proof he had. "There. You see? She's fighting." Teren watched her with a look that might, on anyone else, have been called fond. "I know," he said softly. "That's why she was chosen." The red heat in Loran's arm surged at that, as if the word itself were a spark thrown into dry kindling, and for the first time since the pulses began the pain tipped from bearable to blinding. Fire lanced up from the mark, up his forearm, his elbow, his shoulder, searing nerve and muscle and thought. He choked, doubling over instinctively, shielding Mara even as his own body buckled. The mark flared through his sleeve in bright, bloody lines, its shape no longer just an inked mark but a burning brand, light bleeding between the threads of his shirt as though his skin could no longer contain it. The air around his arm distorted with heat.

Every person near him felt the sudden, sharp change—the way the wrongness of the corruption met something opposite, something that was not clean but different, and both recoiled. Black tendrils of shadow that had been lazily edging along the planks toward Mara jerked back, hissing like steam hitting forged metal. The nearest knot of corruption around Teren's feet shuddered, its edges fraying for a heartbeat. Teren's smile faltered. Just a fraction. His eyes snapped to Loran's arm, pupils narrowing. "Ah," he breathed. "There it is." Ryn, still half supported by Arlyn, dragged himself to a sitting position and stared, the blue in his eyes flaring despite his exhaustion. "Loran," he rasped. "Listen to me. You must calm it—you must breathe—if you let it run wild it will burn through you like oil—" "It hurts her," Loran choked, every word squeezed between clenched teeth.

He could feel it, the way the flare of red in his arm sent a shiver through Mara's body, the way her breath hitched harder, the way her brow furrowed even in unconsciousness. The same force that pushed the corruption back also scraped against whatever thread had sunk into her. It was like trying to hold a torch close enough to light someone's way without burning their skin. "I can't—if I let it—" "You will kill her if you touch her with it," Teren said matter-of-factly. "Your light is poison to what lives inside her now. That is its purpose." He tilted his head, fascinated. "Do you know what you are, Loran?" "Shut. Up." "You cling to her as if you were meant to save her," Teren continued, as though Loran hadn't spoken. "But you were never forged to be her shield. You were forged to be her opposite. A weight on the other side of the scale. When one rises, the other must burn."

His gaze flicked toward Ryn, and something cruel and amused twisted through his expression. "Isn't that right, old one? Tell him. Tell him what mark he bears." Ryn's hands shook where they gripped his knees. For a long moment he said nothing, his jaw working, his throat bobbing as if the words refused to come. Arlyn looked between them, confusion and dread knitting in her brow. "Ryn," she said. "What is he talking about?" The wizard closed his eyes briefly, drawing in a breath that sounded like it scraped his ribs on the way down. When he opened them again, the blue in them was not bright but steady, a hard, thin line of resolve.

"The giants were not the only seals the first war left behind," he said quietly. "They were the great ones. The anchors. But the world is not foolish enough to rest all its weight on a single pillar. In some bloodlines—in some lands—their power left... splinters. Shards of the same force, sleeping under the skin. Most never woke. They were never needed." His gaze fixed on Loran's burning sleeve. "Yours did." Loran stared at him, breathing hard, feeling the fire in his arm pulse in time with his own anger. "What does that make me?" Ryn hesitated. Teren did not. "A counterweight," he said. "A breaker. The red mark is not corruption and it is not purity. It is rupture. It is what the world shaped to tear us down if we ever broke our chains again."

He smiled, slow and delighted, as if he had just found a particularly sharp knife in an old drawer. "You are the knife at our throat, little ember. That's why the corruption tried to kill you before your mark woke. That's why you survived when you should have broken." Loran's stomach lurched. For a dizzy heartbeat all he could think was that he wanted to claw the skin from his arm and throw it into the river, to be free of whatever fate had been tucked into his blood before he took his first breath. Then his gaze dropped to Mara's pale face, to the faint shadow of green and black that still clung to the veins at her throat, and the world narrowed back down to a single point.

"If I am a knife," he said, each word ground out like it hurt, "then I will cut you out of her." "You'll cut her," Teren said. "That's the beauty of it. The Vessel and the Blade were never meant to touch. That was the giants' burden—to hold the balance between them so they would never meet. But your giant is dead." The words rolled through the air like thunder muffled by distance, but everyone felt the truth of them in their bones; the tremors underfoot, the strange tilt in the wind, the way the sky itself seemed a little sicker with every passing breath. Ryn's shoulders slumped. "He was supposed to last another generation," he whispered, more to himself than to anyone. “We were supposed to have more time.”

“Time,” Teren echoed, looking almost amused again. “You fragile things always think you have more of it than you do.” Vale finally found his voice, rough and frayed but still carrying the spine of a commander. “Enough,” he snapped, stepping forward with his sword drawn, the tip steady despite the sweat shining along his brow. “You walk into my hold, you tear my people, you talk about fate like it’s a game. I don’t care what chains you broke or what giant died. You stand here as a threat to my walls, to my people, and to her.” He jabbed his chin toward Mara. “So hear this: if you take one more step, every arrow on this wall finds you.” His hand went up, and along the parapet archers lifted their bows in a trembling but unified motion, strings creaking as they drew.

Teren looked at him as one might look at a particularly tenacious insect. “You already tried arrows,” he reminded him gently. “They do not stick.” “Then we’ll keep shooting until one does,” Vale said. “If my men die doing it, they die on their feet. That’s more than I can say for you.” For the first time, a flicker of honest irritation crossed Teren’s face. The corruption around his feet stirred, rising a little higher, licking at his calves like dark water. “Your defiance is tedious,” he said. “Valor does not impress the corruption, Captain. It simply makes your screams more satisfying.” He took a single, slow step forward. “Loose!” Vale roared.

The air filled with the snap of bowstrings and the hiss of arrows slicing through the dark. They flew in a line that would have been beautiful in any other world, a sharp, dark rain aimed straight at the thing standing in the breach. Shadows surged up to meet them. The corruption coiled and thickened, fog becoming tendon, smoke becoming muscle. Arrows vanished into it with wet, muffled sounds, some dissolving midair, others dropping to the stone as shafts of blackened rot. One managed to pierce Teren’s shoulder—only for the flesh to ripple and reform, spitting the shaft back out like a splinter. He did not even flinch. “Stop,” he said, and the word carried. The archers’ hands locked on their strings as if their fingers had frozen. Some tried to draw again, faces contorted with effort, but their muscles refused.

“You see?” Teren continued calmly. “You can do nothing I have not already died to. Your walls will fall when we are ready. Your captain will scream when we are ready. Your hammer will break when we are ready.” His gaze slid back to Mara—always to Mara. “But she...” He took another step, savoring every inch. “She must not be rushed.” Ryn forced himself up higher, Arlyn’s hand braced at his back, the shattered half of his staff scraping against the planks as he dragged it toward him. “You’re not taking her,” he said, and though his voice shook, the blue light in his eyes flared in a sharp, clear line. “If the Vessel walks north, it will be when I say, not you. The old treaties still hold. You have no right to breach this hold.”

Teren laughed softly. “Old treaties,” he repeated. “Ryn, the ink on those treaties dried on bones no one remembers. The giants who signed them are dust. The gods who watched have turned their faces away. All that remains is hunger and the shapes it chooses to wear.” “Even hunger obeys rules,” Ryn snarled. “Or it chokes on what it tries to swallow.” The broken staff in his hand flared briefly, blue sparks snapping along the carved runes, but the light guttered quickly; he had burned too much in that failed dome, poured too much of himself into the wrong shape. His well was nearly empty and everyone could see it. Teren did too.

“You are finished for tonight,” he said. “You cannot stop me and you know it.” He looked down at Mara again, at the faint green threads under her skin. “But as I said—I will not take her. Not yet. The Vessel must choose to walk. Dragging her would waste her. She must rise when called, on her own feet, with her own grief.” His smile went soft and terrible. “We are very patient.” Something in Loran snapped at that, a soundless fracture inside his chest. “Then hear me,” he said, his voice low and shaking, the words trembling not with fear but with a fury so deep it felt like it came from the same earth that had just lost a giant.

He shifted, cradling Mara closer with one arm while his other hand clawed at his sleeve, ripping the fabric away from his mark. The night drank in the sight of it—the red mark bared to the cold air, lines jagged and bright like fresh cuts that refused to bleed. The skin around it was raw and flushed, veins standing out dark beneath, as if his body did not quite know how to hold what was inside it. Heat radiated from it, a dry, furnace heat that made the corruption nearest him shiver. "You say the Vessel must walk," he said. "You say she will answer when you call." He lifted his gaze to the torn piece of sky around Teren, to the faintly pulsing seam, to the way the world seemed to lean toward it. "Then listen to this: if she goes north, I go with her. If she walks into your darkness, I will burn in it. You will not have her alone."

Teren watched him, fascinated, like he was watching a moth fly into a forge. "You will kill her," he said again, almost gently. "Then I will learn not to," Loran snapped. He turned his head, pinning Ryn with his glare. "You said I had to shape it. Then teach me. Now. Tomorrow. Until my bones break. I don't care. I am not letting this thing in my arm hurt her without also hurting you." His gaze snapped back to Teren. "All of you." For a long moment, something like silence fell, though the world was anything but quiet; the ground still trembled faintly underfoot, the sky still bruised green at the edges, somewhere beyond the ridge a chorus of distant corrupted voices still howled in answer to their herald. But on the wall, between the boy with the burning arm and the man made of borrowed flesh, there was a held breath.

Then Teren smiled. Not the mockery, not the soft pity. Something sharper. "Good," he said. "Hate us. Shape it around that. It will make the fall more interesting." He stepped backward, not turning away from them, retreating into the pale smear of light. The corruption around his legs rose higher, swallowing his calves, his knees, his hips, as if the night were welcoming something beloved home. "I will come back when she can stand without shaking," he promised, and the promise felt like a curse. "When the north pulls so hard she cannot sleep. When your lessons have progressed just enough that you believe you can save her. When the rest of your walls have rotted a little more." His gaze dipped to Mara one last time. Something that might almost have been affection passed over his face. "Dream of the northern pass, little Vessel," he murmured. "Listen for the river under the ice. When you hear it clearly, walk." With that, the seam behind him flared, a sudden vertical wound of sickly green, and then snapped shut like a mouth. The light went out. The corruption that had been coiled thickest around him thinned, receding along the stones, slinking back into cracks and shadows, leaving only a faint greasy residue on the wood where it had pressed hardest.

The pressure in the air eased by a degree, enough for archers to gasp and drop their bows, for Braum to sag against the railing, for Vale to finally lower his sword. No one cheered. The absence he left felt worse than his presence. It felt like the silence after a knife is driven in. Loran realized he had been holding his breath and exhaled shakily, his whole body trembling now that the immediate storm had passed. The red in his arm dimmed from blinding to bearable, the mark still hot but no longer trying to claw its way out of his skin. The loss of that sharp pain made room for a hundred smaller ones—bruises, cuts, the ache in his shoulders from holding Mara too tight.

He looked down at her. She lay limp against him, lashes still, lips parted just enough to let shallow breaths through. The faint green ring that had rimmed her pupils was gone for now, buried deep, but he knew better than to think that meant anything had truly left. Whatever had knocked on the inside of her skull now had her scent. "Is she—?" Arlyn began, voice small. Loran swallowed hard. "She's alive," he said. "For now." "For now," Ryn echoed, and there was so much guilt wrapped around the words that Loran almost flinched.

The old man dragged himself closer, his steps uneven, one hand on the wall, the other clutching the broken staff. When he reached them, he sank to his knees opposite Loran with a muttered groan, joints protesting. "Let me see her," he said quietly. Loran's first instinct was to clutch her tighter, to bare his teeth like a cornered animal. "You've done enough," he snapped. "You nearly—" "Yes," Ryn cut in sharply. "I nearly killed her. I nearly saved her. I failed at both. Do you think that is news to me?" His voice cracked on the last word. He forced himself to steady it. "But I am the only one in this valley who has seen a Vessel chosen and lived long enough to talk about it. If you want her to have any chance at all, you let me look."

The words were a blade laid on the table between them. Loran stared at him for a long, hot second, lungs heaving. Then, slowly, he loosened his grip just enough for Ryn to place trembling fingers against Mara's temple, her throat, the center of her chest. Blue light flickered weakly around his fingertips, not a blaze now but a pale halo, like the last frost clinging to the edge of a leaf. He closed his eyes, his brow furrowing, as if listening to something far away. "The tether is not complete," he murmured at last. "The corruption has its hook in her, but it does not yet wear her name. It whispers. It does not command." He exhaled in something like relief and despair tangled together. "We have time." "How much?" Loran asked, and the hoarseness in his voice made him sound older than he was. Ryn opened his eyes and looked toward the north, toward the unseen pass and the place where a giant's heart had just stopped beating. His gaze was distant and haunted. "Not enough," he said. "But more than none."

Vale scrubbed a hand over his face, leaving a streak of grime across his cheek. "Then we use every breath of it," he said, forcing his tone back into the shape of command. He straightened, turning to the soldiers who still clustered along the wall in shell-shocked silence. "Get the wounded down," he ordered. "Check the supports. I want eyes on every post and every gate. If anything moves out there, I hear about it before it takes a second step. No one stands watch alone. No one sleeps without someone beside them." Braum grunted in acknowledgment, already limping toward the nearest ladder, shouting at the nearest recruit to stop staring and start moving. Arlyn squeezed Ryn's shoulder once, hard enough to hurt, then set about triaging with new, brittle efficiency, her hands already reaching for bandages, salves, whatever small work she could do to hold back the larger tide. People moved. Slowly, stiffly, like their limbs were thawing from ice.

The wall began to empty in staggered clusters, some down the ladders to the courtyard, some along the parapet to other posts. The noise of it—boots on wood, murmured voices, the clink of armor—should have sounded normal. It didn't. Everything seemed too loud and too far away at once. Loran stayed kneeling where he was, the world narrowing to the stretch of planks beneath him and the girl in his arms. Ryn remained opposite him, staring at Mara as if trying to memorize every line of her face before something else took it over.

"You said you'd teach me," Loran said quietly, not looking up. "To shape it. To stop it from hurting her." Ryn's mouth twisted. "I said I would try," he corrected. "You may burn out before you learn. Your mark is not meant to be gentle. It was made to cut, not to cradle." "Then I'll learn to make it do both," Loran said. "Or I'll die trying. Either way, it won't sit in me useless while she..." His voice broke. He swallowed. "While she becomes theirs." At that, Mara stirred faintly, a tiny whimper escaping her lips, as if some part of her heard the word and recoiled.

Loran bent his head, his forehead resting against hers, closing his eyes as tightly as he could, as if he might press his will into her skull by force alone. "You're not theirs," he whispered. "Do you hear me? I don't care how loud they are. You are not theirs." He felt rather than saw the way Ryn watched him, a mix of pity and something harder. "She will hear them more than she hears you soon," the wizard said softly. "That is not a cruelty. It is simply how the tether works. The call is constant. You are not." "Then I'll make myself constant," Loran snapped, lifting his head to glare at him. "I'll be there when she wakes, when she sleeps, when she screams. I'll be there every time it whispers. I'll stand between them and her until they choke on my name."

Ryn studied him for a long moment. "That will break you," he said at last. "Good," Loran said. "Then it can break me instead of her." For the first time that night, something like reluctant respect flickered in Ryn's eyes. "Very well," he said quietly. "At first light—if there is still such a thing—we begin. You will not like what I have to teach you." "I don't like anything about tonight," Loran said. "Teach me anyway."

Below them, Ashwood Hold creaked and groaned, a tired beast trying to shift its weight around a wound it could not reach. Fires were relit. Tents were checked. Children were gathered and counted twice. Somewhere a man began to sob and did not stop for a long time. Somewhere else a woman laughed, the high, hysterical kind that sounded like it might tip into screaming at any second. Above it all the sky hung bruised and heavy, green still pulsing faintly at the horizon where the mountains hid the dead giant's body. The night did not end. But something in it changed. A line had been crossed; an old guardian had fallen, a Vessel had been marked, a Blade had bared its edge, and a herald had walked back through his door with the certainty that he would not need to knock next time.

Loran shifted, carefully slipping one arm under Mara's knees, the other around her shoulders. His muscles protested, every bruise a separate throb, but he pushed through it and rose to his feet, cradling her against his chest. Her head lolled against his shoulder, hair tickling his jaw. She made a soft, broken sound when he moved, and he murmured nonsense in response, the kind of soothing, meaningless words you offer to frightened horses and children and yourself.

"Where are you taking her?" Ryn asked, levering himself upright with a grimace. "Somewhere the wind doesn't hit her face," Loran said. "Somewhere that doesn't smell like him." He glanced once toward the place on the wall where Teren had stood. The planks there were darker than the rest, stained faintly, as if the corruption had left fingerprints in the wood. Someone would have to cut that section out and burn it. He added it to the list in his head of things that needed doing when the world stopped shuddering quite so much. If it ever did.

"I'll bring her to the healer's tent," he said. "You can poke at her there in the morning. But tonight she sleeps. Even if what's inside her doesn't." Ryn nodded slowly. "I will ward the tent," he said. "It will not keep the whispers out, but it will make them... quieter." "Do that," Loran replied. He took one careful step, then another, his boots leaving faint smears of corruption-dust on the boards where it had settled. Each footfall felt like a promise hammered into the wood. He would carry her off. He would keep her breathing. He would learn to wield the fire in his arm until it cut only what he aimed at. He would go north if he had to, into the mouth of whatever waited there, and if the corruption wanted to use Mara as its Vessel it would have to deal with the fact that its chosen host came with a blade welded to her side.

As he reached the top of the ladder, Vale appeared, one hand gripping the rung, the other braced on the wall, his face drawn with exhaustion. He looked at Mara, then at Loran, then at the empty stretch of ridge where the seam had closed. "Is he gone?" he asked. "For tonight," Loran said. Vale exhaled, the sound more like a groan. "Then we have until tomorrow to decide how we live with what he left." His gaze dropped to Loran's bared mark. "And with that." Loran met his eyes steadily. "I'll make sure it hurts them more than it hurts us," he said. Vale gave a humorless huff that might have been a laugh in a better world. "See that you do," he said.

He stepped aside to let Loran pass. As Loran descended the ladder, each careful step jostling Mara just enough to make his heart clench, Ashwood Hold swayed around him—wounded, terrified, not yet broken. The night pressed close to the walls, thick with the promise of more. Above the valley, unseen beyond the clouds, something old and watching turned its attention toward the place where a giant had fallen and a Vessel had been marked, and waited for the first footstep on the northern road

CHAPTER SEVENTY-ONE
The Purpose

Mara came back to herself slowly, as though rising through layers of cold water, her breath catching on every fragile inch upward, and Loran held her as if afraid the slightest shift would shatter her completely, his hands trembling against her skin while her eyelids fluttered in weak, irregular motions; dawn had not yet come, though the air carried a thin silver haze that did not belong to the sun, a residue of whatever had ruptured the night, and the wall around them was eerily quiet, soldiers whispering prayers or sitting with heads bowed, no one daring to look too long at the girl who had screamed with the voice of something that did not belong to her.

Mara's chest rose in one shallow tremor, then another, and Loran leaned in so quickly he nearly knocked Ryn's broken staff aside, whispering her name in a shaking breath. Her eyes opened. For a heartbeat–just one–they were her own. Soft, dark, confused. Then a faint ring pulsed at the far edge of each iris, not a mark, not a stain, not a sigil color–just light, thin as the rim of a distant star, and she flinched, shoving a hand against Loran's chest as if something inside her recoiled from his touch.

He froze, horrified. "Mara?" he whispered, but she shook her head, gripping her temples, breath stuttering. "Too bright," she choked, voice cracking. "You're... too bright." Loran looked down in disbelief at the faint glow leaking from his sleeve—the sigil burning red-gold through the torn fabric, not bright to the eye but apparently blinding to whatever now lived inside her. He snatched his arm away instinctively, heart lurching when she gasped in relief, shoulders unclenching as though he had stopped pressing a hot iron to her skin.

Ryn crawled closer, battered, blood drying on his lips, each breath shallow as he fought through the backlash of his own broken magic. “She is hearing them more clearly now,” he rasped. “The whispers. The pull. The breach in the north is growing thinner, and she is tied to it whether she wants to be or not. She must not touch your mark until you learn to control it.” Mara shivered violently, hugging her arms around herself as though she were freezing despite sweat soaking her hairline, and she whispered something that twisted Loran’s stomach into a fist: “It’s calling again.”

Ryn blanched. “Already?” “It never stopped,” she whispered, eyes unfocused, pupils widening, that faint ring pulsing like a heartbeat she did not own. “It’s... murmuring through the trees. Through the stones. I can feel it behind my teeth.” Loran reached toward her instinctively before remembering—before seeing her flinch—and folded his hand into a fist against his chest. “You don’t have to listen,” he said, forcing the words through a trembling throat. “Fight it. Stay with me. Stay here. Don’t look north.” Her breath hitched, and for the first time since waking she truly looked at him—saw him—not as pain, not as brightness stabbing through her skull, but as the boy she had grown up with, the one whose voice she trusted even when the world collapsed around them.

“I’m trying,” she whispered, voice small, cracked. “Loran, I swear, I’m trying, but it feels like I’m standing in a river, and the current keeps dragging me even when I dig my heels in.” Ryn pushed himself upright with trembling arms, his broken staff hissing faint sparks as the runes died. “Then we give you something to hold onto,” he said, turning to Loran with eyes that burned faintly blue despite exhaustion. “Your mark is tied to the last breath of the guardian. If you can learn to shape it—to wield its power with intention instead of instinct—you may be able to anchor her. A counterweight to the corruption’s pull.”

Loran frowned. "How long?" Ryn's jaw tightened. "We don't have long. Hours. Perhaps less. When the seal fully breaks, the corruption will not whisper. It will command. And she..." He looked at Mara, something like grief twisting through his expression. "...she will obey." Mara jerked as though struck, tears filling her eyes. "I don't want to," she whispered, voice trembling with terror so pure it made Loran feel sick. "I don't want to go anywhere. I don't want to hear it. I don't want to be anything." Loran reached for her hand—slowly, gently—and she let him touch it, just their fingertips brushing, and that small permission felt like a victory he did not deserve. "You won't be," he said. "Not while I'm alive." But even as he said it, the air changed—soft, cold, wrong—and Mara's breath caught again, her gaze snapping north as though something had tugged a cord tied to her spine.

A whisper brushed the stones, not sound, not wind, but vibration, a hum that only she heard. "It's stronger," she breathed, voice going thin. "Loran... it's stronger now..." Ryn swore under his breath. "Then we begin. Now. Before we lose her completely." Loran stood, trembling with exhaustion and fury and fear. His sleeve burned. His arm pulsed. The mark throbbed like a trapped star begging to break free. Mara looked up at him, tears streaking her cheeks as she whispered, "Don't let me go." He squeezed her hand—carefully, gently—mindful of the pain even the faintest glow caused her. "I won't." But far to the north, something old and broken stirred in the darkness—something that had been waiting for the Vessel to breathe. And Mara felt it. And the corruption felt her. And the night, once again, began to shift.

CHAPTER SEVENTY-TWO
The Red Lesson

Dawn never truly arrived over Ashwood Hold; instead, a gray and trembling half-light seeped weakly across the sky as if even the sun feared to step foot into a world where a guardian had died and a Vessel had stirred, and Loran felt the air tighten around his ribs the moment Ryn led him away from Mara, every instinct inside him screaming that he should not be leaving her side, not even for a heartbeat, but Mara herself had whispered, with a fragile resolve that nearly broke him, "Go—learn—before it takes me," and those words echoed now as he followed Ryn across the ruined north wall toward a patch of open ground still slick with ash from the night's fractures.

Ryn walked as a man decades older than he looked, one hand braced against the stones for balance, blue sparks flickering and dying along the cracks in his shattered staff, and when he stopped, turning to face Loran with eyes dimmed but still burning with desperate purpose, his voice came out thin and uneven. "The corruption will take her," he said without preamble, "unless you learn to become the one thing it fears." Loran's jaw clenched. "And what is that?" Ryn pointed at his arm. "You." Loran peeled back his scorched sleeve, the red mark pulsing beneath his skin in slow, jagged throbs like a heartbeat fighting against its cage; the mark no longer glowed steady red but flared with molten streaks of gold and white, threads weaving outward like cracks in glass radiating from the moment the giant died.

Ryn exhaled sharply. "It's awakening faster than I thought. The giant's fall tore the seal open, and your mark is responding to the shift in the world—or to Mara." Loran swallowed, eyes snapping toward the far corner of the wall where Mara sat bundled in blankets despite the sweat, her hands buried in her hair as if holding her skull together while Vale and Lila watched her like she might vanish between blinks. "What do I do?" Ryn stepped closer, gripping Loran's wrist with shaking fingers, breath hissing as the heat of the sigil pulsed against his skin. "You learn to shape it. To channel it. To command it. Because right now, you are a walking fire with no walls, and every time you get near her you burn her without meaning to."

Loran winced—the memory of Mara screaming at the touch of his mark stabbing through him. "Then teach me. Now." "I am trying," Ryn snapped, frustration and fear twisting his voice, "but you must understand—your power is not meant for you. It was never meant for human hands. It belonged to a guardian older than our histories. You are borrowing the remnants of a dying titan, and if you mishandle it, it will not simply consume you. It will unmake you." Loran's pulse hammered, but he nodded. "Then I'll learn fast." "You must," Ryn said, stepping back. "Because Mara is running out of time." Loran's stomach twisted as Ryn lifted the broken half of his staff, blue sparks trembling across the runes like dying lightning.

"Close your eyes," Ryn instructed. "And breathe. Feel the mark—not as fire, not as pain, but as a shape." Loran obeyed, inhaling shakily, and immediately the world tilted—heat surged through his veins, twisting like molten ropes up his shoulders, across his chest, threads of red light flickering behind his eyelids, forming spirals and jagged arcs he couldn't understand. He gasped. "It's—too much—" "It will always be too much," Ryn barked. "Focus. The mark is not a flame. It is a living essence." Loran forced himself to breathe again, sweat beading at his temples as the pressure mounted, the heat building, consuming, threatening to burst through his skin.

He reached instinctively for Mara—her voice, her presence, anything familiar—and the mark responded violently, flaring with wild red-gold light that shot up his arm and blasted outward in a crack of energy that shattered a nearby stone. Loran staggered, eyes flying open. "I hurt her doing that," he rasped. "My mark—every time I think of her it—" "That is the danger," Ryn said grimly. "Your connection to her amplifies it. Your emotions make the mark burn hotter. Think of her now and you will kill her." The words hit like a blade, and Loran felt the world pitch. "Then how do I help her?" "By learning to think of nothing." Loran stared. "Nothing?" "Nothing," Ryn repeated. "Emptiness. Stillness. You must become a vessel with no desire, no fear, no thought—only control. The red does not respond to love or rage or desperation. It responds to purpose. If you cannot hold a single purpose without letting your feelings spill into it, then you cannot wield it safely."

Loran clenched his fists. "My purpose is her." Ryn closed his eyes in pain. "Then that is why it burns." A sound drifted across the wall—a soft, strangled gasp. Both men snapped toward Mara. She was standing now, barely upright, one hand braced on the stone, her hair falling over her face, her breath fogging in the warm morning air as though she stood in winter's grip. Lila reached for her. Mara flinched away, whispering something Loran felt more than heard: "North." Loran took a step toward her before Ryn's hand slammed into his chest. "STOP."

Loran's breath caught. "She needs—" "If you go near her now with your mark raging like this, you will push her the rest of the way," Ryn hissed. "You will burn the last threads binding her to herself. Do you understand?" Loran's heart cracked. But he nodded. Because he had to. Mara lifted her head slowly, her eyes half-lidded, unfocused—but the faint green ring at the edge of each iris pulsed in steady rhythm now, not flickering like before. Becoming certain. Becoming hers. Or becoming something else's. Ryn whispered, horrified, "It's beginning."

Mara swayed on her feet, whispering again, louder this time, voice thin and shaking: "North... calling... calling..." Loran reached out despite himself—his hand hovering helplessly in the air, trembling with a pain deeper than anything his mark could inflict. "Mara," he whispered. She blinked—and for one fleeting heartbeat she saw him fully, recognition cutting through the haze like a shaft of sunlight through storm clouds. Tears filled her eyes. And she mouthed two words that turned his blood to ice. "I'm sorry."

Ryn exhaled in total despair. "She's hearing the pull directly now. The corruption is not whispering anymore. It's speaking." Mara's breath caught, her body arching in a subtle convulsion as her fingers dug into the wall. "I have to go," she whispered, voice shaking with terror and certainty in equal measure. "I can't—I can't stay—I have to—" "NO," Loran snarled, taking a step forward before Ryn shoved him back again. "You're not going anywhere!" Mara's lips trembled. "I... don't think it's a choice anymore." And somewhere deep in the forest to the north, something ancient and newly awakened exhaled—long, hungry, triumphant. And Mara turned her face toward it like a flower reaching for light. The corruption had begun to call its Vessel home.

CHAPTER SEVENTY-THREE
The Last Night She Was Theirs

Night fell too quickly again, sliding over Ashwood like a lid being shut on a lantern, and Mara stood at the far edge of the courtyard with her back to the firelight, her silhouette trembling as though her bones were arguing with themselves about whether they still belonged to her; Vale had ordered a dozen soldiers to keep watch around her, but none dared to stand within arm's reach because every time someone stepped too close the air around her bent—just slightly, like heat over stone, a ripple you didn't see until you were already too close to whatever caused it, and Loran watched her from across the hold with Ryn's hand clamped around his wrist like a shackle, the older man whispering hoarse warnings each time Loran's instincts tried to shove him forward.

Mara hadn't spoken since her apology, since the moment the last shard of sunset touched her skin and her mind seemed to fold inward, leaving her blinking at the world with eyes that saw too much and too little at once; she moved in small shivers, breaths coming shallow and uneven, head turning north again and again as though answering a question only she could hear. Loran felt his chest twist each time her gaze shifted—like a cord tethered between them pulled taut, ready to snap—and every time the mark beneath his sleeve burned a little hotter, reacting to her fear, her pain, her unraveling.

"She's slipping," Ryn murmured, voice frayed with guilt and despair. "Faster than I expected. The pull is nearly constant now. The breach must be widening even as we stand here." Loran's jaw clenched. "Then we go stop it." Ryn shook his head sharply. "You are not ready. Your mark is volatile. If you go near her you might push her the rest of the way." Loran glared at him. "She doesn't have 'the rest of the way' left. She's barely here." And it was true—because as he watched, Mara blinked slowly and for a long, terrifying moment she didn't breathe, didn't move, didn't even *exist* behind her own eyes; the soldiers near her froze, waiting, afraid to touch her, and then—abruptly—she inhaled sharply as if surfacing from deep water, hands gripping her arms in confusion as though she had no idea how she'd gotten where she was.

"She lost time again," Lila whispered, voice breaking as she hurried to catch Mara's elbow. "Mara? Mara, do you know where you are?" Mara frowned, looking at her friend with dazed uncertainty. "Lila... I was... I was somewhere else," she breathed, and her voice sent a shiver through every person listening—because she did not sound frightened of being lost. She sounded frightened of being found. Vale strode toward them, his face pale beneath the grime of battle. "We can't keep her out in the open. Bring her inside—one of the storage rooms, far from the outer walls. Guard it. Double watch. No one opens that door unless I say." But the moment he reached to guide Mara by the shoulder, she recoiled as if bitten, stumbling back into Lila's arms even as her gaze flicked north.

"Don't put me in a room," she whispered. "Don't trap me. If I'm trapped it gets louder." Vale swallowed hard. "Louder?" Mara nodded, and her hair fell across half her face, shadowing one eye—and for the first time that faint sickly green ring around her iris glowed clearly enough for everyone to see. A few soldiers muttered curses and backed away. One dropped the torch he was holding. Mara blinked at their fear as if she didn't understand it, and her expression flickered—hurt, confusion, then something blank and distant, a shutter sliding down.

Loran stepped forward before Ryn could stop him, voice low and steady. "Mara. Look at me." She did—slowly, like turning through water—and when her eyes locked onto his, the mark on his arm surged with heat and her breath caught in her throat. She took a single step backward. "Loran... you're hurting," she whispered, forehead creasing in pain. "You feel like fire. You're burning holes in everything." His heart cracked in two. "I can control it," he said. "I swear I can. Ryn is teaching me. I just—I need more time." At that, Mara's face softened, and she reached out as if to touch his cheek—but her fingers stopped inches away, trembling violently, her expression twisting with grief.

"I don't think I have time," she whispered. "I think... I think I'm almost gone." "No," Loran said instantly, stepping closer until Ryn physically dragged him back. "You're not gone. You're here. You're right here." Mara's lips twitched. "I was... but then I wasn't. When the sun dropped, I lost myself. I didn't even know it was happening until Lila shook me." Lila wiped her eyes. "You're still you. You're still fighting." Mara pressed a shaking hand to her chest. "I don't know what I'm fighting anymore."

The wind shifted—cold, wrong, carrying the faintest echo of something like a distant sigh from the northern ridge—and Mara stiffened as if pierced by an invisible arrow. Everyone froze. Her eyes unfocused. Her breath stopped. And then she whispered, in a voice not wholly her own, "It's closer." Vale swore. Ryn went white. Loran's vision darkened at the edges. "What is closer?" he demanded. Mara turned her head slowly, like a puppet moved by strings. "The door." Ryn cursed and grabbed Loran's wrist. "We need to move her inside—now—if she hears the door this clearly, the corruption is nearly upon us—" But Mara looked at Loran again—really looked—eyes full of desperation and something deeper, something breaking. "Don't let go," she whispered. "Promise me."

Loran reached out his hand—and this time she didn't flinch from it. Her fingers brushed his—cool, shaking, fragile—and when they touched, she exhaled in relief, leaning slightly toward him as if he were the only thing holding her to this world. But then the corruption answered. A distant pulse—soft, rhythmic, unmistakable—rolled across the trees like a heartbeat the world had forgotten. Mara's pupils dilated. Her hand slipped from his. And she whispered, faint and terrified, "It's calling my name." And before anyone could stop her—before anyone could even decide what to do—Mara turned toward the northern darkness. And took her first step. Toward it. The last night she belonged to them had begun.

CHAPTER SEVENTY-FOUR
The Night She Started Walking

Mara's first step toward the northern dark was small—so small it should not have meant anything—but every soul in Ashwood felt the world flinch at the motion, as if some invisible thread anchoring reality loosened by a fraction; Lila gasped and lunged for her, Vale barked an order no one obeyed, and Loran tore free of Ryn's grip with a snarl that came from somewhere deep and primal, but Mara had already taken a second step, then a third, her feet moving with eerie hesitation, like she was walking underwater, like she was being pulled and resisting at the same time. "Mara, STOP!" Loran shouted, his voice cracking, and she froze mid-stride, not because she obeyed, but because something inside her stuttered—her breath hitched, her shoulders trembled, and she pressed a hand over her mouth as if trying to hold in a scream that had no sound.

She turned her head just slightly toward him, and her eyes—gods, her eyes—were not fully hers anymore; the dark of them looked bruised, the faint green ring pulsing once per heartbeat, too rhythmic, too steady, like the corruption had found her pulse and begun syncing with it. "I don't want to go," she whispered, her voice cracking, and for a heartbeat she looked like the girl who used to sit by the river, kicking her boots in the mud, smiling at him shyly when she thought he wasn't looking. But then she winced, doubling over as if struck by a blow to her ribs, and when she straightened, her gaze snapped north again, drawn like metal to a lodestone buried beneath the mountains. "It hurts," she gasped, fingers digging into her skull. "It hurts when I don't listen."

Loran surged forward, but Ryn shoved him back with more force than his shaking arms should've held. "If you touch her now—IF YOU TOUCH HER NOW—your mark will finish what the corruption started!" Ryn wheezed, sweat dripping from his brow. "You will burn the last of her humanity away!" Loran's vision blurred with rage and helplessness. "I'm losing her!" "We ALL are," Ryn snapped, voice breaking, "but if you reach for her now, you will lose her *faster!*" Mara leaned on the wall to steady herself, her breath coming in short, shallow bursts, and Lila approached her slowly, carefully, tears streaming down her face. "Mara... please... you're scaring us... come sit, come talk to us... we'll help you."

Mara blinked at her friend in confusion, as if unsure why the girl was crying, as if unable to pitch her own fear against another's, and her expression flickered—terror, grief, numbness, then something like awe. "It's beautiful," she whispered suddenly. "The sound... it's so beautiful tonight..." "Mara, no," Ryn said sharply, voice trembling. "That is not beauty. That is compulsion. That is a dead god pulling on your bones." But Mara smiled faintly—small, dreamy, wrong—and Loran felt something in his chest rupture. She had never smiled like that. Not at him. Not at anyone. That smile belonged to something else. "It's getting louder," she said, her voice sliding into a lilting whisper. "Like a voice very far away, but getting closer with every breath I take." Vale cursed under his breath. "We need to restrain her before—" "NO ONE touches her!" Loran snapped, spinning on him with fury savage enough that even Vale's hand drifted toward his sword. "She's not an animal, she's not dangerous, she's—she's Mara." But even he could hear the lie in his voice.

Mara straightened suddenly, her spine going rigid, head tilting slightly in a way that sent chills racing through every person who saw it. She whispered, "The door is open." Ryn's knees nearly buckled. "It isn't. It CAN'T be. It's thinning, yes, tearing, yes, but not open—not yet—" But Mara shook her head slowly, as though listening to something only she could hear, and said, with eerie certainty, "It is waiting for me." Loran's pulse stopped. "Who?" Mara's mouth trembled. "The one who calls me." A sick, cold wave rolled through the hold. Teren. Loran surged forward again, Ryn grabbing his arm desperately. "You can't save her like this!" "LET ME GO!" Loran roared, but then Mara gasped and clutched her stomach, collapsing to her knees.

Lila shrieked and dropped beside her, catching her before she hit the stones. "MARA! Mara, look at me!" Mara didn't look. Her eyes rolled back, then snapped open glowing a hard, sharp green that flickered like a candle in a windless room. Words spilled from her lips in a voice layered with hers and something deeper: "The Vessel walks the shadowed path. The Vessel answers the call. The Vessel... returns." "STOP SPEAKING!" Lila sobbed, shaking her shoulders. "That's not you! That's not your voice!"

Mara blinked, awareness surfacing like a drowning girl pushing upward with fading strength. Tears welled in her eyes. "Lila... I'm scared," she whispered, finally trembling, truly trembling. "It's pulling harder. I'm—" She cut off with a strangled cry as her body arched, her fingers digging into the stone, eyes flashing with green fire. The sleeve of her tunic slid back from her forearm as she convulsed. Dark lines crawled beneath her skin, branching outward in sharp, vein-like patterns that pulsed with the same sick green light burning in her eyes. The mark flared once, violent and unmistakable, and Mara screamed—not in pain, but in terror, as if she could feel it spreading, claiming more of her with every breath.

"MA—RA!" Loran bellowed, trying to break free again, but Ryn locked both arms around him with surprising strength. "If you go near her, you will KILL her!" Mara convulsed once more—and then stilled, shaking violently, panting like she had run for miles. She whispered, barely audible, "Loran..." He froze. "...don't come after me." His heart dropped through his ribs. "Why?" Her breath hitched, and she looked at him with more pain than he had ever seen in another living soul. "Because I don't think I'll be me when you find me." And then—before anyone could move, before Ryn could restrain her with spellwork he no longer had strength for, before Loran could shove past him, before Lila could hold her down— Mara stood. Not in her own way. Not at her own pace. She lifted as though someone had tugged invisible strings. And she began walking. Toward the north. Again. Faster this time. Determined. Certain. Controlled. "MARAAAAA!" Loran screamed, and half the hold echoed him. She did not turn. She did not flinch. She did not break stride. She only whispered, soft as falling ash: "I have to." And the corruption—hearing her answer—moved in the trees. Mara crossed the threshold of the gate. And none of them could make her stop.

CHAPTER SEVENTY-FIVE
Into the Hollowing Dark

Loran cleared the gate before the alarm bell finished sounding, his boots skidding on the wet earth as he sprinted into the tree line where Mara had vanished seconds before, Ryn stagger-limping after him with what little strength he still possessed, Vale and Braum shouting orders behind them as archers formed lines on the wall, torches flaring to life, but the forest swallowed everything—the light, the sound, the sense that the world was still something known. The trees here were wrong; their trunks leaned in unnatural angles, their roots twisted like grasping hands, as if the corruption's breath had warped the very grain of the wood.

Loran didn't see any of that. He saw only the faint imprint of Mara's footsteps in the soft earth—too light, too drifting, as though she wasn't fully touching the ground—and the flicker of pale green ahead, glimpsed through the branches like fire. "MARA!" he bellowed, voice breaking as he vaulted a fallen log. "STOP! PLEASE!" She didn't stop. She didn't even slow. Her silhouette moved through the trees with dreamlike steadiness, that strange puppet-string tension in her spine, head tilted like she was listening to something he could not hear. Ryn gasped, "She's following the call—Loran, it's taken hold faster than I thought—we cannot let her reach the threshold—if she crosses it willingly—" "She won't!" Loran snarled, but the ground shook beneath them, a deep tremor rolling outward like the earth itself exhaling something it was never meant to release. Green mist seeped along the forest floor, curling around their ankles, brushing against Loran's skin like cold fingers.

He shoved forward, coughing as the mist thickened, but each breath only fueled him, sharpened him, drove him harder. "MARA!" he roared again, cutting through brambles that tore at his arms, uncaring of the blood streaking down them. Ahead, she wavered—for the first time. Her steps faltered, her shoulders curled inward, one hand flying to her chest as if something inside her had twisted. "Loran..." she whispered, so soft he barely heard. His heart surged. "I'm here!" But as soon as hope sparked in him, she jerked violently as though yanked forward by a hook in her ribs and stumbled deeper into the dark.

Loran nearly screamed in frustration. Ryn stumbled beside him, sweat pouring down his face, eyes flickering blue only in desperate sparks. "The corruption is tightening its hold—she's resisting, gods bless her, but every heartbeat she fights only makes it latch deeper—Loran, listen to me—if she reaches the veil, she won't come back—" "Then we KEEP HER FROM REACHING IT!" Loran growled, and pushed harder, pouring everything he had left into one final burst of speed. He closed the distance to mere yards—could see the braid falling apart down her back, the dirt smeared on her sleeve, the trembling in her legs—could hear her breath hitching, uneven, terrified—and then the forest opened. Not a glade. Not a clearing. A wound. A wide, circular expanse where the trees had recoiled outward, their trunks bending away as if afraid to stand too near the center where the air shimmered. Not with light. Not with shadow. With something between. A veil. An almost-transparent film of wavering green-black, like the surface of a pond reflecting a stormy sky.

Mara stood five steps from it. Tears streamed down her cheeks though her expression was blank, distant, bewitched. "I don't want to," she whispered to no one they could see. "Please... I don't want to..." Loran broke. "MARA!" His voice cracked raw as he sprinted into the clearing. "DON'T GO!" She flinched. She turned. For one impossible moment, her eyes—just her eyes—were fully, painfully human. “Loran... I’m so sorry.” He lunged for her— “NO!” Ryn screamed behind him— And the moment Loran’s red-lit arm reached for her, Mara screamed—not from fear, not from pain, but from something deeper, like his very presence burned her from the inside. She stumbled backward, hand outstretched as if begging him not to follow—not to touch—not to save her. “You hurt me,” she sobbed. “Your mark—it hurts—it HURTS—”

Loran froze, arm half-extended, devastated, shattered. “Mara... gods... I’m sorry—I’m so sorry—just come back—I won’t touch you—I won’t—I’ll walk behind you—I’ll walk blind—I’ll do anything—JUST COME BACK—” She shook her head slowly, trembling so hard she could barely stand. “I can’t.” The veil pulsed. The corruption inside it exhaled, a soft sound like a thousand whispers sighing at once. The forest tilted. Ryn pulled at Loran’s shoulder, voice breaking. “Loran—we can’t step closer—the veil will take us—it wants ONLY HER—don’t make it choose you too—” But Loran barely heard him, his world narrowing to the single word Mara breathed next, her voice quiet, cracked, doomed: “Goodbye.” And then—she stepped back. One foot. Into the veil. The corruption flowed around her like water accepting a returning riverstone. The green-black light swallowed her shape, her hair, her tears, her trembling hands reaching briefly toward Loran before dissolving into shimmer.

“MARA!!” Loran screamed, the sound ripping something vital from him. He lunged—and Ryn tackled him around the waist with the strength of a man who had spent centuries fearing this exact moment. “LOOORAN!” Ryn roared in his ear as Loran thrashed like a wounded beast. “If you enter—you die! IT WILL TAKE YOU APART!” Mara’s last visible silhouette shivered—one flicker of a girl they loved— Then the veil closed. The forest fell silent. Loran collapsed to his knees as Ryn’s grip loosened. A sound left him no one in Ashwood had ever heard from him. Not rage. Not fury. Not even grief. Something deeper. Something hollow. Something broken. Mara was gone.

CHAPTER SEVENTY-SIX
What Remains

The clearing did not move after the veil closed; it did not breathe, or tremble, or pulse with lingering light—it simply *stilled*, as though the corruption had no further need to announce itself, having claimed what it came for, and Loran knelt in the dead center of that quiet with his hands buried in the dirt, shoulders shaking, breath tearing shallow and uneven through his chest like something was slicing him open from the inside.

The world felt thinner without Mara in it; the lantern warmth she carried, her stubborn hope, her laughter, her certainty that something better could still be fought for—gone, ripped from him so suddenly that his ribs ached from the absence. He pressed his forehead to the cold earth where she had stood and whispered her name over and over until the sound lost meaning. Ryn stood behind him, leaning heavily on a broken piece of his staff he had snapped like a makeshift cane, his breaths shallow, his skin gray with exhaustion and guilt. "I'm sorry," he rasped, voice barely more than a breath. "Loran, I'm... gods help me, I'm so sorry." Loran didn't answer. Couldn't. If he opened his mouth, something inside him might shatter loud enough to bring the forest down with it.

Vale and Braum approached slowly with the others, weapons lowered, expressions stunned into something between terror and mourning, Lila collapsed to her knees a few steps away, sobbing silently into her hands. No one spoke. No one dared to break the silence Mara left behind. Ryn forced himself closer and crouched beside Loran, his joints cracking under the strain. "She isn't dead," he said quietly, as though speaking into the earth itself. "She is inside it now, but not lost. Not yet. The Vessel... still remembers her name. She fought. She is still fighting." Loran lifted his head slowly, his eyes red but blazing. "Then we go after her." Ryn closed his eyes in pain. "We cannot cross the veil." "I'm not asking you," Loran said, each word sharp as a blade's point. "I'm telling you. I'll follow her even if it kills me."

A tremor passed underfoot—soft, distant, like the mountains groaning in their sleep. The corruption shifted somewhere beyond the veil's reach, but for now it did not return. "Loran," Ryn whispered, "if you walk into that place untrained, the corruption will strip you to the bone and wear what's left." "Then train me," Loran growled, turning on him with fury and grief curling into one unstoppable force. "You said the red in me is tied to the last of the guardian's power—so teach me how to use it. Teach me how to survive inside that thing. Teach me how to tear it open from within if I have to." Ryn stared at him, seeing not the boy from the village but the man carved sharp by loss, the man whose mark pulsed with heat even now, threads of crimson burning like live coal under his skin. "This path," Ryn whispered, "will break you." "It already has," Loran said. "So what's left to fear?"

Ryn bowed his head, breath shaking with dread—and acceptance. "Then at first light," he said hoarsely, "we begin." A wind rose through the clearing then, carrying with it the faintest echo of a distant sound—like whispering, like a soft call, like the memory of a voice Mara once used when she said his name. Loran stiffened, trembling as the sound passed, both agony and hope sparking through him at once. "I'm coming for you," he whispered to the empty air where she had stood. "I swear it with everything I am. You are not staying in there. I'm coming."

The veil gave no answer. The forest remained still. But the corruption, far away and yet unbearably close, stirred at the sound of his vow—listening. Waiting. And as the torches from the hold flickered into view through the trees, as Braum lifted Lila to her feet and Vale ushered the others away, as Ryn wrapped a steadying hand on Loran's shoulder and guided him slowly back toward Ashwood, the night seemed to deepen one last shade darker, as if marking the end of something fragile and the beginning of something merciless. Mara was gone. Loran was not. And the world would burn before he let that remain true for long.

CHAPTER SEVENTY-SEVEN
The Vow

Ashwood Hold did not feel like a fortress when Loran returned through its gates; it felt like a mausoleum, a hollowed shell of wood and stone that still echoed with the shape of someone who was no longer inside it, the torches guttering low along the walls as if the fire itself sensed that Mara's warmth had been pulled from the world. Soldiers stepped aside silently as he passed, their eyes lowered not out of respect, but out of fear—fear of the red glow pulsing beneath the torn sleeve of his arm, fear of the way the air around him felt charged, sharp, shifting like heat rippling off stone. Vale met him in the courtyard but said nothing; his stern face was carved with pity he didn't dare speak aloud.

Lila stood near the well, her hands shaking as she pressed them to her mouth, eyes swollen, breath trembling, and when Loran's gaze brushed hers she broke—collapsed against Braum's shoulder with a sob that ripped through the quiet. Ryn kept close to Loran, leaning heavily on his broken staff-splinter, but even he did not try to speak. The night pressed down on them, heavy and expectant, as though waiting to see what the boy with the burning arm would become now that the girl he loved had vanished into the corruption.

Loran moved to the center of the courtyard, the place where Mara once laughed as she helped carry water buckets, where she once sat on the stone rim to scold him for sharpening his blade too close to his fingers, where she once reached out shyly and brushed his wrist, telling him she was glad they somehow managed to remain alive through all of it. The memory struck him so hard he nearly dropped to his knees. Instead, he lifted his face toward the northern ridge—toward the veil she had crossed, toward the wound in the world where she had disappeared—and the grief inside him flared into something that felt like fire breaking its chains.

"Everyone in this hold, listen to me," he said, and his voice carried, low and shaking, but clear. The soldiers turned. The healers. The scouts. The remnants of families clinging to one another beneath the torchlight. Even the wind stilled. Loran swallowed hard, and when he spoke again, it came from somewhere deeper than lungs, deeper than bone, from a place carved open when Mara's hand slipped from his reach. "You saw what happened tonight. You saw her taken. You saw the corruption claim what it was hunting from the moment the world began to crack." His jaw tightened. His hands clenched. His arm pulsed bright red beneath his sleeve, the mark burning like a brand. "Mara is not gone."

A murmur rippled through the courtyard—fear, disbelief, hope warring in the dark. Loran continued. "She walked into the corruption because it dragged her there. Because it lied to her. Because it tore her open and left her no choice." His voice hardened. "But she is still fighting. I know it. And I swear on every breath I have left—I will find her." Vale stepped forward, expression grim. "Loran... you can't promise that— "I will find her," Loran said again, louder this time, cutting him off. "And I will bring her back." Ryn closed his eyes, breath shaking, as if the weight of what Loran was binding himself to was almost too heavy to hear. Loran's gaze swept across the hold, fierce and unbroken even through the tears on his face. "The corruption thinks it won," he said. "It thinks it has taken the girl I love and turned her into its weapon. It thinks the world will kneel because it holds her." The torches flickered—not from wind, but from the sudden surge of energy radiating from his arm, red threads spiraling like fire caught in a gale. "But I am not bending." His voice dropped to a low, grim promise.

"Let the corruption spread. Let the world fall. Let every giant die and every city burn. I will walk into whatever darkness it builds." He lifted his marked arm, and the red light spilled across the courtyard like a rising dawn.

"And I will tear it apart until I reach her." Silence followed. Heavy. Absolute. Loran breathed once, twice, then spoke the final words not to the hold, not to Ryn, not even to himself—but to Mara, wherever she was inside that consuming dark. "This is my vow, Mara Rayne," he whispered, voice barely holding together. "I will not stop. I will not yield. I will not fail you. Not again." Far beyond the northern ridge, where the veil shimmered unseen in the trees, the corruption stirred—slowly, thoughtfully—as if hearing the promise and turning its head toward the boy who dared to make it.

The wind shifted.

The torches bent.

Ryn bowed his head. "Then we sharpen every blade, seal every wall, and train until our bones ache. If the world is falling..." Vale stepped beside him. "...then we don't fall alone." Braum slammed a fist to his chest. Lila lifted her chin with trembling resolve. Ryn looked at Loran. "We stand with you. Until the end." The torches guttered. The corruption whispered far beyond the ridge. Loran lowered his arm. And the last hope of the old world flickered in the dark.

The First Corruption

A year slipped by, piece by piece, as the world fell into shadow.
Fields died. Rivers blackened.
Even the mountains wore a sickness in their stones.
Corruption spread like a second sky stretching across the earth.
But not everywhere. Far from ruined villages and collapsing keeps,
in a corner of the world the corruption had not yet found,
a pulse throbbed.
Once.
Twice.
Steady. Not a warning.
Not a threat.
A beginning. Something new was growing in the dark.
Something that did not belong to the corruption at all.
And when it rose,
the world would change again.

Author's Note This book would not exist without the people who stood beside me long before Loran ever lifted a blade. To my family, who believed in me even when the path twisted darker than expected—thank you for your patience, your encouragement, and your faith. You gave me the courage to see this story through. To my friends and early readers who listened to wild ideas, late-night plot tangles, and endless worldbuilding ramblings—you strengthened this world more than you know. Your excitement kept the fire lit. To those who inspired the characters, knowingly or not—thank you for the sparks, the scars, and the laughter. Every story begins with someone who reminds you why you write. And finally, to every reader who picked up this book and stepped into the shadows with me: thank you. May the road ahead be dark, dangerous, and worth the journey.

www.ingramcontent.com/pod-product-compliance
Lightning Source LLC
Chambersburg PA
CBHW060809310726
48980CB00002B/290
* 9 7 9 8 9 9 4 3 9 3 0 1 7 *